D1234371

# CURSE OF THE REAPER

### A NOVEL

## BRIAN McAULEY

TALOS

Talos Press books may be purchased in bulk at special discounts for sales promotion, corporate gifts, fund-raising, or educational purposes. Special editions can also be created to specifications. For details, contact the Special Sales Department, Talos Press, 307 West 36th Street, 11th Floor, New York, NY 10018 or info@skyhorsepublishing.com.

Talos Press is an imprint of Skyhorse Publishing, Inc.®, a Delaware corporation.

Visit our website at www.talospress.com.

10 9 8 7 6 5 4 3 2 1

Library of Congress Cataloging-in-Publication Data on file.

Cover design by Erin Seaward-Hiatt
Cover photo credit: Jacket photography © Sean Gladwell/Getty Images (background), Thomas Winz/Getty Images (scythe), and Renphoto/Getty Images (smudges)

Print ISBN: 978-1-945863-80-6
Ebook ISBN 978-1-945863-82-0

Printed in the United States of America

For the Halloween People

*Night of the Reaper* (1980)
Script Pages Courtesy of Pinnacle Studios

EXT. CAMPFIRE - ASHLAND SUMMER CAMP - NIGHT

Camp director TIM sits in front of the campfire, surrounded by a ring of TEENAGED COUNSELORS.

                    TIM
          You guys know the legend, right?

Nerdy SHEILA pushes her glasses up the bridge of her nose.

                    SHEILA
          What legend?

                    TIM
          The legend of why Ashland quit
          farming in the fifties. Why
          they turned the cornfields into
          campgrounds. The land is cursed.
          The curse . . . of the Reaper!

Tough guy AXEL flips out his switchblade, carving a stick to roast marshmallows.

                    AXEL
          What the hell's a Reaper?

                    TIM
          Not what. Who?

Tim leans toward the crackling flames.

                    TIM
          His name was Lester Jensen. And
          his bloodline dated all the
          way back to this town's Danish
          founders. But Lester grew up an
          orphaned outcast. A mute who
          lived alone in an old, abandoned

barn and never spoke a word to anyone. Some people feared the man, but others hired him as their farmhand because he worked hard and never complained. Then one year, a blight struck every crop. The corn didn't sprout and the leaves just wilted and died on the stalk. Nobody knew why, but it didn't take long for the rumors to start swirling in town.

A gust of wind HOWLS through the circle as the counselors shiver and the fire flickers.

                    TIM
They said that Lester the mute was practicing animal sacrifice out in that barn of his. That he brought on the blight by worshipping the Devil. Folks worked themselves into a frenzy until that fateful harvest moon, when they all decided . . . Lester Jensen had to pay.

                    SHEILA
What'd they do to him?

                    TIM
This God-fearing community went medieval. And the punishment for heresy meant getting dragged behind a horse into the village square to be dismembered in front of a cheering crowd. So Farmer Joe and his sons drove out to Lester's barn to bring him to justice. They tied a rusty chain to the back of their truck and dragged the accused heretic straight through the rotting

cornfields toward town. Lester may have been a mute, but that night, everyone in Ashland could hear his cries, echoing across the land.

Axel twirls a blackening marshmallow on the end of his stick.

                    AXEL
So did they chop him up or what?

                    TIM
Never got a chance to. Because at some point, that chain came loose. Farmer Joe and his sons, they spent all night searching the field for his body, but Lester Jensen was gone. And so was the rusty chain.

                    SHEILA
You mean . . . Lester survived?

                    TIM
Some say he did. Some say he didn't. Either way, Lester came back . . . for revenge. The next day, the town awakened to a stream of blood flowing down Main Street. They found three gruesome scarecrows hanging in the town square. It was Farmer Joe and his sons. They'd been hacked limb from limb and nailed back together in mismatched pieces. Served up as a grisly message to the people of Ashland. A warning from the monster they now called . . . the Reaper.

A shudder ripples through the circle of teens.

                              TIM
          And every harvest moon, just like
          tonight, they say he's out here.
          Roaming in the dark where the
          cornfields used to be. Hunting
          down trespassers and harvesting
          their souls. They say if you
          listen closely, if it's veeery
          quiet . . . you can hear the
          distant clanking . . . of his
          rusty chain.

Silence falls upon the group, listening for any
sound they can hear over the SNAPS and POPS of logs
between them.

                             AXEL
          Boo!

Axel jumps to his feet, scaring the other counselors
as he laughs in their faces.

                            SHEILA
          That's not funny, Axel!

                             AXEL
          Oh, come on. Are you really scared
          that some freak farmhand is
          gonna--

CLANK! A rusty chain whips out of the darkness,
snapping around Axel's neck. He grasps at the metal
links, eyes bulging until——CRACK!——Axel's neck
snaps and his rag doll body is yanked back into
the shadows.

The counselors are paralyzed in terror as . . .

THE REAPER steps into the firelight! His shredded
face oozes blood as ribbons of flesh hang above

ragged overalls. He growls through shattered teeth,
voice hoarse with gravel.

                    THE REAPER
          Children of Ashland . . . it's
          time to reap what you've sown.

The teens SCREAM and scatter as the monster swings
his rusty chain, CACKLING into the night as the
blood harvest begins.

# PART I:
# RESIGNATION

# 1

"What was your favorite kill?"

Howard had been asked the question countless times over the years. With so many guttings and bludgeonings and dismemberments to choose from, he used to enjoy indulging his fans with a colorful selection from his résumé of mayhem. But today, fifteen years since his last lethal outing, he could no longer hide his weariness as he leaned on a rote response.

"My favorite kill is at the end of *Part IV: The Final Reaping*, when the Reaper himself is finally slain and burned to ashes."

The balding fan on the other side of the table frowned, cracking the foundation of his homemade zombie makeup. "Yeah, but . . . you came back." Zombie Man pointed over Howard's shoulder, where posters for all eight *Night of the Reaper* films hung on display in the cramped convention booth. "The Reaper always rises again."

Howard felt the weight of every flimsy poster like another millstone around the neck of his sunken career as he forced a nod. "Indeed he does."

Zombie Man grinned at the woman beside him, who blushed in her bloodstained prom dress. "My wife, she's too scared to ask," he explained, holding up a digital camera. "But do you think she could get a photo with you?"

"Of course," Howard replied, accustomed to the request. "That'll be twenty dollars." The exchange always felt a bit tacky, but he'd decided long ago that it was a matter of artistic principle to reinforce the worth of a professional actor's labor.

The woman handed Howard a red-tinged bill as he stood beside her now, careful not to bump his freshly pressed slacks against her sticky dress.

At six-foot three, he was used to dwarfing most people with his slender frame as he hunched his head above her shoulder, adjusting his parted silver hair before giving a gentle smile for the camera.

Zombie Man frowned again, lowering his lens. "Sorry, it's just . . . Could you . . ."

"Be the Reaper," Howard blushed. He sometimes forgot that it wasn't *him* the fans were coming to meet. It was the sinister slasher who punished countless teens for trespassing on his land through the entire decade of the 1980s. Howard never wore the Reaper's true face at these horror film conventions, but even without the marred flesh that would've taken five hours in a makeup chair to construct, he still knew how to give the fans their twenty dollars' worth.

He wrapped his hands around the eager woman's neck for a faux choke, snarling the monster's rage toward the camera until Zombie Man finally snapped his photo with a gleeful giggle. The flash lingered in Howard's blurry vision as he released his death grip and the once-silent wife leapt off her feet to plant a kiss on his freshly shaven cheek.

"You're my favorite," she breathily confessed. "Freddy and Jason are scrubs. I know the Reaper could take them in a heartbeat."

Howard offered a gracious, "Thank you," as he backed away from her starry eyes and returned safely behind the fold-up table. He knew not to engage with the die-hard fans too deeply, lest he find himself with a stalker.

"Have a lovely weekend, you two," Howard dismissed Zombie Man and his bloody bride. As they skipped away together, hand in hand, he lowered himself back into the folding chair, arthritic knees creaking. His gaze fell now to the glossy publicity stills on the table, where his alter ego cast a mocking grin up at him, swinging the iconic rusty chain with eternal exuberance. Howard had signed thousands of these grotesque glamour shots over the years, so many that his right hand was now permanently cramped from gripping the black Sharpie as he scrawled:

*Dear So-and-So, Happy Harvest! XX The Reaper.*

It used to be that he hardly had time for a bathroom break as his devotees flocked to conference centers all over the globe, lining up for hours just to meet their beloved monster. But there was no line now as Howard looked up at the scattered attendees, moseying among a few dozen pop-up booths for other cult horror films. This happened to be a local event, which meant returning to the comfort of his own bed rather than suffering the night beneath a scratchy hotel bedspread. The thought of a warm bath beckoned as he decided to call it an early day, packing his tote bag along with the conspicuously light envelope of twenty-dollar bills.

As he lumbered toward the hotel conference room exit, a cleaning crew was already pushing their vacuums along the carpets. The stale smell of sweat seemed permanently soaked into these places, and Howard was desperate to breathe fresh air that hadn't been recycled through mouths that munched on microwaved snack-bar pizza.

A banner thanked him for attending Dead World Weekend 2005 as he stepped through the automatic doors of the airport Radisson into the warm Los Angeles spring. Peeling off the sweater he wore to combat the frigid air-conditioning, he traversed the near-empty parking lot to his brown Cadillac DeVille. He tossed his tote bag in the trunk before easing behind the wheel and turning the ignition, only to be met with a resistant gurgle.

"Come on, old gal," he begged as the hot sun beat through the windshield. "Not today." The car he'd proudly bought after the success of the first film was pushing over 200,000 miles now, but Howard wasn't ready to give up on her yet. Sure, the paint had faded from its original walnut shine into a dull rust tint, but he'd be damned if he ever traded her in for one of those shiny new electric monstrosities. Howard was all for saving the planet, but he resented a throwaway culture that discarded things before they'd lived out their full terms of purpose, always seeking some newer, sleeker model.

After a few more persistent grinds, the engine finally grumbled to life. He exhaled with relief, reaching for the gear stick only to find a Post-it Note there with a reminder spelled out in his own careful cursive: *Cat Food*.

Every time he came across one of these notes, he was reminded anew of Dr. Cho's recent diagnosis of Alzheimer's disease. Howard resented her suggestion that he was already going senile and in need of such degrading mental assistance, but he couldn't deny that he'd been relying on these little yellow squares more and more of late.

It seemed that warm bath would have to wait as he plucked the Post-it from the shifter, steeling himself for the two-hour odyssey of creeping crosstown traffic toward his neighborhood grocery store. As he rolled out of the lot, a departing plane roared overhead, sending a sweeping shadow over the asphalt like the specter of death itself, passing him by.

By the time Howard arrived home, a purple dusk was settling over the old Victorian house at the end of the cul-de-sac. Nestled in the Altadena foothills, his home was just far enough from the madness of Hollywood to make it feel like living in the real world, which is exactly why he and Emma had chosen it. Ascending the porch steps now, he eyed the pair of Adirondack chairs where they used to share their morning tea. Flecks of white paint peeled from the sunbaked wood as the chairs had long since fallen into disuse, but he just couldn't bring himself to throw them away. He half expected to open the front door now and find Emma waiting in the parlor, swaying to a Joni Mitchell record with a smile on her face. But as he entered the silent house, the only one coming to greet him in the foyer was Stanley.

"Hello, my little brute." Howard bent down to scratch his feline companion behind the ears. "You must be famished." He cracked the off-brand can of Frisky Whiskers, releasing a pungent odor into the air as he placed the tin on the hardwood floor. The black cat sniffed at the globby mixture and recoiled.

"They were fresh out of Fancy Feast," Howard explained. "Don't be difficult, Stanley."

The animal conceded, pecking at his subpar meal with a domestic displeasure befitting his namesake. Stanley Kowalski had been Howard's first starring role back at the conservatory when *A Streetcar Named Desire* was chosen for their graduate showcase. The violent character served as a formative challenge then for the bookish young actor. "Stage drama is not real life," his professor had told him. "It's *more* real than real life."

The cordless phone rang to life on the end table as Howard shot across the hall to answer it. "This is Howard Browning."

"Howie!" squawked the voice on the other end.

There was only one person in the world who called Howard "Howie," against consistent requests to the contrary. All Hollywood agents were trained to be schmoozy, but twenty-five-year-old Jake Friedman was a bit too overzealous for someone who'd never landed his client an acting job. As soon as public appearances became Howard's primary occupation, the powers that be at Universal Talent Incorporated began shuffling him from one fledgling representative to another.

"How's my favorite client?" asked this current incarnation of false enthusiasm.

"Fine, Jacob." Howard twisted his vertebrae back into alignment. "Nice of you to return my call, two weeks later."

"Sorry, buddy, it's been crazy. Pilot season and all that."

"That so?" There was a time when Howard wouldn't dream of stooping to the level of televised dramas, but he couldn't help perking up now at the thought of all those new series with dozens of roles, fresh for the casting. "Anything you're sending me out for?"

"Unless you can play a 'twentysomething girl, as smart as she is sexy,'" Jake said, "this may not be your season. But hey, if you're itching to act, I could give Lunatic Pictures a call back. See if they still want you for the mad scientist role in that zombie movie."

"No, no," Howard swatted away the suggestion. After being permanently typecast as a genre villain, the only offers that ever came down the pipeline were slight cameos in direct-to-video horror fare, and even those were few and far between. He'd made the mistake of taking such a job once about ten years ago, still optimistic and eager to practice his craft again in earnest. Instead, he found himself trapped on a shoestring amateur production in rural Bulgaria, where he spent most of his days curled up on the outhouse floor with a crippling stomach bug.

"I'm not that desperate," Howard said.

"Damn straight," Jake responded. "That's because I've been busy booking your ass up and down the coast. How was Death Fest?"

"Dead World," Howard corrected, carrying his tote bag down the hall.

"What?"

"Death Fest was last month in Sacramento," Howard explained. "This weekend is Dead World."

"Right, right, Death World." Still wrong. "So how's it going?"

"I'd say it's aptly named." Howard opened the cellar door and walked down the creaky steps into darkness. He tugged the cord of the swinging bulb as the light dimly illuminated an endless collection of Reaper memorabilia, packed onto shelves and spilling out into piles on the floor. Claustrophobia sunk in every time he came down here, crowded in by boxes of T-shirts and posters, cardboard standees and costume masks, action figures wielding tiny plastic chains, all preserved in pristine packaging. These collectibles only grew more extensive as the sequels got kitschier and the Reaper's hellish charisma earned him pop culture icon status. By the end of the 80s, the monster's image and quotable quips could be found plastered on everything from mugs and beach towels to lunchboxes and watches. Howard sold what he could at conventions and stashed the rest here, in this defunct Reaper museum with no curator.

He dropped his tote bag onto the closest pile of basement detritus, next to a bloodstained basketball. This notable gem was from the '86 Bulls halftime show where he appeared in full makeup to promote *Part VI: Urban Harvest*. He still couldn't believe he'd sunk that free throw over the sound of the arena's electric roar, thousands of voices chanting as their energy pulsed through his fingertips.

*"REAP-ER! REAP-ER! REAP-ER!"*

"So what do you need?" Jake chirped through the phone, shaking him from the visceral reverie. "More publicity stills? I could check with the studio, see if they've got anything stowed away."

"No, I have plenty of photos. That's the problem. I hardly signed half a stack today and I don't even bother lugging the memorabilia anymore. The fans just aren't coming out the way they used to."

Howard suspected the cause for this decline in attendance could be summed up in one word: Internet. Conventions used to be the only place that like-minded oddballs could congregate, but now instant-gratification outlets for fandom were found online. These virtual forums might scratch a temporary itch, but Howard still believed that there was simply no substitute for flesh-and-blood human interaction.

"You short on cash, Howie?" Jake asked. "Times are tight for everyone right now, but if you want to hold on to my ten percent of the autograph cash from this weekend, I'd do that for you, buddy. You know I take care of you."

Howard resisted pointing out what a generous sacrifice that forty dollars would be, as making such a petty jab would have required admitting just how thin his collections had been.

"I appreciate that, Jacob, but it's not about the money. I'm just not sure who I'm doing this for anymore. And I'm tired," Howard finally admitted, still slightly out of breath from descending the cellar steps. "Perhaps it's time I called it quits."

His sixty-fifth birthday had passed quietly like any other day, save for the letter he received from the Screen Actors Guild congratulating him on reaching the union's standard retirement age. The pension benefits could easily cover his modest lifestyle for years to come, but the question remained what he would do with himself if he embraced true retirement. As much as these conventions were wearing him down, they at least provided some semblance of structure and purpose to his otherwise empty days.

"I know the circuit's a grind and turnout can be hit or miss," Jake responded with strained empathy, having never attended a convention with Howard before, "but don't forget we've got HorrorCon '05 just around the corner. The Reaper-heads will be coming out in the thousands for that one, and you can't quit on them now, Howie. I mean, a Lifetime Achievement Award is a serious honor."

"Yes." Howard's eyes caught on a collectible tin lunchbox in the corner. An image of the Reaper impaling a victim through the mouth with an ear of corn as the speech bubble read: *Eat your veggies!* "A serious honor."

"Listen, I've got to hop off for another call right now, but let's just focus on one convention at a time. You give 'em hell at Death Fest this weekend and we'll touch base before the next one, all right? All right! Catch you later, Howie!"

The line went dead before Howard could utter a response. Staring out at the heaps of pop culture relics collecting dust in a dank cellar, he was reminded of his favorite Shelley poem.

*"My name is Ozymandias, king of kings,"* the epitaph of that arrogant emperor read. *"Look upon my works, ye Mighty, and despair!"* But his statue lay shattered and forgotten in the vast desert as the narrator observed: *"Nothing beside remains. Round the decay of that colossal wreck, boundless and bare, the lone and level sands stretch far away."*

Howard looked upon his own wreckage now with the cold realization that this wasn't a museum, no. This was a graveyard. A tomb. He reached up to tug the light bulb cord, casting his haunted history back into darkness as the future grew fainter than ever.

## 2

Howard wasn't sure where the night had gone as he pulled up to the airport Radisson the next morning. He never did take that warm bath, having fallen asleep in the parlor chair with Stanley curled in his lap. Groggily awakening to daylight with Dostoevsky's *Demons* open on his chest, he'd found himself uncharacteristically late. On top of that, there was hardly a free space in the lot this morning, likely airport overflow on a popular weekend travel day.

When he finally found a spot some distance from the hotel entrance, he wished he hadn't skipped his usual English breakfast tea. He'd long given up coffee, finding that it rattled his nerves to the point where he couldn't keep the Sharpie steady, but he yearned for some kind of artificial pep now as he climbed out of his car. Voicing his fatigue to Jake had only cemented his awareness of it as he popped the trunk and stared at his tote bag of publicity stills.

Perhaps he should just play hooky today. Get back in his car and drive away before—

"Howard fucking Browning." The hoarse voice muttered inches from his ear as a hand clamped down on his shoulder.

Howard shuddered, having thought himself well past the days of fans rushing him in the parking lot. But as he turned toward his accoster, he was surprised to find a familiar woman's face, weathered behind thick black glasses and topped with a white crew cut.

"Joan," Howard breathed through a relieved smile.

"Christ, it's good to see you." Joan gave a tobacco-stained grin as she pulled Howard in for a hug against her green army jacket. The smell of Parliament cigarettes wafting from her clothing brought Howard right back to Joan's makeup chair. He'd sit on her throne for hours every shoot day while she painstakingly crafted the Reaper's grisly visage, regaling him with stories from her past life as a Vietnam War combat photographer. There weren't many women on the front lines in those days, let alone openly gay women, but "Jersey Joan" was an Army brat who could hold her own with the foulmouthed grunts. She also snuck her fair share of passionate trysts with lonely nurses when she wasn't documenting the visceral devastation that would someday inspire her gory special effects wizardry.

Joan's work on the Reaper's gruesome demise in *Part IV* rightfully won her a Fexie Award, but it had been years since Howard had seen his old friend on the convention circuit. As he finally released from the hug, he realized it was the first physical human contact he'd had in some time, outside of awkwardly staged photo ops.

"I had no idea you were on the schedule," Howard said.

"I wasn't. They're doing this special effects panel, wanted to have the old guard chatting with the new," Joan explained, lighting a fresh cigarette. "Marty Brogan was supposed to be on it. You remember Marty, right?"

"Of course. He designed the Reaper spawn for *Part VII*."

*Seed of the Reaper* was Howard's least favorite entry in the series, starting with the problematic dream-rape sequence and culminating in the birth of the "Baby Reaper." Marty was nothing if not creative, but the rusty chain umbilical cord was a particularly misguided touch.

"Well, he dropped dead last week," Joan puffed. "Heart attack. Face-first in a plate of eggs, right in front of his poor wife."

"That's awful," Howard replied. Awful, but not uncommon. He couldn't help noticing that the many ailments of old age were starting to pick off his cinematic comrades one by one, like the victims of their films.

"Anyway," Joan explained, "they asked me to fill in, and I figured screw it. Might be fun to jump back into the trenches for a day. It's a trip doing these things every now and then, don't you think?"

"Oh, yes." Howard finally turned to close the trunk and hide his blushing face. "Every now and then." He deftly changed the subject as he motioned to the canvas duffel bag over Joan's shoulder. "Which one did you bring today?"

Joan dug into the bag, unearthing a severed silicon head with its mouth agape in death. The flesh-colored paint was chipping away, but it still looked remarkably convincing with the glistening red splatter at the torn neck giving it that wet feel.

"Ah," Howard grinned, "*Part III*, wasn't it? *Fields of Blood*. I believe the poor fellow's name was Brad."

Joan shrugged. "Who remembers the names?"

"Well, as I recall, the Reaper only tore Brad's head off after giving it a good squeeze," Howard grinned. "So let's see the real effect, maestro."

It was Joan who blushed now, embarrassed of her own work as she reached for a small hand-pump attached to the air tube that ran up the back of the severed head. Joan gave the pump a hard squeeze, sending Brad's left eyeball popping out of the socket to hang by stringy red tendons. Howard let out an amused laugh as Joan muttered, "Old dog, old tricks."

"You *invented* the tricks," Howard noted as they began their walk to the hotel. "How have you been? Last we spoke you were opening a military supply store?"

"Army Navy, yeah," Joan replied. "Business ain't exactly booming, mostly just obnoxious hipsters looking for vintage T-shirts. But it keeps me busy, ya know? At my age, that's all I can really ask for. Especially with these son-of-a-bitchin' cataracts," she motioned to the cloudy eyes behind her glasses. "What about you? Still in the acting game?"

"Yes, of course, busy as ever," Howard responded on reflex, hoping the quick lie wasn't too obvious.

"Glad to hear it," Joan smiled, tossing her cigarette butt as she motioned to the Dead World Weekend 2005 banner over the hotel entrance. "You ready to face the fiends?"

"If today's anything like yesterday, I'm afraid we're in for a rather quiet one."

"Suits me. It'll give us more time to catch up." Joan gave him a sturdy pat on the back.

"I'd like that, Joan. Very much," Howard replied with a grateful smile. The automatic doors whirred open as the sound of a clamoring crowd engulfed them. The place was packed, hundreds of people milling about, far more than yesterday.

"Quiet my ass," Joan muttered.

Howard was stunned, searching for some explanation. "Perhaps there's a memorial for Marty?"

"Perhaps," Joan playfully echoed. "Catch you later, Frasier."

Joan walked off as Howard headed in the direction of his booth, squeezing his way through the throng of masked monsters. The closer he got, the more he saw that the masses were forming into a line, stretching all the way along the wall, rounding a corner and continuing onward. What were they all lined up for? Had the snack bar just restocked with microwaved pizza?

Heads began to turn toward him, whispering and murmuring with a building excitement as he noticed that their attire was becoming more uniform. The T-shirts and masks and swinging plastic chains . . .

These were Reaper fans.

Howard finally arrived at his little fold-up table to see that it was all leading here. This crowd was here for *him*, and they began to cheer now at the sight of him. He gave a confused smile as Jake emerged from the makeshift curtain behind the booth, wearing a suit that was two sizes too big as he talked into his cellular phone.

"Yes, sir," Jake stuttered, wiping the sweat from his boyish brow. "He just got here. I'll take care of it." He snapped the phone shut and rushed toward Howard.

"Jacob? What are you doing here? What's going on?" Howard had to raise his voice over the crowd's growing cheers.

"We need to talk," Jake practically shouted as he moved back behind the curtain, pulling a confused Howard, whose senses were awakened by the exuberant buzz he hadn't heard in ages.

"That was Chuck Slattery on the phone," Jake explained.

"Chuck?"

It had been years since Howard last heard from the franchise executive producer, who made the first *Night of the Reaper* film on an independent budget before selling it to Pinnacle Studios and raking in a small fortune in sequels. Back when the franchise was alive and well, Chuck would treat his slasher star to the occasional dinner in expensive Beverly Hills restaurants. It wasn't exactly a friendship, but at least it was cordial. After the films ended, Howard would sporadically call to suggest a lunch catch-up, but was consistently told that the busy man was "on the other line."

"What did he want?" Howard wondered aloud now, after all those years of call dodging.

"Some news leaked this morning," Jake explained. "Pinnacle was going to announce it at the end of the month, but these kids with their blogs, rumors spread faster than chlamyd—"

"Just tell me," Howard demanded, more curt than he had intended. His head was starting to throb from the cacophony of voices on the other side of the curtain as Jake finally answered.

"They're remaking *Night of the Reaper*."

Howard heard the words, but could hardly process them as they bounced around inside his skull, yearning to land in some place of understanding until one of them slipped its way back out of his mouth.

"Remaking?" Howard repeated.

If there was one thing Howard knew about remakes from his days on the convention circuit, it was that the fans were not fans of this recent trend. There was something sacred about the original texts, however rough around the edges they may be. More often than not, these remakes replaced the grit with gloss, effectively removing the soul of the horror itself. Participating in such an unforgivable recreation of his own work amounted to sacrilege, but even that artistic consideration was secondary to Howard's primary concern at this moment.

"It's been fifteen years," he uttered. "Does Chuck really think I have another one in me?"

The mere thought of chasing teenagers nearly fifty years his younger made his joints ache. Besides, this wasn't the first time Chuck had lured

Howard to return when he thought the franchise was dead and buried. Signing on for *Part V: The New Crop* had been the final straw that broke his marriage's back, and Howard was living with the consequences of that choice every day now. All alone in that big empty house.

"Don't worry," Jake said, as if responding to Howard's inner thoughts. "You're off the hook. They're recasting the role."

The din of the crowd muted and the floor dropped out below him as Howard tried again to grasp what he was being told.

Recasting the Reaper? The character was his creation, painstakingly built through the actor's craft from a mere sketch on the page into a living, breathing thing. From the slow cadence of his gravelly voice to the slight limp in his gait, the Reaper wasn't simply a role he performed. It was a skin he wore, wet and sticky on the inside as latex constricted the blood vessels beneath his face, contributing to the monster's visceral rage. Regardless of whether or not he was up to the task of playing the role again, there simply was no Reaper without Howard Browning.

"The fans don't know yet," Jake continued, "but Pinnacle wants to take the character in a new direction, skewing younger for a new generation." His phone chimed, drawing his attention away from Howard as he flipped it open. "You know how it is."

Jake seemed oblivious to the fact that he was a perfect display of "how it was" with today's youth, clicking away on his phone in the middle of a conversation. Modern technology was making it worse, but the self-centeredness of adolescence was a timeless phenomenon that Howard had witnessed while mentoring so many teen actors throughout the Reaper franchise. He would coach his bright-eyed young costars into professionalism, and they would inevitably graduate into breakout careers, leaving him trapped in the dust of Ashland without so much as a glance over their shoulders. That old wound was being pried back open now as Howard wondered what fresh-faced fool was being groomed to take up the mantle for this wretched remake.

"Who could possibly," came the words from his mouth, which he quickly adjusted for propriety's sake. "I mean, do they have someone in mind?"

"You remember *Family Genius?* Sitcom from the nineties? Little Trevor Mane. 'Indubitably!'" Jake laughed at his own imitation of a kitschy catch-phrase that was utterly lost on Howard.

"I'm afraid I'm not familiar with his work," he coldly replied.

"Anyway, kid's all grown up and into front-page news, so Chuck's making a big push for him at the studio. The teen demographic loves him."

A baffled Howard motioned toward the curtain, where the fans' grumbling impatience was starting to rise. "What about the *fan* demographic? Does Chuck really think they'll accept a new Reaper?"

"He's not concerned," Jake responded dismissively. "Sure, they'll whine in the online comments sections right up until the release date. Then they'll shell out their ten bucks and whine some more when they get home."

Howard bit his tongue, knowing it was true. The fans' distaste for remakes didn't stop them from showing up on opening weekend, if only to confirm their own righteous indignation. "And what, exactly, am I supposed to tell them now?" he asked, raising his voice above the rowdy crowd.

"Got that covered, too," Jake said, reaching into his suit pocket to unfold a printed sheet of paper as he handed it to Howard. "Chuck faxed this over to the business center."

*For Howard Browning—Official Statement Re: Reaper Replacement.*

There it was, in cold black and white. He'd gotten through "remake" and "recasting," only to be stabbed through the heart with this third alliterative dagger.

*Replacement.*

There was something so damningly personal about the word that knocked the wind straight out of him. As Howard struggled to regain his breath, the chanting on the other side of the curtain became undeniable, their raving energy giving a steady shock to his system.

"REAP-ER! REAP-ER! REAP-ER!"

"You better get out there," Jake advised. "The villagers are getting restless."

The single sheet of paper was heavy in his hands as Howard crossed the curtained threshold to face his fans, no longer waiting in a neatly formed line, but eagerly pressed up against the table in a messy mob. All eyes hungrily locked on him as they cheered relentlessly. It was all he could do to stand there and let this wave of adoration wash over him, until Jake finally gave him a gentle pat on the back, pulling him back to earth for the laborious task at hand.

He lowered himself into the folding chair as he clutched the statement in front of him and the crowd hushed, reverently awaiting his words. It was so quiet, he could hear the gentle hum of the air-conditioning vent overhead as he opened his mouth to speak.

"Hello," Howard tentatively began, reaching into his shirt pocket to retrieve his reading glasses. The slight frames trembled as he slipped them onto his face, clearing his throat as he started to read the statement for the first time, aloud.

"As you all know, the news broke this morning that Pinnacle Studios is remaking *Night of the Reaper*. Many of you may be wondering whether or not I will be returning to this iconic role."

The silence gave way as the ravenous group before him once again erupted with expectant cheers. The lump in Howard's throat grew larger as a sad smile crept across his face and he lowered his gaze to press onward.

"I'm sorry to disappoint you all. But the time has come for me to pass the rusty chain." Howard looked up into the crowd, watching in real time as every face turned. Expressions of joy and elation now reverting to confusion and anger as Howard felt the sting of every scowl. Then the shouting began, all voices clamoring above each other so furiously that Howard could barely make out complete sentences.

"Bullshit!"

"They can't replace you!"

"*You're* the Reaper!"

Howard shrank, helpless in the face of their blind rage, some part of him wanting nothing more than to commiserate with them in the injustice of it all. Instead, he read onward, faster now.

"I appreciate your constant support through the years, but it would be irresponsible of me to go on playing the role when I am so far past the years of my prime." His gut churned. Past the years of his prime? Did

Chuck really think this was a fair assessment of his condition? He wanted to rip the statement to shreds, but he knew he just had to get through it, letting himself be dragged along by the words as he white-knuckled the paper in his hands.

"You deserve more. The Reaper deserves more. And I fully support Chuck Slattery and Pinnacle Studios as they plan to give the monster new life with fresh blood." A wave of nausea overtook him as the shouts resounded once again, now muted by the fog in his brain as he looked out at the blur of angry mugs.

"We deserve *you*!"

"You're the best, Howard!"

"Fuck Pinnacle!"

*I'll give them fresh blood.*

Howard shuddered at the sound of the Reaper's raspy voice, booming much louder than all the others. At first, he thought it was a fan doing an impression of the character, but no. That dark declaration came from within, a thought that no one else could hear. As if he'd momentarily slipped into the mindset of the character amid all that commotion. He tried to shake off this frightening mental glitch as his head pounded and he wiped the sweat from his brow, desperate to be done.

"Thank you for your time and remember . . . the Reaper will rise again." The rest of the page was blank as he looked up to the confused crowd. "I'm sorry . . ." he mumbled. "That's all."

The angry mob swelled at the abrupt conclusion and Jake tried his best to corral them back into a line. Howard remained seated as, one by one, they approached his table to hold communion with their elder, venting their outrage as he nodded along with sympathy. The day passed in a strange haze as he signed several stacks of publicity stills, each fan walking away with a head hung low in disappointment until the crowd finally dissipated. Jake was quick to collect his ten percent before leaving for a "drinks meeting" and promising he'd "be in touch." But Howard was cemented to his chair, the weight of the fans' anger pooling within. As if they'd all dumped their rage directly into him and now it was his to sit with, simmering inside with no outlet for release.

"Hey, Browning." The familiar smoky voice shook Howard from his stupor as he looked up to find Joan standing on the other side of the table with a sympathetic smile. "This Dead World got a bar or what?"

## 3

Howard spun his full glass of chardonnay on its coaster, staring absently into the amber liquid as Joan pounded her third bourbon on the stool beside him. He was never much of a drinker and he certainly wasn't in the mood now as his stomach rolled over, urging him to speak.

"I never should have read that statement. 'The Reaper deserves *more?*'" Howard bitterly recited the self-reproach he'd been force-fed. "What does that even *mean?*" He wished he could go back in time and speak from the heart. Not from some cold declaration of defeat.

"Fuck Chuck," Joan muttered through malted lips.

The verbiage was crude, but Howard agreed with the sentiment. Chuck never so much as gave him a warning that this Reaper remake was in the works, let alone that he'd already settled on Howard's replacement. This entire affair had been rudely mishandled, and Howard intended to let Chuck know, if he could ever get past the producer's assistant.

"The whole industry's gone to shit," Joan continued in a booze-soaked lament. "You know they don't even do *zombies* with prosthetics anymore? They've got this bright green paint, do all the rotting flesh in the editing room. Computerized bullshit."

Howard was familiar with the dawning age of CGI, which was used to a regrettable degree in *Part VIII: Moon Reaper.* The effects were nowhere near convincing in 1990, when an intergalactic space crew battled the Reaper's chain with star-sabers and laser guns, and they'd only grown more cringeworthy with time. Howard had always viewed that laborious eighth entry as an unceremonious end for his portrayal of the character, with the

26

Reaper getting ejected from the spaceship's airlock toward his final lunar grave. But here he was now, being jettisoned even farther into the abyss. Where no one can hear you disappear.

"Can I get another, hon?" Joan winked at the woman behind the bar before turning her attention back to Howard. "Point is, horror just ain't what it used to be. That's exactly what we were saying on the panel today. See, the seventies were savage and gritty, like war documentaries. Then came the eighties, when gore FX peaked and real creativity thrived. But when the nineties rolled in with their smug-ass irony, it turned the whole genre into one big self-referential joke. So now we're stuck in the middle of this . . . what'd they call it . . . millennial malaise. The fans feel it, too. You can tell."

Howard hadn't exactly been an avid fan of the genre when he was pigeonholed into it straight out of the New York theater scene, but he'd developed a reserved appreciation for it over the years. For better or worse, horror always seemed to have its finger on the pulse of humanity, projecting our timeliest fears and ugliest truths in bloody Grand Guignol fashion. But what he felt from the fans today was not inert malaise, no. It was active, aggressive.

"You should have heard them, Joan. The anger, the disappointment. I just can't help feeling like I'm somehow abandoning them." Even though the entire enterprise was out of his control, he truly did feel like he was letting his fans down. He understood from their perspective how it seemed as if he were simply giving up, perhaps even eager to "pass the chain."

"What'd you expect, Browning? They love you," Joan said as she reached for her fresh drink.

Howard had always dismissed the "L" word in the context of fandom. Obsession, yes. A form of reverence, perhaps. But was it truly love that they harbored in their hearts for him? He twisted his wineglass, recalling every disgruntled face.

"If they loved me before, they hate me now." He'd given them so much, eight films and so many more years in Sharpie-bound servitude. But it wasn't enough. They wanted him for life.

"They'll come back around." Joan turned to her friend with a smirk now. "I ever tell you how much *I* hated you when we first met?"

"I'm not sure you needed to tell me. I felt it rather strongly."

"'I felt it rather strongly.' See, that's exactly why."

It wasn't the first time Howard had been teased for the not-quite-British elocution he'd picked up while studying classical cinema from the Cary Grant era. He simply believed that in drama, every phrase, every word, every enunciation mattered.

"But it wasn't just the phony accent," Joan went on. "Day one of the first film, you came into my makeup trailer with a stick so far up your ass, I wasn't sure how you were gonna sit in the chair. You were the most pompous son of a bitch I'd ever met, took yourself so goddamn seriously."

"If your goal is to cheer me up . . ."

"But then you took the role seriously, too," Joan explained. "And that's why the franchise went on for all those years. You flipped a switch, and you gave the Reaper life."

Howard smiled. He'd always admired the way Joan had channeled every oozing memory from the battlefield straight into her work through all those ghastly permutations of human anatomy. But he never knew just how deeply this maestro of fatal effects appreciated Howard's own creative efforts. It warmed his heart to hear her support now, if only for a moment, before that warmth gave way to the coldness of his current reality.

"And yet this is the way it ends." Howard looked to the stool beside him, where his tote bag of Reaper stills lay. "Not with a bang. But a whimper."

He finally took a swig of wine, only to find his mouth filled with an acidic swill. He considered telling the bartender that the bottle may have gone bad, but it was his own fault for ordering wine from an airport hotel bar.

"Hey," Joan offered, "just remember that you gave birth to a legend. And no one can take that away from you. Legends are forever."

Joan killed the last of her bourbon and hopped off her stool. "All right, chief. This old lady needs her beauty sleep." She threw a crumpled bill down on the bar before patting Howard on the back. "Take care of yourself."

"You too, Joan." Howard watched his friend walk off, leaving him alone with his stale wine.

"How's your wine, sir?" the bartender asked.

"Wonderful, thank you. Just the check, please."

Howard lay in bed that night, half-watching the end of the evening news in an effort to distract his thoughts long enough for sleep to come. They were reporting the story of a teenaged girl who had been abducted and held captive in a basement for fourteen years. Finally escaping as a grown woman, she told her tale now in a heart-wrenching interview. It was not the abject traumas she had endured at the hands of her captor that struck him, but rather the frightening notion of losing such a huge swath of one's life. He wondered what came next for her. Could she truly reintegrate into the world again? Or would some piece of her always be missing, stumbling through her waking days as an incomplete puzzle? Some people criticized horror films for their ghastly depictions of violent behavior, but the fake terrors of the silver screen paled in comparison to what real-world psychopaths were capable of.

Emma had been one such critic of the genre. She was a women's studies major at Barnard when they met in New York in the 1970s, and Howard was doing meaningful theater that Emma truly admired. When he got a callback for *Night of the Reaper* in LA and returned to their cramped studio apartment with the offer, Emma was wary of his big break. She was concerned about the harm that horror films were doing to our collective culture and psyches, citing the rampant violence against women in exploitation films that screened in the same sleazy Times Square theaters as pornography. But Howard assured Emma that this was the only horror film he'd ever make. The paycheck, he promised, would serve as a down payment on their first house, a shared dream that solidified their big move west.

"Besides," he'd told her as he wrapped his long arms around her. "It's only a movie. And movies can't hurt people."

*"Who will survive? Tune in to find out who's leaving the island on this week's Exile."*

The booming commercial pulled Howard back from the memory as he found himself staring at the empty space in the bed beside him. He finally shuffled toward the television, a boxy old thing with a built-in VCR and a long-defunct remote, but before he could turn it off, the next program began with a cheesy jingle. The title appeared on the screen, bringing him face-to-face with *Family Genius*.

This was the sitcom Jake had mentioned. The one that starred Howard's replacement.

All efforts to push the day's traumatic events into the recesses of his mind came undone now as he squinted at the screen. He'd always despised the sitcom format, oozing with falsely peachy family values as canned laughter dictated to its audience what was funny and what wasn't. The fact that reruns ran endlessly into the night, when insomniacs might use the vapid content to lull their brains into an unconscious state, spoke to the sitcom's true nature as the opiate of the masses. So what possible talent could Chuck have plucked from the depths of this mind-numbing tele-vised diversion as his top choice for the Reaper?

The opening scene unfolded against a cheap plywood kitchen set, where a mother cooking breakfast in her apron fortified golden age expec-tations of a woman's role in society. Was this domestic servitude really a better model than the iconic "final girl" who survived every slasher film, outwitting and triumphantly slaying her masculine attacker?

"Tommy?" the mother called toward the stairs. "Are you ready for school?"

A nine-year-old boy hopped down the steps wearing suspenders and glasses, hair perfectly parted as he adjusted his bowtie with eyebrows raised.

"Indubitably!" the boy replied with glee. The off-screen audience responded with hysterical cheers as Howard glared at a young Trevor Mane.

"Do you want your eggs sunny-side or scrambled?" the mother asked as the child opened a large textbook at the kitchen table.

"Poached please, Mother. And preferably duck," the precocious brat responded. The hammy audience erupted again with laughter as Howard clicked the television off in disgust.

"Genius," he scoffed, climbing back into bed as Stanley purred beside him. Tossing and turning, Howard tried to remind himself that this remake, offensive as it may be, was providing him with exactly what he'd wanted. A way out. He now had a legitimate excuse to move on from the Reaper, retire for the rest of his life and find some respite from the world of the dead.

It was time to just be Howard now. And Howard was free.

But he could not sleep.

## 4

Trevor Mane signed his first autograph at the age of nine, when he'd only just started learning how to write in cursive from his on-set tutor. He'd since honed his swooping scrawl thousands of times on everything from *Family Genius* memorabilia to *Teen Throb* magazines. But the signature he was about to ink at the age of twenty-seven was special.

*This document hereby releases Chrysalis Rehabilitation Clinic from all legal responsibility for the below signed.*

It had been sixty days, the longest stint he'd ever done in one of these places. Even longer than the court-ordered month he got after his coke-fueled twenty-first birthday bash, when he broke into that boutique on Melrose to steal a leather motorcycle jacket. Through all the legal mayhem and fines that ensued, his lawyer somehow managed to negotiate for Trevor to keep the jacket. He was wearing it now, cracked and worn out in all the right ways that only seemed to highlight his still-boyish good looks. But despite the timeless allure of his carefully disheveled black hair, Trevor discovered that people found his sloppy behavior less and less charming as he edged into his late twenties.

And he'd done something a lot worse than steal a jacket this time around.

"It's up to you now, Trevor," his counselor Dr. Liz reminded him as he stared at the release form now. "You've made amazing progress here, but nobody's going to help you on the outside unless you help yourself first."

She had advised him to go to a Narcotics Anonymous meeting on day one, find a sponsor and keep working the Twelve Steps. He'd made it through the first three under her wing, though not without a struggle.

Step One was a no-brainer by now, admitting that he was powerless over addiction and that his life had become unmanageable. But the next two, believing that a power greater than himself could restore him to sanity, and then turning his will and his life over to the care of a God of his own understanding? Those were rough. Trevor didn't believe in God, but Dr. Liz said that his doubt was understandable after they unearthed the trauma of being raised by oppressively evangelical parents.

"Don't worry about finding God," she assured him. "When you're ready, God will meet you where you are."

He doubted that very much, and even if it was true, then Trevor had a big fucking bone to pick with that asshole. Still, he was ready for some sanity and he figured that just about anyone could do a better job running his life at this point. That admission meant he was ready to move on to Step Four, a searching and fearless moral inventory of himself. This is where he had to make a written log of all his resentments and fuckups, a memory lane he wasn't exactly eager to stroll down. But as they said in the meetings: First Things First.

Trevor quickly scribbled his signature on the release form, handing the clipboard back to Dr. Liz with a playful smirk. "Don't go selling that on eBay now."

"I'll resist the urge," she responded with her usual patient smile.

Trevor slipped his shades on despite the late hour. "See you around, Dr. Liz."

"I hope not, Trevor," she called after him.

As he exited through the automatic doors, the cold Malibu night nearly knocked the breath out of him. When he was a kid, Trevor had been so excited to move from the snowy Midwest to sunny Los Angeles, but it turned out that the elite coastal mountains were a frigid place to live. He flipped the collar up on his jacket, protecting his neck as the wind howled through the canyons. A quick scan of the parking lot showed no white Toyota.

Maybe she forgot. Or decided not to come. Maybe she finally decided to give up on him. He wouldn't blame her if she did. Smart move, really.

The wind died down for a moment, just long enough for him to hear a small voice calling through the dark.

"Trevor!"

He swiveled his head toward the far edge of the lot to see Sophie stepping out of her car in purple nursing scrubs. The lone streetlight above made her auburn hair glow like a warm fire. Trevor may not have believed in God, but he was certain that Sophie was some kind of angel. He started toward her as Sophie's white sneakers did a tiny dance on the pavement, unable to contain her excitement.

Of course she hadn't forgotten. She was already here, waiting for him, always there for him, ever since they'd met in high school.

Sophie was the only one who hadn't treated Trevor any differently just because he was on TV. In the social jungle of adolescence, people either latched on to the child star as their king or resented and shunned him. But Sophie couldn't care less about his fame. This bruised Trevor's young ego at first, until he discovered that she actually liked him anyway. She liked something about him that had nothing to do with all that Hollywood bullshit. Trevor couldn't comprehend what that might be, and he spent the bulk of their relationship trying to figure it out, testing her unconditional love every step of the way. Despite all the recovery work, Trevor still didn't feel a single step closer to understanding what made him lovable. But it didn't really matter as he finally came within arm's reach and the great love of his life clutched him tight.

"Welcome back, honeybee," she whispered into his ear as her tears wet his cheek.

Trevor buried his face in her neck, letting out a muffled, "Fuck, I missed you."

He wanted to disappear there, dissolve into her skin, merge with this gentle being who was so much better than he was. With her support, he just might be able to do this. Stay sober, be the better man she believed he could be. He was starting fresh now, and things would be different, they *had* to be different.

Even with his eyes closed, the first flash was blinding. By the time he opened them and pulled away from Sophie, two more cameras flickered around them. The paparazzi emerged from their hiding places behind bushes and cars. Vampires in the night, descending on their prey. Trevor's whole body tensed as they shot their questions like bullets in the dark.

"Trevor, do you think you're really cured this time?"

"Is it true you're in talks to play the Reaper?"

"Are you sure you're ready for a comeback?"

He dodged the flashing lights, strong-arming a faceless body away as he opened the passenger door and dove in. Sophie rushed to the driver's side, stuttering as she started the engine. "I'm so sorry, I looked, but didn't see anyone, they must have been hiding."

One of the bold bastards jumped in front of the car now, snapping another photo as Trevor shouted through the glass, "We will run you the fuck over!" He reached over to slam a fist on the car horn, causing Sophie to shudder and the photographer to vault back into the night.

"Drive," he said as Sophie's foot fumbled for the pedal and they finally started moving. Trevor looked into the side-view mirror, watching Chrysalis recede into the distance as the leeches lowered their lenses. He exhaled deeply, sinking into his seat as he looked over at Sophie. Her hands trembled on the wheel as she carefully navigated the winding road down the mountain.

Great. Five minutes out and he'd already fucked up. Add it to the list.

"I'm sorry," he started. "You know I wasn't angry at *you*, it's just those people drive me crazy."

Trevor didn't realize what a relief it had been to have a two-month reprieve from the leering cameras, eagerly awaiting his next newsworthy embarrassment. But anger was one of the many addictions he needed to keep in check, another adrenaline fix that led him nowhere good.

"No, I know, it's fine." Sophie kept her eyes on the road as she put on a smile. "I'm just happy you're finally coming home." She could smile through anything, but Trevor felt her skin vibrating as he reached out to put his hand on her shoulder.

"Me too," he replied, turning to stare out the windshield at the darkly twisting road ahead.

## 5

The canned laughter from that dreaded sitcom was still rattling in Howard's ears as he tugged the light bulb cord on, standing barefoot on the concrete cellar floor with a box of trash bags tucked under his arm. He'd been too restless to sleep and decided to expend the excess energy by finally cleaning house. If his time as the Reaper truly was over, then there was no sense waiting another minute to wipe every trace of the monster from his home so he could start life anew with a clean slate.

He opened the first trash bag and started to fill it, blindly grabbing whatever he could get his hands on as he tossed it all into the gaping black hole. Action figures, posters, T-shirts. There would be no sorting for the recycling. He just needed everything gone, the space clear. Then perhaps he could find some other filler for this space, some activity to keep him occupied in retirement. He could convert the cellar into a woodshop, for instance. He'd always dreamed of doing something with his hands, creating a concrete product through manual labor that would be of some clear use in the world. Like a chair. Yes, it might be very nice to build his own porch chair so he could finally toss those old Adirondacks. He was already feeling better as he tied off the first full bag, lifting it from the concrete. But the plastic gave way instantly, tearing at the bottom as its contents spilled to the ground.

*CLANK.*

Howard startled at the sharp sound, looking down at the heap of cloth and plastic that had reformed at his feet. He dug his hand into the pile and pulled out the heavy metallic source.

A long, rusty chain.

Not one of the cheap rubber fakes produced for Halloween costumes, no. This was the real deal. Howard had retrieved it from a junkyard ages ago to use for physical character work, to feel the weight of the weapon in his grip.

He didn't even remember putting it in the trash bag, but as he held the iconic chain in his hands now, those rusty links seemed to vibrate against his skin. He dropped it, metal clattering back to the ground as he wiped brown rust from his fingers onto his pajama pants.

The overhead light glinted off something else in the pile. A clunky black box, wrapped in plastic. Howard lifted it toward the bulb to read the crimson lettering on *The Reaper Legacy*. A VHS box set of the entire *Night of the Reaper* franchise, films one through eight.

He ran his hand over the dusty shrink-wrap, realizing that it had been years since he'd watched any of the films. Yes, the sequels had grown increasingly over-the-top as the Reaper became a pun-loving jester of gore, asking a pizza delivery boy for *"a slice"* before carving him up with a sickle, or inviting a hippie girl to *"get baked"* before tossing her into a flaming furnace. But even through the campy one-liners, Howard had always endeavored to imbue the beast with a certain Shakespearean balance of gravitas and frivolity. Finding himself wide-awake now, he decided to postpone his cellar cleanup and revisit the first film, for old time's sake.

Howard carried the box back upstairs and sat on the edge of the bed, picking at the plastic wrap. His well-groomed nails were much too short to break through, but there was Stanley, already purring up against him.

"Stanley. Would you do the honors?" Howard placed the box on the bed and Stanley circled it twice, studying his prey before giving his first tentative paw swipe. When the box did not fight back, a flurry of scratching ensued, plastic shredding until Howard lifted the cat, rubbing his head in gratitude before placing him on the carpeted floor. "Bravo."

Howard pulled the torn plastic off and slid the first tape out of its box. *Night of the Reaper*

The cardboard case had a distinctive scent, not unlike the inky aroma of a new book, and the plastic cassette shined like a pitch-black obsidian jewel. Howard walked to the TV set and slipped the tape into the rectangular mouth below the screen. The machine hungrily pulled the cassette from his fingers, whirring to life before he could even press *Play*.

The screen sparked to life with an ominous techno-tone humming beneath the film's opening image of the harvest moon, a dark orange sphere burning in the night sky. By the time Howard had climbed back into bed, the camera had tilted down to reveal the rotting cornfield, where all was dead and quiet.

*VROOM!*

A pickup truck tore across the field and Howard jumped beneath the sheets, causing Stanley to leap from the bed. Those auditory jump-scares were cheap, but effective. Howard found himself getting pulled into the story like a fresh-eyed newcomer, pulling the covers up as he watched the truck skid to a stop outside a big red barn.

Two teenaged farm boys hopped out of the truck bed like a Frankensteinian mob, pitchforks in hand. The driver's side door opened and out stepped their ruthless patriarchal ringleader, Farmer Joe. His eyes filled with hate as he barked, "Lester!"

Inside the barn, a forty-year-old man in shabby overalls paced back and forth, a nervous tic quaking through his boyish face. Howard looked upon his younger self, the bright blonde hair that had since gone gray, and smiled at sweet Lester Jensen.

When Howard first received the script, the Reaper was nothing more than a soulless ghoul with no backstory. It was he who suggested that a tragic origin story would make for a much more complex viewing experience, endearing audiences to the man who would become the monster. Chuck was reluctant to take notes from the audacious actor, until he realized that if he hoped to build a franchise, the killer would be the only constant. Seeing dollar signs, Chuck gave in to the suggestion and quickly drafted a prologue backstory about the "retarded" farmhand Lester Jensen. Even in 1980, Howard found the term insensitive and unproductive. He wanted to give Lester a full emotional world beyond the reductive stereotype, so he dove into psychological research and diagnosed the character with a severe anxiety disorder that manifested in selective mutism.

Uneducated and ostracized by his fellow townsfolk, Lester only felt safe talking to himself or his beloved animals, often engaging in self-abusive behaviors.

Howard was impressed by his own attention to detail now as he watched Lester hit himself on the side of the head with a weak fist. A sheep bleated behind him and Lester rushed to silently beg his companion to stay quiet as the barn doors rattled.

"We know you're in there, Lester," Farmer Joe's gruff voice resounded. "Just open the doors and we promise we won't hurt you."

Lester looked into the sheep's eyes, as if hoping it might somehow come to his aid, or at least advise him on the best course of action. When the beast offered no guidance, he gave it a big fluffy hug, took a deep breath and turned to face the doors.

Lester slowly lifted the crossbeam, but before he could place it on the ground, the doors flung inward, knocking him down as the scared animals scattered behind him. Farmer Joe stepped in with his boys behind him, hoisting their weapons overhead.

"You've got to answer for the blight, Lester," Joe said while his sons tore through the place with their pitchforks, searching for evidence. One of them opened a steamer trunk in the corner and shook his head at the contents.

"Get a look at these, Pop!" Inside the trunk was a collection of hand-made dolls, woven from hay and dried cornstalks. "Bet he uses 'em in his Satanic rituals."

Tears streamed down Lester's silent face, and Howard's heart ached anew for the poor, misunderstood farmhand. He wished Lester would find his voice and explain that he'd only made the dolls to keep himself company. The only thing Lester Jensen was guilty of was a crippling lone-liness. But Farmer Joe wasn't here to be his friend as he reached down, grabbing Lester by the straps of his overalls and pulling him to his feet.

"You've got an appointment in town. Better not keep them waiting."

As the trio dragged Lester through the barn doors, Howard looked away from the screen and up at the ceiling. He knew what came next and couldn't bear to watch, but the sounds alone were enough to send a chill down his spine as Farmer Joe pulled a rusty chain from the back of his truck with a loud *CLANK*.

That unmistakable sound drew Howard's attention back down to the television. Joe wrapped the chain around Lester's neck while the two boys secured the other end to the back of the truck. Lester was sobbing like an inconsolable child as he reached deep, finding the courage to utter one word to his fellow man. His final hope for stopping this violence.

"Puh-please . . ."

Howard suddenly had trouble breathing, like the chain was wrapped tight around his own neck as he reached up to rub his cramped throat.

Farmer Joe looked into the scared farmhand's face. "That harvest was the lifeblood of our whole community, Lester. It's time to atone. Blood for blood."

Joe got behind the wheel and revved the engine as his sons hopped back into the truck bed. Lester was hyperventilating now as tears streamed down his face, and Howard found himself gasping for breath as well. He watched helplessly as the truck took off into the cornfield.

The chain rattled across the dirt, going more taut with every link as Howard pulled himself out of bed, grasping at his throat, desperate for air. He stumbled toward the television, hoping he could end this madness by turning it off. But before his hand could reach the dial, Lester was violently yanked off his feet, and Howard's own neck nearly snapped from the force as he was thrown back onto the bed.

Lester was dragged by the rattling chain in the vehicle's wake, screaming as his body smashed through rotting cornstalks and his face burned across the earth. Flesh ripped and tore, blood oozing, teeth shattering, the Reaper's gruesome visage being created in real time. Howard felt every sharp pain as his own face burned, body thrashing on the bed, his screams mingling with Lester's across the room until the clanking chain overtook all other sounds and his vision scraped to black.

A sharp ringing startled Howard awake as he bolted upright among a tangle of sheets. He caught his breath as his eyes focused through the dark room on the snowy TV screen, emitting a horrible churning sound.

He must have dozed off while watching the film. But what about that horrible experience, feeling his neck snap and his skin burn with Lester's? He reached up to touch his face, unmarred but damp with sweat. Clearly that was nothing more than a vivid nightmare.

The second ring gave him another fright as he turned to the cordless phone on his bedside table. His arm was heavy as he fumbled to click it on, gasping out a "Yes?"

"Howie! It's Jake."

"Jacob?" Howard glanced at the alarm clock, reading ten thirty-four. "It's the middle of the night."

"It's the middle of the *morning*, buddy," Jake responded. "You rage last night or what?" he quipped as Howard noticed the little red AM dot on the clock. He slept far longer than he realized, which would explain the strange, weighted feeling in his body as he slid from under the covers now, grounding his feet on the carpet. Howard rubbed his eyes.

"Why are you calling, Jacob?"

"Your announcement yesterday, the way the crowd responded? The message boards went wild," Jake explained as Howard lumbered toward the thick drapes covering the windows. "Shook things up all the way to Pinnacle Studios and Chuck just called me with an offer."

". . . an offer?" Howard repeated, tugging the drapes back as morning light blazed into the dark room. He shielded his eyes from the harsh glow.

"You heard me, buddy. Guess he realized he was an idiot for trying to make another Reaper film without you."

Howard couldn't help but smile, feeling a surge of pride that the fans' disapproval of his exclusion from this remake had actually turned the tide. It was still hard to imagine crawling back into those bloody overalls, but he was grateful to at least receive the offer. Even if he respectfully declined, he could now do so with his dignity intact.

"I'm happy to hear Chuck's come to his senses," Howard said as he stared out the window, "but I'm still not altogether certain it would be worth my while to return after all these years."

"I totally understand," Jake responded. "The good news is they only need you for one day of shooting."

Howard cocked his head. "How's that?"

"Chuck wants *you* to play Farmer Joe! A big cameo in the prologue!"

Howard's hand gripped the phone a bit tighter. "He wants *me* to kill Lester Jensen."

"And then *you* get killed by the Reaper! The irony, right? The fans are gonna cream their pants."

Howard paced across the carpet. This wasn't an offer at all. It was an insult. After the embarrassment at Dead World, he couldn't believe Chuck would pour salt into the gaping wound and act as though it were an honor.

"What about the Reaper?" Howard asked.

"I told you," Jake responded, clearly thrown by Howard's unenthusiastic response. "They're closing in on a deal with Trevor Mane as we speak."

"Because of his inspired work on *Family Genius*?" Howard asked as the television hissed in the background.

"He's been front-page news for years now, and people want to see what he'll do next. Look, Howie, it's a pretty tasty offer for one day's work. Chuck just needs a yes or no and then we can negotiate—"

"No," Howard replied.

". . . No?" the infant agent parroted.

"If I'm going to return, it will be as the Reaper." Howard was surprised by his own proclamation, but now that it was out there, he had no choice but to stand strong in his defiance. "Now get me a meeting with Chuck Slattery."

"I appreciate your passion, I really do." Jake said. "But I don't think I can do that, Howie. He's made up his mind and Trevor Mane is the—"

*"I'm the Reaper!"* The words scraped across his throat like they were wrapped in barbed wire. Howard pressed a hand against the window frame for balance in the buzzy aftermath, clearing his raspy voice before speaking again. "Just . . . make the call, please."

"Oh-okay, yeah," Jake stuttered through an audible gulp. "You got it, Howie. I'll call him right now."

Howard hung up the phone as the blood drained from his head, embarrassed that he'd just erupted at Jake like that. It was only yesterday that he thought he was done with the Reaper, ready to retire, yet here he was demanding to play the role once more. He didn't realize how badly he wanted it until the words spewed forth with a life of their own, a voice of their own, like the monster was screaming through him. But was this really what he wanted?

Black and white pixels danced over the screen in their electric sizzle as Howard started toward the television. Before he could reach it to turn it off, his foot kicked against something plastic and clunky, drawing his gaze down to the carpet. He bent down and picked up a video tape, perplexed by the sticker reading *Night of the Reaper*.

That couldn't be. He'd fallen asleep with the cassette in the player, yet here it was with the tape inside spooled to the right, played all the way through. His eyes fell back to the floor, where all eight Reaper tapes had been pulled from their boxes, haphazardly strewn about like discarded shell casings. Howard reached for the next nearest tape.

*Night of the Reaper Part II: The Reaper's Revenge*

Again, the tape was spooled to the right. He quickly checked every cassette.

*Part III: Fields of Blood*

*Part IV: The Final Reaping*

*Part V: The New Crop*

*Part VI: Urban Harvest*

*Part VII: Seed of the Reaper*

One after the other, all spooled to the right, until he finally pressed *Eject* on the player and found himself holding *Part VIII: Moon Reaper*.

Spooled to the right.

Howard's last waking memory was Lester's death scene from the prologue of the very first film, but the evidence in front of him suggested that somehow, he had watched the entire franchise last night. Tape after tape. All eight films. Beginning to end.

He closed his eyes as his mind tried to wrap around that possibility. Flashes of violent imagery flooded back to him, like fresh memories of a nightmare returned, scenes from every film blurring together in a bloody tangle in his mind. A machete slashing an arm, an axe splitting a skull, a post-hole digger exhuming a heart. He couldn't explain it, but it seemed as though he had indeed ingested every last Reaper kill that night, just as the evidence before him suggested.

Dr. Cho had warned him that cognitive blackouts could be the next progression from smaller memory lapses. Still, Howard was deeply unsettled by this development, and there was no Post-it Note large enough to plug a gap of this magnitude. He told himself he'd call the doctor later as he reached to turn the television off, bathing the room in a moment of silence.

The phone rang in his hand and he startled before answering. "This is Howard Browning."

"Well," Jake began with a sigh. "I didn't get you a meeting with Chuck . . ."

A momentary relief settled in Howard's nerves, looking into the black television screen at his own dark reflection. "That's quite all right, Jacob. I'm sure you did everything you could."

"I did. Which is why you've now got an *audition* with Chuck . . . for the Reaper!"

Howard's heart lodged in his throat as his agent prattled on.

"I'm glad you pushed back, buddy, because we're gonna get you the deal you deserve. I gotta jet to crosstown lunch, but my new assistant will be in touch with details. You're gonna crush it, Howie!"

Howard's mind went blank as the dial tone kicked in. It was all he could do to get down on the carpet and start collecting the scattered cassettes. Delicately tucking each tape back into its individual case, a new resolve formed as he held them all snugly together in the box, restored into a complete collection.

Eight tapes. Eight performances. Yet here he was, being asked to audition for the role he brought to life. If that's how Chuck wanted to play it, then fine.

Howard stood erect now, cradling his legacy in his arms.

It was time to bring the monster back out of its box.

*Night of the Reaper Part II: The Reaper's Revenge* (1981)
Script Pages Courtesy of Pinnacle Studios

INT. CABIN - ASHLAND SUMMER CAMP - NIGHT

Counselor Christy tucks little camper Sally into
her bunk bed.

> CHRISTY
> I already told you, Sally. There's
> no such thing as the boogeyman.

> SALLY
> But I saw him out the window!

> CHRISTY
> You were probably just spooked
> by your own reflection. Now go to
> sleep.

Christy ruffles Sally's hair and heads to the door.
She clicks off the light, darkness falling over the
cabin full of young campers.

EXT. CABIN - CONTINUOUS

Christy steps out onto the porch, shivering in the
windy night air as . . . TWO HANDS EMERGE from the
shadows behind her, PULLING her back into the arms
of—

> CHRISTY
> Jim!

Jim laughs as Christy slaps the chest of his var-
sity jacket.

> CHRISTY
> You scared me half to death!

> JIM
> If you're scared now, just wait
> til you see what I found. Come on.

Christy follows Jim, away from the cabins and into the woods.

EXT. DARK WOODS - NIGHT

They duck through the brush toward . . . A BIG RED BARN, the rotting wood strangled by overgrown weeds.

                    CHRISTY
          Wait . . . Do you think this is . . .?

                    JIM
          Lester Jensen's barn. You know the
          story, right?

                    CHRISTY
          I know he was left for dead back
          in the day. But he survived and
          came back to slaughter all those
          counselors last year. Until that
          girl put a sickle through his
          heart and killed him for good.

                    JIM
          I wouldn't be so sure. Legend
          has it Lester's deal with the
          Devil turned him into a zombie.
          My cousin works at the Ashland
          morgue. He says they never
          cremated the body . . . because it
          walked right out of the freezer.

Jim does a zombie-walk with arms outstretched.

                    CHRISTY
          You're just trying to scare me
          again. The Reaper is dead.

                    JIM
          Then he won't mind if we take a
          little tour of his home.

Christy gulps as Jim leads her across the threshold.

INT. ABANDONED BARN - CONTINUOUS

Rusty farm tools line the walls as Jim flops down onto a big pile of hay.

                    JIM
          How about a little . . . roll in
          the hay?

Christy looks around at the cobwebbed space.

                    CHRISTY
          It's creepy in here.

                    JIM
          It's quiet in here. Come on. I'll
          keep you safe.

Jim pulls Christy down to the hay and they start making out.

                    CHRISTY
          Shouldn't we be watching the kids?

                    JIM
          Screw the kids.

They laugh, groping and kissing as they shed their clothes, totally unaware of . . .

A MANGLED HAND grabbing a pitchfork from the wall.

Jim climbs on top and Christy closes her eyes while they make love.

                    CHRISTY
          Yes . . . Yes . . .

She's lost in ecstasy, until she opens her eyes to see . . .

THE REAPER standing over them with his pitchfork raised high!

                    CHRISTY
          No!

The pitchfork SLAMS into Jim's back, sharp prongs PIERCING through his torso and into Christy's chest. The lovers cough blood, entwined bodies twitching until they both go limp.

The Reaper leaves the pitchfork skewering the dead teens as he steps back to admire his grisly handi-work.

                    THE REAPER
          Double penetration.

His CACKLE echoes in the empty barn as the hay runs red.

# PART II:
# RESURRECTION

## 6

Trevor's home in the Hollywood Hills was exactly like he left it, only cleaner. Sophie was good at that, keeping things neat, and with Trevor away these last two months, it must have been a whole lot easier. It was her house, after all. He'd surprised her with it on her twenty-fifth birthday and was still covering the mortgage with residual checks from *Family Genius* reruns. Sophie probably would've preferred something a bit less flashy than the boxy modern home he chose, but it did have a private backyard with room for the garden she always wanted. Trevor tried to convince her that a pool would be more fun than a bunch of plants that were just going to die every drought season, but she assured him that the colorful succulents and cactuses she envisioned wouldn't need much to thrive.

"Anything for you, honeybee," he'd said.

It was their mutual pet name since high school, when they shared their first kiss beneath the bleachers and got swarmed by bees from a honeycomb overhead. Their fateful union was sealed by an afternoon spent holding hands in the nurse's office, the pain from those little pink bumps dulled by the healing power of young love.

Sophie had decorated the house with rustic flourishes from Pottery Barn, but it was Trevor who insisted on the black leather couch he was lounging on now as a Reaper DVD played on the plasma screen in front of him.

A muscular juvenile detention inmate was bench-pressing in the prison yard when the monster appeared over his head.

*"Need a spot, bro?"* The Reaper grabbed the bar, slamming it down and decapitating the inmate as blood sprayed. *"Oops. At least now you'll make weight!"* The monster cackled at the headless corpse.

Trevor couldn't believe *this* was the trash he was auditioning for at this point in his career. Sure, it had been a while since he'd actually acted, and it was true that his current fame was based on fans' titillation that geeky little Tommy from TV had grown up so sexy. But that's exactly why now was not the time to descend further into hackdom. He desperately needed to revitalize his image and take his work in a new, serious direction.

"What happened to the indie recovery drama with that Sundance director?" he'd asked his agent, Greg.

"They want a recovery drama in *front* of the camera, Trev. Not behind the scenes." Greg was an asshole, but that's what Trevor paid him for. He didn't want another smarmy yay-sayer bullshitting him all day. He needed someone to tell him the truth for once. Greg assured him that all publicity was good publicity and this horror remake would put Trevor's name back on the industry map. The actor had been in hiding for too long and he just needed to get his face out there and on the screen. But as Trevor looked at the face of the Reaper on his TV now, covered in goopy red makeup, he wondered how exactly this role was going to help with his brand recognition.

"Which one is this?" Sophie asked, entering from the kitchen with two mugs of tea.

"Five, I think?" Trevor responded. "I don't know, they all sort of blur together into one unwatchable mess." He took the offered mug from Sophie and put it on the table without sipping, next to the DVD box set of *The Reaper Legacy.*

Sophie picked up the open DVD case, reading the description on the back in her best movie trailer voice. *"Night of the Reaper Part V: The New Crop.* With the Reaper dead and buried, Ashland finally thought they were rid of the monster for good. But when a juvenile detention center is built on the haunted cornfield, the Reaper returns for bloody justice . . . and this time, *everyone's* getting a death sentence!"

Trevor laughed at the hokey copywriting, though it dredged up a memory of being a teenager, scared shitless in court as he faced a month in juvie for possession. Of course, he didn't serve any time because being a white boy with a TV network paying your legal fees meant dodging a whole lot of consequences. But it felt like all that owed debt was catching up to him now as he picked up the box set to check its contents.

"I can't believe I still have three more to go."

He'd been binging on the franchise all day while Sophie worked a double shift at the hospital, though that didn't stop her from calling him every hour to check in like a worried mother. Maybe that's what attracted Trevor to her in the first place, Dr. Liz had suggested. His real mother never really gave a shit, so he sought a partner who was nurturing in all the ways he'd never experienced.

Sophie gasped at a cheap jump-scare on the screen.

"Okay, this is actually pretty scary, though," she said, snuggling up to Trevor's shoulder.

"You're scared of tiny little spiders," he said.

"Well, I had to step it up while you were gone. Killed a few with my own bare hands."

"You monster." He prodded her ribs to incite a playful giggle.

"Careful!" she squealed, nearly spilling her hot tea as the Reaper bellowed from the TV.

*"I said 'lights out,' inmate!"*

Trevor looked up to see the monster hurling the body of another inmate against a giant electrical switchboard, which lit up with blue flashes as the teenaged victim caught fire and began to scream. It was actually kind of unsettling to see a real stuntman flailing in the flames, rather than the cheap CGI of modern movies.

"I give up," Trevor said, picking up the remote and pausing it. "I don't think watching this shit's gonna help with my audition."

"We don't have to watch anything," Sophie suggested. "We could just talk." As she inched closer to Trevor, it felt more encroaching than the paparazzi the other night. Fear of intimacy is just a defense mechanism, Dr. Liz would have reminded him, and the only way to get through the discomfort was to practice being vulnerable.

Trevor tried not to flinch as Sophie reached out to touch the hair that hung over his ears. "You've been letting it grow out."

"Yeah, well. The on-call stylists in rehab are trash," he joked. Another defense mechanism.

"I like it. Reminds me of your shaggy high school days." She smiled, ruffling the black mop on his head as the yellow rubber bracelet bounced on her wrist. It was last year's trend, but the cause really meant something to Sophie. Her father died of cancer when she was young and now she worked at Cedars-Sinai's treatment center. Trevor admired her dedication, but he knew better than to trust flashy charities after witnessing his parents prop up plenty of "good Christian causes" as false fronts to line their pockets.

A pregnant silence filled the air and Trevor could tell that Sophie was hesitant to ask. It irritated him when she was hesitant. He just had to wait until she finally found the courage to open her mouth and ask a simple question.

"So how are you feeling?"

"Great," he answered too fast, "I feel great." He put on a smile, hoping that would be the end of it.

"Tell me more." She was so sincere, open as a book. "What was it like?"

"Pretty cushy, actually. My roommate, Ryan, brought his Xbox, so we played a lot of *Call of Duty*. Guy did a tour in Iraq, so I mostly got my ass kicked." Trevor was being avoidant and Sophie wasn't about to let him get away with it.

"And the therapy? Do you feel like you learned anything?" she asked.

"I mean, nothing new by now, right? Same old talk about this terrible disease of addiction." He hated that idea, the sickness, the affliction. People with cancer were sick. He was just a selfish asshole. The only thing Trevor hated more than all the disease talk was all the God talk.

"I was thinking maybe we could try praying together," Sophie offered. Sometimes it was like she could read his mind but always landed on the wrong button to push.

"Maybe, sometime," Trevor replied, "but I should really keep preparing right now." He picked up the remote and started clicking through the main menu. "Ooh, Special Features. *The Reaper Speaks*. This should be interesting."

As he clicked play, Sophie quietly deflated beside him. He could almost hear Dr. Liz's voice reminding him that expressions of gratitude were the key to a recovered relationship.

"Thanks for the tea, honeybee," he said, throwing Sophie a bone as he lifted his mug for a sip, repulsed by the pungent floral aroma.

"You're welcome," she smiled back.

Trevor fixed his attention on the flat screen, hardly recognizing the man being interviewed as the face beneath the Reaper's shredded mug. Howard Browning looked like the stereotype of a coffee shop beat poet in his black turtleneck sweater.

"Wow," Trevor laughed. "Is this guy for real?"

"So Howard," the interviewer asked, "how exactly do you tackle a role as dark and violent as the Reaper?"

"Well, the craft is the craft, and I approach every role with the same sense of integrity," he replied, uncrossing and recrossing his legs. "The wonderful Jack Lemmon once said that acting is the ability to be totally vulnerable, to be emotionally naked in front of an audience in an act of public intimacy."

The I-word made Trevor shift on the leather couch as Howard rambled on.

"You see, most people think of acting as putting *on* a mask. But the truth is, it's in our daily lives that we wear the most masks. And in a raw, honest performance, we shed them. We pull back the curtain, unleashing our truest selves."

"Wow," Sophie breathed. "That's kind of beautiful."

"It's kind of pretentious," Trevor replied, pressing *Stop* and tossing the remote into her lap. "You wanna find something to watch that's not total shit? I'll be right back."

Trevor was desperate for air as he rushed up to the bedroom and opened the sliding glass door, stepping out onto the small balcony where steps led down to the dark garden below. From up here, the larger cactuses looked like they were reaching up at him with their big spiny arms, yearning for a prickly hug. A cold dip in a pool would've felt really nice right now.

Instead, Trevor closed his eyes and started counting long deep breaths, just like they practiced during meditation sessions at Chrysalis. He'd been out for three days now and hadn't gone to a meeting yet. This is exactly what Dr. Liz had warned him about.

Get to a meeting. Find a sponsor. Keep working the steps.

But Trevor wasn't that desperate. He was stronger than those other head cases in group therapy, didn't need as much help. Or maybe he was just too stubborn to admit it. He was already feeling irritable and he didn't want to lash out at Sophie. She didn't deserve that.

He would've killed for a cigarette right now, just to feel the warm smolder down his throat. They didn't allow smoking of any kind at Chrysalis, and Sophie didn't approve of it, either, but he couldn't quit everything cold turkey, could he? His whole body itched now for that gentle tobacco buzz as his thoughts wandered straight down the road to a stronger fix, to the thing that would really set him straight with one deep hit.

It struck him like lightning in the night, his eyes shooting open. This was a craving, his first honest one in weeks. And it scared him. Trevor finally had to admit to himself that if he was actually going to stay clean, he needed to get his ass to a meeting.

Fast.

## 7

Howard's study didn't get much use these days as the burgundy leather chair gathered dust at the oak desk, surrounded by bookshelves teeming with the classics. He took great pride in his library, never adding a text he hadn't read, which would've been cheating. There was a sense of comfort in being surrounded by the inspiring words of all those great artists as he ran his fingers along the spines now, arriving at a shelf full of course books from his conservatory days in New York.

*Respect for Acting.*

*Building a Character.*

*The Development of the Method.*

Howard fondly remembered sitting in Washington Square Park as a youth, reading these life-changing words as the squirrels bounced around him.

"Actors need a kind of aggression," Stella Adler wrote, "a kind of inner force. Don't be only one-sided, sweet, nice, good. Get rid of being average. Find the killer in you."

Howard's young mind had slowly cracked open as he was called upon not simply to assume the skin of another, but rather to find the character within. The books were just the beginning, the homework in between endless hours spent practicing in workshops, running lines and rehearsing scenes in a community of like-minded individuals. They ate, slept, breathed their craft together. Blood, sweat, and tears funneled into an off-off-Broadway play, performed in some leaky-pipe theater in the bowels of the East Village. Twenty fold-up chairs in a room so dark, you could hardly tell if anyone was occupying them. But it didn't matter. You weren't performing for them. You were offering up your energy to something much greater than yourself, to the creative force that lived and pulsed through all things.

Even more unseen labor took place off the stage, through hundreds of humiliating auditions while working dead-end jobs to make ends meet. One had to earn those moments of glory beneath the lights, and Howard doubted very much that little Trevor Mane, whose career was handed to him on a silver platter, had ever gone through the grueling wringer of being a starving artist.

He moved to another shelf now, finding thick tomes of the psychological variety. There were the mental health texts that helped him understand Lester, *Speaking without Speaking* and *The Fear Behind the Silence*, offering details of the anxious preoccupations that lay behind the troubled farmhand's selective mutism. Other books with titles like *The Psychology of Evil* and *Meeting Your Own Shadow* were for discovering the Reaper, a sadistic personality who delighted in toying with his prey, for whom violence was its own cheerful art form.

Howard had always treated the character with a sense of duality, the yin and the yang inextricably bound. The Reaper was born of Lester, of some dark place within the benevolent man. The monster had lain in wait since the very beginning, eagerly anticipating its opportunity to rise to the surface, to take the helm. It was in Lester's humiliating and undeserved death that the reins of life were seized by the rageful Reaper.

Howard found many names for it, this "chaos, a cauldron of seething excitation" that Freud dubbed the Id and Jung called "the shadow," shunned and yearning for recognition. This dark side existed within every human being, and Howard had plumbed the depths of Lester Jensen in order to find the Reaper all those years ago. He did so by devising his own creative approach to "the method" taught by Stanislavski, who encouraged every actor to find their own conscious process for unlocking a character's subconscious world.

Howard was in search of the tangible results of that method now as he bent down to the cabinets below the bookshelf, opening one to find a cardboard box taped shut. He dragged the heavy box out to the rug, then grabbed a letter opener off the desk to cut the tape, unearthing his treasure trove of creative gold. Dozens of marbled notebooks were resting inside as he dug to the bottom, plucking out the first one to read the words written in Sharpie on the cover:

*THE LESTER LOGS—March 1979*

Here in plain black and white was the evidence of his commitment to the character, the laborious work of a serious actor's craft. Journal after journal, dated through the years, all the way through to the end of the franchise. This was how he, in Joan's words, gave the character life. Creatives often talk about how their best work is not so much a conscious effort as it is a process of channeling something larger than themselves. Howard discovered that the more he practiced being a conduit for the character, the easier it was to click into that headspace between action and cut.

He flipped the notebook open now, revealing the childish scrawl of Lester's innermost thoughts. His uneducated, but emotionally raw words.

The anumuls ar MY Frends. Thay keep me cumpuny. But I stil git lonly sumtimes.

This was the secret to Howard's portrayal of the character. He never played the beast outright without first tapping into the man *beneath* the monster, where the true emotional bedrock lay. The Reaper gave voice to the voiceless, and in order to get back into character after all these years, Howard would have to summon this stream of consciousness, to meet Lester Jensen within.

He found a blank notebook resting atop the others and took it to the desk, settling into the old groove of the worn leather chair. In the early days, he would lock himself in here for days at a time to dive deep into his method, communing with Lester and transcribing the character's free-flowing thoughts and feelings. Emma respected his need for space when he worked, but that didn't stop her from lovingly teasing him, sometimes knocking on the door and pretending to be a prison guard.

"Prisoner 623, it's time for dinner in the mess hall. And no funny business or it's back in solitary." She always knew how to pierce through his severity and make him laugh, something he hadn't done much since she left. Sure, he'd faked plenty of half-hearted chuckles for the sake of social decorum, but he could no longer remember what it felt like to experience the genuine gut-busting laughter that only pure joy could engender.

Howard tried not to think about how humorless his life had become in Emma's wake as he refocused on the task at hand, opening to the first page of the journal, its white glow almost blinding. He reached for his trusty fountain pen, which was still getting plenty of use on daily Post-it Notes, and uncapped the arrow-like head. Armed and ready, he closed his eyes and began his measured breathing.

Meditation was the beginning. Follow the breath. Go inward.

He expected it would take a long while, perhaps hours, to shake out the mental cobwebs and create that empty space for Lester to meet him. Howard's own thoughts passed through and he let them go, one by one, seeking the blank canvas of his unconscious mind.

Time slipped away until he finally arrived at that serene inner sanctum, the black box theater of his deep psyche. He stood in the darkness of his mind's eye now, in the safe space he'd imagined for him and Lester alone. Howard spent years breaking down the mute character's emotional walls here, encouraging him to speak so that he could get to know the real Lester Jensen.

"Lester!" he called, voice echoing in the abyss. "Lester, are you here?"

A rustling came in response to his call as a solitary hay bale materialized in the ink black nothingness.

"Come on out, Lester," he gently called, sensing a body hiding behind the hay, shaking and afraid. "You're safe. I promise."

Howard moved closer and closer, finally rounding the hay bale to find Lester, trembling in his overalls, rocking back and forth. That same younger version of himself from the first film.

The old method was working.

"Talk to me, Lester. I'm here to listen."

"You don't care about me," Lester lamented in his soft whisper. "Nobody does." He turned away from Howard and curled into an even tighter ball. Lester was talking to him, which was a good start, but Howard still needed to rebuild trust.

"That's not true, Lester. You're very important to me, and I care about you very much." Genuine guilt swelled behind his words as Howard reached out a hand, placing it on the younger man's shoulder.

"Then why'd you leave me here?" the character responded through quiet sobs. "In the dark. With that scary man."

"What scary man?" Howard asked, having never encountered another character in this inner space before. "Farmer Joe?"

"No. The man with the scratchy face." Lester replied. "That's who you're really looking for, ain't it?"

A sudden chill rippled down Howard's spine. It didn't make sense. The characters were not separate beings, and the poor farmhand shouldn't have any awareness of the monster he would someday become. This was not how the method worked. How could Lester have met the dark flipside of his own coin?

"Lester," Howard tentatively asked, "Have you seen the Reaper?"

*CLANK.*

The deafening sound of the rusty chain rang out in the blackness as Lester grabbed Howard, pulling him down to hide behind the hay bale.

"Shhh!" Lester whispered. "You'll bring him out!"

No. The Reaper shouldn't be here, *couldn't* be here.

*CLANK.*

But the sound of his death knell was inching closer as Howard tried to stay strong, quivering with fear. "I'll protect you."

*CLANK.*

So close now as Lester frantically shook his head, low voice trembling. "It ain't me he wants. You gotta leave, before it's too late."

*CLANK.*

Just on the other side of the hay now as Howard asked, "Too late for what?"

Lester pulled Howard close for an urgent whisper. "Run."

*CLANK.*

The rusty chain whipped down between them like a blade, severing the hay bale in half as strands of yellow puffed into the air and Howard fell into the abyss.

His eyes shot open, back in the study now as his rolling chair pro-pelled backward, bumping to a stop against the wall behind him. Catching his breath, he pulled himself back to the desk and looked down at the notebook, where one tiny word was scrawled in the center of the page in Lester's primitive handwriting.

run

Howard shivered as he grounded himself back in the conscious world. Something had shifted in that inner space. No longer a sacred meeting ground for the actor and the sweet farmhand, it was haunted by the spec-ter of the monster now as the yin and yang of the character had somehow ruptured.

Could it be that the Alzheimer's was compromising his method? As much as he hated to admit it, if his brain cells truly were degenerating, it stood to reason that the boundaries of his unconscious process were dete-riorating as well. He still owed Dr. Cho a call, but there was no time for that now. His audition was tomorrow and he needed to find some easier way to prepare without returning to that unstable space within.

Unless he decided to forget the audition altogether, just give up and walk away now. He hung his head as those three letters stared up at him.

run

No. He couldn't run now. His entire life's work was at stake, his leg-acy. He wasn't going to sit quietly in his study while they took it all away from him.

## 8

"So when the PA came to bring me to set, he saw smoke coming from my trailer door." The man who called himself Danny A relayed his story to the group. "I was inside, high as a fuckin' kite, facedown on the couch. And the microwave was in full-on flames, burning like a bonfire five feet away. Turns out I thought it would be a good idea to reheat my Chipotle burrito, still fully wrapped in tinfoil."

Trevor laughed at the story, along with the dozen or so people around him, all sitting in a circle of fold up chairs in the dimly lit church basement. They didn't do last names in these anonymous meetings, but Trevor recognized the lead speaker with his flawless bronze skin and carefully trimmed goatee as Danny Alvarez. The famous actor first found success in the independent film boom of the 70s, when he earned a Best Supporting Actor Oscar playing a street-hustling teen addict in *Youths*. He spent the next decade typecast in the same role, until life imitated art and he started slipping in and out of rehab. But Danny made a huge comeback last year playing the lead in a gritty comic book reboot of *Nightshark*. Now in the prime of his forties, everyone in town wanted to work with Danny Alvarez, and Trevor could understand why as he listened to the performer bring his yarn to an end.

"The poor PA put out the fire and started to drag my dumb ass out of the trailer, but I insisted on taking my lunch with me. So I popped open the smoking microwave and grabbed my burnt burrito." Danny held up his right hand to reveal the burn scar covering his palm, prompting winces from the group. "Guac is extra. But scars are fuckin' priceless."

Everyone was fighting hysterical tears now, plastic chairs creaking as they doubled over in laughter. Trevor appreciated that people on the outside had a sense of fucking humor. In rehab, it was all doom and gloom. As the laughter died down, Danny looked around at the group, easing into a quiet sincerity.

"But today, with the help of the steps and my Higher Power, I don't have to be the asshole in the flaming trailer anymore. I get to have integrity. And that's a word I couldn't even spell before I got clean and serene in these rooms six years ago. So thanks."

The group clapped in support. Trevor always heard that when you're looking for a sponsor, you should pick someone who has what you want. The life, the perspective, the energy. Danny Alvarez seemed to have it all as he confidently leaned back. "Room's open for sharing."

The hands flew up around him as Trevor shoved his fists into his pockets, sinking deeper into his chair. It was his first meeting since Chrysalis, and he wasn't ready to open up to a room full of strangers, so he decided to just wait it out.

The truth was, Trevor's story wasn't all that original. It started with alcohol, drinking at parties just like everyone else, until he realized that alcohol didn't affect him the way it affected everyone else. He couldn't stop himself from gulping down drink after drink until the blackness washed over him and he woke up the next morning with a laundry list of stupid shit to apologize for. As his fame grew, so did the parties, and with that came more colorful options for fun. For a while, he was all about the coke, chasing that dopamine high he used to get from live studio audience tapings. But eventually, his anxiety got too much to bear, and he needed a different fix, something to bring him down and level him out.

He remembered the night he was first offered heroin at a Victoria's Secret poolside bash. He thought it was only for homeless junkies who shot up with syringes in back alleys, but when he first snorted that golden powder, and later upgraded to freebasing to savor the euphoria, Trevor discovered a whole different kind of high. Alcohol and cocaine only seemed to make Trevor more of his asshole self, but when the opiates hit his bloodstream, he separated entirely from that asshole self. Drifting away without a care in the world, watching from a hazy distance. *That* was the ultimate freedom. The freedom he yearned for right now.

But he wasn't about to admit that to a bunch of church basement rejects as Danny stood now to lead the group out with the Serenity Prayer. Trevor moved his mouth to make it look like he was joining them, but he refused to pray out loud as they all chanted together.

"God, grant me the serenity to accept the things I cannot change, the courage to change the things I can, and the wisdom to know the difference."

With the meeting over, Trevor drifted over to the coffeepot, watching from afar as people shook Danny's hand and thanked him for his lead. He wanted to approach, to ask Danny to sponsor him, but now this seemed stupid. This guy didn't know him, didn't care about him. None of these people did. He decided he should just take his Styrofoam cup and leave. He almost made it to the steps when he heard Danny's voice calling after him.

"Hey. New guy."

Trevor stopped, turning on his feet as Danny approached.

"Oh, hey." He tried to sound casual, but he could feel his cheeks flaring like a cartoon character.

"What's your name?" Danny asked, extending a hand from his muscled arm, covered in badass tattoos that made him all the more intimidating.

"Trevor Mane. Fuck, I mean . . . Trevor M," he corrected, shaking Danny's hand and feeling that soft scar.

"It's all right, kid," Danny laughed. "I know who you are. It's just common courtesy to pretend we can be anonymous in this town."

"Right. Well, in that case," Trevor said, gathering the courage, "can I ask you something?"

Danny nodded as he started to refill his coffee. "Shoot."

"When you were offered Nightshark, were you worried that it was somehow . . . I don't know . . ." He tried to choose his next words carefully. "Beneath you?"

"Beneath me?" Danny repeated, stirring the creamer in.

Trevor quickly back pedaled, worried that he'd offended the great actor. "I just mean . . . Not that you—"

"You bet your ass I did," Danny responded. "I'm an addict, man, my ego's bigger than this fuckin' church. I watched that cheesy '60s show and those campy '90s movies and thought 'How the hell am I gonna rehab my career by beating up bank robbers with a fuckin' fin on my head?' But at some point, I just had to surrender, put my ego aside and have a little faith in my Higher Power's path for me. And once I got out of my own fuckin' way, wouldn't you know it, things actually started happening for me."

Trevor nodded along. 'Higher Power' was easier to swallow than 'God,' but he still cringed at the spiritual talk.

"So . . . Do you . . ." Trevor's throat closed up like he was about to ask his crush to the dance. "Do you sponsor people?"

"That depends," Danny said, tapping sugar into his cup.

"On what?"

"On their willingness."

Trevor's back straightened up to attention like a soldier ready for battle. "I'm willing."

"Then why didn't you share today?" Danny asked without missing a beat.

Trevor shrugged in response. "I didn't have anything to say."

Danny studied him with unflinching eyes. "Look, kid. You're desperate, I can see that. My G.O.D. when I got in here was the Gift Of Desperation, too. And it's a good place to start, but it's not enough. Because if you get a little better, and you feel a little less desperate, then you might start to think you've got this thing under control. And that's when it's *really* got you."

It was a recipe for a relapse that Trevor knew all too well.

"Recovery's a true commitment," Danny continued. "Good days and bad. The long haul."

"I'm in it for the long haul, I am," Trevor promised.

"Then share something with me," Danny crossed his arms in front of his barrel chest.

Trevor wanted to run from this invitation, but he finally understood that there was no running from himself. So he kept his feet planted firm as he dug deep for something honest, something real.

"I'm just . . . I'm fucking sick of it, man. Sick of my own bullshit. I don't want to go back to rehab again, I can't. And I don't want to lose my girlfriend. I love her so fucking much, and I need things to be different this time, I need *me* to be different now." He forced himself to look Danny in the eyes. "And I'm willing to do the work, whatever it takes. I'm serious."

Danny's piercing gaze held for a few endless seconds before finally cracking into a smile.

"Sounds to me like you've got plenty to say. So if I take you on, you open your mouth and share something, anything, at every meeting you go to. And that's a meeting a day to start, ninety in ninety."

"Does that mean you'll sponsor me?" Trevor asked, hope trembling in his voice.

"I got you, kid." Danny finally took a sip of his coffee and grimaced, tossing the full Styrofoam cup directly in the trash. "First things first, what say we go get some real coffee? You can tell me your story and we can take it from there."

"Great," Trevor said, brimming with relief. "Yeah, let's do it." As they climbed the basement steps into the sunlight, he watched his new sponsor light up a cigarette. "So you're cool with cigarettes?"

"I'm sober, not suicidal," Danny responded, offering the lit cigarette to Trevor. He smiled and took his first drag in months, nerves instantly calming as he held the smoke in his lungs for a moment before exhaling.

Dr. Liz would not have approved, but the rules were different on the outside, away from that sheltered Malibu enclave. If Danny could find balance in the Hollywood machine, then Trevor was going to follow in his footsteps. Then maybe, just maybe, he could get out of his own way long enough to get a taste of that thing they called serenity.

# 9

As Howard rolled through the gates of the Pinnacle Studios lot, a wave of nostalgia washed over him. He'd spent so many days and nights filming among this large cluster of buildings in the heart of the valley, contributing to its rich history of the cinematic arts. The studio's output of late mostly pandered to adults in arrested development, as the silver screen became a second home to student wizards from children's books and toy cars that transformed into fighting robots. But as Howard parked his car and stepped onto the pavement, he thought about how he and Marlon Brando had walked these very same paths on their way to work. It had been a long while since Howard felt like a true actor, and nothing jump-started that feeling quite like being where the magic happened.

He tried to follow the convoluted map the security guard had given him at the gate, but got turned around among the towering stages as the valley heat began to creep under his brown tweed suit. Once he finally found the right building, he was relieved to step inside the air-conditioned space.

"Good morning, Mr. Brownie." A clean-cut receptionist in a button-down shirt greeted him from behind the desk with a cold bottle of sparkling water. "Hot out there, isn't it?"

"It certainly is, thank you," Howard replied, accepting the beverage before gently correcting the young man. "And it's Browning."

"Right, I'm sorry," the receptionist blushed. "It's my first week. If you'll just have a seat here in the waiting area, I'll let them know you're here. It shouldn't be too long."

"Of course," Howard nodded as he settled into a leather chair, feeling the sweat pooling inside his suit. Why had he picked such heavy fabric on such a hot day? He wanted to appear professional, but now he was afraid he'd overdone it as he nervously tugged at his scratchy collar.

After that frightful failure to connect with Lester through his writing exercises, he had tried against his better judgment to prepare from the outside in, to force his body into the Reaper physically. He chased Stanley around the house as he swung the heavy chain, trying to find the monster's voice, but his throat couldn't recall the shape that evoked that gravelly growl. It seemed there was nothing he could consciously do to click himself back into the groove of the character. What if the years, along with his disease, had simply eroded that groove and he would never find it again?

He was eager to distract himself now by browsing through the literature on the coffee table before him, disappointed to find there was no newspaper among the cheap magazines. Only aspirational titles like *Fit* and *Stylish*, where airbrushed images perpetuated impossible standards for beauty. Shuffling through the glossy covers, he stopped cold as he found himself face-to-face with Trevor Mane.

Howard wiped his eyes, hardly trusting what he was seeing, but the little boy from the sitcom was indeed a thumbnail photo in the corner of *FameUs* magazine. The blown-up cover was a paparazzi photo of what must be Trevor now, sloppy-haired and scowling at the lens with a red-haired girl in the car beside him.

"Family Genius *Star Leaves Rehab*," the headline read.

Howard flipped to the article, where another photo showed the red-haired girl in a hospital bed. *"Mane was serving a court-ordered rehabilitation stint after the DUI accident that nearly killed passenger and longtime girlfriend Sophie Boyd."*

The image of this poor girl, broken and helpless with tubes and wires extending from her body, made Howard ill. He knew Chuck was tasteless, but was his first choice for the role really this irresponsible train wreck, stepping straight out of rehab and into the Reaper?

Howard felt a swell of confidence now, knowing just how unequipped his competition was. Until he heard the door open and saw the young man swagger through, as if he'd just leapt from the page and into the room.

"Hey," Trevor Mane announced to the receptionist. "I'm Trevor Mane."

Disheveled in ripped jeans with a worn leather jacket over his wrinkled white T-shirt, Trevor looked as though he'd just crawled out of a Goodwill pile. Howard wished he could duck for cover like Lester behind the hay bale, but he was trapped in his chair as he wondered what Trevor was doing here in the first place.

"I know who you are, Mr. Mane," the young man behind the desk beamed with starry eyes. "It's such an honor, really. If you'll just have a seat along with Mr. Browning, I'll let you know as soon as they're ready for you."

Howard raised the magazine to cover his face as he heard Trevor's footsteps moving toward him. Easing into the chair right across from him, Trevor squinted past the edge of the magazine at Howard's face.

"Browning?" he repeated. "Wait, you're the guy, right?"

Howard lowered the magazine, reluctantly surrendering to the awkward moment. "Sorry?"

"Shit, yeah, I recognize you," Trevor said, running a hand through his greasy hair. "You're the old Reaper. I mean, not *old* old, just . . . you used to play the Reaper."

This amendment didn't make Howard feel any better, but he forced a smile in response.

"I am Howard Browning, yes." The one and only Reaper, he wanted to add.

"Wow," Trevor extended his hand for a shake. "So great to meet you, man." Howard was reluctant to touch the fingers that had just combed through that shaggy black mop, but did so anyway. "Wait, are you . . ." Trevor began to fill in the blanks himself. "Are you here to watch my audition? Like, to judge me?"

It was a reasonable assumption, and Howard was about to correct him, until he realized that this misunderstanding offered a unique opportunity. Trevor had no idea that Howard was still in the running for the role, that they were in direct competition. Of course, he didn't want to lie outright, so he simply smiled in response and let Trevor confirm his own assumptions.

"Wow," Trevor said, "Performing in front of the OG. No pressure, right?"

Howard cleared his throat, glancing at the distracted receptionist before he decided to run with it. "No need to be intimidated, Mr. Mane. Chuck just wants my expert perspective on hand to assess your performance."

Trevor was visibly sweating now as he nodded along. "Right. Well, your work was really inspiring to watch."

Howard could sense that Trevor was lying through his teeth, but it only gave him more license to lie back. "Thank you. I'm glad we're having this opportunity to speak before you're thrown to the wolves. Perhaps I can prepare you with a few questions, just to ease your nerves?"

Trevor exhaled. "That would be great, yeah. Thanks, man."

"What makes you think you deserve this role?"

The question caught Trevor off guard, just as Howard had hoped. "Deserve?" Trevor responded. "I mean, I've watched all the movies and I—"

"Millions of people watched the lunar landing. Should we make them all astronauts?" Howard asked.

Trevor let out an uncomfortable laugh. "Wow. Okay," he said, taking off his leather jacket.

"I hope you don't think I'm being too hard on you," Howard said. "It's just that Chuck has a habit of being rather ruthless, so it's best that I prepare you for the worst."

"No, it's cool, I appreciate it," Trevor said, sitting up a little straighter as he puffed up his chest with confidence. "I've been acting since I was nine, so I have a ton of experience. And I never had a single lesson, it all just came naturally to me."

"Indubitably," Howard smiled, using the cheap catchphrase to prod the unschooled amateur. The blow seemed to land as Trevor forced a fake smile before blathering on.

"Right. Anyway, I've had a lot of success in comedy so far, but I'm looking to change up my image right now. And I think the Reaper is the kind of role that could help me do that."

"You want the Reaper to help *you*," Howard leaned back. "That's interesting."

Trevor seemed irritated now, perhaps catching on to Howard's dismissive tone. "What's so interesting about that, Mr. Browning?"

"Well, you're telling me what you hope to get out of this. But what are you going to do for the Reaper?"

Trevor shook his head. "I'm not following you."

"The fans have waited over a decade for the monster's return. There's a legacy to fulfill, to be respected," Howard explained. "The Reaper is the spine, the lifeblood of the franchise, more central to the films than any final girl."

"Final girl?" Trevor echoed back.

"Yes, final girl. The archetypical heroine of every slasher film. Weak at first, but pure of heart. She endures the trauma to discover her inner strength and, in the end, slay the beast. You really haven't done your research, have you?" Howard shook his head. "I'm sorry. But I just don't see very much evidence that you take your*self* very seriously, let alone the opportunity that's being presented to you."

"Okay, I get it," Trevor laughed. "You're fucking with me, right?"

Howard could no longer hold back his distaste for the crude charlatan as he leaned in. "Mr. Mane. I've seen your work on *Family Genius*, and it's all very cute. You make a delightful little jester."

Trevor's face went red as Howard pressed onward.

"But the Reaper is a role for a true actor, one with the strength and experience that comes from years of practicing the artist's craft. Now, you may see this as another fine opportunity to get your face on the cover of *FameUs* magazine," he said, motioning toward the coffee table, "but true creation demands a selfless commitment. And, given your track record, I just don't think you're ready for that type of responsibility. Perhaps you should play it safe and stick to your . . . situational comedy."

Trevor was silent now as Howard eased back in his chair, satisfied with the monologue that had flowed forth quite naturally. It wasn't personal, really. The young man was simply out of his depth, and the role was not meant for him.

"Here's a comedic situation for you." Trevor leaned forward. "A pretentious old actor thinks he's actually achieved something in his career, but he has no idea how much of a joke he really is. Hilarity ensues."

Howard's fingers dug into the armrests, fuming at Trevor's smug grin. *Let's see if he's still smiling when I rip his jaw from his—*

"Mr. Browning?" the receptionist chirped and Howard's head swiveled to look at him. "They're ready for you."

Howard was shaken in the aftermath of hearing the Reaper's voice again, just as he did during the Dead World announcement. These intrusive violent thoughts were not a part of his method, but he hoped they were a sign that he was more prepared for this audition than he realized as he cleared his throat and got to his feet.

"Well, Mr. Mane." Howard adjusted his suit jacket, looking down at Trevor. "I suppose I'll have to let Chuck know just how much of a *joke* you think the Reaper is."

Trevor's face paled as Howard smiled, having successfully thrown his opponent off balance. But as he headed for the door, he carried with him the humiliating truth that he was no gatekeeper. For the first time in decades, Howard Browning was just another actor walking into an audition, praying he'd get the part.

## 10

Trevor couldn't believe he just stepped in shit thanks to his big fucking mouth. He rushed out of the waiting room, back into the midday heat, and lit a cigarette as he took out his phone to call Danny. He didn't know what else to do and Danny said that when you don't know what else to do, you pick up the phone. So here he was now, ranting to his sponsor about how he'd just fucked up and insulted Howard Browning, even though the guy fucking deserved it, but now Trevor was fucked because the pompous asshole was about to judge his audition.

"Slow down," Danny responded. "Take a deep breath and listen."

Trevor took that deep breath through the filter of his cigarette, exhaling smoke.

"I know you're only on Step Four," Danny explained, "but you're about to make an emergency Ninth Step."

"An amends?" Trevor scoffed. "To that asshole? But he fucking started it."

"He *started* it? What are you, nine years old?"

Trevor often felt that way, like his life stopped cold the first day of filming *Family Genius*, forever trapping him in emotional adolescence.

"Besides," Danny continued, "him being an asshole has nothing to do with you being an asshole. Can you do anything about him being an asshole?"

"No," Trevor responded.

"Can you do anything about *you* being an asshole?"

"Yes," Trevor sighed. He hated being spoken to like a child, but he hated even more that it was exactly what he needed.

"Great. So the second you walk into that room, you're gonna clear the air and take responsibility for your side. Go ahead and rehearse it with me now."

Trevor grit his teeth as he dug deep, tossing his cigarette into a nearby bush. "I'm sorry if I offended you, Mr. Browning. I was just . . . nervous for my audition. And I got defensive. I was out of line."

"Wow. That sounds something like integrity to me," Danny replied. "You'll survive, kid. Call me after to bookend it."

Trevor hung up the phone, annoyed at what he was being asked to do. The thought of making an amends was so humiliating that he considered just walking straight to his car, driving off the lot, and leaving it all behind.

But that would've just proven Howard right. Trevor *did* know about serious commitment, and that's why he was going to ignore his first impulse to jump ship and instead do what his sponsor told him to do. Because that was recovery.

After sucking down a second cigarette, he went back into the waiting room, where he paced in front of the receptionist's desk for what felt like forever.

"Can I get you anything, Mr. Mane?" the receptionist offered, concern in his voice.

"I'm fine. How much longer before they call me in?"

"That all depends on how long Mr. Browning's audition takes."

Trevor stopped in his tracks. "Wait, he's *auditioning*? For what role?"

"Um . . ." The kid blushed, probably a college intern still learning the office ropes. "I guess I really shouldn't say."

"Oh, come on." Trevor flipped the switch on his trademark charm as he sidled up to the desk. "It'll be our little secret." Trevor gave his best sitcom wink and the live studio audience of one melted before him.

"Okay, fine," the kid whispered, biting his lip at the intrigue of it all. "He's auditioning for the Reaper."

Trevor's body twitched with a spark of anger. "Son of a bitch."

"But please don't let them know I told you," the receptionist begged. "Also, I'm sure you're gonna get the role."

"So am I," Trevor asserted, moving back to the waiting room chair.

He kicked his feet up on the coffee table now, easing back into self-confidence. Howard Browning tried to get in his head, but he failed. Trevor didn't owe the sneaky old bastard an amends after all. In fact, he hoped that asshole ate shit and bombed in there and Trevor would be here waiting after. Not with an apology, but a big fucking grin.

## 11

"Howard! Christ, you look great!" Chuck Slattery rose from the other side of the long table, looking exactly as Howard remembered him with his cheap smile and thick brown hair.

"Ah, so do you, Charles." But as Chuck approached for an empty hug, Howard could see more clearly that the hair was plugged and painted, the smile frozen in place from years of plastic surgery. "You don't look a day over twenty."

"My guy works wonders." Chuck motioned to the skin stretched so tightly over his skull that it looked on the verge of snapping. "You should've seen me two years ago. My old mug had so many cracks, I looked like the Reaper himself."

"Nonsense," Howard laughed, thinking that Chuck surely looked more monstrous now than he did before a dozen facelifts.

"You wanna see *true* beauty, look no further than Mandy Ray here," Chuck said as a young girl appeared over his shoulder in pink sweatpants and a white spaghetti-strap shirt. "You may recognize her from season two of *Pop Idol.*" He didn't. "Mandy's gonna be reading with you today."

"How do you do, Ms. Ray?" Howard greeted the would-be actress who truly didn't look a day over twenty with her bleached hair and shiny lip gloss.

"Oh my god, it is *so* good to meet you!" Mandy smiled, giving a tug on his tweed jacket. "And can I just say that I am officially *obsessed* with this vintage jacket?"

"You may," Howard awkwardly offered back, catching a strong whiff of her sickly sweet perfume. He was all too familiar with Chuck's penchant for casting his young girlfriends as one-line fodder for the Reaper's blood-lust, but Howard was shocked that this trend had continued onward into Chuck's elder years, and even more disturbed that the girls seemed to remain the same age. Howard's eyes moved past Mandy now, landing on the curious man who remained seated behind the table.

"And this," Chuck motioned to the stout stranger with dark hair and a thick furrowed brow, "is the most talented director Romania has ever seen. Andrei Dalca." Andrei gave a stern nod in Howard's direction. "Guy was nominated for a Foreign Picture Oscar in oh-one."

"It's an honor, Mr. Dalca," Howard said to the stony man who gave no acknowledgment in response.

"I gotta say," Chuck said, throwing his arm around Howard's shoulder, "I was surprised to hear you were still interested in the role. You know we would've called you sooner, we just figured you were through with this stuff, on to bigger and better. And I didn't want to insult you by asking you to do *another* Reaper flick."

Howard wasn't buying Chuck's shrewd cover, especially considering the insulting cameo offer, but he had already prepared one of his own.

"Yes, well, I have been awfully busy. I was set to play Richard III in a rather large production up in the Bay Area, but the funding fell through at the last minute. You know how fickle the theater can be." It sounded convincing enough, and Howard knew that Chuck didn't know the first thing about theater.

"I sure do. Well, lucky for us, right?" Chuck gave Howard a pat on the shoulder.

"That being the case, is it quite necessary that I audition?" Howard asked, a last-ditch effort that he hoped wouldn't sound too desperate.

"Preaching to the choir, buddy. I know it's ridiculous, but the studio has its reasons," Chuck explained.

"That boy out there being one of them?" Howard motioned toward the waiting room. He was surprised to see that Chuck was capable of blushing through the constricted nerve endings on his shiny new face.

"So you met Trevor," Chuck responded through an awkward smile. "Look, they're just testing out a marketing strategy. Floating some buzz and seeing if the youth demographic bites." Howard loathed industry terminology that sounded like it was devised by a sixth grader. "But nothing's set in stone. I mean, do you really think I'd bring you in just to waste your time?"

"Of course not," Howard responded, knowing full well that Chuck would do exactly that.

"Mandy," Chuck turned to the bright-eyed actress. "You ready?"

Mandy nodded eagerly as she bounced her way to Howard's side. Chuck moved back to the other side of the table, taking a seat next to Andrei as Howard attempted to slow the train that was rolling into motion.

"Jacob never received any sides for me to study." It may have been a long time since his last audition, but surely providing the actor with a portion of the script to prepare their performance was still an industry standard.

"The script is still being written," Chuck explained. "Rewritten, really, so we don't exactly have the words down yet. But an old pro like you doesn't need sides, right? Just improvise and give us your best Reaper."

The harsh overhead fluorescents seemed to be giving off heat as Howard's mouth went dry. All of his preparation had failed, and he feared that his best Reaper was years behind him, but it was too late to back out now.

"Mandy's gonna feed you some familiar inspiration," Chuck offered. "And 'Drei?" he turned to the director. "You got anything for him?"

The intense auteur locked eyes with Howard, speaking in a thick accent. "In the field. She runs. A mouse. In the night. You. The cat. Find your mouse." He threw up his hands like claws. "*Kill* . . . your mouse. And *live*."

Howard had never been directed via haiku before, but it seemed there was a first time for everything. "Very well," he replied. "Thank you. I'll just need a moment to get into character."

He went off into the corner of the room, took a deep breath, and closed his eyes. He could do this, he'd done it a million times before. But if he really wanted to capture the character's essence, he'd have to return to that inner sanctum to find Lester again, and that hadn't gone so well the last time.

Howard tried to lean into the darkness and shut out the sounds around him as a pen scratched on paper. Was Andrei taking notes, judging him already? The receptionist laughed in the next room and was quickly joined by Trevor. That charming little punk was going to take the role from him if he didn't find it now, if he didn't dive deeper into the abyss and shut everything out until there was nothing. He squeezed his eyes tighter as his breath left his body and total silence overtook him, a darkness enveloping.

He found himself in the black space within, standing at the edge of an endless cornfield, the dry husks glowing gold.

Good. He was here. Now all he had to do was find Lester. Howard slowly entered a narrow passage between two rows and began calling out.

"Lester! Lester, where are you?" Walking through the maze of high cornstalks, he quickly got lost, turning around in circles as the rough leaves scratched his skin.

"Lester!" he called.

A harsh cackle resounded in the darkness, and Howard stopped short.

*"Lester can't come out and play . . ."*

The Reaper's gravelly voice rang out from somewhere in the distance as fear seized Howard's heart.

*". . . but I can!"*

The voice was right behind him now as Howard spun around, just in time to see the scythe cutting through the cornstalks at him. He jumped back, barely dodging the blade before turning to run through the field. The scythe sliced through the air at his back, inching ever closer as the monster laughed behind him until Howard tripped, face-planting in the dirt. He flipped around to face the beast, but no one was there in the motionless stalks.

This wasn't right. He was trapped with the Reaper somewhere in his own subconscious and he needed to get out, back to reality before—

Two dirty boots stepped on either side of Howard's head and he looked up to see the Reaper's upside-down grin. A glob of loose flesh fell from that shredded mug, splattering against Howard's forehead.

*"It's showtime!"*

The monster reached down and pressed his ragged thumbnails into Howard's eyes. A piercing pop sent blood oozing over his cheeks as he screamed into the darkness and the Reaper cackled until—

Howard's eyes flipped open, back in the silent audition room now.

Awake. Alive.

He tried to move, but he couldn't. Like the internal wires had been severed. Looking through his own eyes, he was somehow removed, at a distance. Trapped inside his own body as his arms stretched overhead, muscles aching as if being used for the first time in ages. His jaw creaked open like a rusty hinge.

*"Ohhh, it's good to be back!"*

It wasn't Howard's voice that issued forth. It was the Reaper, only somehow more primal and raw as it scraped up through his aged innards. Howard was a helpless spectator with another force at the helm, his eyes locking in on Mandy as his legs took their first steps.

*"And what's your name, little seedling?"*

The muscles in his face twisted into a painfully wide grin as Mandy looked at him in true horror. Too startled to speak, she finally cleared her throat and forced herself into the moment.

"Muh-Mandy. You're . . . the Reaper. Aren't you?" she said in monotone. "What do you want from me?"

Howard's feet crept toward her, body slinking without his control. He was nothing more than an observer as his fingertips drifted through Mandy's fried blonde locks, feeling her scalp tremble as his face leaned in for a deep inhale.

*"Mmmmm. So delicious. Your fear."*

He didn't know where the words were coming from, but Howard really did smell it. Not the sweet perfume he'd smelled earlier, but a sulfuric scent, like the dizzying aroma at a gas pump. This couldn't be happening. He was sure it was a nightmare from which he'd soon awaken, but it all felt so real as the words clawed up his throat and over his tongue.

*"Do you know what they did to me, Mandy?"*

His fingers extended, clasping around her skull now. Mandy tried to speak, but her jaw was frozen as her eyes moved over to the table where

Chuck and Andrei sat. Howard wanted to follow her gaze there, but the muscles behind his eyes wouldn't budge, firmly homed in on his prey. He shook Mandy's head like a snow globe as he shouted into her ear.

*"DO YOU?!"*

The poor girl shrieked and Howard wanted desperately to stop this, but he didn't know how. He'd lost all control over his body, his voice. All he could do was listen to himself speak, listen to the Reaper speak.

*"Year after year, I toiled in the hot sun. Planting and harvesting. Working my fingers to the bone."*

His fingertips gently danced along her cheeks now, down to her neck.

*"I gave my life to Ashland. And they killed me for it. Does that seem fair, Mandy?"*

She sputtered a helpless "No . . ."

Howard finally heard Chuck's voice. "Okay, I think that's enough."

Yes, please, someone stop this. Because Howard couldn't stop himself as he hissed into Mandy's ear.

*"I will not be put down. I will not be buried. I will reap the flesh from your bones."*

His fingers pinched Mandy's cheeks now, moist with tears.

*"Such a lovely face . . ."*

"Please . . ." Mandy begged, reality piercing through performance.

*"I think I'll try it on."*

Howard's fingernails dug into her skin.

"For fuck's sake, *cut!*" Chuck shouted.

Howard's whole body suddenly went slack, nearly collapsing to the floor before he caught his own weight with a stumble, finally back in control. Chuck pulled Mandy away as Howard gasped for air like he'd just emerged from being held underwater.

"Christ, Howard. That was a bit much, don't you think?" Chuck held Mandy as she trembled in his arms.

"I'm sorry," Howard stammered. "I didn't . . . mean to . . ."

Another strange smell breached his nose now as he looked down and saw that Mandy's pink sweatpants were soaked with urine. The poor girl was petrified.

Chuck held Mandy at arm's length, grimacing at the stench as he turned to Howard with a cold finality. "I think we've seen enough for today. Goodbye, Howard."

Howard hung his head, shuffling toward the door in shame as he heard Andrei jump to his feet at the table. "Why does he leave? This is our monster!"

"Not now, Andrei," Chuck shut the man down.

Howard pushed through the doors, wanting to flee the scene as quickly as possible as the blood surged back into his head, making him dizzy, almost high as he found himself face-to-face with the last person in the world he wanted to see.

## 12

"Mr. Browning!" Trevor beamed as he jumped to his feet, stepping right in Howard's path to deliver a gut punch to the bastard's ego. "How was your *audition?*"

But Howard bulldozed right past him with a distant look in his eye, nearly knocking Trevor off his feet as he disappeared through the exit. Before Trevor could say another word, a blonde girl burst out of the audition room, sobbing as she ran into the bathroom. Was that piss Trevor smelled? What the hell just happened in there? He turned to the receptionist now, who seemed just as confused.

"I guess they're ready for you?"

Trevor collected himself and entered the room to find Chuck engaged in a heated argument.

"That's too fucking bad, Andrei," the producer said in a hushed tone. Trevor recognized the other man as Andrei Dalca, the director whose work he'd studied to prepare for this meeting. The films were raw and verité, but the subtitles were a strain.

"That was *brilliant* performance, evoked true *fear!*" Andrei gushed.

Trevor awkwardly waited for someone to notice his presence.

"I don't care if you—" Chuck started before seeing Trevor, turning to greet him with a big smile, "There he is! Our big star!"

"Good to see you again, Mr. Slattery," Trevor said, though the sight of Chuck's plastic surgery always gave him the creeps. He'd considered getting some work done himself, just to tighten the crow's-feet that were already starting to form at the corners of his eyes. When Sophie said he was way too young for that, Trevor quoted Indiana Jones back to her, "It's not the years, it's the mileage." In Chuck's case, it must've been both.

"Thanks for taking the time to come in," Chuck said through porcelain teeth.

"Thanks for the opportunity. I have to say, though, I was surprised to see Howard Browning here. I didn't realize he was still up for the role," Trevor said, fishing for more details.

"Look," Chuck replied, putting his arm around Trevor's shoulder, "I'll be straight with you. We did get some fan blowback when they heard Howard was out. So I had to throw the old dog a bone, give him a fighting chance. But what we just saw," Chuck went on, shaking his head. "Well, let's just say I think his Reaper may have gone a little rusty over the years. Maybe even lost a screw or two."

Trevor was tempted to pile on and gossip about Howard's waiting-room mind games, but his sponsor would remind him that feeding a resentment was like drinking poison and hoping the other person dies. So he just nodded respectfully and listened to himself force out the kind words, "It was generous of you to give him the opportunity."

"Hey, I'm a generous guy. But what this franchise really needs is fresh blood!" Chuck exclaimed. "Right, Andrei?" he said, turning to the director, who sulked in his chair like a child denied a new toy.

Trevor tried not to be discouraged as he reached into his back pocket and pulled out a few pages of notes. Despite Howard's assumptions, Trevor actually had done his research. He may not have watched every terrible entry in the franchise, but he saw enough to know that he wanted to do something fresh and different. Now was his chance to show the director just how seriously he was taking this opportunity.

"Mr. Dalca," Trevor said. "If you don't mind, I had some questions I'd love to discuss with you before the audition. Just to make sure we're on the same page creatively before I give you my take on the character. I know there's a legacy to fulfill," he went on, cribbing Howard's words now, "and I want to respect it."

Chuck just laughed. "That is so damn sweet. Isn't he sweet, 'Drei? But there's no need to suck up now. This isn't an audition. It's an offer. The part is yours for the taking."

Trevor's shoulders slumped as he took in what was supposed to be good news.

"Really?" he questioned. "It's just . . . you haven't actually seen me perform this kind of material, so I'd love to show you what I can—"

"I'm sure you'll do great," Chuck interrupted, "Bottom line is everybody loves a good comeback story, and the masses can't get enough of you right now. I mean, between you and Brangelina, the tabloid industry might not be so dead after all."

And there it was. Trevor's true claim to fame. His blood boiled as he thought of those greasy photographers, sneaking photos for a few hundred bucks, destroying any semblance of a private life. The yard he was so happy to give Sophie wasn't even safe as he once caught a creep who'd hopped the fence and hidden in the garden to snap his secret photos. Trevor chased the son of a bitch halfway down Mulholland before losing him. He understood that there was a sick fixation for people in seeing the wholesome young boy they watched on television grow into a mug-shot fuckup. He just wished there was an easier way to wash away the past.

"So what do you say?" Chuck asked. "Are you ready to reap?"

As Trevor looked into Chuck's Cheshire grin, some part of him felt like he was about to sign a deal with the Devil. Was he really this soul-crushingly desperate?

"Sure," he found himself answering aloud.

"Great!" Chuck replied, unfazed by Trevor's lack of enthusiasm, "Just one thing I want to make clear." His voice lowered as he clamped a hand down on Trevor's shoulder. "I'm giving you a shot here. But you pick up that pipe while you're on *my* payroll? I will bury your career and shit on the grave. Got me?"

Chuck was still smiling his plastic smile as he waited for Trevor's reply.

"I'm clean," Trevor said with confidence. "And I'm staying that way."

Chuck's wicked grin widened even further than Trevor thought possible. "Attaboy! We're already in production on the announcement trailer, so we'll need you in the studio for a little voice-over action soon."

"Okay," Trevor replied, turning to Andrei once more, "Then maybe we could start with some voice work?"

Andrei muttered something in Romanian as Chuck led Trevor back toward the door. "We've had a long day here, Trev. Right now, all you need to do is go home and celebrate."

As Trevor walked away, he knew exactly how he wanted to celebrate. How to make all those ugly feelings go numb and bright. A soft voice inside was telling him to just give up and do it, but he swore he wouldn't listen, wouldn't cave to his worst instincts. Not this time.

He was stronger than the voice inside his head.

## 13

Howard drove home from the Pinnacle lot feeling like every vein in his body had been flushed with fire. He'd never had such an out-of-body experience before, like the Reaper had climbed behind the wheel and thrown Howard out of the speeding car.

As soon as he entered the house, he went upstairs to take a cold shower, only to find a Post-it Note on the bathroom mirror reading: *Buy Soap*. Not only had he forgotten to do so, but he didn't even remember writing the note. Further proof that his mind was fading and what happened in that audition room was just another slip. Surely a phone call to Dr. Cho would help explain these mental and physical manifestations. But first, he climbed into the shower and let the frigid water pelt his skin, calming his scorched nerves until he was numb all the way through.

He went down to the kitchen afterward, whole body shivering from the chill as he put on a kettle and made the call. The receptionist on the other end said that the doctor was busy and would call him back, but Howard told her that it was an emergency and he'd wait as long as he had to. After what felt like an eternity of excruciating hold music, Dr. Cho finally came on the line with her reassuringly tranquil tone.

"Howard. What's the emergency?"

"Good afternoon, Dr. Cho," he said, pacing in the kitchen as he tried to remain calm. "I'm sorry to bother you, but I'm afraid my condition may be worsening. The Post-it Notes are a great help, but I've started to experience the blackouts you warned me about."

"A little ahead of schedule, but it's not altogether abnormal with your condition."

"Yes, well, today I experienced something else, something rather disturbing. In an audition, I sort of . . . detached from myself. As if I were an observer, watching my body move and speak without me."

"Mm-hm," the doctor matter-of-factly responded to what Howard thought was rather unusual behavior. "What you're describing sounds like a depersonalization episode, which can be triggered by acute stress. Unfortunately, it's a common symptom of a deeper decline into Alzheimer's and it often coincides with the cognitive blackouts."

Howard breathed a sigh of relief. The news was unfortunate, but also strangely comforting. At least he could understand his experience now as a symptom of his illness brought on by the stress of the audition and nothing more.

"Is there anything I can do to help alleviate these symptoms?" Howard asked.

"I know you're resistant to medication," the doctor began, "but I think it's time you came back in to talk about some treatment options."

Howard had always been wary of letting any unnatural chemicals into his bloodstream. He hardly ever took an Advil for a headache, let alone anything that might actually alter his brain chemistry. "I'll come in as soon as I can," he promised, "but in the meantime?"

"In the meantime, some patients find it useful to keep a journal of their thoughts and feelings. It helps them hold on to their memory and maintain their identity when it feels like it's starting to slip away."

"Yes, of course," Howard said as he stopped pacing.

"I've got a patient waiting right now," the doctor said, "but just hold tight and Diane will be on the line to set up an appointment."

"Thank you, Dr. Cho," Howard said, grateful for the quick solution as the hold music kicked back in. After spending all those years journaling as Lester Jensen, it should be easy to start writing for himself. Yes, a little creative exercise to reconnect with Howard and he'd be right as rain in no time at all.

The kettle began to whistle, drowning out the cheesy jingle in his ear and the anxious thoughts in his mind as Howard let it scream.

## 14

The restaurant was too noisy, and Trevor really wasn't in the mood to celebrate, but Sophie had already made a reservation at his favorite spot even before she got the good news. She just believed in him that much.

"I'm so proud of you," Sophie said as they squeezed into the red leather booth at Musso and Frank's. The old Hollywood steakhouse was a favorite haunt for famous actors and writers through the ages, including Charles Bukowski, who used to regularly drink himself stupid on Heinekens at the bar. Trevor wasn't much of a reader, but Ryan at Chrysalis had lent him a book by the infamous alcoholic poet. It wasn't hard to see the appeal of those unpretentious tales of drinking and womanizing. Bukowski was long dead now, his spot at the bar currently occupied by two overweight Midwesterners in scuffed-up Keds, racing toward heart attacks as they chomped through steaks the size of their faces.

"I don't think landing a trashy B-horror remake is really cause for celebration, babe," Trevor muttered.

"Don't be so hard on yourself. This is just the start of your comeback." Sophie was always looking at the positive side. It was a trait he admired in her, especially when all he could see was the shitstorm ahead.

"I'd rather do another *Family Genius* reunion special. It would be less embarrassing," Trevor said.

The sound of a gunshot made Trevor jump in the booth, until he saw the waiter in a red jacket holding up the popped bottle of champagne.

"I hear there's cause for celebration," the waiter smiled.

Sophie grinned across the table as the waiter poured the bubbly amber liquid into her flute before tipping the bottle toward Trevor's glass.

He quickly covered it with his hand. "Not that kind of celebration."

"Babe," Sophie said, "It's okay. I called ahead."

The waiter twisted the bottle so Trevor could see the label, not for champagne, but for sparkling apple cider. He gave Trevor a wink as he filled the flute.

"And what will we be having for dinner this evening?" the waiter asked.

"I'll have the chicken Caesar salad, dressing on the side, please," Sophie said, "and he'll have the prime rib, rare."

First she got him his apple juice, then she ordered his meal for him. What came next, a paper place setting with a box of crayons? He told himself to stop being such an ungrateful brat as Sophie continued her words of encouragement.

"I know it's hard to see right now, but you've come a long way in the last year. And landing this role just proves that you deserve a fresh start."

But Trevor didn't feel like he deserved anything. He hadn't earned his career, he was just a lucky kid whose parents dragged him to the right audition at the right time. He often wondered what his life would've been like if they'd never taken him that fateful day. If he'd avoided Hollywood altogether and lived a normal life, only visiting this awful town as a tourist, just like those Midwesterners at the bar. But he wasn't normal and he'd been infected with the fame bug too young to shake it now.

"I just want to do something great," he admitted, "I want to *show* people that I can do something great. That I'm more than they think I am."

"And you will. One day at a time," Sophie responded.

Trevor cringed at the familiar mantra. He wondered if she was still going to her own group meetings, the ones that gave emotional support to people with addicts in their lives. He was afraid to ask, and more than a little ashamed at the ripple effects of his own bullshit.

"To you," Sophie said, raising her glass. Trevor nodded, raising his glass and taking a deep swig. Shit. For a moment there his mouth was still expecting champagne. Sophie probably thought it was a cute substitute.

What she didn't realize was that the mere sight of a glass bottle, let alone the feeling of a bubbly liquid sliding down his throat, was dangerous for an addict at this stage. A slippery slope toward the real thing, which eventually led to the *real* real thing.

"Excuse me?"

Trevor quickly registered the Midwestern accent as he turned to see the two round tourists hovering over his table now.

"Oh my God, it *is* you! Tommy Hooper!"

"Not for a long time," Trevor responded. "We're actually out to dinner right now, so . . ."

"Oh, we don't want to interrupt," the round man said. "We'd just love it if we could get a picture with you. We watched *Family Genius* with our kids and now they watch reruns with their kids and it's just a real family tradition."

"So you *do* want to interrupt," Trevor said, watching their faces fall.

"Trevor." Sophie gave him her "be nice" look.

This was a moment of choice. He could either swallow his pride and bite his tongue, or be a total fucking prick and ruin the night right now. It should've been an easy decision, but it was always so goddamn hard.

"Sure," he said, standing to face the couple. "Let's get a picture."

Sophie wound up their disposable camera and snapped the photo. As the fans thanked him, Trevor noticed the round woman eyeing the green bottle on the table with concern. They walked off as he slid into Sophie's side of the booth, leaning on her shoulder.

"That was very nice of you," she said, kissing his head.

"Ya know, I thought five seasons of *Family Genius* was a prison sentence, I couldn't wait to get out," Trevor said. "But today I met Howard Browning, the guy who played the Reaper for ten fucking years. And there he was, this pathetic old man, still trying to crawl back into his tired ass franchise. I don't know, Soph. It was just sad."

"Wait, you beat the original guy for the role? You didn't tell me that!" Sophie lit up. "See, you obviously earned this, sweetie. Your audition must have blown them away."

Trevor didn't have the heart to tell her what had actually happened. That there was no audition, that he'd been offered the role not because of his acting talent, but because of his tabloid sideshow status. He hated the way those tourists looked at him, like he was supposed to keep being some perfect little child who wasn't allowed to make mistakes for the rest of his life. What did Howard call him? "A delightful little jester." He was done with that shit, ready to shed his old identity and embrace a new one. The Reaper probably would've sliced those tourists' heads off and served them on a silver platter to the next table over. *"Midwestern cow brains, extra rare!"*

"You know what?" Trevor said. "I do deserve this role." He grabbed the bottle, condensation wetting his palm as he refilled Sophie's flute. "But I don't deserve you. You know that, right?"

"Too bad. You're stuck with me," Sophie smiled. Sometimes the way she smiled at him made Trevor feel worse. Like the light within her was shining deep into his own dark pit, its warmth wasted in the bottomless abyss, illuminating nothing. But tonight, it reminded him of a Bukowski poem. He couldn't remember the exact words, something about how even a little bit of light beats the dark.

Trevor knew that he needed to lean into Sophie's light if he ever wanted to beat his own darkness, so he reached for the bottle and held it up ceremoniously. "Here's to the Reaper."

Sophie smiled and clinked her glass against it as Trevor took a deep swig, the acidic bubbles tumbling once more into his stomach. He felt like he might vomit just as Sophie leaned in close to whisper. "You don't *fear* the Reaper . . . do you?"

"What?" Trevor said. "No, I'm not afraid of anything."

And then she started singing. Softly at first, but getting louder with each line of the familiar chorus while Trevor held back a grin, shaking his head. "Please don't . . ."

But she was already doing it, full-on serenading him in public now. She stopped short of the final line as she held her flute to Trevor's mouth like a microphone, waiting for him to pick up the tune. He could feel onlookers turning to stare, but as he gazed into Sophie's sparkling eyes, the whole restaurant faded out of focus.

He wrapped his hand around hers, pulling the flute close to sing off-key. "Baby, I'm your maaaaan!"

Sophie laughed and Trevor kissed her on the lips, feeling pure joy wash over him for the first time since he left Chrysalis. He didn't give a shit about anything or anyone outside of this little red booth as they sang their la-la-las.

## 15

The storm inside had given way to a heavy fog as Howard sat in his silent study with a steaming mug of tea. He was determined to clear his mind and fill up on himself as the doctor had suggested, opening the notebook to find that first page still tainted with Lester's handwriting.

run

Was this what the character had tried to warn him about? That the Reaper had separated from Lester and was coming to seize control of Howard now?

What a ridiculous thought. There was no Lester, no Reaper. It was all make-believe. There was only Howard and this would be *his* journal now. He tore the page out, starting fresh.

*"My name is Howard Browning,"* he wrote in his own controlled cursive, *"and I am an actor."*

It was strange, writing about himself, and he hardly knew what to say, but he already felt more calm and focused as he took a soothing sip of tea and placed pen to paper again.

*"I enjoy fresh vegetables, chamomile tea and—"*

CLANK.

Howard dropped his pen. It was the same sound he heard when he was hiding in that inner space with Lester. Only he wasn't there, he was here. In his home, fully conscious.

CLANK.

This wasn't in his head. The sound of the rusty chain was coming from somewhere in this very house. Somewhere downstairs, beneath the floorboards. He quietly moved to the study door and opened it to the dark hallway.

A Post-it Note was stuck to the wall in front of him with words scratched in a feverish handwriting that he did not recognize.

WHEN THE SEEDS ARE SOWN

A little further down the hall, on the opposite wall, another Post-it.

BUT THE STALKS GROW DRY

Howard was familiar with the words. The first line of a playground rhyme, sung by the children of Ashland throughout the franchise. A warning that with every harvest season, the mythical killer would return for new blood. But who wrote these notes?

He looked ahead and saw another yellow square at the top of the staircase.

AND THE HARVEST MOON BURNS IN THE SKY

Drifting down the staircase, another message awaited him at the bottom. Could Howard have written them and forgotten?

DON'T SET FOOT ON LESTER'S LAND

But this manic handwriting wasn't his. The final Post-it, stuck to the wall above the phone on the foyer table, brought the grim rhyme to a close.

LEST YOU'RE SLAIN BY THE REAPER'S HAND!

The cellar door was ever so slightly ajar. It was possible he'd left it open himself, but unlikely. He always kept it securely closed to prevent a cold draft from creeping up through the whole house. He hadn't ventured down there in days and he surely would've noticed before now.

Yet here it was. Open. So he must have opened it. Because who else could have?

*CLANK.*

It was coming from the cellar, he was sure of it. An intruder. Someone had broken in and they were in the house now, leaving these threatening notes. That was the only explanation that made sense.

"Who's there?!" he called toward the cracked door. Silence answered back.

*BRRRING.*

He jumped at the phone ringing on the table beside him. Then stared at it, waiting for a second ring, unsure if the first had really happened.

*BRRRING.*

Howard quickly pressed the answering machine button to cut off the call. He wasn't ready to speak to anyone, not right now.

*BEEEEP.*

"Howie, it's Jake. Listen, I just got off the phone with Chuck . . ."

Howard was yanked back to earth by the message. He'd been in such a tense state since the audition, so caught up in himself, he'd almost forgotten about the mortifying public experience. Mandy's terror. Chuck's anger. Trevor's smug grin.

"It sounds like you definitely made an impression today," Jake continued, "but they still want to take the character in a new direction. Nothing personal."

How could it not be personal? Howard's hand began to shake as he stared down at the blinking red light, barely listening as the message continued.

"But the good news is, we've got a year's worth of fresh appearances to milk out of this thing. I know things have been slow, but Pinnacle wants the OG Reaper making the rounds at every convention in the nation, giving the remake his blessing—"

Howard's fist slammed down on the answering machine, plastic shattering as Stanley yowled near his feet and leapt under the table to hide.

"Oh, Stanley!" Howard was startled by his own violent outburst as he dropped to the floor and scooped the traumatized cat into his arms. "I'm sorry . . . I'm so sorry, I didn't . . ." His whole body shook, rocking the cat back and forth like a scared child clutching his teddy bear. "That wasn't me . . . That wasn't me . . ." He hit himself on the side of the head with a weak fist, giving Stanley an opportunity to scurry away.

Howard's gaze moved back to the cracked cellar door now. He climbed to his feet, creaking the door wide and looking down into the inky depths. The impenetrable darkness summoned him, yearning to pull him inside, across the threshold of the monster's lair.

Howard turned away, only to find himself face-to-face with the inside of the cellar door. Every inch was covered in overlapping Post-it Notes with one word repeated in the same screeching scrawl as the sound over-powered him . . .

CLANK CLANK CLANK CLANK CLANK CLANK CLANK
CLANK CLANK CLANK CLANK CLANK CLANK CLANK
CLANK CLANK CLANK CLANK CLANK CLANK CLANK
CLANK CLANK CLANK CLANK CLANK CLANK CLANK
CLANK CLANK CLANK CLANK CLANK CLANK CLANK
CLANK CLANK CLANK CLANK CLANK CLANK CLANK
CLANK CLANK CLANK CLANK CLANK CLANK CLANK
CLANK CLANK CLANK CLANK CLANK CLANK CLANK
CLANK CLANK CLANK CLANK CLANK CLANK CLANK
CLANK CLANK CLANK CLANK CLANK CLANK CLANK
CLANK CLANK CLANK CLANK CLANK CLANK CLANK
CLANK CLANK CLANK CLANK CLANK CLANK CLANK
CLANK CLANK CLANK CLANK CLANK CLANK CLANK
CLANK CLANK CLANK CLANK CLANK CLANK CLANK
CLANK CLANK CLANK CLANK CLANK CLANK CLANK
CLANK CLANK CLANK CLANK CLANK CLANK CLANK
CLANK CLANK CLANK CLANK CLANK CLANK CLANK
CLANK CLANK CLANK CLANK CLANK CLANK CLANK
CLANK CLANK CLANK CLANK CLANK CLANK CLANK
CLANK CLANK CLANK CLANK CLANK CLANK CLANK
CLANK CLANK CLANK CLANK CLANK CLANK CLANK
CLANK CLANK CLANK CLANK CLANK CLANK CLANK
CLANK CLANK CLANK CLANK CLANK CLANK CLANK
CLANK CLANK CLANK CLANK CLANK CLANK CLANK
CLANK CLANK CLANK CLANK CLANK CLANK CLANK
CLANK CLANK CLANK CLANK CLANK CLANK CLANK
CLANK CLANK CLANK CLANK CLANK CLANK CLANK
CLANK CLANK CLANK CLANK CLANK CLANK CLANK
CLANK CLANK CLANK CLANK CLANK CLANK CLANK
CLANK CLANK CLANK CLANK CLANK CLANK CLANK
CLANK CLANK CLANK CLANK CLANK CLANK CLANK
CLANK CLANK CLANK CLANK CLANK CLANK CLANK

Howard nearly toppled down the stairs, catching himself on the door-frame as he pushed back, slamming the door closed to an abrupt silence. He dragged the heavy foyer table across the hardwood until it pressed against the cellar door. The darkness was locked away now and the only sound that remained was his own heavy panting.

Exhaustion settled deep into his bones as he moved toward the banister and pulled himself back up the stairs. Drifting toward his bed, he hoped the quiet would last long enough for him to finally get some rest. Perhaps that was all he really needed to get his head right. A long, deep rest. And when he finally awakened, he would discover that all of this was nothing more than a bad dream.

*Night of the Reaper Part III: Fields of Blood* (1982)
Script Pages Courtesy of Pinnacle Studios

EXT. CORNFIELD - NIGHT

Amid a sea of healthy green cornfields . . . A PARTY
RAGES in an open clearing. The DJ blasts new wave
tunes as TEENS in neon clothing dance under flashing lights.

At the edge of the cornstalks, fraternity brothers
BRAD and GARY share a joint.

> BRAD
> It used to be a summer camp,
> but the counselors kept getting
> killed. So the town tore down the
> cabins and started growing corn
> again. Guess they thought the
> monster would leave them alone if
> they just gave him his land back.

Gary exhales smoke.

> GARY
> Did it work?

> BRAD
> That depends.

> GARY
> On what?

> BRAD
> On whether or not you believe any
> of that horseshit. I think our
> folks are just trying to scare us
> into not partying out here.

He tosses Gary a beer can.

> BRAD
> Shotgun?

                         GARY
             You're on.

They use car keys to stab holes in their cans, then
ready their fingers beneath the tabs.

                         BRAD
             One, two, three, pop!

The cans POP and the boys chug. Brad wins, CRUNCH-
ING his empty can and tossing over his shoulder
into the cornstalks.

                         BRAD
             Gonna have to drink faster than
             that if we wanna beat Delta Phi at
             the Greek Games.

Gary belches.

                         GARY
             I want a rematch.

They prep a second round of beers, fingers tucked
under tabs.

                         BRAD
             One, two, three—

THE REAPER bursts out of the cornstalks behind
Brad, latching on to the frat boy's head.

                       THE REAPER
             Pop!

He gives Brad's skull a CRUNCHING squeeze until an
eyeball POPS out of its socket, dangling by red
tendons. Brad SHRIEKS as the Reaper RIPS his head
clean off in a shower of blood.

                       THE REAPER
             Heads up!

The Reaper tosses the dripping head to a trembling Gary, who instinctively catches it. He SCREAMS, dropping the severed head and running into the party.

> GARY
> The Reaper! He's here!

But nobody seems to care as they bump and grind to the beat. Gary rushes up to the stage and pushes the DJ aside, grabbing the microphone as the record SCRATCHES off track.

> GARY
> Everybody, listen! The Reaper is here and he's gonna kill us all!

The crowd BOOS as the DJ grabs Gary by his shirt.

> DJ
> All right, joker. Show's over.

He tosses Gary from the stage into the arms of the partygoers, who crowd-surf the buzzkill away. The DJ yells into the mic.

> DJ
> Hello, Ashland!

The crowd CHEERS.

> DJ
> What do you say we get this party back on track? Can you dig it?

The crowd SCREAMS in response just as——

A SHOVEL BLADE ERUPTS FROM THE DJ'S CHEST, splattering blood into the crowd. The dead man collapses on his turntable, revealing the Reaper behind him.

                    THE REAPER
          I can dig it!

The partygoers SCREAM in horror now, scurrying
away under flashing lights. The monster grips the
microphone with rock star verve.

                    THE REAPER
          Goodbye, Ashland!

# PART III:
# REPULSION

## 16

"Howard," a soft voice beckoned in the dark.

He slowly awakened to find himself in bed, sunlight slicing through the white curtains. Rolling toward the voice, Howard found a familiar radiant face resting on the pillow beside him.

"Emma?" he uttered in disbelief, heart thrumming.

Emma's cheeks curled into a smile, framed by her long black hair.

"Who else would it be, sleepyhead?" she teased, kissing his wrinkled brow.

"Oh, Emma," he buried his head in her chest, breath deepening. "I had the most awful nightmare."

"It's okay." Emma gently stroked his hair. "You're awake now."

"Please," he begged as tears welled in his eyes. "Don't leave me."

"I would never leave you, silly," she assured him in her silky tone as he closed his eyes tight. *"Never,"* the now-harsh voice breathed into his ear. Howard opened his eyes to find the Reaper's bloody face staining the pillow where Emma once was, broken grin stretching wide. *"You're mine."*

Howard opened his mouth to scream as the Reaper's jagged teeth sunk into his neck, cutting his cry short with blood gurgling in his throat. He choked for air as he jumped awake, flailing beneath the sheets and pushing himself up to look at the bed beside him.

Empty. Alone.

Touching his neck, he found no bite marks among the stubble. The dream was over, but now he was back in reality, where he had been hiding away from the world for more days than he could keep track of. It was hard to mark the passage of time when he wasn't sleeping, plagued by nightmares that ripped him awake every time he slipped from consciousness. Howard swung his heavy legs over the side of the bed as his head began to throb. The thoughts were rushing up again, pulsing in his brain, straining against his skull.

Dark thoughts, horrible thoughts.

The Reaper's thoughts.

He had to get them out.

He rushed into the study, jumping into his chair and flipping the journal open. It was filled with the same jagged handwriting as those Post-it Notes that sang the monster's rhyme. He knew now that there had been no intruder in his house. Only in his mind. The Reaper was writing through him, just as the character had spoken through him, moved through him during the audition. He quickly turned page upon page of the hastily scrawled words that had been spilling out of him, day after day, transcribing the wicked voice in his head.

I'VE BEEN WAITING ROTTING IN THE DIRT THIRSTING FOR BLOOD BUT EVEN IN THE DARKNESS OF DEATH I SMELLED YOUR FEAR GROWING I STALKED THROUGH THE SHADOWS OF YOUR MEMORY TENDING TO YOUR TERROR RIPENING YOUR SOULS FOR THE COMING HARVEST SWEET CHILDREN OF ASHLAND THE TIME HAS COME THE REAPER HAS RISEN AND I WILL HAVE MY REVENGE HAHAHAHAHAHAHAHAHAHAHAHAHAHAHA

The pen trembled in Howard's hand as he kept flipping through the vile stream of consciousness, desperate to find some blank space to unload his pounding head until he finally arrived at the final page of the notebook.

Where the Reaper's chain was scratched in an endless spiral.

He reached for a pad of Post-its, but even those had been corrupted and converted into a flipbook where a stick-figure drawing of the Reaper stabbed his victim over and over and over.

Howard sank back into his chair, realizing that every blank scrap of paper in his study had been consumed with black ink, every page a dumping ground filled with violent thoughts. There was nowhere left for him to empty his ragged mind as it oozed with all that nastiness.

If he wanted some relief, he would have to risk going out into the world for more notebooks while his brain buzzed like a nest of bees, ready to swarm and sting.

Howard kept his head low as he moved through the supermarket, pushing his cart on a fervent mission. He needed to get in and out as quickly as possible, minimizing human contact for fear that it wouldn't be him that surfaced to speak.

His first stop was in the small stationery section, where he cleared out every marbled notebook they had. That should keep him busy for a while with plenty of empty space to dump the detritus that clamored in his skull. It was being drowned out now by the awful pop music that blared overhead as he moved into the next aisle to stock up on cat food. When he finally made his way to the fresh produce, he found himself uninspired by his usual vegetarian diet. His gaze drifted away from the leafy balls of cabbage toward the butcher's counter, where raw red slabs glowed under white lights.

Had fresh meat always looked so delicious?

He could almost taste the sinews of flesh between his teeth as his mouth watered. Shoveling a dozen thick steaks into his cart, he watched the blood glide along the plastic wrap as he wheeled up to the register.

With these supplies, he wouldn't have to leave the house again anytime soon. It wasn't much of a plan, but he was hoping that this was nothing more than a passing phase. After such a long hiatus from acting, he'd simply pushed himself too far in that audition and was now in need of a brief break from the world to get his head right. Eventually, his imagination would slow down, the seething swamp of his unconscious would settle, and everything would return to normal.

He unloaded his cart onto the conveyer belt as the teenaged checkout boy stared at a hanging television set, blindly dragging the notebooks over the red light.

*BEEP.*

*"It's not too late!"* the commercial blared. *"Text now to vote for your next Pop Idol!"*

BEEP.

Pop Idol. Howard couldn't help being reminded of poor Mandy and the horrible way he'd treated her. Perhaps he could send her a handwritten apology note through the studio once he got on the other side of this. For now, he tried to stay focused on finishing his grocery run as the cashier rang up the first can of Frisky Whiskers.

BEEP.

Stanley had been unusually reclusive ever since Howard's outburst in the foyer, and he'd hoped to mend the relationship with a can of Fancy Feast. It was a risk speaking to the cashier now, but Howard missed his sole companion too much not to ask. "I had a question about the cat food," he furtively began as the cashier's eyes remained glued to the television.

BEEP.

"Do you know when you'll be restocking on Fancy Feast? I'm just wondering about the quality of this . . . Frisky Whiskers."

BEEP.

"I don't know, man." The boy's eyes finally met Howard's with a dead-pan glare. "But if you wanna crack open a can and try it, I won't tell my manager."

Howard's stomach churned as a monstrous thought sprang up.

*I'd rather crack open your ribs and make a fancy feast of your innards.*

The Reaper's voice, knocking at the door.

"That won't be necessary," Howard managed to utter instead. "Thank you." He should have just kept his mouth shut, but the boy was nearly through ringing up his steaks now and all he needed to do was pay and leave.

"Total is sixty-five twenty-two," the cashier said as Howard pulled out his wallet. "Unless you want us to slaughter another innocent cow for you?"

Howard noticed the MEAT IS MURDER pin on the boy's apron now. He struggled to keep a lid on the cauldron within as he handed over the cash, but he couldn't stop the response that hissed over his lips.

*"Yesss . . ."* The Reaper's gravelly voice gushed forth. Howard's hand clamped down on the cashier's wrist, pulling him close while his other index finger grazed along the boy's ribs like a blade. *"Let's slice some fresh flanks, shall we?"*

The cashier shook under his grip as Howard's face trembled into a grin.

"Everything okay over here?"

Howard was pulled back into his body as he turned to face the store manager, who crossed her arms with a concerned scowl.

He quickly cleared his throat, discovering his own voice again. "I just . . . asked for paper bags." Howard quickly shoved everything into brown bags as the cashier rubbed his wrist.

"No, Bethany, everything is not okay," the cashier said, taking a step back. "This guy's being a total creep."

Howard quickly threw a handful of bills onto the conveyer belt as the manager stepped closer. "Sir, I'm going to have to ask you to—"

"Keep the change and have a wonderful day," Howard said, grabbing his groceries and rushing out the door.

He was flushed with shame, mortified by his own actions as he crawled back into his car. But as he leaned his head against the steering wheel and exhaled deeply, the tension in every muscle discharged in a swell of relief he hadn't experienced in days. It was as if giving voice to that nastiness actually discharged some of the pressure that had been building up inside. Those dark impulses weren't his true thoughts, but if they were spilling out of his mouth, he had to take responsibility for them and deal with the consequences. He couldn't risk letting something like that happen again, but what if scribbling in notebooks wasn't enough to give him the sense of clarity that he felt now? This cleansing sensation of true bodily release.

As he drove his Cadillac toward the freeway entrance, he changed his mind at the last second and took the southbound ramp, away from home. He couldn't remember when his appointment with Dr. Cho was, but he would spend all day in the waiting room if he needed to. Howard couldn't deal with this alone anymore. Never in his life had he ever been called a "creep," but that's exactly what he was becoming. He needed help before he became something much worse.

## 17

*"A clown can get away with murder."*

The John Wayne Gacy quote was printed below the creepy clown painting. Trevor stared into those dead black eyes framed by blue makeup for so long, he started to feel like they were staring back. According to the rest of the display placard, Gacy had painted the self-portrait from death row, where he landed himself after killing thirty-three young boys. Trevor didn't understand why they let the sick fuck breathe, let alone paint.

He was in the Museum of Death, a Los Angeles staple he'd driven past many times but never had any reason to enter. After Andrei's rejection during the audition, Trevor decided he'd take it upon himself to build his own take on the character. He wanted to ignore all the supernatural nonsense and start with the grim reality that the Reaper was, if nothing else, a serial killer. Trevor moved to the next wall, where the Son of Sam's handwritten letters to the police had been framed.

*I LOVE TO HUNT. PROWLING THE STREETS LOOKING FOR FAIR GAME. TASTY MEAT. POLICE—LET ME HAUNT YOU WITH THESE WORDS. I'LL BE BACK! YOURS IN MURDER, MR. MONSTER.*

Trevor figured the Reaper must think the same way, must get off on hunting his victims. He wondered what it took for someone to truly crack like David Berkowitz, to imagine that a talking dog was commanding you to kill. That was some next-level insanity.

He moved into the next room, dedicated entirely to the Manson family, followed by actual beds from the Heaven's Gate cult. This breed of crazy was easier for him to wrap his head around because the recovery rooms often felt like a cult. There was a certain relief that came from being part of a clan and just following orders. Of course, Danny Alvarez was probably a healthier choice for a sponsor than Charles Manson. Or at least Trevor hoped so.

The sign above the next room stopped him cold.

The Suicide Room.

He peeked across the threshold to find the walls plastered with crime scene photos of people who had blown their own heads off, hanged themselves, leapt from buildings. He didn't want to admit it, but something about this imagery was even more relatable than the Cult Room as Trevor felt dizzy. Checking the time on his watch, he realized that he needed to get to the studio soon anyway. He decided to blow right past Suicide and the two rooms after it, working his way back to the entrance gift shop.

"How was your journey down the River Styx?" the goth girl behind the counter asked with silver lip rings clacking around her black lips.

"Delightful," Trevor responded, eyeing the glass case of souvenirs. "You have any documentaries on serial killers?"

The goth girl grinned, opening the case. "We've got 'em all. Dahmer, Manson, Gacy, Berkowitz. Pick your poison."

"Give me everything you've got," Trevor said, pulling out his credit card.

She rang up the purchases and handed Trevor his card back. "Before you go, can I get a picture?" Trevor tensed as she lifted a Polaroid camera from behind the counter.

"Why, so you can sell it to the press, tell them Trevor Mane's got a death fetish?"

Her black-rimmed eyes blinked in confusion. "Um. No. For the Victim Wall."

She pointed over Trevor's shoulder, where Polaroids were plastered of every gift shop customer holding up their purchases.

Wait. Did this girl really not recognize him at all? Maybe there was hope for a clean slate after all.

"Sure," Trevor shrugged with relief, holding up his DVDs with a performative mug-shot grimace as the camera flashed.

The goth girl pulled the Polaroid photo and started shaking it as she squinted at Trevor, straining to recognize him. "You *from* something?"

"Yeah. A dysfunctional family," Trevor responded, collecting his DVDs. "Just like the rest of these deviants."

Trevor headed for the door as he heard a rehearsed farewell over his shoulder. "Thank you for visiting the Museum of Death! Have a killer day!"

*"And the Reaper . . . will have his revenge . . ."*

Trevor whispered harshly into the microphone. He was trying something different with his Reaper voice. A bit more childish and uncertain. He still didn't understand why they were recording voice-overs for a trailer before he'd even seen a script, but he didn't want to rock the boat now as Chuck clicked through on the other side of the recording booth glass.

"That's great, Trev. But can you make it a bit more . . . Reapery?"

"Reapery. Right." What the fuck did that mean? "Sure thing, Mr. Slattery."

He tried to ignore grumpy Andrei seated next to Chuck on the other side of the glass, still looking disappointed by the casting choice that was forced upon him. Trevor just needed to focus on his performance now. He imagined that Lester Jensen had swallowed a lot of dirt and rocks when he was dragged by the chain, so the Reaper's raspy voice was the result of shredded vocal cords. He tried to contract his esophagus a little tighter, straining out the words.

*"And the Reaper . . . will have his revenge . . ."*

Spittle flew from his mouth onto the mic, sending feedback through the system. Chuck winced as he snapped his headphones off and Andrei let out some silent curse.

"Great, Trev," Chuck said into the mic after a moment's pause. "Excellent. It's just . . . we'd really like you to sound *just* like the Reaper we know and love."

"Oh," Trevor's shoulders slumped. "I just thought, this being a remake and all, that you might want me to try something different."

Andrei tried to speak up next to Chuck, who quickly quieted the director before clicking back into the mic. "It *will* be different, it absolutely will. But for now, we really just need to sell the classic. So why don't you just give us your best impression of the Reaper?"

"You mean . . . my best impression of Howard Browning as the Reaper?"

"I guess you could say that, yeah," Chuck shrugged, losing patience.

Why the fuck did they hire Trevor if they just wanted the same old shit? He grit his teeth, not wanting to blow it now. Taking a deep breath, he leaned into the mic.

*"And the Reaper . . . will have his revenge!"*

It was so over the top, he couldn't help feeling like he was doing a parody.

"I'm sorry, Mr. Slattery. It just doesn't feel natural."

"You're right. Just give us one second over here."

Trevor wished he could hear what they were saying on the other side of the soundproof glass as Chuck turned to the bearded sound mixer for a brief exchange. All he could do was watch their hand gestures as the mixer nodded and Chuck smiled, pressing the intercom again.

"Okay, let's get one totally clean take. Just say the words."

"No Reaper voice?"

"Totally clean."

Trevor took a sip of bottled water and cleared his throat before speaking in his own voice.

"And the Reaper . . . will have his revenge."

The mixer gave a thumbs-up and Chuck smiled, pressing the intercom. "We got it!"

"I'm sorry," Trevor responded. "How did we get it?"

"Our sound guy can just make a composite Reaper filter from the old flicks. We'll slap it on in post, make a few adjustments, and be off to the races."

Trevor felt water spilling over his fingers as he realized he was clenching the Poland Spring bottle in his fist. "I mean, I can find the voice. If I could just do a few more takes."

"You'll find it in filming, we know that," Chuck said as everyone on the other side of the glass started to stand. "Thanks for coming in!"

Fuck. This was Trevor's first chance to actually show them what he could do, and he screwed it up. Now was the time to step up his game. He was tempted to skip his NA meeting and go home to do character work, but he knew that was a bad idea. He couldn't make this job his Higher Power, Danny had warned him about that.

Recovery came first, and the Reaper would have to wait.

## 18

Howard sat on the examination table, the paper sheet crinkling under his body as he shifted uneasily, thinking about that poor cashier. The boy was rude, yes, but he didn't deserve to be attacked like that. Of course, it wasn't Howard who had done it, who had said those awful words. He couldn't seem to shake the Reaper from his mind or stop himself from slipping in and out of the character. That was why he was here to see Dr. Cho, to help redraw the lines, bold and dark.

The wall in front of him was covered in cheesy motivational posters. Stock images of sunsets and bald eagles with words like OPTIMISM and LEADERSHIP along with an inspirational quote. When his attention landed on a photograph of a blue butterfly above the word CHANGE, he was surprised to find a Socrates quote below it. *"The secret of change is to focus all of your energy not on fighting the old, but on building the new."*

"Howard."

He hadn't even heard the door open as he turned his head to find Dr. Cho standing before him, smiling beneath her black bangs. "I'm glad you came in," she said, shaking his hand. "We missed you last week."

So he already missed his appointment. He couldn't even recall how long ago that last phone call had been.

"Yes, I'm sorry about that. I'm afraid I'm still having those troubling blackouts," Howard explained. He was hesitant to dive into the extent of his struggles. It all sounded so absurd. "I'm also experiencing some . . . aggressive thoughts."

"I know it can be scary, but mood swings are fairly common with your condition."

This was more than a mood swing. Howard would have to climb out of his well of shame and share more if he wanted to get help. "Well, I tried keeping a journal, like you suggested . . ."

"Okay," the doctor responded, jotting notes in her little pad. "And how's that been working?"

"It certainly helps to clear my mind, but the thoughts that are coming out . . . well, they're not my thoughts, not my voice. They're not even in my handwriting."

Dr. Cho stopped writing as her brow raised. "How exactly do you mean?"

"You see, when I told you that I felt outside of myself during that audition, I wasn't merely disconnected. I was watching the Reaper, the character, take the wheel. And it happened again today at the supermarket. I was saying things, doing things with no control over my own body."

The doctor lowered her pen, a grave expression overtaking her. "Howard. What you're describing goes a bit beyond depersonalization. The idea that a character is somehow in control of your body and mind is a serious delusion. Now, it's possible for Alzheimer's patients to experience psychotic symptoms, usually in later stages—"

"Psychotic?!" Howard was shocked by the word as he quickly back-pedaled. "No, no, you misunderstand." He had read those psychology books in his study from cover to cover and dog-eared his own copy of the DSM for character research. He knew how mental illness was diagnosed and every ounce of his being resisted the label of insanity. "I've merely fallen into a . . . creative rabbit hole, that's all. It's an actor's job to assume different identities, wouldn't you agree?"

"That's true, yes," the doctor conceded. "And it was Van Gogh's job to paint landscapes, which he eventually did through the window of Saint-Paul Asylum."

"A flattering comparison, Doctor, but all I really need is a way to reel myself back in, to calm my nerves."

She eyed him seriously in response. "Are you experiencing any hallucinations, seeing anything out of the ordinary?"

"Of course not," Howard replied, "Nothing like that." Surely nightmares didn't count as hallucinations.

"And these . . . aggressive thoughts you're having, the character's thoughts. Do you hear them inside your head or as an external voice, telling you to do something?"

Howard knew which one was worse, and gratefully the truth was the lesser of the two. "The thoughts are internal."

"Good," she scribbled with a nod, bringing Howard some relief. "So no auditory hallucinations, strange sounds without a clear source?"

The *CLANK* that had permeated his house was still fresh in Howard's ears, but he wasn't ready to believe that the sound was only in his head. The old house had old pipes, after all.

"No," he quietly answered, "not hearing a thing."

"Any history of mental illness in your family?" Dr. Cho asked, running through a clinical checklist now. Howard rarely thought about his mother and the erratic moods she would storm in and out of when he was a child. The nightly fights between his parents were a real chicken-or-egg mystery. Did her mood swings set off his drinking or did his drinking trigger her mood swings? No one had ever been diagnosed as they kept it all behind closed doors, but it was all too distant to seem relevant now as Howard shook his head.

"Not that I'm aware of."

"Okay," Dr. Cho gently nodded, taking out a different pad as she began to write. "I'm going to prescribe you a medication called Rispoquel. We'll send you home with some samples today to get you started."

"Rispoquel?" Howard repeated, shifting again on the crinkly paper sheet. "What's it for?"

"Well, it has an antianxiety component that should bring some immediate relief to your nervous system."

"Component. Meaning that's not its primary purpose?" Howard could read between the lines of her dodgy answer.

"It's going to take a few weeks to fully kick in, but Rispoquel is primarily prescribed to help settle disorganized thinking, dissociation, aggression . . ."

"Psychosis." Howard shook his head, compelled now to declare aloud, "I'm not crazy."

"I'm not saying you are, Howard. Antipsychotics are prescribed to treat a wide range of conditions these days," Dr. Cho assured him, "but given your rapid cognitive decline, I can't recommend that you live alone anymore."

"Oh, I'm not alone. I have Stanley," Howard half-heartedly replied.

"Stanley? Is that your partner?" Dr. Cho asked.

Howard caught himself before correcting the doctor. He had no qualms about his perceived sexual orientation and he certainly wasn't about to move into some dreadful assisted living facility. "Yes," he lied, "Stanley is my partner."

"Well, I'd like you to bring Stanley in for your next checkup so we can bring him up to speed. In the meantime, I highly recommend finding yourself a therapist, someone to talk to."

Howard bit his tongue at the suggestion of paying someone just to listen to him talk. That seemed even more desperate than taking antipsychotic pills when he wasn't psychotic.

"Thank you. I'll do just that." Howard had no intention of doing either as he pocketed the prescription along with the drug samples for decorum's sake before leaving the office.

The doctor clearly didn't understand what he was going through. How could she?

How could anyone?

# 19

"I've never felt more alone than I did in that moment." The young newcomer sharing was a twitchy mess in his early twenties, still coming down from his last high. "And I didn't know what to do, but I knew that I needed help. So that's why I'm here."

The room clapped with echoes of "Welcome" and "Keep coming back." Trevor understood now why Danny had told him to go to a meeting every day, to embrace the warmth of fellowship. Despite the voice-over fuck up, he was feeling sturdy in his recovery, and things with Sophie were solid as ever. He even surprised her with flowers at work, where he wasn't even bothered by the judgmental glares from her coworkers who hated Trevor's guts. He knew he was on the right path, working the steps with his sponsor and feeling supported on his journey.

As the meeting ended, Trevor emptied and cleaned the coffeepot. This small commitment helped him remember to get out of his own selfishness and be of service to others. Danny approached and wrapped those tree-trunk arms around him for a hug, a warm gesture that Trevor was finally starting to tolerate.

"How're you filling it today?" Danny asked his sponsee this question every day, the "it" being the "God-shaped hole" inside. He explained that getting clean doesn't make that empty feeling go away. It's still there, gaping wide in all of us. You just have to find a healthier way to fill it than with drugs. That's the path to true sobriety.

Trevor still shied away from the G-word, but he couldn't deny that he felt that black hole gaping somewhere inside his chest. Not quite in his heart, but somewhere just next door, more central to his entire being. That's where the emptiness lived and it was screaming out to be filled with something, every second of every day.

"Today, I'm filling it with service," Trevor said, rinsing out the sponge.

"Good man," Danny said, patting him on the back as the newcomer approached with an empty coffee cup trembling in his hand.

"Sorry, man," Trevor said, "We're fresh out."

"Just my fuckin' luck," the kid grumbled, tossing his cup in the trash and heading for the stairs. Trevor wanted to tell the brat to fuck off and buy his own coffee if the service wasn't up to his standards, but that wouldn't have been very welcoming.

"You recognize him, don't you?" Danny said, watching the new kid walk off.

"I don't think so," Trevor responded, searching his cinematic memory. "He an actor?"

"No, I mean do you see anything familiar?" Danny clarified.

Trevor watched as the kid cursed under his breath with his head hung low, heading up the steps. He saw a reflection of himself at that first meeting as he nodded in understanding to his sponsor. "Oh yeah. I recognize him."

"Well, go fuckin' talk to him already," Danny said. "He needs to know he's not alone. That's the real service work right there."

Trevor dropped the sponge and hustled up the steps into the daylight, catching the newcomer in the parking lot with a "Hey."

The kid spun on his feet, on high alert with a clenched fist ready to fight. Trevor recognized this hypervigilance, too. "Easy, man," he said reassuringly. "You're safe here. I'm Trevor."

"That's great, Trevor. I just . . . I don't think this place is for me." The kid started walking, and Trevor thought about just letting him go, but something told him to walk beside him instead.

"What's your name?" Trevor asked.

"Max."

"I've been there, Max. Looking at all these sad sacks talking about God in a church basement, wondering what the fuck I'm doing here. Truth is, I still don't really buy it."

"Really? Because you sure seem to drink their Kool-Aid," Max spat back.

"And how's *your* Kool-Aid working out for you?" Trevor asked with a hint of tough love. This stopped the newcomer cold, allowing Trevor a chance to take his best shot. "Look, I can't make you any promises. All I can tell you is that when I keep coming back, I feel better. And somehow, it just fuckin' works. One day at a time."

Trevor felt like he was listening to someone much kinder and wiser than himself speak the words. He wondered if this is what people meant when they said their Higher Power spoke through them, that they were just a vessel for unconditional love.

"I need help," Max said, tears welling in his eyes. "Will you help me?"

"Yeah, man," Trevor said, stepping closer. "I'm here."

Max dug into his jacket pocket and Trevor's own startle response kicked in, expecting a knife or a gun. But it was something much worse.

The kid opened his clenched fist to reveal a dime bag of golden powder, along with a small glass straw, a lighter, and a little strip of tinfoil. The H-fiend's starter kit.

"Please," Max begged, "Just take it. I'm not strong enough."

Trevor looked at the stuff like it was contagious, afraid of what might happen if he touched his kryptonite. But he knew that he was at least stronger than this kid was right now, so he closed his eyes and grabbed the whole stash, shoving it into his jacket pocket and zipping it closed to lock the poison out of sight.

"I'll take this," Trevor said, "if you take my number. And call me, any time, day or night."

After giving Max his phone number, Trevor watched the kid walk off, his steps a little lighter than before. Danny and the others emerged from the basement behind him.

"How is he?" Danny asked.

"He's gonna keep coming back," Trevor answered. He wanted to tell Danny exactly what happened, to pass that shit in his pocket to his sponsor like a hot potato, on to the next strongest man who might not let it burn him. But something wouldn't let him. Something wanted to keep that little baggie zipped tightly in his jacket pocket, close at hand.

"Good," Danny said. "Nick's for lunch?"

"Sure," Trevor responded, zipping his other pocket closed to match, just in case anybody noticed. "Split a stack of chocolate chip pancakes?"

Danny shook his head. "You're on your own there, Peter Pan."

Trevor laughed nervously, wishing he'd never touched the bag of pixie dust that was hiding in his pocket, weighing him down as it promised to make him fly.

## 20

A craving rumbled through Howard's guts as he turned onto his street. He was looking forward to a hot steak dinner alone with no more human interaction, but as he pulled into the driveway and saw a familiar blue truck waiting, he knew his day was long from over.

Joan sat waiting on one of the porch chairs, cigarette hanging from her lips as she waved. Howard forced a smile through the windshield with an uneasy wave back. His mind was quiet for now, but the hunger pangs were subtly stirring something else as he checked himself in the rearview mirror to confirm that it was still Howard behind those eyes. He took a deep breath, hoping he could hold himself together as he gathered his groceries and stepped out of the car.

"Joan," he said, in his own voice. A good start. "What a surprise this is."

"Hey pal." Joan lifted a boot sideways to crush her cigarette against the sole. Howard appreciated the conscientiousness, until she aimed to flick the butt over the railing.

"Not in the azaleas, please," Howard requested. There were no visible flowers on the dry shrubs that hadn't been watered in days, maybe weeks, but he'd eventually get back to regular maintenance and didn't want trash floating around when he did.

"Right. Sorry," Joan nodded, tucking the crushed butt back into her pack. "I tried calling, but your machine wasn't working."

"Is that right?" Howard asked, taking a seat in the other Adirondack chair as he placed the brown bags on the porch between them. "I'm afraid

I don't always remember to clear the tape," he explained, knowing that the broken machine was still in pieces on the foyer floor.

"You know I prefer face-to-face anyway," Joan said, pushing her big black glasses up on her face. "So I figured I'd just swing by, see how you're doing."

"Oh, I'm doing quite well," Howard lied. "Though I can't help but assume you've heard otherwise."

Before their run-in at Dead World, Howard hadn't seen Joan in years, and though their rapport had always been timelessly effortless, this sudden house call reeked of a concerned check-in.

"You know Jake's my agent, too," Joan explained, confirming Howard's suspicions. "He told me about the Reaper audition, how you went MIA after."

Hearing the monster's name out loud prodded Howard in an unexpected way. He'd been grappling with the voice in his head, but having an outsider remind him that this thing did indeed exist in some way in the outside world, that the Reaper wasn't entirely a figment of Howard's imagination, sent a shiver down his spine.

"I don't know exactly what you heard," Howard began, "but it was hardly an audition. I was there, at Chuck's request, to make sure the remake is on the right track," he explained, regurgitating the same lie he'd fed Trevor. "Protecting the legacy, you know."

Joan just nodded in response, though Howard could tell she either wasn't buying it or knew more than she was letting on. Either way, Howard was too exhausted to hold up the ruse as he let his shoulders fall. He leaned back in the chair, fingers grazing the peeling paint.

"All right, yes, I auditioned," he admitted. "And it was a mistake. I don't want the role anymore. I just want to get away from it all, leave the past in the past and move on with my life. You know, Socrates said that the secret of change is to focus all of your energy not on fighting the old, but on building the new."

"I did not know that," Joan replied. "Those Greeks really knew their shit, huh?"

"I just hope it's not too late for me," Howard lamented, staring out at the eucalyptus tree at the edge of the yard.

"Come on," Joan nudged him. "It's never too late for something new, even for old farts like us. Maybe pick up a hobby. A man should have a hobby."

Howard looked down into his grocery bag, the blank journals staring back up at him. His new hobby, filling his days, line by line, word by word. Then he remembered Dr. Cho's suggestion.

Find someone to talk to.

If anyone could understand Howard's true struggle with the monster, it would be Joan, the artist who crafted the Reaper's visage. Yes, maybe his old friend could provide some solace after all.

"Joan," Howard sheepishly began. "Do you remember saying that when I played the Reaper, that I flipped a switch? Gave it life?"

"Of course," Joan replied. "It's the damn truth. Nobody could've done what you did."

"But what if the switch is . . . broken, somehow?" Joan's blank stare gave Howard pause, but it was too late to turn back now. He'd have to push full steam ahead and hope against hope that he was making any sort of sense. "You see, in that audition, I went deeper into the role than I've ever gone. Perhaps too deep, gave it too much life."

"I get it," Joan nodded in a moment of understanding that gave Howard a glimmer of hope.

"You do?"

"Sure. You went a little over the top, botched the audition, and now you're beating yourself up over it."

No. She didn't get it.

"But it's not your fault," Joan assured him. "It's just the usual studio bullshit, totally out of your control."

"It's not that, Joan, it's . . ." Howard found himself at a loss for words, no longer capable of holding himself together as he leaned forward in the chair to bury his face in his hands.

"Shit, okay," Joan said, putting a hand on Howard's shoulder. "So it's more than that. Just talk to me, no more beating around the bullshit bush."

Part of him wanted to retreat from his friend's affection, but he was in desperate need of some kind of warmth and understanding, so he opened himself to it.

"My mind isn't right, Joan. The Reaper is haunting my every thought and I'm losing control. The doctor thinks I'm going mad," Howard confessed, "that I need medication, therapy."

He was sure that Joan would scoff at the notion, but when he looked into her haloed eyes, he watched them soften behind the glass.

"Look, I never told you this," Joan began, "but when I got back from 'Nam, from all the blood and the muck . . . I was out of my goddamn mind. Having PTSD flashbacks every day, seeing and hearing things that weren't there. It took some heavy-duty meds and serious therapy to get me back on track."

"Really?" Howard was surprised by this admission from a woman who had trained with the Marines to strengthen her nerves in live combat scenarios.

"Really. And I learned a thing or two about grief, about catharsis. You're wrestling with this thing, trying to push it all down, right?" Howard nodded in response, feeling the cauldron lid rattle inside. "But it's gonna keep bubbling up until you find a way to just let it go."

"I've tried, Joan, I have, but *how?*" Howard begged, unabashed in his desperation, knowing that the notebooks were nothing more than a half measure.

Joan thought for a moment. "Jake mentioned you've got HorrorCon next month, they're giving you a Lifetime Achievement Award?"

"No," Howard shook his head, "I couldn't possibly go. I need to move *away* from the Reaper, not toward it."

"The Reaper was your life, Browning. And I know more than anyone just how much you sacrificed to keep those movies going."

Emma.

She and Howard used to invite Joan and her rotating "roommate" over for dinners on those rare nights when production wrapped early, the four of them laughing and drinking wine in the parlor. Howard could almost hear that long-gone mirth through the window now, but he pushed the happy memory back. There was no time for reminiscing as he listened intently to Joan's guidance.

"You gave it everything and now they're taking it from you. That's a real loss, a death, and it hurts like hell, I'm sure." Howard had never felt so

understood as Joan spoke the words matter-of-factly. "But you can't stop
loss. The only thing you have control over is how you let things go. So go
to HorrorCon, accept that award. Recognize a whole goddamn lifetime of
achievement. *Then* walk away, on *your* terms. It's unfinished business is all,
for you *and* your fans. Like you said, you gotta go out with a bang, not a
whimper. A proper fuckin' send-off."

It was a brilliant idea, in theory. If he wanted to get his mind right and
rid himself of the Reaper once and for all, perhaps a theatrical grand gesture
was just the ticket to redraw the boundaries between fiction and reality.

"Not just a proper send-off," Howard said aloud now. "A proper
burial."

"Hell yes," Joan affirmed. "A proper fuckin' burial."

Howard was suddenly filled with hope and a warm gratitude for his
only friend in the world. "Thank you, Joan."

"Hey, us freaks gotta stick together, right?" Joan smiled. "If you want,
I can hang around for a while."

*SCREE . . . SCREE . . . SCREE . . .*

Howard almost didn't hear it at first, the soft metallic squeaking. But
it only grew louder until his gaze followed the sound toward the eucalyptus tree once again. His throat closed tight at what he saw.

*SCREE . . . SCREE . . . SCREE . . .*

The rusty chain was tied up in the overhanging branches, squeaking
as it swayed with the weight of Joan's dead body. The chain links wrapped
around her neck, squeezing her face into a deep shade of blue while her
glasses magnified bulging red eyes, blood vessels about to pop.

*SCREE . . . SCREE . . . SCREE . . .*

Howard closed his eyes to the horrible sight of his friend's corpse
swinging back and forth, cold and lifeless.

"Browning?" he heard Joan say. "You want me to hang?"

"No!" Howard jumped to his feet, opening his eyes to the eucalyptus
tree as the leaves swayed in the gentle breeze. No chain or body hanging
from its branches.

"Whoa. You all right, big guy?" Joan asked from the chair beside him,
alive and well.

"I'm sorry," Howard stuttered, "I just realized I've hardly eaten all day."

"Okay." Joan stood up next to him, persistent as ever. "Maybe we go down to Cafe Santorini, grab some gyros in honor of ol' Socrates—"

"No, no," Howard put on a smile as he ushered Joan down the porch steps to her truck. "I've got groceries to cook and you've been kind enough with your time already."

"All right then." Joan finally took the hint as she got behind the wheel and leaned out the window. "Come swing by the store sometime, will ya? Let me know you're still alive?" She handed him a business card for Poletto's Army Navy with the hand-drawn image of a zombie in a soldier's uniform. "Drew him myself. I call him Sargent Flesher."

"Very good, Joan. I'll see you soon, thanks for stopping by," Howard replied, desperate for her to escape as he walked back toward the house. He listened to the engine rumble as Joan's truck pulled out of the driveway and off down the road. Turning to take one last look at the bare eucalyptus tree, Howard watched the sun set over the quiet yard, leaving him alone with the coming night.

## 21

"Just steer clear of the fan sites," Trevor's agent warned him at the end of their call. "The horror community is a bunch of maniac trolls."

"Got it. Thanks, Greg." Trevor hung up the phone in his upstairs office, the one room in the house that didn't have any windows. He liked it that way and kept the space mostly bare, with a computer on the desk and an uncomfortable office chair to keep him focused.

Of course, he'd never actually "worked" in here before. He just wanted to have his own space in the house, a place to escape and be alone. But now that he was committed to the role of the Reaper, he decided that this would be his creative haven.

The serial killer DVDs sat in a stack next to his computer, but he wasn't ready to go there yet. He *was* ready to immediately ignore Greg's advice, though, and take a deep dive down the rabbit hole of the online horror fan community. Chuck seemed to think the fans just wanted their same old Reaper, but Trevor wanted to see for himself.

He was familiar with intense fandom, like the obsessive freaks who would show up to live studio audience tapings of *Family Genius* with homemade shirts, screaming in ecstasy for their favorite characters. This Beatlemania-like fervor was mostly focused on Keith Cosmos, who played Trevor's cool Uncle Mikey on the show. Trevor idolized his on-screen uncle, who gave him his first sip of beer at the age of twelve and taught him how to pick up chicks at fan signings. It was Chris he was thinking of when he saw that leather motorcycle jacket through the Melrose store window and decided he had to have it. To be like Uncle Mikey.

Keith Cosmos hanged himself two years after the show wrapped. When Trevor skipped the funeral to go on a bender up the Santa Barbara coast, the rest of the *Family Genius* cast officially excommunicated him from their little clique. They were already embarrassed by his antics at that point, but the selfishness of skipping their costar's memorial really cemented that Trevor was not a part of their family. He wasn't a part of his own family either, after successfully suing his parents for squandering his show profits on a megachurch investment. Trevor was better off without them anyway. Family was overrated.

He clicked his way through BloodHound.com—*Your Cutting-Edge Source for Horror News*—until he came across a recent article: *Reaper Remake Casts Sitcom Star.*

This was exactly the association Trevor was trying to shed, his identity forever entangled with the world of dad jokes and laugh tracks. The article itself was mostly tame, although it did suggest that replacing Howard Browning in the title role was a shocking travesty. Trevor didn't understand what his agent was so worried about, until he arrived at the bottom of the article, where the "Comments" section was waiting.

*RustyChain99: Reaper without Browning? Fuck that.*

*DeadHeadX: Trevor Mane couldn't act his way out of a rehab center.*

*HellVixen: Here's hoping he overdoses and dies before they start filming.*

Jesus. Trevor had received some negative attention before, but these disembodied online voices were way more vicious than he expected. Who the fuck were these assholes anyway? Probably a bunch of ugly nerds jerking off to scary movies in their parents' basements.

He didn't want to let it bother him, but it did, and now he wanted to call Greg and back out of the contract, walk away. Chuck said that the whole point of making an announcement trailer was to give time for the fans' excitement to build up, but they were clearly already excited. Excited to see Trevor crash and burn.

He closed out of the site and opened up a new browser, navigating his way to PornPics.net. He hadn't been down *this* rabbit hole since he got back from rehab. Trevor clicked on his go-to fetish for MILFs, but as he waited for the first pixelated photo to load, he was reminded of what Doctor Liz said about his mommy issues. Fuck. She was right. How pathetic was he? Those Internet trolls were right, too. He couldn't get their cruel words out of his head now, the hatred that had seeped through the computer screen and settled into his blood.

Trevor flicked off the computer, swiveling away in his chair as he found himself staring at his jacket, hanging from the door, the pockets zippered closed. The stuff the newcomer gave him was still in there, waiting.

Why hadn't he just tossed it in the trash, gotten rid of it immediately?

He knew why. It gave him comfort to have an out. Plan B, right there in his pocket. An escape hatch, a golden rip cord. In case of emergency, break glass and self-sabotage.

Trevor stood up, feeling shaky as he ran his hand through his hair. He needed some kind of fix, something to feed into the void.

He went into the bedroom, where Sophie was sleeping after a long day shift, and crawled under the covers, pressing up against her from behind until she stirred awake.

"You coming to bed, baby?" she asked.

"Mm-hm," Trevor nodded as he began to kiss her neck, wrapping his arm around her to cup her breast over her shirt.

"I've got an early shift," she groggily replied.

"But I want you so fucking bad," Trevor whispered, his nerves on fire now as Sophie rolled to face him with a tender kiss. He was looking for a quickie, but she always wanted sweet and present lovemaking. This was not Trevor's strong suit, but he surrendered control now as she tossed her shirt and climbed on top. Sliding into pure bliss, it wasn't just about the high of sex for Trevor. When he was inside Sophie, he wanted to rip out his raw beating heart and give it to her, a sacrificial offering to this perfect being. He felt so vulnerable now, he wanted to cry as he squeezed his eyes shut and let his hands roam up over her naked body.

That's when he felt it. His fingertips grazed the jagged raised skin on her chest, just above her left breast and below her neck bone. He opened his eyes and saw the zigzag scar clearly in the moonlight.

The scar from the car accident. The scar that was his fault.

Trevor could feel himself going limp in shame, until he forced himself to think about something else. He closed his eyes again and started fantasizing about Dr. Liz. He imagined bending her over her desk in the middle of a session and fucking her right there. He finished quickly, basking in the release as Sophie leaned down to kiss him on the forehead. She went into the bathroom to clean herself up, then crawled back into bed and pulled Trevor's arm around her.

"I love you," she yawned, slipping back into sleep.

"Love you, too," he replied, spinning in a whirlpool of self-loathing, wondering if that was even any fun for her. He got what he wanted, but he resented her for giving it to him, and he resented himself for resenting her for it. He knew that Sophie loved him, but was Trevor even capable of loving someone? Or only using them, scarring them?

As the afterglow faded from his nerves, he was restless again and wanted to go back to the office, to his jacket, to what waited in the pocket. But he stayed, reminding himself that he only needed to get through this night. If he stayed in bed and waited until morning, it would be a new day. One more "One day at time."

Trevor wrapped tightly around Sophie's body, soaking up her warmth, clutching her like a life raft in an endless dark ocean as he waited a sleepless night for sunrise.

## 22

"Are you experiencing any hallucinations, seeing anything out of the ordinary?"

Dr. Cho's question stuck in Howard's brain as he frantically gulped down the sample medication before getting into the hot shower. He closed his eyes to the rushing water, but the image of Joan's body hanging from the tree was still emblazoned behind his eyelids. That violent vision was more troubling than the dark thoughts or even his outburst at the grocery store. Hallucinating things that weren't there was a classical sign of insanity, straight out of a Shakespearean tragedy, like Hamlet haunted by his father's ghost.

As much as he resisted the damning diagnosis of psychosis, Howard wasn't taking any chances as he stayed in the hot shower for what must have been a full hour. He took long steady breaths in the steam, waiting for the antianxiety effects to kick in. His empty stomach must have aided the speed of the drugs coursing through his bloodstream as a soothing wave of relief washed over him. Getting out of the shower, he wrapped himself in a plush robe, feeling every thread in a big cushy hug.

Floating back downstairs, he moved to the record player in the parlor and put on Chopin's *Nocturne No. 2*. The delicate piano meanderings crackled to life as Howard smiled, feeling the tune in his stride as he swayed into the kitchen to cook himself a hearty dinner.

As he heated olive oil in a pan and rubbed salt into the steak, he was delighted by how quickly the medicine was taking effect. Like a balm rubbing over every shattered nerve ending. He forked the meat into the pan, listening to the slow sizzle over the fluttering high keys in the next room. Perhaps this medicine was the solution after all. The stress of preparing for the audition and then the audition itself, it was all just a compounded strain on his rattled nerves and fading mind. There was no shame after all in some prescribed chemical relief to get him back on track. Howard was calm now, at peace. Even a little hopeful.

*THUMP-SCRAAATCH.*

Howard froze in the kitchen, untrusting of his own ears as he slowly moved into the parlor doorway. Something had bumped the record player, its needle swaying off to the side now as the black disc spun in silent circles. He waited for something, someone to reveal themselves.

". . . hello?" he asked the empty room.

Stanley darted from behind the record player with a hiss, revealing himself as the clear offender. The cat was giving chase to some unseen prey, now scrambling behind the reading chair. Was Stanley seeing things as well? No. Howard saw it now, too. The little gray blur that Stanley was chasing.

A mouse.

When he and Emma first moved in, they were infested with the little buggers, leaving droppings in every kitchen cabinet. Howard laid spring-loaded traps all throughout the house and Emma always hated coming upon a tiny rodent with its neck snapped beneath the metal bar.

"Isn't there a better way?" she asked, but Howard assured her that it was a quick and painless death.

He hadn't seen signs of the critters in years, but as Stanley barreled after the mouse, Howard was compelled to save the helpless rodent from its feline predator.

"Stanley!" The mouse darted around the corner and through the open cellar door as Stanley ignored his master's call, stalking his prey down the steps into darkness.

Howard stopped cold at the sight of the wide-open door, a gaping maw.

When had he moved the table away and removed all those Post-it Notes?

Were it not for the calming effect of the medication, he might start to panic, but he quickly reasoned that he'd simply had another lapse in memory. He didn't remember taking them down the same way he didn't remember putting them there in the first place. Regardless, he was glad that they were gone and there was nothing inherently sinister about an open door now.

He looked down into the darkness as the hall light shined down the steps, illuminating a spot of concrete floor at the bottom. There, Stanley had caught his prey and was batting it back and forth with glee.

"Stanley, no!" Howard rushed down the steps, nearly stumbling over his own floating feet as he finally reached the ground and scooped the mouse into his hands.

Its sleek gray body was streaked in bloody gashes as it squealed in pain, tiny heart racing with rapid breath. One of its paws was nearly severed, dangling by a stringy red thread. Howard became entranced by the sight of the glistening crimson.

*Its blood is ripe for the harvest.*

The Reaper's hoarse voice was no longer within, but right beside Howard's ear now. As if the killer was standing right behind him. But he couldn't turn to look, too spellbound by the reddened rodent in his hand as he lifted it even closer to his face. He gazed into the creature's beady little eyes as its panicked screeching finally calmed into a whimper. The crippled prey felt safe in Howard's palm as Stanley pawed at his master's leg in frustration, wanting his plaything back. Howard was utterly intoxicated by the blood, giving off a strange shine in the near darkness, glowing with some holy light. It was the most beautiful thing he'd ever seen.

*Let's see if the juice is worth the squeeze.*

The devilish voice breathed hotly on his shoulder in the dark. Without a second thought, Howard gave in to the Reaper's demands, curling his fingers around the mouse's little body. The screeches rose once again as his fist clenched and those baby bones crunched and cracked, tiny organs popping like wet balloons beneath the strain of his grip. The squealing stopped as blood oozed between his fingers, trickling down to Stanley's eager face as the cat lapped up the crimson droplets.

Howard wanted to vomit, but something else was surging up from the depths of his bowels now. Clogging somewhere in his chest before pushing its way up his throat and out his mouth. A deep, guttural laugh, low at first and then rising in pitch into a feverish cackle.

The Reaper's cackle.

His ribs ached, but he couldn't stop laughing, trapped in hysteria as tears streaked across his face. Through watery eyes, he saw a shadow move. The shape of a person, darting from one corner of the cellar to another. He gasped as he suddenly regained his breath, snapping back into his body and dropping the dead rodent to the floor.

"Who's there?!" he asked of the darkness as Stanley snatched the broken mouse off the ground and scurried up the steps with his prize clenched tightly in his jaws.

Howard stepped closer to the corner, where the shadow figure now stood erect in motionless defiance. "I'm calling the police!" Howard threatened.

The shape did not move.

Howard took a cautious step back now, keeping his eyes on the intruder as his hand reached up for the light cord, yanking it to illuminate the Reaper, sickle raised high.

Howard gasped at the life-sized cardboard cutout, standing still with its frozen grin. He caught his breath now, shoulders relaxing as he realized that the inanimate object posed no threat. He swore he'd seen something move, but it was probably just a trick of the light.

*BEEP. BEEP. BEEP.*

Howard cocked his head at the piercing sound. His alarm clock? Was this all just another dream? He remained still for a moment, waiting to awaken.

*BEEP. BEEP. BEEP.*

But still he stood, very much awake in the cold basement as something frantically beeped upstairs and the smell of burning flesh reached his nose.

The smoke alarm.

Howard scrambled back up the steps and into the kitchen, where smoke plumed from the frying pan. He threw the charred steak and pan into the sink, turning on the cold water. Seeing the red residue left on the faucet handle, he looked at his hand. Coated in blood. He had killed that mouse, a living thing, with his bare hands.

Because the Reaper's external voice had told him to.

He started scrubbing his hands with soap, washing the blood away, desperate to cleanse himself of sin like Lady Macbeth and that damned spot. He reached for the phone next, hands still dripping wet as he called Dr. Cho to come clean about his violent madness.

But as he listened to the ringing on the other end, he remembered Van Gogh. Howard pictured himself locked away in a padded cell, the Reaper whispering in his ear as he rocked back and forth in a fetal ball for an eternity of starry nights.

"Doctor Cho's office, how may I assist you?"

Howard clicked the phone off. There had to be another way.

After a moment's thought, he dialed another number. "Jacob. It's Howard."

"Jesus, it's good to hear your voice, buddy. I've been worried—"

"HorrorCon, the Lifetime Achievement Award. I'll do it. But let it be known that this will be my last public appearance, my final words on the Reaper. You can tell Chuck that it will make Pinnacle's remake all the more official. Only this time, I write my own speech."

"Okay, Howie. If that's what you want. But we should at least discuss—"

"That will be all, Jacob, thank you." Howard hung up the phone.

He wasn't entirely convinced that Joan's suggestion would work, but he had no other plan of action. Could a cathartic gesture actually heal his fractured psyche, dispel the delusion of the monster's influence? The Reaper wasn't anything real, after all, so reckoning with the character on symbolic terms, meeting it on the plane of the collective unconscious where it *did* exist, seemed to make some sort of sense.

Even still, his next call was to the pharmacy to fill the prescription Dr. Cho had given him. He couldn't tell the doctor what had happened, but he could keep taking the medication in the hopes that the antipsychotic might kick in and clear his head for long enough to use those blank notebooks. Not as a dumping ground for the Reaper's thoughts, but as a drafting space for Howard's grand farewell speech.

HorrorCon was the altar upon which he would exorcise the Reaper once and for all, with thousands of fans there to bear witness.

A sacred audience to his final offering.

*Night of the Reaper Part IV: The Final Reaping*
(1983)
Script Pages Courtesy of Pinnacle Studios

INT. ABANDONED BARN - NIGHT

Gina trembles with fear as she backs against a hay bale in the corner of the barn. The Reaper stalks toward her, dragging his chain across the dirt.

              THE REAPER
    Nowhere left to run, little piggy.

              GINA
    You're right.

Gina drops the scared act, reaching behind the hay bale to retrieve the double-barrel shotgun she planted there.

              GINA
    I'm done running.

The Reaper's eyes go wide as—

BANG! Gina blows his left arm clean off. The Reaper looks down at the bloody limb, twitching in the dirt.

              THE REAPER
    I'll never play piano again! You'll
    pay for that.

He rears back to swing the rusty chain in his right hand as—

BANG! The second blast tears his right arm off. The Reaper frowns at the blood spurting from his shoulder.

              THE REAPER
    This bites. But I bite harder!

The Reaper gnashes his teeth as he stalks toward Gina. She aims for his head this time, pulling the trigger as——CLICK.

> THE REAPER
> What's the matter? Shooting blanks?

Gina pops the empty shells out, trying desperately to reload the weapon as the armless monster charges toward her and——

WHOOSH! He steps on the false floor, hidden beneath scattered hay, falling into Gina's trap below with a SHUNK!

The Reaper SCREAMS as Gina approaches the pit. The monster lays IMPALED on the sharp tines of a spike-tooth harrow.

> THE REAPER
> Hoisted by my own petard!

Gina kicks the severed arms into the grave with him.

> GINA
> I figured out your secret. The key to your immortality.

She dangles the rusty chain, taunting him.

> GINA
> Without your rusty chain, you're nothing. You're shit.

Fear flashes behind the monster's eyes before his face twists with a venomous rage.

> THE REAPER
> You can't bury me!

                    GINA
          No.

Gina lifts a can of gasoline.

                    GINA
          But I can burn your ass to the
          ground.

                  THE REAPER
          Go ahead. Light me up. But I will
          rise again. I am etern——

Gasoline splashes in the Reaper's mouth, choking
him as he coughs and sputters.

                    GINA
          Ya know, for a mute . . . you talk
          too much.

Gina soaks the monster in the flammable liquid,
tossing the empty can and pulling a pack of matches
from her pocket. She lights one as the tiny flame
flickers in her eyes.

                    GINA
          Go to Hell, Reaper.

The Reaper spits blood and gasoline.

                  THE REAPER
          I'll save you a seat, bitch.

Gina tosses the lit match into the pit and the
Reaper BURSTS INTO FLAMES. He SCREAMS as his skin
burns and his flesh melts into the earth.

What's left of his face slides off to reveal the
skull beneath, jawbone flapping wildly in one final
CACKLE as the monster quietly smolders into dust.

# PART IV:
# REFLECTION

## 23

On the morning of HorrorCon, Howard was prepared. He'd taken the medication like clockwork every day for the last two weeks and now the intrusive thoughts were barely humming in the background, rather than clawing their way to the surface. The hallucinations had stopped, both auditory and visual, and he was back to his normal self. Perhaps focusing his energies on the farewell speech had also helped.

While drafting his words in the study, pacing beside the bookshelves as he spoke aloud, he had come across a book he didn't recognize entitled *The Magic of Intention*. It must have been a remnant of Emma's New Age phase, mixed in with Howard's old texts and left behind. He could smell her lavender scent between the pages as he flipped through the book, a most apropos reading for the cathartic speech he was creating.

"When you tap into the energy field of intention," the author explained, "you realize the natural power of birth and death are within the realm of your personal magic."

Howard now firmly believed that since he had given birth to the Reaper with his creative energy, he also possessed the power to give it death, if he focused his intentions strongly enough. With the help of that book, he'd honed the words of his speech like a magical spell, confident that he had hit the right combination of notes to banish the beast.

Embarking on the long drive to San Diego, he practiced his words out loud as he navigated traffic. He was cutting it close now, having spent the last half hour bumper-to-bumper on I-5, repeating one line over and over again. An intentional mantra.

"I lay this monster to rest. I lay this monster to rest. I lay this monster to rest."

He was still repeating the phrase as his Cadillac rolled up to the edge of the Gaslamp District, where a sea of horror fans had overrun the streets. He'd forgotten just how massive this convention was, the mothership of horror fandom for the entire nation and beyond. Fans shelled out hundreds of dollars on tickets that sold out in minutes and then spent all year preparing their costumes, some of them so shockingly professional and convincing, even Joan would be impressed.

As Howard drove through the crowds, he felt as though he were entering a post-apocalyptic wasteland filled with hordes of the undead. But he brightened at the sight of them all. Perhaps Joan was right that their fandom wasn't sheer insanity, but actually love. Pure, unadulterated love and community, the likes of which many of these people simply didn't experience in their day-to-day lives. They were understood here, welcomed here, and the ones who came for the Reaper deserved a heartfelt farewell.

After retrieving his badge at the private entrance, Howard was soon on foot, wending his way through the back tunnels of the convention hall. He was late now, struggling to navigate an endless cavern of cold cement walls as claustrophobia seized his breath. He shuddered to think of what might happen if he missed his window for closure, rendering him stuck with the beast forever. Rounding a corner, he found the entrance to Hall Q, where Jake was waiting to usher him past security.

"There you are," Jake said. "I was worried you wouldn't show."

"I wouldn't miss it for the world," Howard replied, catching his breath on stage behind the big red curtain. "This was my idea after all."

"Right. About that. Are you sure you want this to be your final farewell, Howie? It's not too late to back out of that part. You can just accept the award, say thanks, and we're back on the circuit," Jake suggested, his voice thick with desperation.

Howard's public appearances hardly provided a steady income flow, so the young agent must have really been struggling if he was trying this hard to keep the old cash cow on his roster.

"I'm sorry, Jacob," he said, placing a sympathetic hand on the shoulder pad of Jake's ill-fitting suit. "It's over."

*"You can't kill me."*

Howard recoiled at the Reaper's voice. "Dear God, no . . ."

*"I am immortal!"*

"What's wrong?" Jake asked. "If you don't want them to play the supercut, I'll tell them to hit stop right now."

"Supercut?" Howard asked, confused as another line resounded, this time more clearly through speakers on the other side of the curtain.

*"It's time to fear the Reaper!"*

"Yeah," Jake explained, "they edited a bunch of clips from every film into a little video intro for you. Wanna go watch?"

Howard was awash with relief to discover that the voice was not a mental manifestation. Still, he wasn't keen on exposing himself to the films right now for fear that it might trigger something when he was so close to doing what he came here to do.

"No. No, I'll just wait until it's done."

He tried to ignore the symphony of slashing and screaming as he paced back and forth, thinking of all the lives the Reaper had claimed. Purely fictional, yes, but the weight of all that death suddenly fell on Howard's shoulders as the announcer's voice kicked in.

"Ladies and gentlemen. Here to accept a Lifetime Achievement Award for his contribution to the genre . . . the Reaper himself in his *final* public appearance . . . the one . . . the only . . . Howard Browning!"

Howard didn't even wait for the applause as he stepped through the curtain, eager to deliver his grand goodbye. The lights blinded him for a silent moment before the bulbs swiveled back to illuminate his audience. But the small spattering of costumed attendees in a roomful of empty seats hardly qualified as an audience. A few half-hearted claps echoed across the space as Howard turned back toward Jake, who shrugged helplessly at the low turnout.

Howard had hoped to go out with a bang, but the gathering before him represented a whimper of the grandest scale. Where were all those fans he had given so much of his time to over the years? Why couldn't they be bothered to show up for him now, to support him, to show him their love in this most pivotal moment? They'd been so outraged at the remake announcement, but now it was Howard who felt abandoned as his anger swelled.

He swallowed that rage deep down, fearing what it might bring as he approached the podium, where the announcer handed him the award. A shiny golden skull, true to life size and heavy as a bowling ball, with his name engraved on the base below: *Howard Browning.*

Holding the skull in his hands now, Howard thought again of Hamlet's madness. *"Whether 'tis nobler in the mind to suffer the slings and arrows of outrageous fortune . . . Or to take arms against a sea of troubles, and by opposing, end them."* It was time now to take arms, to oppose this specter in his mind and end his troubles, once and for all. Howard placed the skull on the podium as he cleared his throat into the microphone, sending a feedback screech across the nearly empty room.

"Thank you. My dear . . . dear fans. It truly is an honor. Your support is what has kept me going through all these years." He looked out again at the meager crowd, the empty plastic chairs mocking him as he refocused himself.

He was not here for the fans. He was here for release.

"I can't tell you exactly what this award means to me. But I can tell you that when you give your whole life to something, as I have to this role, you make a certain sacrifice. As you do in any relationship."

A muffled snickering emanated from someone in the audience. Howard scanned the dozen or so masked attendees, but couldn't tell which one it was. He wanted to scold them for their disrespect, but decided to ignore it and press onward.

"When you truly dedicate yourself to a character for the length of eight films, you give up a little bit of yourself to make room for this . . . other person. I have shared my mind, my heart, my *soul* with the Reaper for twenty-five years now. But my term of service has ended. I promise you, my friends, that I have given it everything I possibly could. But the honest truth is, I have nothing left to give. I am but an empty vessel. Hollow. Drained."

"HA!"

The sharp laugh caught him off guard. A man in a hockey goalie mask stood at the back of the room now, pointing his finger at Howard and laughing out loud.

"Hahahaha!"

Howard looked around at the other fans, none of them even turning their heads to look at the heckler, all focused on Howard, whose face was twisting in confusion. But the sinking feeling in his gut told him that this wasn't happening at all. He was imagining things again, hallucinating. The drugs clearly weren't working anymore, but then, some part of him had expected that. That's why he was here, wasn't it? He had to keep going.

"And you, my dear fans. It is truly you who wield the power of immortality. It is you who can galvanize a corpse, bring the dead back to life. But there comes a time when every creature must meet his maker."

Another masked attendee with a blank white face and a shock of brown hair rose now, pointing and laughing alongside the hockey goalie. The next laugh came from a burned face beneath a brown brimmed hat. Then a hook-handed man in a long coat. A sad ghost and a ginger doll. A bald head of nails and a stitched face of human skin. An ax-wielding Santa and a goggled miner. The whole audience of ten masked killers all pointing and laughing at Howard as they stalked their way down the aisle now, swinging knives and machetes, meat mallets and pickaxes.

Howard tried to ignore it as he continued onward.

"Perhaps Frankenstein's monster put it best before he and his bride met their own poetic demise. 'We belong dead.'"

"Hahahahaha!"

The mob grew more manic now as it neared the stage and Howard spoke louder to overpower their mocking mirth. "And so I lay this monster to rest! The Reaper dies here, today! And should he crawl out once again from his endless grave . . ."

The monsters crawled up to the podium, circling Howard as their collective cackle took on one cohesive tone. The Reaper's cackle emanated from their mouths as they pointed their deadly tools in Howard's face.

*"HAHAHAHAHAHAHAHAHA!"*

". . . it shall not be through my hand that he finds resurrection! Because Howard Browning . . ."

The slashers dropped their weapons to paw at him now, tugging at his limbs, fingers digging into his skin.

"*HAHAHAHAHAHAHAHAHAHAHAHAHAHAHA!*"

". . . is the Reaper . . ."

They were trying to tear him apart, rip his flesh to shreds. Drag him straight to Hell.

"*HAHAHAHAHAHAHAHAHAHAHAHAHAHAHAHAHAHAH AHAHAHAHAHAHAHA!*"

He squeezed his eyes tight as he screamed, "NEVERMORE!"

Howard's whole upper body collapsed on the podium as he panted, out of breath. He looked up, only to find the small crowd still in their seats, their wide eyes visible through the slits in their masks as they looked around in dismay at what must have seemed like a very strange performance.

But it was over now. Howard uttered a weak "Thank you," garnering some awkward claps from the room as he lifted the golden skull, cradling it in his arms like a newborn as he walked away from the podium.

Jake was on the other side of the curtain, snapping his phone shut now to pretend he'd been paying attention. "That was beautiful, Howie, really. Best speech I've ever heard. I'm just sorry there wasn't a bigger turnout."

"It doesn't matter," Howard replied. And it really didn't. Yes, his ego was wounded, but his unconscious was calm. Even in the face of that monstrous hallucination, he had done what he came here to do. Imbued with the power of intention, the words seemed to have worked their magic as he now felt delicious tranquility coursing through his veins.

"Ya know," Jake began, ever relentless, "since there are only so many fans out there, we could still set up a table for a quick final signing and photo-op. Special limited edition pricing. What do you say, Howie?"

Howard looked at the golden skull in his hands, feeling its heft as he stared into the dark eyeholes. Those two empty pits surrounded by all that glittering gold. He ran a finger along the nameplate.

"My name is Howard," he responded, soft but firm as he handed Jake the skull. "And I say it's over."

With that, Howard walked away. Only this time, he didn't want to take the cavernous back route to his car. He walked straight through the main hallway of the convention center, the humming artery off of which every conference room lay.

Weaving his way through the throngs of fans, he felt like a ghost. The weight of the world had been lifted from his shoulders and he was merely passing through this space, no longer fated to haunt it for eternity. The masked demons around him only added to the feeling that he was passing out of Hell, or perhaps through Dante's Purgatory, toward some brighter existence in Paradise.

He soon found his way toward the front of the building, where the sun blasted through floor-to-ceiling glass windows.

A radiant white light at the end of the tunnel.

His freedom lay on the other side of those doors, but he no longer dreamed of the possibilities that came with it. He didn't think about new hobbies like building a chair or even returning to his evening routine of books and records. After all this chaos, the only thing Howard wanted to do was rest. A deep slumber like he'd never experienced before. This is what he was dreaming of as he drifted toward the glowing doors, twenty feet away now, when a muffled sound stopped him in his tracks.

"REAP-ER! REAP-ER! REAP-ER!"

The chanting came like a cult of religious fervor as Howard stood rooted in terror, fearing the noise in his head had returned. But then he saw two fans open double doors beside him and enter Hall H, the largest of the lot, where the sound leaked out, loud and clear.

"REAP-ER! REAP-ER! REAP-ER!"

No, this wasn't a hallucination. This was really happening.

He was relieved to know he wasn't hearing things. But then what was going on in that room? Why were they chanting for him?

A surprise. Perhaps Jake had planned a surprise. It was a clever ruse, pretending that nobody had come to see him for the award when they were all gathered in another, much larger room, waiting to shower him with praise. Yes, that must be it.

Howard looked to the sunlight outside, inviting him into a world of endless brightness. Then he turned back to the doors of Hall H.

"REAP-ER! REAP-ER! REAP-ER!"

He was being summoned, but he need not heed the call. He could still walk away, leave it all behind. Howard walked onward, getting close enough to the glass entrance to feel the sun's rays on his skin now, warming him to the bone.

But he could still hear them, even at a distance, faint but forceful.

"REAP-ER! REAP-ER! REAP-ER!"

They wanted him, needed him. As he watched the sun hang above the building tops, he had a strange feeling that this might be the last time he ever saw it.

Howard spun on his feet, away from the light as he walked back toward the double doors to Hall H. Gripping the handle, cold against his skin, he thought no more of the warmth of the sun as he pulled the door open, stepping across the threshold to whatever lay waiting on the other side.

As he stepped into the enormous room, Howard found himself at the back of a packed house. Thousands of people were crammed in with standing room only behind endless rows of filled seats. A convention worker beside the door handed him a pair of black sunglasses, only adding to his confusion as he squinted over the sea of heads toward the stage, where a giant screen was flanked by posters, too far to read.

Howard gently tapped the shoulder of a young woman who was wearing no costume, but plenty of makeup, as if waiting in line for a dance club.

"Excuse me," he said as she turned to him with no attempt to hide her instant disgust. "What's going on here?"

"It's the teaser for the new Trevor Mane movie," she said, turning her attention back toward the stage as Howard's heart sank. A fan on the other side of him interjected, plastic chain wrapped around his neck as he rolled his eyes at her answer.

"It's the new *Night of the Reaper* movie," he corrected with fanboy authority.

Howard waited for chain-neck to recognize who he was talking to, but the moment never came. Instead, the lights went dim and the crowd roared as everyone lifted their sunglasses and put them on their faces, as if readying to gaze into a solar eclipse. Howard couldn't fathom what was going on here as the screen lit up.

The image was blurry and out of focus. He could barely make out some kind of building at a distance, but it appeared in double vision. Howard placed the cheap plastic glasses on his face and everything came into startling clarity in three dimensions.

A dirt road led to a lone barn in the distance, dry cornfields on either side as the harvest moon glowed in the sky. Howard's heart stopped at the familiar imagery as the generic movie trailer voice-over boomed.

"Lester Jensen was a good man."

A figure ran toward the screen, toward Howard in crystal-clear 3D. The figure was Mandy, her shirt conveniently torn to reveal the black lingerie cupping her breasts.

"Lester Jensen never hurt anybody."

Howard felt like he was going to vomit, but didn't know if this urge came from the dizzying effect of the glasses or the awful content of the trailer itself.

"Lester Jensen is gone now," the voice-over continued as Mandy kept running, closer and closer to the camera. Close enough now to see the desperation in her eyes and the tears streaking across her cheeks. Then came a different voice, a monstrous growl.

*"And the Reaper . . . will have his revenge . . ."*

Howard's gut sank at the unmistakable sound of Trevor's Reaper. Familiar on the surface, but different at its core. Mandy was about to collide with the camera, the audience collectively braced for impact as *THWACK!*

The glossy CGI chain snapped around her neck from behind and Mandy's eyes shot wide before *CLANK!*

The chain was pulled and Mandy flew backward like a rag doll through the air, across an impossible distance, into the barn as the doors slammed shut and the image cut to black.

The crowd let out a collective gasp as the words crashed into the screen.

*Night of the Reaper 3D*

*The Reaper . . . REBORN*

The speakers boomed with the Reaper's cackle, only this time Howard was certain the sound had been stolen from his own performance. The lights flicked on over the screaming crowd and he stood frozen in the aftermath. The fans erupted with cheers, tossing their 3D glasses into the air like graduation caps as Howard wiped away the tears he didn't know had fallen. He looked to chain-neck and makeup girl, both shrieking with glee. They loved it, both Reaper-fan and Trevor-fan alike. They actually ate it up, just like Jake had suggested. They didn't care about Howard, standing in their midst, utterly unknown.

It had been a mistake coming into this room. He should have kept walking straight out that front door. He wanted to leave now, to get away from this demoralizing experience and forget all about it. As he turned, stepping toward the door, the announcer kicked in.

"Ladies and gentlemen, please welcome . . . the Reaper himself . . ."

Howard stopped with his hand clenching the door handle.

"Trevor Mane!"

## 24

Trevor heard his name through the curtain, followed by the roaring crowd, and he wanted to turn and run. But he remembered what Danny had told him.

"You're never alone. Your Higher Power's gonna be with you on that stage, making sure you don't fuck up."

Trevor was finally starting to believe that something bigger than himself might actually give a shit about him, might want to see him succeed. It gave him some comfort as he took a deep breath and stepped through the curtain, coming face-to-face with the biggest crowd he'd ever seen in his life.

*Family Genius* tapings brought in two or three hundred people max, but he was now staring down thousands of screaming faces. With the lights blinding him, they looked like one amorphous blob of limbs with glinting eyes and chomping teeth. A ravenous group, ready to devour him at any moment. He smiled and waved awkwardly for what felt like several minutes until the interviewer finally began.

"So, Trevor." The crowd died down to listen intently. "What was your first reaction when you were offered the role?"

"I was just totally honored," Trevor lied. He feared the collective crowd could read his mind, that they knew he really thought these movies were trash. But he couldn't tell them the truth now, so he just piled on the bullshit. "The original films are such absolute classics and they were a huge part of my childhood."

Not only had he never seen a Reaper film before his agent pitched him the part, but he still hadn't finished watching the entire franchise. Once he got to the ridiculous entry where a voodoo priestess exorcised the monster's soul from Chicago straight to Hell, he had to call it quits.

"And what can fans expect from this remake? How is it going to be different from the original?" the interviewer continued as the sweat pooled under Trevor's leather jacket. Why were these lights so fucking bright?

"Well, I think we can all agree that the films got a little more kitschy toward the end of the franchise, and the Reaper became more silly than scary."

The crowd was silent in response and Trevor could hear his own gulp echo through the microphone.

"Which is great. I mean, we all love that stuff. But my approach is to go back to the core, to the horror, and make the Reaper scary again."

"What do you guys think?" the interviewer asked the crowd. "Are you ready for a scarier Reaper?"

Trevor waited with bated breath for what could have only been a second before the crowd exploded with cheers, champing at the bit. He wiped some sweat from his brow and relaxed his shoulders at their approval.

"I'm gonna be honest," he said, testing new waters, "When I first found the online fan base for these films, I was terrified." He looked out into the dark sea of fans. "I was sure you guys were gonna burn me at the stake, and some of you were promising to do exactly that in the comments section."

This brought some laughs from the crowd, which didn't exactly make Trevor feel any better.

"If there's one thing I've learned preparing for this role for the past few weeks," Trevor continued, "it's that there's a legacy to respect with the Reaper. And I don't wanna be the guy who fucks it up." He turned to the interviewer. "Sorry, can I say fuck?"

The whole room laughed at this, which made Trevor feel at ease, growing more comfortable and conversational.

"Hey," the interviewer joked, "I'm not gonna say no to the Reaper!"

"I just want to do right by you guys," Trevor said to the fans, "and with Chuck Slattery on board producing, you know we're not trying to fuck with the original. Fuck, I did it again."

More laughter, genuine laughter, not like that canned *Family Genius* shit. Trevor was feeling good now, actually bonding with the fans by being himself. Maybe they wouldn't tear him apart after all. Maybe he could actually do this.

"I'd love to hear from you guys now," Trevor said. "Maybe answer some—"

The crowd cut Trevor off in an eruption of fresh cheers. Confused, he turned and saw that Chuck had just emerged from behind the curtain, waving to the adoring crowd.

"What a treat!" the interviewer announced. "Legendary producer Chuck Slattery, everyone!"

This was not part of the plan, and Trevor was annoyed at the interruption. Hearing his name out loud must have triggered Chuck's oversized ego to rush out and soak up some attention. The producer roughly pulled the microphone from Trevor's hand now.

"I hate to interrupt, but some whispers in the crowd have just made their way up to the stage," Chuck explained. "As we talk about the original, it seems we have a special surprise today." The producer cued a tech assistant and a light swiveled, spotlighting someone in the back of the crowd that Trevor couldn't quite make out.

"Everyone say hello to the *original* Reaper . . ." Chuck exclaimed.

The blood drained from Trevor's face as he realized who it was. Even at a distance, he could see the old man's eyes going wide like he'd just shit his adult diaper.

"Howard Browning!"

## 25

Howard stood frozen for a moment before spinning on his heels for the exit. But a thick layer of fans had already flanked up behind him and were physically pushing him back toward the stage. He was the lamb being led to the slaughter, dragged past hundreds of hungry faces until he finally stumbled his way up the side stairs and onto the stage.

Trevor forced a feeble smile, jutting out his hand for a shake. "Mr. Browning. So great to see you again."

Howard shook the hand as he swallowed deeply and the crowd cheered. He was confident that his verbal spell had worked, but that confidence was waning now as his nerves began to prickle. He wanted to get off this stage as fast as possible before something bad happened.

"A handshake?" Chuck scoffed, inserting himself between the two actors. "Are you kidding me? Let's get a proper photo op here. Give us Reaper versus Reaper!"

Howard winced at the suggestion. Chuck had no idea what he was asking for, what he was summoning as the ravenous crowd cheered, eager to meet their monster.

*My children are waiting.*

The Reaper's dark whisper returned, louder than all other sounds. Howard could no longer discern if it was internal or external as it vibrated through his entire being. All he knew was that no one else could hear it as he shook his head, denying the command.

He took a step back, but not far enough as Trevor raised his hands to Howard's throat, barely making contact for a camera-friendly faux choke.

"How's that?" Trevor smiled at the crowd as they all went wild.

Howard felt their electric energy coursing through him now, galvanizing the creature.

*"My turn!"* The Reaper's voice burst forth from Howard's lips. His hands flew at Trevor's neck, as if pulled by a puppeteer's strings.

"That's more like it!" Chuck exclaimed over the roaring audience, delighting in the performance.

But Howard wasn't performing as his hands squeezed tightly against his will. Trevor's eyes swelled with confusion as Howard fought to loosen his own grip, but he couldn't regain control as his veins surged with untold energy.

His knuckles went white, choking the life out of Trevor before the insatiable crowd. Howard wanted to fight it, but there was no use. He was about to murder this young man on stage in front of thousands of people, but they were asking for it.

The villagers of Ashland demanded their sacrifice.

## 26

Trevor's hands were still wrapped around the saggy flesh of Howard's neck, but he wasn't squeezing. He was too shocked by the pressure he felt from the old man's grip.

Was this some sort of intense method acting? Trevor didn't want to seem weak, but he was having trouble breathing now. Maybe Howard was just trying to scare him, teach him another lesson, but this was way more extreme than the waiting room trash talk.

He knew this was serious when he looked into Howard's eyes and saw something he recognized. There was a struggle going on in there, an internal war being waged as he watched light and shadow flickering back and forth.

In one moment, Trevor saw the weak silver-haired man, terrified, seemingly on the verge of tears. In the next, it was blind rage, a monstrous glint flashing as he felt those leathery hands go tighter around his neck.

Trevor had seen enough frantic junkies in his day to know that this was a man crashing toward his bottom, grasping at the edge and struggling to hold on. Only instead of holding on, he was squeezing Trevor's neck, causing black spots to crowd into his vision.

This wasn't method acting. This was dangerous desperation.

Trevor's knees began to tremble as he saw a grin stretch across Howard's face and he realized that the internal war may have just ended, with the darkness winning out. The crowd kept cheering, camera's flashing, oblivious to what was happening as Trevor finally came to his senses and made a choice.

He wasn't going to die here.

He summoned all his strength as he grit his teeth and squeezed back. Howard's loose skin was slippery and Trevor had no choice but to dig his nails in. He was losing his sight entirely now, gasping for air. Just before the blackness became total, Trevor saw the grin disappear from Howard's face as the death grip released from his own neck.

Trevor regained his breath as he seized the opportunity to keep squeezing, filled with fresh rage at the madman who had almost killed him. But Howard wasn't even struggling against him now, legs buckling as he fell to his knees at Trevor's feet. Howard's arms dropped limply to his sides, just letting himself be choked as he closed his eyes. Trevor had the strange thought that maybe the old man wanted to die, here and now.

But that was too crazy. This was all too crazy. He finally released his grip and Howard collapsed to the stage floor, coughing on hands and knees.

"Ladies and gentlemen!" Chuck announced with glee. "Trevor Mane is *your Reaper*!"

The crowd responded with a voracious uproar, wanting more. They might have been happier if someone actually had died on that stage. Even though Howard had almost choked him out, Trevor felt sorry for the sad bastard as he watched him shuffle off the stage on all fours like a wounded animal, disappearing behind the curtain.

## 27

Howard was still coughing when he burst into the private backstage bathroom, splashing cold water in his face at the sink. His whole nervous
system had been hijacked again and every nerve felt like it was being
singed with a cauterizer. The cold water eased the heat under his skin
until his face went numb, then he turned off the faucet and looked at his
dripping wet hands.

The hands that had nearly choked the life out of Trevor Mane on that
stage.

It had taken every ounce of his being to fight his way back into consciousness, to stop what was happening and regain control. When he
finally did, he was glad that Trevor fought back. Howard had come to
HorrorCon for relief, and in that moment, as his breathing slowed under
Trevor's grip, death seemed like it might just be the sweet release he was
seeking. He remembered Hamlet once more, "To be or not to be." If this
madness continued, if he posed a real threat to the people around him,
then Howard no longer wished to be.

*CLANK.*

Howard spun on his feet to face the solitary stall, checking underneath to find no feet there. He was alone.

*CLANK.*

He had to be imagining it, but it sounded so real, so close.

*CLANK.*

He could hear it echoing off the tile walls around him, sure that the
rusty chain was in this room with him.

"I don't hear you," Howard said, addressing it out loud for the first time as he squeezed his eyes shut. Surrender had failed, so he decided he would stand up to it now, shut it down by force. "I don't hear a thing."

*"Open your eyes, Howard."*

The Reaper's voice was coming from directly in front of him as Howard shook his head in refusal.

*"Open your eyes . . . or I'll slice off the lids."*

Howard relented, opening his eyes to the mirror to find the Reaper staring back. A flap of cheek hung loosely from his torn face, exposing jawbone and shattered teeth.

*"That's a good boy."* The beast's grin was stained red.

"This isn't happening," Howard uttered to the monster that stood where his own reflection should be. He looked down at his own pressed suit, then up at the reflection of dirt-caked overalls. "I can't . . . I can't be seeing you. You're not real."

*"You made me real. Now stop ignoring me. It hurts my feelings."*

The Reaper frowned like a demonic clown as Howard reached into his pocket for the bottle of antipsychotics, fingers fumbling over the safety cap.

*"You and your silly pills. The good news is . . . you're not crazy. The bad news is . . . I am!"*

The Reaper laughed as Howard finally gave up, shoving the bottle back into his pocket. Some part of him knew that the monster was right, that the pills would solve nothing now. He'd been taking them steadily for weeks and the vision he was now reckoning with was far worse than anything that had come before.

"What do you want from me?" Howard asked, afraid to find out the answer.

*"I want more. Play the role, give me life. I've been waiting so very long."*

Howard shook his head. "It's not my role, not anymore. Go bother Trevor Mane."

He couldn't believe he was actually trying to reason with this monstrous reflection, but he saw no other recourse at this point.

*"I would break his feeble mind in two. You're my vessel. And I'm your ball and chain."*

The Reaper playfully swung his rusty chain.

"Please," Howard began, exhausted with desperation, bargaining with the beast in the mirror like it was the most natural thing in the world. "I have given you everything. Just . . . give me peace."

As he held the Reaper's unwavering gaze, Howard noticed a piece of gravel lodged in the monster's eyeball, oozing with pus. Could his own mind have conjured up such a sickening detail?

*"One last harvest,"* The Reaper replied. *"And then I'll let you rest in peace."*

As the specter gave a sinister grin, Howard knew that this was the best deal he was going to get. But these demands still seemed impossible. The trailer was a success, Trevor was the Reaper now.

"I've already tried to get the role back, you know that. There's nothing I can—"

*CLANK.*

The Reaper swung his chain against the floor, shattering tile with a sharp sound that pierced Howard's brain and sent him leaning against the sink for balance.

*CLANK.*

The next swipe cracked through the sink, knocking a huge chunk of porcelain to the floor as Howard stumbled backward.

"Okay, okay!" Howard covered his ears.

*CLANK.*

A third swing cracked against the mirror, a few shards of glass shattering into the broken sink.

"I'll find a way, I promise!" Howard shouted, desperate to make it stop.

The Reaper grinned through the cracked mirror, a dozen shattered smiles all reflecting back at him.

*"I can help . . ."* The monster reached behind his back for a curved sickle, the old blade worn with nicks from carnage past. *". . . clear the path."*

Howard was horrified by the implication as he shook his head, firm with resolve as he leaned threateningly toward the monster in the mirror. "No. If you try to act through me, I will fight you and you will lose. Just as you did on that stage."

The Reaper chuckled.

*"My sweet little puppet. I let you win. But the seed has only just begun to sprout."*

Howard knew in his gut that this nightmare was far from over and the Reaper had him desperate and cornered. Then again, perhaps desperation was Howard's secret weapon.

"I'll give you what you want," Howard promised, "only if you stay out of my way, out of my mind." He reached into the sink and grabbed a shard of glass, holding the sharp edge to his own throat. "But if I hear another word from you, I will end us both."

The Reaper snarled in response, gripping the sickle tight. The devil did not like to be challenged. Howard only hoped that his opponent couldn't sense the terror beneath his defiant words as he pressed on with his ultimatum.

"You will stay mute, Lester." The Reaper recoiled at his true name. "That's the deal. Take it or leave it."

Howard could feel the beast's rage swelling in his own blood, but he maintained its glare, standing his ground and squeezing the sharp glass until he felt blood drip down his hand.

The Reaper finally relented with a light chuckle.

*"Oh, I'll be quiet. Quiet as a mouse."*

The chuckle grew into laughter as Howard tried not to think about the poor creature he'd killed in his cellar. He was terrified at the thought of killing something much larger than a mouse as the monster's laughter bubbled into a cackle. That deep, mocking cackle.

A thrumming pain splintered through Howard's skull, suddenly overcome with nausea as he dropped the glass shard and it clattered into the broken sink. He closed his eyes as the cackle faded away, receding into the unknown recesses of his own mind.

When he finally opened them again, he found his own reflection there, staring back through the unbroken mirror. No shattered glass, no blood on his hand. The monster was gone, but the face that stared back was still haunting. His own gaunt visage, dripping with sweat.

Howard darted into the stall to vomit, a deep and painful purge.

## 28

Trevor couldn't believe how long the Q&A session went on after Howard left the stage. He had no choice but to stand up there, speaking through a sore throat as if he hadn't almost been choked to death in front of the crowd. The fans weren't giving him any softball questions either, and he was totally unprepared for the onslaught of nerd-dom.

"Are you going with the continuity from *Part V* that the Reaper can teleport at will?"

"Is it true that you're changing Lester Jensen's backstory to imply that he was sleeping with Farmer Joe's daughter?"

"Will we finally find out what happened to the Reaper's spawn?"

"Will Howard Browning have a cameo in the new movie?"

He knew the answer to that last question was "Absolutely fucking not," though his response aloud was a judicious "Unfortunately not."

With every other question, Trevor was clueless, leaning heavily on his "I don't want to spoil anything" crutch, which seemed to satisfy their eager appetites. He couldn't very well admit that he hadn't even seen a script yet and that the film was being fast-tracked in the most backward way he'd ever seen.

When the barrage was finally over, Trevor stepped off the stage, away from the shrieking crowd. He barely took his first breath backstage before Chuck put an arm around his shoulder and started walking beside him.

"You *killed* it, Trev. Way to keep 'em teased."

"I didn't really have a choice. Why'd you pull Howard Browning up on stage?" Trevor asked, rubbing his neck.

"Just playing to the masses," Chuck grinned.

"To the masses, *that* guy's the real deal. You stand him next to me, I look like a fucking fraud," Trevor admitted, his own insecurity shining through.

Chuck pounced on it like a dog on a bone as he stopped short. "Christ, you kids are so soft these days. Don't tell me you're already getting cold feet."

"I'm not getting cold feet. It just feels like we're putting the cart before the horse here, amping up publicity before production even starts rolling."

"Trust me, I've been doing this a lot longer than you have," Chuck said, adjusting the wave of fake hair on his head. "We just heard straight from the horse's mouth what the fans wanna see. So now we feed that info to our writer, he scribbles it out in a week and they'll get exactly what they want on opening day." He took a step closer to Trevor now, arms crossed. "You are right about one thing, though. Production hasn't started yet. Which means you're still replaceable. And if you can't even handle the fans, how can I trust you to—"

"I can handle it," Trevor snapped back.

Chuck's eyes narrowed and Trevor had to look away from the producer's piercing gaze. He was desperate for an escape as he spotted the bathroom sign over Chuck's shoulder.

"I gotta piss," he said, walking off.

"Poster signing starts in ten," Chuck called after him, "Don't be late."

Trevor waved over his shoulder before ducking into the bathroom and quickly locking the door behind him. Panic welled in his chest as he went to the sink and splashed cold water in his face. He'd never actually done this before, it's just what people always did in movies when they were stressed. But it didn't help one fucking bit now as he gave himself a hard look through the mirror, water dripping down his cheeks. He was in way over his head, drowning with no lifeboat in sight.

Jesus, it smelled like puke in here. The stench brought him back to his senses.

"You've got this," he assured himself aloud. "You're not sinking yet, so don't jump ship now, you fucking coward."

He remembered what Kevin M shared in the meeting this morning, about how fear has two meanings. Fuck Everything And Run or Face Everything And Rise. The choice is yours.

Trevor just couldn't face it all alone. But that's what the fellowship was for, right? The solution was in the community. He took out his phone and flipped it open to call Danny, finger hovering over the send button. But he knew what Danny would say.

"Your Higher Power's got your back."

Trevor wasn't in the mood for that Obi-Wan bullshit right now. He just wanted to escape. He wanted to be outside of his body, floating somewhere above it, looking down. From up there, everything looked okay.

Yes, the program was one solution, but there was another one still waiting inside his jacket pocket. It was stupid to keep carrying it around, especially to a convention like this where he could have easily been frisked by the swarm of security guards. But after a quick wave of the wand and an autograph for the guard's daughter, Trevor had passed right through the gate.

He unzipped the pocket slowly now, every *click-click-click* echoing off the walls until he pulled out the pipe, the lighter, the slip of tinfoil, and the little baggie of heroin, placing it all on the sink's edge. He still couldn't believe the newcomer had just handed him everything he needed to relapse, right outside a meeting.

What if this was a test from his High Power?

No, it felt more like a message, a gift.

What if he wasn't supposed to be sober after all? What if smoking right now was the only way he was going to get through this day?

Trevor was bargaining now and he knew it. Exactly the right time to pick up the phone and call your fucking sponsor. But he also felt pretty damn comfortable with the justification he'd just cooked up. It felt airtight, snug.

The real question was whether or not he was ready to give up those two-plus months of sobriety. He could always start over, he'd done it before. The stress was just too much right now and he only needed one fix, one hit, then it would be straight back to the straight and narrow.

Of course, he could never tell Danny. Or Sophie. God, she would be so disappointed in him. It would shatter her. No, Sophie could never know. This would be his little secret, nobody else would ever have to know about it. "We're only as sick as our secrets," Danny would say.

Fuck Danny.

*squeak.*

Trevor spun back to face the stall behind him. "Who the fuck's there?"

He dropped down to look under the stall door for feet, but none were there. Must've been the plumbing. Or a mouse. Or it was just in his head. Shit, he was already getting paranoid. Now he really needed it, just to quiet his mind, to ease his racing heart before he had a full-on fucking panic attack.

Trevor tapped the powder onto the foil, flicking the lighter and holding the flame underneath as he watched that golden dust bubble into a syrupy mixture. That part always made him think of when his grandma used to make him chocolate chip pancakes after Sunday church. Those pure childhood days before he got paid to pretend to be somebody else.

Trevor didn't hesitate now as the smoke rose from the foil. He put the glass pipe in his mouth and took a strong, deep pull. His first taste in months, that beautiful burn, coursing through his lungs. He held it in as long as he could, feeling it blossom in every nerve ending, wishing he never had to let it go. When he finally exhaled, all that stress flooded out of him as a cloud formed in the mirror, his own reflection disappearing behind it. He didn't want to see himself anyway. One more swift hit and then Trevor just let the euphoria sink in, melting him in place until the smoke finally dissipated and he saw his own face smiling back at him again.

This was a good idea. He held on to that self-righteous feeling as tightly as he could, knowing that the shame would flood in soon after. He grabbed everything, the pipe and the lighter and the baggie and the tinfoil, and turned back to the stall, thinking he should flush the evidence. With his hand on the stall door, he stopped.

What was he thinking? This stuff would obviously clog the toilet.

Catching his own high logic, he couldn't help but laugh as he went back to the sink and wrapped everything in paper towels, twenty times over, shoving the large mass deep into the bottom of the trash can. Just for good measure, he wet a few more paper towels and piled them on top, because nobody wants to go digging through wet paper towels. More high logic.

He took a breath to compose himself, then splashed cold water on his face again. It actually did feel nice this time, igniting his nerves as an empty clarity settled into his mind. He put his sunglasses on, confident that he could face the fans now. Settling into a sweet semi-conscious state, he could sink into that chair and sign as many fucking posters as they wanted.

Trevor unlocked the door and stepped back out into HorrorCon, ready to be their Reaper.

## 29

When Howard finally heard the door close, he waited a moment in silence just to be safe before lowering his legs to the floor in the bathroom stall. His arthritic knees had been aching ever since he'd pulled them up to the toilet he was crouching on, just fast enough to not get caught. He didn't even have a chance to flush the vomit in the bowl before he'd heard someone rush into the bathroom, so he pressed the lever now before opening the stall door and approaching the mirror again. He was still in shock at what he'd just witnessed through the crack of the door.

Howard had seen Trevor Mane's *hamartia*, his fatal flaw. Every tragic character in Greek drama had a human weakness intrinsic to their being, a quality that both defined who they were and also provided the fateful key to their grand undoing. It seemed that Trevor wasn't so recovered after all and Howard had seen the crack in the glass. One pointed tap and the whole thing would shatter.

He took no joy in the thought of ruining Trevor, but the alternative was so much worse, the violence suggested by the beast in the mirror. Howard imagined himself on the stand in a court of law, desperate to explain, "The Reaper made me do it!"

No, that wouldn't go over well at all. But it was true, yes, he was certain of that now as he pulled the bottle of pills out of his pocket. The antipsychotic antidotes had proven themselves useless because Howard wasn't crazy or delusional or psychotic.

The Reaper was real. And now that he had reached an agreement with the beast, he had everything under control. He could handle this on his own.

Howard emptied the bottle into the sink, pills clanking down the drain as he flipped the faucet on to flush them away. He looked at himself in the mirror, wetting a paper towel to dab the flecks of vomit from his chin. Fixing his disheveled silver hair, he saw that the color was already returning to his cheeks as he felt a renewed sense of self. Vindicated in his mind and clear in his mission, Howard walked away from his own reflection.

*Night of the Reaper Part V: The New Crop* (1985)
Script Pages Courtesy of Pinnacle Studios

INT. ASHLAND JUVENILE DETENTION CENTER - NIGHT

Prison guard Danvers drags inmate Cameron along
the upper catwalk toward his cell.

> CAMERON
> I'm not crazy!

> DANVERS
> Sure. A ghost with a bloody face
> and dirty overalls is haunting a
> juvenile detention center.

> CAMERON
> He killed Paul and he's not gonna
> stop there! He's feeding on us, on
> all of our fear!

Danvers tosses Cameron into his cell and slams the
barred door shut.

> DANVERS
> I don't blame him. The food here
> sucks. Now keep quiet or it's back
> in the hole.

Danvers walks away as Cameron hangs his head.

> THE REAPER (O.S.)
> Poor little Cameron.

The familiar gravelly voice echoes off the cinder
block walls as Cameron turns to see . . .

THE REAPER materializing in the shadows like a
ghost in the dark cell corner.

> THE REAPER
> Nobody will ever believe a screwup
> like you.

                    CAMERON
        Help!

Cameron BANGS on the cell door bars.

                    CAMERON
        He's here, the ghost is in here!

                    DANVERS (O.S.)
        Tell Casper to keep it down!

A desperate Cameron turns to face the Reaper.

                    CAMERON
        Please. Just leave us alone.

                    THE REAPER
        Leave? But it's the best buffet in
        town! All this pain and misery. It
        brought me back. It gave me life.
        And once I'm done feeding, I'll
        finally be whole again.

The monster extends his arms to the sky.

                    THE REAPER
        The Reaper will rise!

Cameron turns to BANG against the bars again.

                    CAMERON
        Let me out of here! Please!

The Reaper glides up behind Cameron, clamping his
hands down on the helpless inmate's shoulders.

                    THE REAPER
        I can help with your great escape.
        But it's gonna be a tight squeeze.

                    CAMERON
        No, no, no . . .

Danvers stomps back along the catwalk toward Cameron's cell.

> DANVERS
> I told you to shut—

SQUELCH! Cameron's body is forced through the bars like a gruesome cheese grater, chunks of meat pushing through metal and PLOPPING to the catwalk on the other side.

> DANVERS
> Oh my God . . .

> THE REAPER (O.S.)
> Clean up, Cell Block Five!

Danvers stomachs vomit as he draws his gun, stepping over the gory mess to aim between the blood-soaked bars at the killer within.

> DANVERS
> Hands on your head!

> THE REAPER
> Which ones?

The Reaper holds up Cameron's severed hands. Danvers cocks his gun.

> DANVERS
> What the hell are you?

> THE REAPER
> I'm the ghost of harvest past . . .

Danvers fires three quick shots—BANG-BANG-BANG!—but they pass straight through the ghostly Reaper.

> THE REAPER
> . . . and you're Scrooged.

The specter FLIES through the bars and pushes Danvers over the catwalk railing.

He SCREAMS all the way down until his skull CRUNCHES against the concrete floor in a splatter of brains.

The inmates all CLAMOR against their bars now, CHAOS rising in every cell.

> THE REAPER
> Prison's a riot!

The Reaper CACKLES, soaking up their fear as the monster grows stronger and stronger.

# PART V:
# REPRISAL

## 30

"I really never thought I'd make it this far," Max confessed. The newcomer who gave Trevor his stash was now leading the meeting, sharing his sobriety story, no longer a twitchy mess. It was Trevor who shifted uncomfortably on his plastic chair now. It had been two days since his secret relapse and he wanted to crawl out of his skin. Or better yet beat the shit out of this kid for giving drugs to an addict outside a Narcotics Anonymous meeting.

Max looked him directly in the eye now as he spoke. "But this group has really showed up for me, since day one." Trevor looked down at his shoes, avoiding eye contact. "And I'm just so grateful."

The claps resounded as Trevor kept his arms crossed, knee bouncing, just wanting to get the hell out of there.

"Thanks for sharing," Danny said. "Trevor? You got something you want to share with the group?"

Trevor looked up to meet eyes with his sponsor from across the circle.

Shit. He knew. Of course he did. Trevor was awash in anxious shame, and sober old-timers like Danny can smell the stench of disgrace from a mile away. He shouldn't have come here, but he needed help. He didn't want to smoke again.

"I . . ." Trevor stumbled over his words, weighing the unbearable possibility of confessing his relapse to a room full of fellows.

"He doesn't want to admit it," Danny spoke for him, "or maybe he just forgot. But today marks ninety days clean for Trevor." Danny held up the red plastic coin, dangling from a beaded keychain, and the room clapped with support.

Fuck. Trevor didn't realize he was that close to his three-month chip when he threw it all away.

"Come on," his sponsor motioned for him to stand, crossing the room to give Trevor a hug and place the cheap plastic coin in his hand.

The room fell silent as he found himself in the center of the circle, everyone waiting for him to speak. He didn't deserve their support, didn't deserve their kindness. He wished they'd all just pull big fucking rocks from their pockets and stone him to death right there.

"Thanks," Trevor eked out as he tucked the red chip into his now-empty jacket pocket. "I'm gonna keep coming back."

Everyone clapped as they stood, circling and holding hands to end the meeting with the Serenity Prayer. Trevor felt like he was hearing the chant that followed for the first time now.

"It works if you work it, so work it 'cause you're worth it."

Maybe that was the problem. Trevor hadn't really been working his program. He told Danny that he'd started his Fourth Step, the searching and fearless moral inventory, but that was a lie. He didn't want to look that closely at himself, to see all his human flaws laid bare, especially not now. But maybe that's exactly what he needed to get back on track.

Trevor's whole body tensed as Danny approached. "Surprised I didn't hear from you this weekend. It was HorrorCon, right?"

"Yeah, well. It wasn't as bad as I expected."

"Most things aren't, especially with three months under your belt," Danny replied, beaming with pride.

Trevor couldn't maintain eye contact, and some part of him was still sure that Danny knew, that he was pointedly prodding him now.

"How about some chocolate chip pancakes, on me?" Danny offered. Trevor wished he could say yes, wished he could celebrate his progress with the stranger who had already shown him more love than he could ever hope to expect.

"Actually, I was thinking I'd skip fellowship and go get some step work in."

"Look at you, the overachiever now. How's that Fourth Step going?"

"Fucking brutal," Trevor replied, sipping his coffee, the caffeine buzzing in his brain. It was something, but he wanted more.

"Just remember," Danny said, placing a gentle hand on Trevor's shoulder. "You're not as big a piece of shit as you think you are, okay?"

Trevor nodded, but he didn't believe it. Maybe Danny didn't know about his relapse after all, because if he did, he wouldn't be saying that. Trevor *was* a piece of shit, a fucking fraud, and he didn't belong here, where people were actually trying to get better.

"I'm gonna run," Trevor said, starting toward the basement steps.

"If the step work gets too much, just put it away and do something fun. Easy does it."

Trevor nodded at the program slogan. They had so many dumb fucking slogans.

"And don't forget to check in every night," Danny reminded him, gentle but firm. He really was the perfect sponsor. Too bad Trevor had already fucked it up.

"Will do," Trevor promised. Anything to get away right now, to go back to his office and hide.

"Trevor." Max stepped in front of him. "I wanted to thank you again for taking that—"

"You're welcome," Trevor cut him off so that Danny wouldn't hear. "Just don't . . ." Don't say another fucking word. "Don't mention it." Trevor forced a smile, patting the bright-eyed newcomer on the shoulder before circling past him.

It may have been the paranoia setting in, but he swore he felt Danny's eyes boring into his back as he hustled up the stairs, away from that church basement, away from the loving fellowship as he found himself alone again.

## 31

Howard was finally ready to reach out to a friend for help as he pulled into the tiny strip mall at the edge of Hollywood, an area of Los Angeles that he rarely frequented. The dingy neighborhood possessed none of the glitz and glamor promised by its historic name. Instead, it was overcrowded with street level criminals who profited off the steady stream of clueless tourists with conspicuously bulging fanny packs.

Tucked between a donut shop and a laundromat lay the storefront for Poletto's Army Navy. There was only one other customer milling about when Howard entered with the dinging of the overhead bell, startling Joan out of a midday snooze at the counter.

"Browning!" Joan jumped to her feet, visibly embarrassed that she'd been caught off guard. "You snuck up on me."

"Hello, Joan," Howard smiled, giving her a hug. "The place looks fantastic." He meant it. She really had done an excellent job of organizing the cramped space into neat little sections, which greatly helped Howard in his secret purpose. "Why don't you give me the grand tour?"

"Right this way." Joan smiled, leading Howard to the zombie manne-quin at the front of the store. "First, I'd like to introduce you to Sergeant Lou Flesher." The gruesome makeup effects were as impressive as ever with the undead soldier's jaw hanging loose as shrapnel peppered his face.

"Sergeant. Thank you for your service." Howard saluted the manne-quin, which got a chuckle from Joan.

"I'm sorry, but did Howard Browning just make a *joke?*"

"You were right, Joan." Howard had practiced his pitch many times before coming here. He needed Joan's help, but he had to be sly about it. "Accepting that award at HorrorCon worked like a charm, very cathartic. I feel a million times better now that all is said and done."

"Well, shit, pal. I'm glad to hear it," Joan smiled, so genuinely happy for her friend that Howard felt guilty about the lie he was about to tell.

"And now that I'm officially retired, I've decided to pick up a hobby, like you suggested. Something fun to pass the time."

"Sounds like a great idea. What'd you have in mind? I could set you up with a pump gun, take you skeet shooting. Or maybe a knife for whittling. You strike me as the whittling type."

The mere mention of these violent tools should have garnered some reaction from the Reaper, but Howard was relieved to find the voice stayed quiet, their agreement upheld.

"I was thinking more along the lines of bird-watching," Howard replied.

Joan's brow furled. ". . . bird-watching."

Howard was already kicking himself. It was a ridiculous story, of course she wasn't buying it. "Yes," Howard swallowed hard, doubling down. "Bird-watching."

Joan stared at him over the rims of her glasses before breaking into joyful laughter. "Now *there's* the Browning I know and love. Only you would call that a fun hobby."

Howard might have been offended, were he not so relieved. He chuckled along with Joan as she led him over to the surveillance section, just as he'd hoped.

"These babies are classics," Joan said, pulling a clunky old set of binoculars off the shelf.

"Same ones we used in the jungle."

Howard put the heavy binoculars to his face and aimed them over Sergeant Flesher's shoulder, through the store window and across the busy street, where a tourist in flip-flops was taking a photo of a celebrity star on the ground. He couldn't read the name from this angle, but he doubted he'd recognize it anyway. Nowadays, the city dished out those iconic plaques as casually as after-dinner mints.

"The distance is quite remarkable." Howard lowered the binoculars. "I'll take them."

Joan cocked her head, overtly suspicious now. "Okay. Be honest."

Howard braced himself for the question to come.

"Are you just buying shit because you think I need the help? Because really, I know it doesn't look busy, but I'm doing just fine."

"Joan," Howard reassured her, "I would never insult you like that."

"Good. I would never insult you either," Joan smiled. "You patronizing prick."

They both shared a laugh before Howard continued. "How about a camera?"

"Now you're *really* speaking my language. But it's gonna be film, none of that digital crap. And I can recommend a good developing shop, run by an old roommate of mine."

"What if I want to develop the pictures on my own?" Howard asked. He didn't want someone seeing what he was photographing. No, he needed to be very careful and calculated with this whole operation.

"Birdwatching *and* photography?" Joan marveled. "That's *two* hobbies. Better slow down there, old man."

"I'm afraid I have a lot of time on my hands," Howard admitted.

"Well, I can outfit you with everything you need to set up your own darkroom at home."

"Excellent. I've got the perfect space for it." Howard was thinking of the windowless cellar, an ideal place for a darkroom. Then again, he hadn't been back down there since the incident with the mouse. He had no intention of awakening the darkness that dwelled in that subterranean hole, teeming with the Reaper's artifacts. Besides, there were plenty of other spaces in the big empty house that would do just fine. The cellar would remain off limits.

"Hey." The only other customer in the store interrupted them now, a scrawny teenager with a skateboard under one arm, holding up an old army jacket on its hanger. "You got this in an extra small?"

"What I got is what I got," Joan huffed irritably.

The kid rolled his eyes with a dramatic sigh, tossing the jacket atop the nearest rack before skating out of the store. Joan shook her head as she stepped over to the rack, putting the jacket back on its hanger and replacing it on its proper rack. "Punk-ass kids. No manners."

Howard nodded in agreement, justified in the secret knowledge that he was about to teach one punk kid a lesson he wouldn't forget.

# 32

*"Police entered the house to find a grisly scene . . ."*

Trevor sat in the dark cave of his office, hunched over a notebook at his desk while the documentary DVD *Inside the Killer's Mind* played on the computer screen. The gory details of how Jeffrey Dahmer lured men into his house of horrors to dismember them and do fucked-up shit with their corpses was a bit too disturbing to give his full attention to, but it served as a good background distraction from the Fourth Step journal he was working on.

Step Four involved airing all of his resentments on the page, anyone who had let him down, taken advantage of him, betrayed him, hurt him. Only by acknowledging his role in every dynamic and letting go of these resentments could Trevor be free of the turmoil that drove his addiction. It sounded like a promising exercise, but Trevor's list was long.

He resented his parents for treating him more like an ATM than a son, and the *Family Genius* cast for turning away when he needed them the most, and every rehab center he'd ever been to for never actually fixing him, and the paparazzi for feeding off his misery for a paycheck, and Chuck Slattery for being a fucking bully, and Howard Browning for trying to sabotage his audition and choke him out on stage. The list went on and on. Trevor didn't realize how much anger he was harboring below the surface until he was forced to spell it all out in black and white. He wasn't even ready to look at his side yet, how he was the common denominator and therefore bore some responsibility for the shitshow that was his life.

There was one name on the list that he was most surprised by, someone he was holding the deepest grudge against. He resented her for loving him, for giving him hope that he could change for the better, because it only hurt more every time he fell short.

The light rapping on the office door now made Trevor go tense as he wondered if she somehow knew that he was writing about her.

"Trevor?" Sophie's unsure voice came from the other side. "Dinner's ready."

"I'll eat later," he called back to her. The thought of sitting across the table from her right now was too much to bear. She'd see through him, ask what was wrong and then something would spill out that he couldn't take back.

"It's gonna get cold." One of the things he resented: her sheepish relentlessness. He didn't know the two could go hand in hand, but it drove him fucking crazy.

"I'm not hungry," he replied, trying to stay calm as he turned up the volume on the computer and Dahmer's voice crackled through the speakers.

*"It's hard for me to believe that a human being could have done what I've done. But I know that I did it."*

"How about some tea?" Sophie asked, louder but still soft.

"I said not *now*!" Trevor boomed. Shit. He didn't mean to shout, but he was edgy as fuck in the wake of his relapse. He knew another fix would soften those edges, but he promised himself that the HorrorCon hit was a one-off. Regret swelled in his chest as he listened to Sophie's soft footsteps padding away.

"Sophie . . ." He rushed to follow her down the stairs.

She spun to face him in the living room, tears streaming down her face. She always got to tears so quickly, she could've been an actress herself. Except it was never an act. Sophie's deep well of sorrow was always just a scratch beneath the surface, and it came pouring out of her now, running down her cheeks.

"I'm sorry," Trevor started. "I'm just really stressed from work and it's making me a little extra irritable."

"Well, I don't think the cigarettes are helping with that." Sophie shook her head. "I've been smelling them on you for weeks."

"Then why didn't you say anything?" She was so passive-aggressive, holding on to a piece of information until she found the right moment to sneak-attack him with it.

"Because I trusted you," she threw back at him. "Because you promised me things would be different this time."

"And they will be. That's why I took this role, why I need my space to prepare. So things can be different."

"I'm not talking about your career, I'm talking about *us*. You're already keeping secrets from me and we haven't even *talked* about the accident. I mean, aren't you supposed to . . ." Sophie stopped herself, but Trevor knew exactly what the rest of that sentence was.

"Say it. Apparently, you're the recovery expert, so just say it."

"Aren't you supposed to make amends?" she asked, crossing her arms over her chest.

She was talking about Step Nine. Trevor couldn't tell her how far he was from making things right with her, how he was only just now entering the swamp of anger and resentment toward her and everyone else in his life with no idea how to drain it.

"I'm sorry I almost killed you. I'm sorry I'm such a fuck up and I can't do anything right. Happy?" Trevor walked away from her, standing at the sliding glass doors in front of the dark garden. He was practiced at turning these tables, at somehow making himself out to be the victim in the end. All he had to do now was wait.

"Oh baby, you are not a fuck up." Sophie's turnaround was even faster than usual as she rushed to wrap around him from behind. "I'm sorry, I love you so much. I'll try to be more patient, okay?"

It worked every time, and normally Trevor would have been satisfied with this deft emotional deflection. She was kissing him on his cheek now and he could probably leverage this into some makeup sex, then go back to his study and be left alone for the rest of the night. But his old friend shame came creeping over his shoulders, making him feel like a manipulative asshole, undeserving of her love.

Was this the gift of recovery? Getting sick of your own bullshit, no longer comfortable playing the same old games?

*CLICK.*

He heard the metallic sound through the glass door, coming from the garden, where he saw a shadow move in the night.

"Son of a bitch." Trevor pulled away from Sophie's embrace, flipping the yard light on before throwing the sliding door open. "I see you, motherfucker!"

Nothing moved beneath the bright light and all was silent in the garden.

"Trevor, what are you doing?" Sophie asked.

"You didn't hear that sound, like a camera? I saw someone out there, it's the fucking paparazzi in the yard again."

"I didn't hear anything." Sophie said.

Trevor stared at the cactuses, brightly lit with their arms raised in silent surrender. Was that all he'd seen? Not a person, but a fucking succulent? Paranoia was clearly setting in from fresh withdrawal, a stage where hearing and seeing things wasn't entirely out of the ordinary. He was living in a perilous purgatory, yearning for his next fix, but praying he wouldn't get it. He just needed to get over the hump, into the clear.

Trevor took a deep breath and turned to Sophie, rubbing her arms. "I'm sorry. You're right. The nicotine must be messing with my nerves. No more cigarettes."

"And no more secrets," she said.

Trevor silently nodded in response. He was pricklier than those cactuses right now and he didn't want to stick Sophie again with his shitty little spines.

"You know what?" he said. "I think I'm gonna go catch a meeting."

"I think that's a good idea, sweetie."

"And thank you for making dinner. I'll eat when I get back." Trevor kissed her on the head before grabbing his jacket and ducking out the front door.

His BMW was waiting in the driveway, the one he'd nearly totaled in the accident. The one that Sophie got fixed for him when she was finally released from the hospital, while he was still in rehab. It looked brand new now, like nothing had ever happened. A fresh coat of paint to cover up the trauma. He got behind the wheel, even though there was no meeting he knew of tonight. He just needed to get out of the house. Maybe take a drive up into the hills with the windows down, letting the cold air blast away the itch that was creeping up under his skin.

But as Trevor pulled out of the driveway and stopped at the corner of the street, he felt his hands turn the wheel down the hill in another direction. Almost like he had no control, like something else was guiding him, pulling him down.

He knew where he was headed, and there was no stopping it now.

## 33

Howard had gotten too close. What was he thinking, sneaking into Trevor's backyard like that? But there were hardly any windows at the front of the hideous modern house, and the garden provided the perfect cover while focusing his camera through floor-to-ceiling windows.

After watching Trevor's girlfriend cook in the kitchen for an hour, he'd actually considered sneaking up the steps to the balcony to see if he'd find his target up there. Thankfully, Trevor came down to the main floor before Howard made that dangerously conspicuous move. It was dark enough that he hardly needed to hide, but he wasn't prepared for the loud clunky sound Joan's old camera made as he clicked the button. When Trevor rushed out, screaming into the yard, Howard barely had enough time to duck behind a large cactus.

He was plucking the sharp spines out of his arm now as he crept back across the street, and he didn't even have any good photos to show for it. All he saw was what appeared to be an argument between Trevor and his girlfriend. The scene looked like good drama from afar, but it wasn't the brand of hamartia he was after.

As he climbed safely into his Cadillac, he still couldn't believe that Jake's fumbling assistant had been able to pull the address so quickly, and that he'd given it to Howard so freely. All he had to say was that he wanted to send a congratulatory gift to the new Reaper and now here he was, at Trevor's house. But he'd already botched the plan and hadn't gotten the photos he needed. Perhaps he could come back tomorrow night.

He was about to start the engine when Trevor came out of the front door, jumping behind the wheel of his BMW. As the car backed out of the driveway, Howard knew he had to follow. It wasn't part of the plan, but time was not on his side. He turned the ignition and his Cadillac gurgled, but didn't start. No, it couldn't give up on him now. Not right in this moment after all these years.

Trevor's BMW zipped past, and Howard quickly bent down toward the passenger seat to hide. He waited a few seconds, then popped back up and turned the ignition again, and again, and again. Nothing. He was stuck. If he needed a tow, he'd have to call now or Trevor might see him when he got back. Howard gave it one last hopeful turn and the engine started with a roar as he exhaled with relief. He pulled the gearshift into drive and sped around the first corner to catch up, staying at a distance from the flashy black car as they wound down the hill toward the city.

Howard tailed Trevor straight through the main drag of Hollywood Boulevard now, where the masses swarmed the sidewalks beneath the flashing lights of El Capitan Theater. The historic cinematic temple where Orson Welles premiered his magnum opus *Citizen Kane* was now screening the sequel to an adaptation of a theme park ride about pirates. Howard was so distracted by the mockery of this landmark edifice that he almost lost sight of Trevor's car getting onto the 101. But he made up ground on the freeway, following the red brake lights as they pulled off now into downtown Los Angeles.

Howard often forgot that there was a metropolitan heart to this sprawling city, where businessmen had business meetings in business centers. But Trevor was driving straight past the towering skyscrapers, deeper south, where Skid Row lay.

It was a city unto itself, made up of tents and homeless encampments, and authorities had long stopped providing aid to those in need. The destitution in plain sight was heartbreaking, and Howard understood why most people just chose to ignore it, walking or driving right past rather than looking cold misery in the eye. A stark reflection of the fragile truth that any of us could fall this far and end up invisible, forgotten.

Trevor pulled over, parking his car on a street corner just past a large blue tent as Howard stopped a half block behind. He watched as Trevor got out of his BMW and approached a hooded figure on the corner. A brief conversation ensued, hands quickly slapped, and then Trevor walked away and got back into his car.

Howard was stunned. Was a drug deal really as simple as they portrayed it in the movies? He waited for Trevor to start the car again, prepared to follow him back home, but the BMW stayed quiet. Trevor was probably too desperate to wait the long drive home before getting his fix, meaning Howard's moment was already slipping away. He got out of the car and locked the doors, walking hurriedly along the opposite sidewalk with his head low. Ducking behind a parked car, he aimed the camera over the hood, through the driver's side window of Trevor's car.

Carefully zooming and adjusting the focus, just like Joan had taught him, he watched as Trevor flicked his lighter. The small flame was just bright enough to illuminate that famous face taking a deep pull from the pipe, all in one crystal-clear frame. Howard didn't hesitate to take his shots.

*CLICK. CLICK. CLICK. CLICK.*

"Can you see them?" A hoarse voice whispered just over his shoulder as Howard turned to see a face full of open red sores above tattered clothing. But it wasn't the Reaper, no. It was just a man, twitching with abject paranoia. "The aliens. They're here, aren't they?" He grabbed for the camera with wild eyes. "Let me see. Let me see them!"

"Let go," Howard said in a panicked whisper as blackened fingernails latched onto the camera, wrestling him down to the hard concrete sidewalk.

## 34

Trevor was in a haze, car filling with smoke as he settled into his heavy body, mind floating above. He actually forgot where he was until he heard the sounds of a struggle from across the street. It brought him back to earth as he looked over and saw what looked like two homeless men, fighting over something behind a car in the darkness between two streetlights.

He heard a heavy *thump* before one of the shadowy figures scurried away into the night with some clunky object tucked under his arm. A prize that he was probably going to pawn for a few bucks to get his next score. The other body lay motionless, facedown on the sidewalk.

Trevor's first instinct was to go see if the guy needed help, but he quickly ditched that idea. He hated it down here, but Skid Row was always the quickest place to get a fix. Especially because he didn't trust the "discreet" Hollywood dealers who had sold him out to the press more than once already. He often had nightmares that someday, he'd end up an addict on the streets himself, desperately wrestling behind cars or doing something much worse to get his next hit. That's why Trevor never touched a needle, a line he refused to cross, because then he would *really* have a problem. Smoking was much classier anyway. He heard that even Charles Dickens used to dip into London opium dens to fuel his creative process. Trevor hadn't actually read any Dickens, but the guy wrote a shit ton of famous books, so how could he be wrong? And Trevor Mane was a Hollywood fucking star, a professional who had an important role to play, and he was going to do it well. He just needed a little help, to ease his rattled nerves. That's what he told himself as he took the second hit and his vibrating phone made him jump out of his skin.

How long had he been gone? Was Sophie already looking for him?

When he saw Danny's name on the screen, he laughed out loud. Another great joke from his Higher Power, making his sponsor call the moment he took a hit. Good one.

The next thought was a paranoid one. The thought that it wasn't a coincidence, that his sponsor had caught him, knew exactly what he was doing, was watching him now. Trevor was sweating as he looked around outside the car again at eerie strangers milling about. He realized he was being ridiculous when he remembered that he was supposed to call Danny tonight to check in. But he couldn't talk to him now, no. He'd call his sponsor back in the morning, after he sobered up. Then he could start over again, get clean for real.

Trevor started the car for the long drive home and told himself that this was the absolute last time he'd ever come down here again, and no one would ever have to know about it.

He didn't have much of an appetite when he got back to the house, but when he saw the dinner Sophie left in the oven, he had to have one bite. It was mac and cheese with a corn flake crust, his absolute favorite. He didn't even bother to reheat it as he shoveled a forkful of crunchy cold noodles into his mouth, reveling in the texture and the taste. She was the best fucking cook.

He quietly stripped and put his clothes in the washing machine before heading into the shower, scrubbing relentlessly at his hair to wash out the stench of smoke. He couldn't afford to get caught. Naked and still half wet, he crawled beneath the sheets, rubbing Sophie's shoulder as she stirred awake.

"Sorry, babe, I'm too tired," she whispered in response to his assumed advances. But he didn't want sex this time.

"Will you hold me?" he asked, feeling vulnerable in his secret high, hoping she wouldn't notice through her sleepy fog.

She rolled over to face him, but he quickly turned his back to her, allowing himself to be spooned and coddled like an infant.

There was so much he wanted to say to her right now. *I'm sorry, I love you, I don't want to hurt you, I'm so scared of losing you, I'm drowning, Please help me.*

But he couldn't bear to speak a word of it as he stuffed every feeling deep inside, into that endless dark hole. He knew the tears were coming, but he held those back too, until he felt Sophie slipping back out of consciousness behind him. Once he was sure she was asleep, he let them go, trying to keep his body from shaking so he wouldn't wake her.

It was over quickly, this sad release he hadn't experienced in so long. He dried his face on the pillowcase, quietly erasing the evidence. Just another little secret that nobody would ever have to know about.

## 35

Howard locked the front door behind him, still shaking with adrenaline from his struggle with that man in the street. He wasn't even sure how he'd escaped the tense fray, his memory already a spotty blur. But as he looked at the camera strapped around his neck now, he saw that the lens had cracked amid all that flailing. He only hoped that the man wasn't hurt, and that he'd captured what he needed as he carried his busted camera upstairs to the spare bedroom.

He'd converted the space into his makeshift darkroom by blacking out the only window with a large dark sheet. The room had lain empty since the day he and Emma moved in, though they had big plans for it. Those plans dissolved with her departure and he couldn't bring himself to do anything with the room after that. There was no proper way to fill a space that was intended for new life. But he'd found a way, a new purpose now.

The room glowed red with the special bulb he'd bought from Joan, and all of the other necessary equipment was spread out on a folding table he'd found in the garage. He'd shot a test roll earlier in the week, mostly photographs of Stanley lounging around the house, but that development experiment revealed some amateur mistakes with many of the shots ending up out-of-focus or underlit. He'd also forgotten to wear the rubber dishwashing gloves when pouring the acetic acid into the tray, resulting in a mean blister when it splashed back on his wrist. He hoped this second attempt would go more smoothly as he carefully cut the acid with water.

Pressing the first image into the chemicals now, he waited as it slowly came into focus. It was Trevor and his girlfriend, mid-argument, the photo he'd taken from the backyard. He looked at the young girl's face, twisted in pain and sorrow, as Emma's words from long ago came back to him.

"It feels like you don't even want to be here anymore, with me, living your own life."

Howard grimaced at the memory as he hung the photo from the string he'd stretched across the room, moving along now to the next print. As he used the tongs to press the paper into the liquid and the photo started to come into focus, he was worried that the lighting just wasn't enough. Could you even tell who it was in the picture? The image slowly got clearer and clearer, the darks and the lights gaining harder edges until Howard knew that he had it.

An undeniable photograph of Trevor Mane smoking heroin in his car.

Howard's excitement peaked, but as he hung the photo from the line and stared at it, a deep sympathy settled in. The desperation in the boy's eyes was palpable, trapped in a prison of his own making.

Could Howard really go through with this? Destroy a young man's life? What would the consequences be, not just for Trevor, but for that poor girlfriend of his as well?

He hung his head, questioning his plan as he looked down into the tray of chemicals. The Reaper's horrid grin was reflected back, dancing in the watery mixture as a grim reminder.

"I know," he said aloud to the silent beast, remembering his bargain.

If Howard didn't get Trevor out of the way and reclaim the role, the Reaper would do it himself, in a much more decisive fashion.

He tapped the tongs into the water, rippling through the monster's image until the liquid settled again and it was Howard staring back. The fumes made him dizzy as he quickly left the darkroom and headed into the study.

He had an important letter to compose.

## 36

Trevor hadn't been to a meeting in days, and he'd long stopped returning Danny's calls, but at least he was still working on his Fourth Step inventory. The more he identified his role in every resentment, the more he realized that the person he had the most resentment against was himself. Scribbling pages upon pages of self-loathing in his notebook, he understood now that he truly was his own worst enemy.

Any time this self-reflection got to be too much, he'd switch gears to Reaper prep, which now included reading a dense book on abnormal psychology. This wasn't exactly the fun alternative that Danny had suggested, but studying the mind of a psychopath somehow made him feel a little less sick himself. The back and forth between recovery and character prep, punctuated by the occasional hit of H, filled the God-shaped hole inside seamlessly. He did still want to get sober, eventually, but he decided that he just needed to get through the shoot first.

After all that waiting and buildup, the film was suddenly in full-tilt rush mode. Coming off the success of the HorrorCon presentation, Pinnacle decided to move the release date for *Night of the Reaper 3D* a month ahead of schedule. Their latest *Roadmorphers* flick flopped and they needed a quick revenue injection to fund their next Oscar-bait drama in time for awards season. Chuck promised them he could deliver and now everyone involved was in high-tension mode.

"Again!" Andrei shouted at Trevor in the lot's rehearsal space now.

They had barely a week to prepare together and progress was nonexistent, thanks to Andrei's impossible standards.

"Come to me, Reaper!"

Trevor did his best to embody the monster, lurching across the empty space toward the pacing director. But it all felt so awkward and laborious, like he was a dancing puppet in a children's show.

"No, no, no!" Andrei shouted, confirming Trevor's insecurity.

He wished he could just go into autopilot mode, like he did on the last few seasons of *Family Genius*. Even as a kid, he could memorize a script while playing Super Nintendo in the morning and then spit it out in front of a live studio audience that afternoon with all the requisite facial expressions to make it seem fresh and alive.

But Trevor hadn't come this far just to phone it in. He knew he had to do better, to *be* better, and he'd done his fucking homework.

"Again!" Andrei shouted before mumbling a frustrated string of Romanian words that Trevor was glad not to understand.

"I'm trying, Mr. Dalca, but this miming stuff doesn't help me," Trevor explained. "Can we please *talk* about the character? I think I'm finally starting to get into his head."

The more he could get into the Reaper's head, the more he could get out of his own, which was the worst place to be right now.

"Your culture, too much emphasis on mind," Andrei said, tapping the side of his skull. "Much more wisdom in *body*. Physical exercises are doorway to character *essence*. You must *feel* the monster, in your *bones*."

"It's just, I've been reading this book on abnormal psychology and I think maybe the Reaper has a sadistic personality disorder." Trevor related more to the masochistic side of the spectrum, ever the glutton for punishment, but the more he did his Fourth Step work on himself, the more he felt a vague connection to the spiteful beast.

Andrei scoffed, waving his hand to shoo away the diagnosis. "Psychology was invented to justify weak constitutions. Did you watch what I tell you?"

"National Geographic? Yeah, a little." Trevor had been on the nod in his office the other night when he tried to watch the slow hunt on the Sahara. Waking up to a lion's roar as it tackled a gazelle and bit through bloody tendons was a serious buzzkill.

"Predator! Prey!" Andrei threw his hands in the air. "The dance of life and death!"

"Animals kill to survive, it's pure instinct," Trevor argued. "Humans are more complicated than that. I need to know *why* the Reaper kills, what his motivation is." He was growing frustrated now at having to explain the basic premise of acting to his director while his body ached for the sweet release of another hit.

"Action *is* motivation," Andrei said.

Trevor wanted to tell him he was full of shit, but he took a deep breath instead. "Can I take a smoke break?"

"No. You show me walk. Now!" Andrei gave Trevor a little shove on the shoulder, something that may have translated as gentle encouragement in his culture. But Trevor's body instantly tensed with the memories of every bully who ever picked on him in high school. *Look who it is! The Fairy Genius!*

Trevor's jaw clenched, swallowing rage as he walked back across the room, then turned to face Andrei.

His prey.

A sudden heat channeled through his veins and into his legs as he stalked across the floor, body buzzing, brain going blank.

"Yes!" Andrei screamed as Trevor advanced toward him. "There is monster! Cut!"

Trevor stopped short, catching his breath. He had tapped into something, something much deeper than his bones, an almost out-of-body experience. That's where he wanted to go, where he needed to go to reach the monster. He smiled with relief at the breakthrough.

He could do this, he *was* doing this.

Trevor was the Reaper.

This bright spot lasted only a moment before the door flew open behind him and Chuck burst into the room.

"Hey, Mr. Slattery," Trevor said before seeing the rage in the producer's eyes. Chuck clutched a rolled-up magazine in white knuckles as he charged Trevor like a bull.

"You're *dead*!" he shouted as he hurled the magazine, glossy pages slapping Trevor in the face before fluttering to the floor.

Trevor stood rooted in sheer shock for a moment before bending down and picking up the latest issue of *FameUs* magazine. His heart thumped in his chest as he looked at the cover photo. Of Trevor. Smoking H in his car.

Trevor wanted to rip the magazine in half, straight through the headline—*REAPER OFF THE WAGON*—but he swallowed his fury, gulping deeply as he looked up into Chuck's unforgiving face. "I can expl—"

"I fucking warned you . . ."

Chuck continued to rage, but all his words blurred into the background as the air left Trevor's body. He didn't need to listen to every nail being driven into his coffin to know that he had finally done it. He had fucked up his last chance at resurrecting his career, at starting over.

Trevor wasn't the Reaper. He was nothing, a nobody.

He was dead.

Trevor drove home from the Pinnacle lot in a fog of rage and self-pity, feeling like he'd been ripped to shreds like a Saharan gazelle. He found Sophie waiting for him in the living room, sitting calmly on the couch as she sipped a mug of tea.

"I just had the worst fucking day," he said, crawling across the couch toward her, desperate for the comfort only she could provide. But she scooted away from his touch, didn't even look him in the eye. That's when he saw the open *FameUs* magazine on the table. Fuck. He was hoping to earn some sympathy points before she found out, but it was too late now. Trevor sat up, slouching into a seat.

"Go ahead," he sighed. "Might as well pile on and say it. I'm a fucking asshole."

Sophie shook her head. "I'm not playing this game anymore, Trevor."

"What game?"

"The one where you say shitty things about yourself, and I say no you're wrong, and then we make up and act like everything's fine. It's not fine." Her voice took on an unaccustomed edge. "From now on, I just want you to be honest with me."

"Okay," Trevor nodded, nothing left to lose. "Let's be honest."

She stared him in the eye now. "How long have you been using?"

That term always seemed backward to Trevor. In his experience, it was the drugs that used the addict, not the other way around.

"Since HorrorCon," he answered.

"And that night, when we fought and you left for a meeting . . ."

"I went to get high." Wow, honesty really was a whole lot easier.

Sophie lowered her head. "So this is the real reason you've been so agitated lately."

Trevor realized that she was still trying to give him the benefit of the doubt, blaming his behavior on the drugs. By her logic, Trevor was an asshole because he was using, but the truth was that he was using because he was an asshole. She was right about one thing, though. It was time to be honest with her. Maybe that would finally push her away for good and he could just be left alone in his misery.

"No, Sophie." He got to his feet now, tapped out and tired of tiptoeing. "I've been agitated lately because you agitate me. The drugs are actually the only thing that make you remotely tolerable anymore. Because I can't stand you breathing down my fucking neck all day, hovering over me, like I'm some puppy that's gonna shit the rug if you turn your back for one second."

Sophie looked like she'd just had the wind knocked out of her.

"Baby, I just want to *help* you." She reached out for him, but he dodged her touch, disappointed that she'd given up so easily. That strength looked good on her, but she wasn't standing up for herself anymore and he wanted to make her.

"I don't want your help, Sophie. I don't need it," he spat back.

"Why don't you just sit down, I'll make some more tea and we can talk—"

"I don't want to talk!" Trevor shouted, reaching down for the hot mug. "And I sure as shit don't want any more fucking *tea*!" he roared, smashing the mug down on the table. Shards of porcelain shattered as hot tea splashed in Sophie's face and she shrieked, jumping to her feet.

"Oh my God . . ." Trevor was beside himself at the violent outburst. What the fuck was that? "I'm so sorry, honeybee. I didn't mean to . . ."

He reached out for her, but she was the one recoiling from his touch now, climbing over the back of the couch in terror.

"No. No, I can't do this anymore," she said, seemingly to herself as she grabbed her keys.

"Sophie, please." It was always Trevor who ran away, he was the one with one foot out the door their entire relationship, but now the tables had turned and he didn't like it. He jumped between her and the door, grabbing her arm. "Don't leave me, not now."

She looked down at his hand, clamped around her wrist, and fresh horror filled her face as she spoke firmly. "Trevor. Let go."

It took every ounce of his energy to release his own grip, like something in him was desperately latching onto her, knowing that if he let her go now, there was no hope for him. But his better self wanted her to run far away, to escape the blast zone of his pathetic implosion.

So he let her go, and she left.

The silence in Sophie's wake was deafening as Trevor rushed to his jacket, digging into the pocket and pulling out the red NA keychain.

Shit. Wrong pocket.

He tucked the chip back inside, stomaching his shame as he quickly unzipped the other pocket, pulling out his stash and lighting up as quickly as possible for a deep hit. The euphoria barely lasted ten seconds before the emptiness of his life began to suffocate him. Chuck hated him, Sophie hated him, everyone fucking hated him. But not as much as he hated himself.

He wished he hadn't just smoked. He'd already built up a tolerance, so the H didn't even numb him out, just sucked him into a muddy undertow of shitty feelings. He took out his phone and called Danny, the hardest call he'd ever made in his entire life.

"Danny. I fucked up, big-time," Trevor ran his hand through his hair.

"I saw the article." There was no judgment, but maybe hint of sadness in his sponsor's voice.

"I need help," Trevor begged. "Sophie left, for good, I think. And I don't know what the fuck is wrong with me, but I—"

"Are you high right now?"

Trevor's first impulse was to lie, but he skipped it. "Yeah."

"Okay. I've got my daughter tonight, otherwise I'd come get you. But you shouldn't be alone right now, so I'm gonna call another one of my sponsees to come help you."

"Okay, yeah, great."

"You remember Max?"

That fucking idiot. "I remember him."

"He's got a service commitment at the nine o'clock Laurel Canyon tonight. I'll have him come pick you up, take you to the meeting with him. Then you go back to his place and sleep it off. There's an 8 a.m. on Highland tomorrow morning. I'll meet you there, and we'll get you back on the wagon, okay?" Trevor nodded, but Danny needed verbal confirmation. "Trevor. Okay?"

"Yes, okay, I'll be there. Thanks, Danny."

"Hang tight, kid. This too shall pass."

Trevor hung up. All he had to do now was wait for Max. But fuck, he didn't want to be high in front of that asshole, the one who handed him his relapse on a silver platter. Max was on his resentment list and he didn't have the energy to play nice. Besides, the newcomer couldn't possibly understand what Trevor had been going through, the pressures of preparing for the role as he trudged through the endless mire of his Fourth Step. He wondered if Danny could, either. Nightshark was a loveable superhero in a PG-13 comic book movie. Nothing like the murderous psychopath that Trevor had spent weeks digging into. He thought of Dr. Liz next. She could help him. She'd done it before and she could do it again. He flipped his phone open and called.

"Chrysalis Rehabilitation Clinic," the receptionist answered.

"Yeah, hi, this is Trevor Mane calling for Dr. Liz."

"Oh, hi Trevor! She's off tonight, but would you like to leave a message?"

"No, can you just . . . can you give me her home number, please?"

"I'm sorry, I can't give out the personal information of our staff. But we just had a room open up today if you'd like to— "

"Fuck no, I'm not coming back there," he responded on reflex. "I'm sorry, I just . . . Nevermind." He snapped the phone closed as he sat back down onto the couch, sinking into the cold reality that he truly was alone. That's when his eyes fell on the open magazine. He hadn't actually read the article after Chuck threw it in his face.

*"An inside source reports that Howard Browning had always been director Andrei Dalca's top choice, which means the veteran bogeyman might be back in the running now."*

This time, Trevor actually did rip the magazine in half, straight down the binding. But the more he sat there and thought about it, the more it gave him an idea. Probably a bad idea, but those were the only kind he seemed to have left these days as he threw on his jacket and headed out the door.

## 37

"In light of this startling revelation, the question on everyone's minds is: Will Pinnacle Studios stand behind Trevor Mane in their upcoming *Night of the Reaper* remake? Or will Howard Browning swing the rusty chain once again?"

Howard read the *FameUs* article aloud to Stanley in the parlor, in utter disbelief that his plan had actually worked. He'd mailed the photos anonymously with his "insider" note, thinking it would be a long shot that they'd ever print it without a nameable source. But it seemed the magazine's bar for integrity was even lower than he'd anticipated.

He took no pleasure in hurting Trevor's career, but he hadn't forced the pipe into the boy's mouth after all, and he couldn't help but feel some sense of satisfaction, vindication after all this. Everything had gone according to plan and no blood needed to be shed.

Howard decided to celebrate by putting on a Vivaldi record and cooking himself a healthy dinner of stuffed artichoke hearts with a side of quinoa. He'd gratefully lost his taste for meat, now that the hungry beast was back in its cage, and he'd finally regained total control of his own senses. Enjoying the warm meal alongside a tall glass of chilled chardonnay, he savored every bite, every sip, all the textures and tastes grounding him in his body. Most importantly, his mind was quiet, the peace that he was promised with the Reaper appeased. He indulged in a second glass of wine, carrying it into the parlor to listen to his record.

*KNOCK-KNOCK.*

A rapping at the door gave Howard pause before he could even sit. He turned off the music, waiting a moment to listen again.

*KNOCK-KNOCK-KNOCK.*

Louder this time and definitely not in his head. He moved to the door and peered through the peephole, wondering who could be visiting at this late hour.

No, it couldn't be. The Reaper was playing with his mind again. There was no possible way that Trevor Mane was standing on his doorstep right now.

But that's exactly who Howard was seeing through the peephole as the nervous boy mumbled, "What the fuck am I doing here?" and started to turn away.

There was only one way for Howard to know if this was really happening, so he opened the door, catching Trevor halfway down the porch steps. "Mr. Mane?"

Trevor spun back, face pale. "Hi."

"This is unexpected." Was it possible that Trevor knew what he had done, that he was here to confront Howard? He searched for anger in the young man's countenance, but found only sadness.

"Sorry to just drop by unannounced. I found your address in the White Pages. Dot com," Trevor clarified.

"I wasn't aware I was listed." Howard was mortified to know that his address was just floating about on the Internet, and also a little surprised that it hadn't resulted in more unexpected guests from online fandom. "How may I help you?"

"Look, I know you don't like me. And I get it. Truth is, I don't really like me, either. I'm just here to make amends, for the way I acted toward you. And I was hoping we could talk."

"I was just settling in for the night," Howard responded. He couldn't believe how gracious a loser Trevor was being, but letting him into the house now seemed too dangerous a proposition.

"Right, okay," Trevor nodded. "It's just . . ." His eyes were wet and glassy and he looked down, as if to hide them. "I could really use someone to talk to right now."

Disarmed by the young man's candor, Howard couldn't very well shut Trevor out in the cold now after taking his job from him. "Of course." He stepped to the side and opened the door wide. "Please, come in."

"Thanks." A visible relief settled over Trevor's body as he headed into the parlor. "Nice place."

Howard blushed, seeing his home through the eyes of the hip young man. The old quilt draped over his reading chair next to the reading light with the frilly lampshade wasn't exactly haute couture. When Trevor took a seat in Howard's chair, he just smiled, ever the cordial host.

"I was just having a glass of chardonnay, if you'd like to join—" Howard caught himself, remembering who he was talking to. "I'm sorry."

"It's fine, really."

"Perhaps a cup of tea?"

"No tea." Trevor shook his head with a strange insistence, just as Stanley purred up against his leg and he nearly jumped out of his skin. "Fuck!"

"Oh, that's Stanley. I'm afraid he has always depended on the kindness of strangers," Howard joked, anything to lighten the tension.

The reference was clearly lost on Trevor, who was sweating now as he pulled his feet up onto the chair, his dirty sneakers rubbing against the fabric. "I'm allergic."

"Very well." Howard gently shooed Stanley away and the cat reluctantly slinked upstairs.

"Anyway," Trevor began, "I'm sorry I was a dick to you at the audition. And then at HorrorCon, things got way out of hand. I want to take responsibility for my side of that."

"I think we both went a bit over the top," Howard confessed, trying to keep the peace without revealing too much. "Please accept my apology as well."

Trevor rubbed his visibly sweaty palms along the armrests. "So are we cool?"

"Yes. We're cool." The words felt unnatural on Howard's lips.

"Cool," Trevor repeated, sinking deeper into the chair. Howard noticed the young man's heavy eyelids, like he might nod off at any moment. Of course. He was high. That much was clear now, but it still didn't explain what he was doing here.

"Is there anything else?" Howard asked.

"Well," Trevor cleared his throat, sitting up straighter to finally get the words out. "I guess I just wanna know . . . how you did it."

Howard swallowed hard, body stiffening. Here it was. He'd been caught after all and this was the slow burn confrontation. "Did what?"

"How you became the Reaper," Trevor answered. "I mean, you were right. It's a serious role, and I guess I just wasn't taking it seriously enough."

Howard's shoulders relaxed. This was no confrontation. He took a seat in the adjacent couch as Trevor continued.

"In your audition, you scared the piss out of that girl. I mean, literally. And at HorrorCon, you scared me, too. There was something in your eyes, it was like you . . . tapped into something. Something deep and dark and . . . real."

"Thank you." Howard accepted the compliment on his acting despite knowing that what happened on that stage was something much more than a performance.

"I want to know how you do it," Trevor repeated, leaning forward.

At this, Howard became the shifty one, recrossing his legs. He feared all this Reaper talk was bound to bring the monster forth. Best to dismiss, divert, in any way possible.

"It's just a role, Mr. Mane," Howard lied through his teeth, though he still didn't fully understand the nature of the beast.

"Call me Trevor. Mr. Mane is my father." Trevor got to his feet. "And I fucking hate my father."

Trevor buzzed over to the mantel, where the golden skull award rested. Jake had mailed it to Howard after HorrorCon and he was too afraid to put it in the cellar where it belonged. He regretted placing it in plain sight now in what appeared to be an egoistic emblem of self-congratulation. Trevor ran his fingers along the skull, continuing his rant.

"I've been doing some research, reading that psychoanalysis stuff you talk about in all your interviews. Like how Freud talks about the death drive, fueled by these primitive, destructive instincts."

Howard was impressed by the boy's research. "I said a lot of things back then. I don't think I truly understood any of it."

"It's not just destructive, though. It's *self*-destructive, too, right?"

"Yes. That's right." Howard couldn't help being drawn into the conversation now.

"But where does it come from? Where do you find all that in the Reaper?" Trevor asked, humble as a pupil. "I just, I don't see the motivation. Like, Manson got off on controlling all those girls, and the Zodiac wanted to show the cops how smart he was. But what does the Reaper *want*?"

"You mustn't jump straight to the Reaper," Howard said, eager to share the method he'd spent years honing. Perhaps in doing so, in verbally retracing the character's evolution, he could get some better understanding of what he was dealing with himself now. "The motivation, the rage, it all begins with Lester Jensen."

"The mute? He barely has one line."

"Lester was a quiet man, but he was a *good* man. The mythology got muddled in later entries, but at his core, he was a hard worker who dedicated his life to the people of Ashland. And what did he receive in return from this town full of takers? Rejection. Humiliation. Abuse."

Trevor was still pacing, clearly struggling to wrap his brain around it. "I don't get it," he admitted.

Howard stood up, desperate to reach some mutual understanding. "The people of Ashland are doomed to be haunted by the Reaper because they *created* him. When they killed Lester so unjustly, they planted a dark seed deep in that good man's soul. A seed of shame, of hatred. And when he died, the seed gave birth to a violent monster, gave voice to a vengeful beast."

Howard could see the light of recognition in Trevor's eyes, listening intently. He felt deeply vulnerable as he swallowed the lump in his throat, a truth flowing out of him that he hadn't yet articulated to himself, let alone to another human being.

"But I think you're right, Trevor. It's not just hatred. It's self-hatred. Perhaps some part of Lester believed that the blight *was* his fault. That he deserved what came to him." Howard looked around at his hollow home, the barren cornfield of his life. "But Lester, like any good character, is just the gateway to an actor's personal emotional well. When you tap into your *own* self-loathing . . . when you find yourself rejected and alone at the breaking point of utter despair . . . consumed by your darkest fears . . . then you truly open yourself to the monster. Then you will know the Reaper."

Howard swore he saw tears in Trevor's eyes as the young man choked out the words, "Hurt people hurt people."

Howard cocked his head, unfamiliar with the expression.

"It's an NA thing," Trevor admitted, stealthily wiping his eyes as he cleared his throat and dropped back into the chair, looking overwhelmed. "I just don't know if I can do this anymore."

"You don't have to," Howard reminded him.

Trevor looked up at him, confused. "What do you mean?"

"Oh, I just . . ." Howard fumbled, "I read the article. And I suppose I assumed that . . ."

"That Chuck would kick my ass to the curb? Yeah, I thought so, too. Part of me actually hoped that he would. But I guess all press is good press after all. I'm on thin ice, for sure, but production starts next week."

No. Howard's plan hadn't worked after all. The revelation made him dizzy, squeezing his eyes closed as Trevor continued to talk.

"That's why I came to you for advice. Because I feel like I'm losing my fucking mind over here and I just needed to spill my guts to someone who might actually understand."

*Yes. Let's spill them.*

The Reaper's voice in the room forced Howard to open his eyes. The monster stood behind Trevor's chair, raising the sickle high, and before Howard could speak, the curved blade swung down into Trevor's stomach, ripping upward as intestines tumbled to the carpet in a bloody splash.

Howard gasped, but the gory vision was gone in the blink of an eye. The monster disappeared and Trevor looked confused with his guts fully intact as Howard spun to catch his hand on the mantel for balance.

*You failed, Howard.* The Reaper exhaled in his ear.

"No, no, please . . ." Howard said aloud to the eager voice.

*I won't.*

## 38

"Are you okay?" Trevor asked.

It may have been a cliché, but Howard really looked like he'd seen a ghost when he turned away to grip the mantel and started mumbling something to himself. He straightened up now, speaking toward the wall in a soft voice. "You came to me for advice."

"I did," Trevor responded. After their conversation, he actually kind of liked the guy. Trevor felt seen, understood, and he really did want Howard's help.

"I have only one piece of advice," Howard said, slowly turning back toward Trevor to reveal haunted eyes. Something had shifted inside him, but it wasn't the rage Trevor saw at HorrorCon. It was something else. Trembling, but forceful as he commanded. "Surrender the role to me. And walk away."

A laugh jumped from Trevor's throat, a truly guttural reaction. "You're joking, right?"

But Howard looked dead serious as he took a step forward from the mantel. "If you continue to stand between me and the Reaper, I'm afraid bad things will happen."

Trevor leapt to his feet. "Are you threatening me?"

Howard's hands shook and Trevor feared that the old bastard might have a stroke. If he did, it wouldn't be Trevor's fault. This guy was clearly unwell.

"I'm trying . . ." Howard muttered. "to warn you . . ."

"Let me give *you* some advice," Trevor responded. "Let it go, man. Chuck never even considered giving you the role back. And I'm sorry, I know he's an asshole, but you're only embarrassing yourself now."

"You don't understand," Howard said, grabbing Trevor's shoulders.

Trevor flashed back to his father coming home from a "church event," several scotches deep as he grabbed his son by the shoulders, screaming into his face about scattered LEGOs. Trevor took it then, but he wasn't going to take it today as he shoved Howard back.

"Don't fucking touch me. I understand perfectly. You're pathetic. I can't believe I actually came here for *help*." Trevor wanted to keep laying into him, to make him feel ashamed, but he swallowed that rage. What he wanted more was another hit to ease his nerves, once he got the fuck out of this creepy-ass house. "Thanks for nothing, dick."

Trevor turned away from a trembling Howard, almost at the door when he heard a familiar voice over his shoulder. A voice that wasn't Howard's. A voice he'd only heard in movies, only harsher, more chilling in person.

*"Then scurry on back to Skid Row. I love a good chase."*

It was the Reaper's voice.

Trevor turned back to see Howard covering his mouth in horror, like he couldn't help the words that had just escaped his own lips.

"I'm sorry . . ." Howard quickly apologized. "I didn't mean that . . ."

"What the fuck is wrong with you?" Trevor asked.

"Please, Trevor," Howard was begging now. "You have to leave, now. Run."

"I'm gone." Trevor started out of the room, but he stopped when his eyes landed on the table next to the chair. He hadn't noticed the *FameUs* magazine resting there and it sparked something for him now.

"Wait. Skid Row?" Trevor said. "The article didn't say *where* the photo was taken." He turned back to Howard, whose nervous eyes were the opposite of a poker face. "Son of a bitch. It was you, wasn't it?"

Howard squirmed like a mouse caught in a trap, and Trevor's whole body shook at the revelation. The calming H in his system was no match for the rage that was pulsing hot through his veins now, all that energy ramping up to an almost maniacal glee.

"Wow," Trevor said, gliding toward Howard like a shark. "You're even more pathetic than I thought." He was channeling something again, locked in on Howard with primal clarity.

Predator. Prey. The dance.

"You know what?" Trevor continued. "I'm glad I came here. This is exactly the inspiration I needed. I'm gonna play the role so well, nobody will even remember the original. It'll be like you never existed."

Howard stumbled backward and tripped over his own feet, falling to the floor. Good. Trevor wanted him to hurt as he leaned over him, fists clenched tight.

"Your time is over, old man. You're nothing, a nobody. So why don't you just stay up here alone with your sad little cat and *rot*!"

The last word scraped out of Trevor's throat like it was covered in nails. The shocking pain of it brought him back to his senses as he looked up to see his own fist raised over Howard's head. Was he actually about to hit the poor bastard? Trevor quickly shook the tension out of his hand as he stepped back. He'd gotten carried away in the current, but seeing the sad sack of a man on the ground before him now, he was awash with remorse.

Trevor cleared his throat, holding back the apology that begged to be voiced as he walked away. He just needed to get the hell out of here. Heading straight for the front door, he took one step onto the porch into the chilled night air when he heard the raspy voice rushing up behind him.

*"And the award goes to!"*

Trevor heard a dull *thud* as a crackling pain flared at the back of his head. A white light flashed behind his eyes and when it faded, he found himself collapsed on the porch. He was looking up at Howard, who clutched the shiny golden skull award with both hands. There was fresh blood smeared across the bony nose-hole and Trevor knew that it was *his* blood. He wondered how much more might be spilling from his head right now, but he couldn't feel a thing.

As his vision began to fade, Trevor had a strangely lucid moment, picturing his final frontpage headline. *Desperate Actor Beat to Death by Desperate Actor.* At least it had a real punch line. He could almost hear the laugh track as he fell headlong into that God-shaped hole.

*Night of the Reaper Part VI: Urban Harvest* (1986)
Script Pages Courtesy of Pinnacle Studios

INT. L TRAIN - CHICAGO - NIGHT

Lisa and Mark squeeze through the closing train doors, panting with terror and exhaustion.

> LISA
> I think we lost him.

Lisa looks back at the crowded platform to make sure.

> MARK
> Great. But what are we gonna do now?

The train RATTLES along the raised tracks as the Chicago skyline glows through the car windows.

> LISA
> We have to get back to Madame Moreau. Now that we know the truth, that Lester Jensen really was practicing dark magic, we have to fight fire with fire. And she's the only one who knows how to perform the ritual to stop the Reaper.

> MARK
> The ritual that requires your blood? Lisa, I can't let you do that.

The train takes a hard curve and Lisa stumbles. Mark catches her in his strong arms.

> LISA
> Farmer Joe was my great grandfather, Mark. I have the power to end this, once and for all. And I can't just walk away now.

                         MARK
              Then I'll be right by your side.
              To the end of the line.

Mark leans in for a kiss just as——

The door to the next train car SLAMS open and THE
REAPER enters, snarling at horrified commuters.

                     THE REAPER
              Is it just me or does this city
              have an overpopulation problem?

The monster unsheathes his hand-scythe as a mohawked
STREET PUNK stands to face him.

                     STREET PUNK
              Yo, Old MacDonald. Halloween ain't
              'til next week.

                     THE REAPER
              Then I better start carving my
              jack-o'-lantern.

The Reaper SLASHES his scythe across the punk's
mouth, carving a gruesome gash, followed by——SHUNK!
SHUNK!——two quick stabs through the punk's eyes.

                     THE REAPER
              Trick or treat!

He spins the wavering dead man to show off his
gruesome masterpiece as passengers SCREAM, rushing
past Lisa and Mark toward the next car.

                     THE REAPER
              City folk sure are rude.

The Reaper tosses the bloodied punk to the floor as
Lisa steps forward, protecting Mark behind her.

                    LISA
     Don't take another step closer,
     Reaper.

                  THE REAPER
      Or what? You'll collect my fare?

The Reaper licks the fresh blood from his scythe
blade.

                  THE REAPER
      Here. I'll come give it to you.

The monster charges across the empty train car as
Lisa reaches into her jacket. She pulls out one of
Lester Jensen's old hay dolls, extending it like a
talisman toward the beast.

                    LISA
     Evil demon, do no harm! I send you
     back to your rotting barn!

                  THE REAPER
     Noooooo!

The Reaper's whole body SPARKLES into a blinding
white FLASH before disappearing into thin air with
a puff of smoke.

                    MARK
     It worked!

                    LISA
     It won't hold him forever. But
     Madame Moreau's spell will.

Mark looks at the L Train map on the wall.

                    MARK
     How much longer 'til we get to her
     shop?

Lisa grabs him by his shirt.

                         LISA
          Long enough.

She kisses him passionately as the train screeches
into a dark tunnel ahead.

# PART VI:

# REVELATION

## 39

Trevor slowly came out of the fog to the smell of dank earth. He couldn't feel his body, and everything was still black as his first thought arrived.

He was in Hell. He died and he was in Hell now where he belonged, lost in an infinite abyss, awaiting eternal punishment. Just like he was promised every Sunday as a kid.

As his vision returned from blackness, he saw a figure in the shadows. Was this the Devil, here to take inventory of his sins? His eyes honed into focus, registering the mangled face above shabby overalls.

It was the Reaper, standing there in front of him. He stared into the monster's unwavering gaze, thinking the Devil had a wicked sense of humor, coming to him in this form.

Trevor tried to stand, only to find that his body was tied securely to a chair. He was surprised to discover he still had a body and wasn't just a ghost floating in the ether. Blood was flowing back into his limbs now as a sound echoed from somewhere above.

A door creaking open as light cast down into the darkness. Footsteps coming downstairs. Another figure arriving, surrounded by a glowing light. A guardian angel coming to rescue him? Yes, God made a mistake. This one really tried to be good. The angel reached up, tugged a cord and a light clicked on. Blinded for a moment, Trevor found himself looking up at his savior.

No, not an angel. Just Howard Browning.

The man who killed him.

He looked over to his Devil, the Reaper, and saw that it was nothing more than a life-sized cardboard cutout, standing among a clutter of other movie memorabilia.

Trevor understood now that he wasn't dead. He was alive, captive in Howard Browning's basement, in what looked like some creepy little shrine to the Reaper. And this was much worse than any Hell he could dream up.

"How are you feeling?" Howard asked, stepping out of sight behind Trevor.

"If you're gonna kill me, just get it over with," Trevor muttered as something cold and lumpy was placed on his head.

"The bleeding stopped," Howard spoke. "But you may be concussed. I'll get you some anti-nausea medicine." He came back around to face Trevor. "And I have no intention of letting any more harm befall you."

"Then what the fuck do you want?" Trevor demanded, feeling bold despite being incapacitated.

"I warned you," Howard replied, a frank emptiness behind the words. "But you didn't listen. The role is mine."

Trevor shook his head and the cold object resting on top of it fell to the ground.

A bag of frozen peas. The sheer insanity of it all was just too much.

"You fucking psychopath. You're holding me hostage over a role?" Trevor vaguely remembered Howard speaking in the Reaper's voice last night, but it was all pretty hazy now. Either way, this guy clearly had attachment issues. "Take it, it's yours, I don't give a fuck."

Howard shook his head. "It's too late for that now, Mr. Mane. This all could have been much easier if you'd only heeded my warning. But I can't let you go now."

"You'll never get away with this." That's what victims always said in the movies, but Trevor really believed it. "My girlfriend will go to the police when I don't come home tonight."

As soon as the words left his mouth, doubt set in. The finality of that last fight meant that Sophie might never wait for him again. For all he knew, she was packing her bags and leaving for good right now, writing a farewell note that he'd never get to read.

"You can't just make me disappear," Trevor said, as if to reassure himself.

"Sources close to Trevor Mane have reported that the actor has gone missing." Howard spoke as if reading the next *FameUs* article. "But his car, found abandoned on Skid Row, contained more than enough evidence to suggest that the troubled star is off on one of his infamous benders, confirming recent speculation that he will no longer be playing the Reaper—"

"Fuck you!" Trevor seethed, every muscle in his body straining against the ropes in a unified desire to punch this son of a bitch in the face. He never should've turned his back and given the coward a chance to strike. He should've beaten him to a pulp and left him for dead.

"I will play the Reaper one last time," Howard explained, "and when filming is complete, I will release you. After that, you can do what you wish."

"That's your big plan?" Trevor was stunned as Howard just stared in response. "Well, then I hope you like prison."

He watched Howard's eyes move around the room, at the strange collection of all things Reaper. "I've grown accustomed to it."

Howard started up the stairs, halfway to the top when Trevor called after him, "Just because I'm out of the way doesn't mean they'll cast you."

Howard stopped mid-step. The cocky bastard hadn't thought about that, had he? But after a momentary pause, Howard spoke over his shoulder.

"We'll have breakfast at seven." He continued up the steps and through the door, closing it behind him without another word.

Trevor struggled against his bindings again, the rope burning his skin as his head throbbed. He looked down at the frozen peas, already gathering condensation as they melted in the subterranean warmth. He regretted knocking them away. Anything to numb the pain.

Anything.

## 40

As Howard closed the cellar door behind him, he noticed the golden skull still lying on the hardwood floor where he'd dropped it, just inside the front door. He tried to remember exactly how it had all happened. Trevor was shouting in his face in the parlor when his vision went black, and then Howard found himself standing in the front doorway with the golden skull in his hands and Trevor collapsed on the porch in front of him.

The Reaper had attacked.

When Howard came back to his senses, he'd panicked for a moment, but then knew exactly what needed to be done. Dragging Trevor's body back inside, he was surprised at the hefty weight of the sleight-framed young man. Getting him down the basement stairs was easier, with gravity on his side. Then it was only a matter of retrieving one of the Adirondack chairs from the porch along with the old rope from his car trunk. Keeping Trevor's unconscious body in place while tying off the rope was a struggle, but Howard was impressed by his memory of clove hitch knots this many years out of the Boy Scouts.

As he lifted the golden skull from the floor now, he saw the small indentation it left in the hardwood and shuddered to think of what might have happened had he not regained control after that first blow. Yes, keeping Trevor hostage was awful, but it was better than the Reaper smashing the boy's brains all over the front porch.

He took the golden skull to the kitchen, pulling a bottle of extra shine spray from under the sink to polish the small spattering of blood away before bringing it back to the parlor. As he placed the award back on the mantel, the reflective surface revealed the warped visage of the Reaper staring back at him.

*"You should have kept swinging."* The words hissed through broken teeth. *"Finished what I started."*

"No." Howard stared into those vengeful eyes. "I am not a killer."

*"Yes, we are."* The Reaper grinned.

Howard stiffened at the implication that he and the monster were somehow one, destinies entwined, the true yin and yang. He knew where he stood, and Trevor being alive proved that he still maintained some control over the situation. He would not be bullied by the beast into questioning his own identity. Right now, it wasn't the Reaper, but Trevor's words that were troubling him as he spoke to the demon in the golden skull.

"He's right, you know. Just because he's out of the picture doesn't mean they'll take me back."

*"We always come back."*

"There is no 'we,'" Howard spat back, turning away from the skull.

*"Don't turn your back on me."* The monster growled, no longer playful. *"You're nothing without me."*

"I'm nothing *because* of you!" Howard shouted as he turned to face the Reaper. But he was only shouting at his own reflection now, alone in the parlor. He hung his head, desperately tired, but he still had to dispose of Trevor's car and make a stealth return home while it was dark out. The monster was sloppy, but Howard had to be careful to cover their tracks well.

## 41

Trevor couldn't believe he actually slept through the night, but it wasn't much less comfortable than sleeping on an airplane. If the stewardess had tied your hands behind your seat before takeoff. What was more surprising was waking up to a disheveled Howard Browning holding out a hot plate of scrambled eggs.

"They're slow-cooked," Howard said, lifting a forkful to Trevor's mouth. "I would've added a bit of shredded cheese, but I didn't know if you were lactose intolerant."

Trevor was sick to his stomach, his appetite totally gone from the morning-after withdrawal. But he opened his mouth anyway, gathering a mouthful of moist eggs.

"How are they?" Howard smiled before Trevor spit the eggs into his stupid face. The eager chef looked more sad than angry as he wiped the yellow goo from his cheek. "Very well."

Howard started toward the stairs when a phone started ringing. It was Trevor's, in the pocket of his jacket, crumpled on the floor where Howard must have left it after tying him up.

"They're looking for me," Trevor smiled.

Howard bent down and reached into the pocket. Flipping open the phone, he squinted at the caller ID as the ringtone blared. "Who's Danny?"

"My NA sponsor. I was supposed to meet him this morning. He's gonna be worried that I didn't show. I talked to him last night before I came over here," Trevor said, which was true. "I told him I was gonna go see Howard Browning for some advice," which was not true. "It shouldn't be long now before he comes looking for me."

Howard just stared at him, uncomfortably long, phone still ringing in his hand. Trevor tried to hold the gaze, but couldn't help shifting in his seat.

"You better let me talk to him," Trevor said, "smooth things over."

Howard seemed to be considering it for a moment. Then he snapped the phone shut and tucked it back in the jacket pocket. "A valiant effort, Mr. Mane. But you really could stand an acting lesson or two. I doubt very much that you told anyone about your impulsive visit, and not showing up this morning will only feed the story of your relapse."

Trevor knew Howard was right as he watched him start back up the stairs, holding the plate in one hand with the jacket draped over the other. He thought about what was in the other jacket pocket and his whole body tingled.

"Wait!" Trevor shouted, a desperate cry. "If you're gonna keep me like this, the least you can do is give me a little relief." Howard turned back as Trevor felt his face flush with shame. "In the other jacket pocket."

Howard checked the pocket and pulled out the little baggie of heroin. He looked Trevor up and down. "You're going through withdrawal already?"

Trevor nodded, feeling the sweat collect on his forehead. "Please. Just hold it under my nose, one little bump." The delivery method didn't matter at this point, he just needed a fix.

"I would never enable your addiction," Howard self-righteously proclaimed. "You might view your time here as a blessing. You'll get through this ordeal and be clean on the other side."

"Don't act like you're helping me," Trevor spat back.

"I hope your appetite returns in time for dinner," Howard calmly changed the subject. "I'm making a harvest vegetable casserole and there's always too much for one person."

Trevor just shook his head in disbelief, watching Howard disappear up the stairs as his body began to shiver beneath the bindings. "Can I at least have my jacket?"

But the door closed halfway through his request, leaving him cold and alone as the fever set in, knowing the pain would come next.

All of it.

## 42

Two days. That was all it took for the call to come from Jake.

"I know you're done, Howie, but Chuck's got a new offer, a *real* offer, and I just couldn't forgive myself if I didn't let you know."

Howard played dumb on the phone as Jake told him how Trevor Mane's car was found abandoned, how he was likely on another bender, how Chuck was beyond pissed.

"The circumstances are truly dreadful," Howard responded, "but I suppose it couldn't hurt to hear Chuck's offer."

Mere hours later, Howard found himself back on the Pinnacle Studios lot, sitting across the big desk from Chuck Slattery with a pile of likely-unread scripts between them.

"I'm gonna be honest with you, Howard." That would be a refreshing change of pace. "We've got a lot of money invested in this thing and the kid screwed us over, big-time. What we need is a quick fix. Andrei loves you and I know you want the role, so let's just have Jake fast-track the paperwork and get this show on the road."

It was all so matter-of-fact, so emotionless. Like nothing had ever happened. But so much *had* happened and Howard could no longer let it go unsaid.

"I will consider bailing you out of this mess," Howard replied, "if you admit what you did and apologize."

"What I did?"

"Let me be more specific. You milked me like a cow for ten years, kicked me to the curb as soon as the money stopped flowing, and then you sought to *replace* me." The word still tasted bitter on his tongue, but Howard felt clear-headed. This was not the Reaper speaking. This was Howard Browning, years of unspoken resentments finally airing out.

Chuck defensively crossed his arms in front of his chest. "You're right. I did try to replace you. And let me be clear, I still can." He held up a printed list. "I've got at least a dozen hungry actors who would kill for this role."

*Not if we kill them first.*

Howard took a moment to suppress the voice. He didn't need the Reaper to fight his battles for him as he leaned forward, voice firm. "You may have won the fans over once, Chuck, but they won't go for it a second time. It reeks of a bomb in the making, no matter who's on that list of yours. At this point, they will only show up on opening night to see their one, true Reaper." Chuck visibly grit his teeth at the truth. Howard had him exactly where he wanted him. "Now. Apologize."

The stubborn producer finally threw up his hands. "Fine, I'm sorry."

*Make him beg. On his knees.*

Howard hesitated to take commands from the monster, but he wasn't altogether opposed to this particular suggestion as he recited the cold demand. "On your knees."

Chuck laughed out loud. "You're kidding, right? I'm not getting on my knees."

*Then we'll break them backward.*

Howard rose to his feet against his own will. He could feel the Reaper wanting to pounce across the desk and crack every bone in Chuck's body, but he managed to steer himself toward the door, dragging the beast within.

"Good luck with the film, Chuck," he called over his shoulder.

"Okay, okay, Christ." Chuck leapt from his leather chair. His stretched face went a fresh shade of red as he came around the desk and dropped to his knees at Howard's feet. "I'm sorry, Howard. I treated you like shit and you didn't deserve that. I should have been more . . . respectful."

Howard didn't realize how badly he needed to hear that apology until it finally came. Forced, yes, but there was an unexpected sincerity behind Chuck's words.

*Good. Now snap his neck like a wilted cornhusk.*

Howard watched his own hands move threateningly toward Chuck's head.

*Make him suffer. Like I suffered.*

He feared what might come next if he couldn't stop the Reaper, but he realized in this moment that it wasn't the monster who had suffered, who needed atonement now.

"To Lester," Howard commanded while his hands pressed against Chuck's cheeks. "Now apologize to Lester."

Chuck's brow furled. "You want me to apologize to the character?"

*"Say you're sorry."* The hoarse voice took the place of his own as Howard's thumbs slid under Chuck's upper lip, pushing the wet flesh back to reveal those bright porcelain teeth. *"Or I'll pull these pearly whites, one by one."*

Chuck swallowed the lump in his throat, terror in his eyes as he forced out the words, "I'm sorry, Lester, I'm so sorry!"

Howard closed his eyes, digesting the apology into the pit of his churning stomach, hoping it would save Chuck's life.

*By the skin of his teeth.*

The voice returned safely within as the tension in Howard's hands released.

"Thank you," he said, pulling a visibly shaken Chuck to his feet.

"Are we done now?" Chuck dusted off the knees of his slacks. "Can we save the performance for the cameras, please?"

"For now," Howard replied. He had successfully avoided violence, but he wasn't happy about how seamlessly the Reaper's influence was now weaving into his life. He just had to press onward, so close to the finish line now.

"Good," Chuck said as he moved a little too quickly back behind the safety of his desk. "Principal photography already started with the kids and you're scheduled to hit set in three days. They need you in wardrobe right now to fit the costume."

*Yes . . .* The Reaper groaned. *Bring me to my skin.*

## 43

The cellar was cold, but Trevor's chill ran deeper than his skin, itching its way into his bones. He was familiar with the aches and pains of full-on withdrawal, having ridden those crashing waves all the way to shore at Chrysalis. But that was in a cushy facility with couches and chocolate. A shit ton of chocolate. And support. He could no longer deny that Dr. Liz was a literal lifesaver. She gave him a new reason to live, a reason to believe that he *deserved* to live, and he really had believed that he could keep it up on the outside.

Yet here he was, back in the throes of his tiresome addiction, dying for a hit. He hated himself for caving like a coward after three months of sobriety. He never should've taken that red chip, never should've lied in front of all those people. Even though a maniac had tied him to a chair in this basement, Trevor only had himself to blame for his misery now. At least he finally had something to put in that self-reflection column of his Fourth Step.

"Trevor?"

The voice cut through the dark, soft and sweet. It couldn't be. "Sophie?"

The light bulb clicked on and there she was, standing in front of him, bathed in white light. He'd been in such a haze, he hadn't heard the door open or the footsteps down the stairs.

"You found me," he said, on the verge of tears.

"Oh, sweetie," she said, rushing to hug him.

"How did you find me?"

"You were struggling so much with the role, I figured maybe you came to talk to Howard Browning about it."

Trevor had never been more grateful for her limitless intuition.

"Let's get you out of this chair," she said, moving behind him to undo the bindings.

"Baby, I'm so sorry. For everything. I will never take you for granted again, I love you so much."

"If you love me, then why'd you try to kill me?" she asked in a tone soaked with sadness.

"What? No, honeybee, that was an accident." He needed to see her face, to explain. He never meant to hurt her, to leave her scarred.

"So you don't want me dead? Out of the way?"

"Of course not." Trevor's hands popped free and he was ready to wrap them around the only thing that mattered and never let go. "I want to spend the rest of my life with you." He stood, turning to Sophie, but her face was a shredded mess now, dripping with torn flesh as she grinned wide and the Reaper's voice emerged from her throat.

*"What life?"* Sophie's bloodstained hands grabbed Trevor's head and gave a hard twist. He heard his spine pop through the pain of tearing tendons as his limp body collapsed to the floor and he awoke with a start.

Trevor was still tied firmly to the chair, soaking in a pool of his own sweat as he scanned the dark space with panicked eyes.

No Sophie. No Reaper. Just a feverish nightmare.

Nobody else was here because nobody was ever going to find him here. He couldn't wait for someone to come rescue him.

He had to get himself the fuck out of this basement.

## 44

Howard buttoned up the flannel shirt, running his fingers along the familiar checkered pattern of red and black. The fabric was brand new and still had some creases in it from being folded in a warehouse somewhere. Stepping into the blue overalls next, he slid the crisp denim straps over each shoulder and looked down at the full costume.

All the pieces were there, but he couldn't help feeling that something was off. He pulled back the curtain to face the costumer, a short woman with cat-eye glasses.

"It's a bit too . . . fresh, isn't it?" he asked, squirming in the itchy fabric.

"Don't worry. Once we know it fits, we'll tear it and dirty it up real good for you," she assured him as he stepped in front of the full-length mirror. She adjusted the overalls with pins as Howard moved his arms around in circles.

"If you could adjust the right sleeve to be just an inch shorter than the left," he requested. The costumer gave him a confused look over the rims of her glasses. "Makes it easier to swing the chain," he explained.

"Sure." She tugged at his sleeve, pinning it back as Howard gazed into the mirror before him. Standing there in the Reaper's iconic costume, it was still Howard staring back. He waited for the voice in his head to speak up, but nothing came.

"Are you happy?" he whispered to his own reflection, prodding the monster.

"I'm happy if you are," the costumer responded, taking a step back. "Give it a go."

233

Howard blushed as he shook out his arm, then gave an empty-handed swing of the phantom chain. "Yes, that should do quite nicely. Thank you."

He left the wardrobe office with a renewed sense of confidence. The experience with Chuck had been frightening, but Howard had managed it well, and the beast was quietly appeased now. Yes, there was still a young man tied to a chair in his basement, but it wouldn't be long now before filming started and soon thereafter ended.

As he headed toward his car in the lot, he knew that he couldn't worry too far ahead. He just needed to take this one day at a time, focusing now on what Trevor might like for dinner. The vegetable casserole had not been a hit, so perhaps the boy would prefer some fast food or—

"Mr. Browning?" The soft voice startled him as he turned to see a timid young woman whose face he recognized all too well. "I'm sorry," she went on, "you don't know me." But he did. He knew her from the magazines. He knew her through the lens of his camera.

"My name is Sophie Boyd," she explained, "I'm Trevor's girlfriend. Trevor Mane." The girlfriend of the young man he'd kidnapped. The poor sad soul he saw crying that night as he hid in her backyard, stealing photos like a sleazy voyeur.

"Hello," was all he could muster in response.

"I heard you might be taking over the role," she said, dabbing at her eyes with a tissue. Howard had tried so hard not to think about the collateral damage of his actions. The young girl must've been up every night, losing sleep with worry, wondering if the love of her life was dead or alive.

"I'm just . . ." Howard started, "filling in until Trevor returns."

"I was actually just on my way to ask Mr. Slattery if he'd heard from Trevor at all," Sophie said, desperation trembling in her tiny voice. "I've been trying to call, but I couldn't get past his assistant."

"That sounds like Chuck," Howard replied. The shrewd producer had no time for concerned girlfriends and probably wouldn't care much if Trevor was found dead in a ditch somewhere. "But I've just come from his office and I'm afraid there's been no word."

Sophie nodded as Howard watched whatever hope she'd come here with get dashed away. "Right," she said. "Well, I'll let you go. Thanks. And good luck."

"Thank you. Take care."

Guilt swelled in Howard's chest as he turned away from the girl, heading for his car, but there was nothing he could do. Best not to get involved, it would only complicate matters at this point, make things worse.

"Actually," she squeaked behind him, stopping him in his tracks. "Would you like to get a cup of coffee with me?"

Howard turned back to see her eyes welling with fresh tears, putting all her energy into trying to keep it together. "I don't drink coffee . . ." he muttered, a delicate decline.

"I'm sorry. You're busy, forget it. It was nice meeting you." She shuffled away, palpably embarrassed.

"But tea would be wonderful." The words jumped to Howard's throat despite himself.

The girl spun back on her feet, a grateful smile brightening her face.

He couldn't help it. He felt he owed her something for the trauma he'd inflicted, and perhaps he could somehow ease her pain. Besides, what harm could come from one cup of tea?

## 45

Time moved strangely in the dark, but a long stretch had passed with no footsteps overhead, meaning Howard was probably out of the house.

If Trevor wanted to make his move, now was the time.

He tried to wiggle his hands free of the knot, but the friction only burned his skin. It was too tight, no hope of slipping free. He'd have to untie it. Reaching up with his fingertips, he could feel the neat interlocking loops. Ironclad. As he picked at the cracks between the knots with his fingernails, he wondered how many other people Howard had tied up before. The tip of Trevor's finger caught on the edge of the knot, until his nail bent backward with a sharp pain.

Fuck. No wriggling free, no untying it. He was stuck.

"You're not giving up that easily, are you?"

The voice startled him as Trevor looked up to see little Tommy Hooper, the *Family Genius* himself, sitting on the basement steps with an open textbook in his lap. It wasn't the first time Trevor's strung-out brain had conjured the character while wrestling with opioid withdrawal. Detox was a bitch.

"Got any recommendations?" Trevor asked his nine-year-old self, dressed in full costume with his red suspenders and bowtie.

Tommy held up his physics book, featuring diagrams of the chair with calculated angles. "The seat of this craftsman Adirondack chair is sloped backward at a forty-five-degree angle, making it rather difficult to fight the gravitational pull, especially in your weakened state."

"Yeah. I noticed," Trevor responded.

"In order to accommodate for the uniquely sloped seat, the rear legs are not built straight like most chairs, but rather angled back in the same direction." Tommy flipped a page in his book to show new diagrams of the chair with arrows and measurements of velocity. "Which means if you push up with your feet and tip back against the sloped legs, you should be able to build enough momentum to—"

"To fall backward and break the chair," Trevor cut him off. "You're a fucking genius!"

Tommy shook his head. "Mother wouldn't like that language. And I was going to say—"

"Fuck your mother. I've got this." Trevor slid his feet down, pushing off the tips of his shoes to tilt the chair back against the angled legs. His muscles were weak and his joints were throbbing from withdrawal. Sweat poured down his face, stinging his eyes as the front legs barely lifted. But when he let go, the chair tilted forward and he leaned with it, adding another inch or two. The chair swung back and then forward again, gaining a little further each time with momentum building now, nearing the tipping point on either end.

He gave one final tip back. This was it.

The chair hovered on its hind legs, but didn't fall. It swung forward again, a surge of unstoppable momentum pitching the wooden frame headlong. Trevor's face smashed against the hard cement as hot pain shot up his nose. He knew from one too many bar fights that his nose was broken for sure.

"I was going to say . . ." Tommy laid on the cement next to Trevor. "You should be able to build enough momentum to pitch the chair *forward*. But you'll need to brace for impact."

"Do me a favor, Tommy." Blood oozed in Trevor's mouth as he tongued his chipped front tooth. "Get lost."

Tommy sighed. "Indubitably."

As the hallucination faded from his drug-addled mind, Trevor began to think that he might actually die here. Like one of the thirty-three victims found buried in Gacy's crawlspace, except that Trevor was alone in his soon-to-be-grave.

Something fluffy rubbed up against his side with a soft purr.

Maybe he wasn't alone after all. This *was* real, Trevor was sure of it. Even through his smashed-up face, his allergies were kicking up as he saw the black cat out of the corner of his eye.

He tried desperately to remember the little creature's name. "Sammy! It's Sammy, right? Come back here, I've got a treat for you." Trevor started snapping his fingers behind his back.

Cats loved scratching things, right? If he could get the little clawed beast to scratch at the rope for long enough, he just might be able to escape.

Yes, this was an insane plan. But it was better than Tommy's shit idea.

"Come get your treat!" He kept snapping until the cat finally slinked toward his back, disappearing from view. Then he felt the soft pawing at his hands.

Holy shit. It was actually working.

"Come on. The rope, the rope." This was it. Talking to a cat was his only chance. If it actually worked, he swore he'd adopt a whole litter of the fuckers and become a Claritin junkie if he had to. Until the claws came out and the little monster started scratching away like crazy. Trevor couldn't tell if it was even striking any of the rope because all he felt were tiny razor blades slicing the flesh below his palms. Pain pulsed up his arms, straight to his head as he screamed into the cement floor.

Trevor really *was* going to die here. Because this fucking cat was going to slit his wrists and make him bleed out on the basement floor.

"Stop, fuck!" He tried to swat the beast away with his fingers, but the cat kept clawing and Trevor could feel his own blood spraying over his hands.

Rage welled in his chest, his frantic fingers finally wrapping around the cat's little skull. With a quick hard twist, the clawing instantly stopped. He released the limp corpse behind his back and sighed into the puddle of blood that was forming around his own broken face.

Trevor had never killed anything bigger than the spiders Sophie was so afraid of, and the thought of what he'd just done caused vomit to rise up from his stomach. He choked it down and swallowed it, not wanting to drown in a pool of his own disgusting fluids on this cold basement floor. He felt awful, snapping little Sammy's neck like that, but it wasn't Trevor's fault he'd been forced into this position. And if killing Howard's cat brought the old man just one ounce of pain, then it would be worth it just to see the look on the fucker's face.

# 46

Howard smiled nervously as he dunked his tea bag and Sophie wrapped her small hands around a mug of chai latte across the table from him. The coffee shop just off the Pinnacle lot was bustling with aspiring actors running lines and would-be screenwriters clacking away on clunky laptop computers as Sophie finally spoke up in her barely audible voice.

"Have you ever been married, Mr. Browning?"

Unprepared for the personal question, Howard hoped to buy time by lifting the hot tea to his mouth for a sip, but only scalded his lips in the process.

"I'm sorry," she said, noting his discomfort. Apologies seemed to drip from her like a leaky faucet. "I'm being rude."

"It's quite all right," Howard assured her through stinging lips. "Yes, I was married once. Her name was Emma." He hadn't spoken her name aloud in years

"How did you meet?" she asked, summoning a memory he'd tucked away long ago.

"Emma worked at a café across the street from my theater group in New York. Every day, I'd enter and order the same sandwich: egg salad on whole wheat. And every day, I would try to woo her with some romantic verse. One day it was Shakespeare, the next it was Byron. *She walks in beauty, like the night / Of cloudless climes and starry skies / And all that's best of dark and bright / Meet in her aspect and her eyes.*"

"Wow." Sophie's own eyes were twinkling now. "That is so romantic."

"I thought so, too," Howard smiled at the warm memory. "But every day, she turned me down. Until finally, I just walked right up to her and said, 'Hello. My name is Howard Browning. Would you like to go to dinner with me?' She looked me in the eyes for a long beat. '*There* you are,' she said. 'What took you so long?'"

Sophie exhaled in deep understanding. "She just wanted to see the real you."

"And she did." Howard swallowed the lump of regret in his throat. "But I'm afraid it didn't last."

Sophie nodded in response. "Both my parents and Trevor's got divorced when we were young. It's one of the things we bonded over, why we decided we'd never get married. So that every day, we would have to *choose* to be together. Like it would mean more that way."

"It's a romantic notion," Howard offered.

"It's easy to be romantic when you're young, right? But life just gets so complicated as you get older."

Howard nodded at a truth more potent than she could possibly know.

"How did you know that it was over?" she asked.

He knew the exact moment. But he couldn't share that now, couldn't even think about it. Still, he was compelled by her warmth to speak honestly. "I suppose you could say that Emma kept choosing me, every day. But at a certain point, I chose my work."

Sophie looked him straight in the eye. "You mean you chose the Reaper?"

Howard's mouth went dry as the voices in the shop around him fell out into silence. Perhaps he hadn't heard her right or it was another auditory hallucination. Either way, he didn't want to keep having this conversation. He just wanted to leave.

"I'm afraid I really don't have too much time . . ."

"Of course, I'm sorry. Can I just ask you one more thing?" Sophie urgently reached into her purse and pulled out a black notebook, placing it on the table between them. "I'm not sure if I should show you this. I really shouldn't have read it myself, but under the circumstances . . ."

"What is it?" Howard asked, curiosity rising as he opened the notebook.

"It's Trevor's Fourth Step journal, his personal moral inventory from NA."

Howard flipped through the pages, reading Trevor's words. An outpouring from the deep well of self-hatred the young man had described. *"I'm a piece of shit who ruins everything. I don't deserve Sophie. I don't deserve to live."*

"At least, it starts out that way," Sophie explained with a shiver. "But then it becomes . . . something else."

The further Howard flipped, the more ragged the writing became, the tone growing darker, pages inked in rage as a familiar wretched scrawl took shape.

THEY THINK I'M A JOKE BUT I'LL BE THE LAST ONE LAUGHING WHEN I REACH DOWN THEIR THROATS AND SHUT THEM UP FOR GOOD HAHAHAHAHAHAHAHAHA HAHAHAHAHAHAHAHAHAHAHAHAHAHAHAHAHAHA

No. It couldn't be. Trevor's words were etched in the same handwriting as Howard's notebooks. Because these were not Trevor's words.

They were the Reaper's.

*Surprise.* The beast whispered in Howard's skull. *I've been a busy boy.*

His hands began to quake as he came to a page filled with the Reaper's chain in an endless spiral. A carbon copy of his own sketch. He could barely hear Sophie as she continued to speak.

"I mean, I know it just looks like preparation for the role. It's just so . . . dark. Have you ever had these kinds of thoughts before?"

*Go ahead. Tell her.*

"No." Howard responded firmly to the voice, to Sophie.

But she kept pushing, desperate for validation. "So you don't think it's possible that the role is somehow . . . doing something to him?"

*Ripening his soul.*

"I'm sorry, Sophie." Howard snapped the notebook shut, trapping the darkness within, trying to hide the shudder that rippled beneath his skin. "But it's just a role, nothing more."

He only wished that were true as Sophie's face went flush.

"Right," she said. "Hearing myself out loud now, I realize I must sound like a crazy person to you."

"You're not crazy," Howard assured her, perhaps trying to assure himself.

"Neither is Trevor," she went on. "I mean, he's never been the most stable person in the world, but there have always been limits, boundaries with me. The night he disappeared, he was angrier than I've ever seen him. The way he treated me, the look in his eyes when he . . ." Sophie rubbed her wrist at some visceral memory. "Well . . . he wasn't himself. And I'm just scared that he's all alone in a really dark place right now."

Howard looked down at the notebook. "If it would make you feel better, I could take a closer look at this. See if anything strikes me. Does that sound all right?"

Sophie nodded, grateful through the tears that brimmed in her eyes, unable to speak as Howard stood up, hoping to escape before she found her words again.

"I really must be going." He gripped the notebook in his right hand as she reached out to squeeze his left.

"Thank you." Her voice was so quiet, barely more than a whisper, but filled with a depth of gratitude. With those bright eyes beaming up at him, Howard was compelled to comfort her.

"Just be patient. He'll come back to you, safe and sound, I'm sure of it. And when he does, you take him away, far away from here. Leave this toxic town behind and never look back."

Before Sophie could respond, Howard slipped from her grasp and hurried out of the coffee shop. Passing so many hopeful writers and actors already poisoned with Tinseltown's promises, he wanted to warn them all that chasing their dreams was a trap filled with untold nightmares. But he focused instead on the one soul he could still save. Howard only hoped he hadn't just lied to Sophie and that Trevor, all alone in that very dark place, wasn't dead yet.

## 47

"Trevor!"

The blood had dried and caked around his face by the time Trevor heard Howard's footsteps rushing down the wooden steps.

"What happened?" Howard lifted the chair upright.

"Sammy tried to kill me. But I got him first." Trevor was rubbing it in, reveling in the moment as he watched Howard's eyes fall toward the dead cat on the floor.

"Oh, Stanley." Howard dropped to his knees and scooped the little beast into his arms. "No, no, no." He buried his face in the black fur, convulsing with a deep sadness.

It didn't feel as good as Trevor had hoped, seeing Howard suffer. He thought the crazy bastard would be more pissed, but it was just sad to see the tears running down his wrinkled cheeks now. Howard reached for a Reaper beach towel from a pile of junk and wrapped the fury corpse with it.

"Look, I'm sorry." Trevor felt the need to justify his actions now. "But he almost cut my wrists open."

"It's quite all right, Trevor," Howard responded, still choked up as he swaddled the cat like a baby now. "I know it wasn't you."

"What's that supposed to mean?" Was Howard going to blame the disease of addiction now, too? Trevor was tired of being let off the hook for everything he did.

"You know, my parents never let me have a pet growing up," Howard said, eyes distant. "My mother thought they were too dirty, uncivilized. But one day, I found a sweet little bunny in the backyard. I snuck him into my bedroom and stole carrots from the fridge. When Mother caught me, she wanted to teach me a lesson. So she cooked the rabbit for dinner with a side of roasted carrots. I wasn't permitted to leave the table until I cleared my whole plate."

"Jesus," Trevor responded. "That's fucked up, man."

"And that was before my father got home to give me the belt," he went on, turning to Trevor now. "Did your father ever use his belt or just the back of his hand?"

"What makes you think my father hit me?" Trevor asked. His family drama had been pretty public back in the day, and maybe Howard was even more of a stalker than Trevor realized. But something about the old man's tone and the way he was ignoring the question again made him uneasy as Howard turned his attention back to the lump of dead cat in his arms.

"I'll find you a sunny spot beneath the azaleas," Howard whispered as he planted a kiss inside the towel before placing the corpse on the bottom step. A steaming mug was resting there and he retrieved it now, wiping the tears from his eyes.

"I can't fault you for trying to escape," Howard said. "It's a horrible position I've put you in, and I want to apologize."

"Great," Trevor responded. "You can start by letting me go."

"Not for keeping you here, no. I see now just how much this truly is for your own good."

Howard brought the mug to Trevor now. "But I thought you might like some hot cocoa. I read that withdrawal can be rather chilling and the sugar might help even you out."

Howard's compassion only made him seem crazier, but Trevor's whole body shivered as he stared at the steam rising from the mug. He imagined the sweet taste on his lips and he wanted it bad, but he looked away. He couldn't give the bastard the satisfaction.

"Trevor, please. There's no sense making this any more difficult than it need be."

Trevor held strong for a moment before finally giving in, turning his head back as Howard gently tilted the mug to give him a sip. He couldn't deny it. The instant that warm sugary mixture filled his mouth, he felt a rush of warmth and joy, taking him back to Wisconsin winters as a child. It was damn good hot chocolate, but he bunched up his face in performative disgust as he swallowed.

"It's too sweet," he lied.

Howard didn't seem offended, probably seeing straight through Trevor's bullshit as he looked him in the eye. "I used real chocolate, not that horrid powder. Just the way your grandmother used to make it."

Trevor's chest burned with a different kind of heat now. "What the fuck did you just say?" How could Howard know all of this personal shit?

"As I was saying, I want to apologize . . . for underestimating you. I thought you couldn't possibly understand the true depths of the Reaper's madness. But it seems I was wrong."

Howard held up a black notebook, a Moleskin, just like the one Trevor had been doing his Fourth Step in. Then he noticed the slight bend on the corner of the cover, from when he'd thrown it across the room while doing character work the other night. That *was* his notebook. From the desk in his office, from inside his fucking house.

"How the fuck did you get that?!" Trevor barked. He'd bared his whole fucking soul in those pages, every memory and grievance from childhood to now. That was how Howard knew so much.

"Sophie gave it to me," Howard calmly replied.

Trevor's blood surged like a hurricane. "If you laid a hand on her, I will fucking kill you, do you hear me?! I'll kill you!" he screamed, his muscles straining against the bindings, wanting to burst free and finish what he'd started on that HorrorCon stage.

"Relax, Trevor. You don't seem to believe me, but I'll tell you again. I have no intention of hurting you, or anyone else for that matter."

Howard was right. Trevor didn't believe him. "Then why the fuck were you talking to my girlfriend, Howard?"

"She found your notebook and was distraught. She just needed someone to talk to."

Trevor was crushed by the thought of Sophie reading all his resentments about her, but it must have crushed her more. Still, why would she want to talk to Howard about that?

"Talk to me, Trevor. That's what you came here for in the first place, isn't it? So why don't you tell me what this is?" Howard opened the Moleskin.

"It's called recovery, working the steps. And it's none of your goddamn business."

"I'm not concerned about that part," Howard said, going deeper into the notebook. "I'm concerned about this."

He held up a page of angrily scratched words that Trevor hardly recognized as his own. From where he sat, he could only make out one line. PAIN AND SUFFERING FESTERS IN MY HEART BUT I WILL GIVE IT ALL BACK TO THEM WHEN I FLAY THEIR SKIN AND SHOWER THE CROPS WITH THEIR BLOOD

Trevor had almost forgotten those late nights when he'd unconsciously slip from Fourth Step work into role preparation, drifting along in a cloud of H. Chasing the dragon and finding the monster as the Reaper's thoughts flowed out of him and onto the page. It felt like he was connecting with something larger than himself, like some Higher Power was helping him bring the character to life while he just stood by and watched from the sidelines.

"Despite what everyone thinks," Trevor replied, "I *am* a fucking professional who knows how to prepare for a role."

Howard kept flipping, holding up another page, where the Reaper's rusty chain spiraled out in a circle of black ink. Trevor vaguely remembered drawing it, but it felt like a distant dream. There'd been something entrancing, soothing about drawing the endless chain as he zoned in and zoned out, link by link.

"Have you heard it yet?" Howard asked.

"Heard what?"

"The Reaper's chain. Clank. Clank." There was a haunted look in Howard's eyes as he held up a different notebook, opening the marbled cover and flipping to a page with the same image of the spiraling chain.

"What is that?" Trevor asked.

"*My* preparation."

It was strange, for sure, but obviously just a coincidence. The same character with the same iconic weapon was bound to inspire the same imagery.

"Have you seen him?" Howard took a step closer. "Has he spoken to you?"

"Howard . . . Are you hearing voices?"

"Just the one," Howard replied, as if it was the sanest thing in the world. "I know you must think I'm crazy. That's what Dr. Cho thought and so did I, for a little while. Until I realized that the Reaper is something much more than a role. And this is proof."

Trevor realized now just how far Howard's mind had cracked. Sure, Trevor may have had a harmless vision of little Tommy Hooper, but that was just his detoxing brain trying to regulate its dopamine. What Howard was describing amounted to a Son of Sam level schizophrenic delusion. Trevor was terrified to be in the grips of a violent madman, but at least he knew his angle now. He'd seen Dr. Liz deal with his roommate Ryan's PTSD flashbacks in group sessions. He watched the way she gently guided him out of his hallucinations and back to reality. If he could walk that tightrope with Howard now, he might be able to negotiate a truce.

"What is he saying to you, Howard? What is he making you do?" Trevor asked.

"I gave him everything, but it wasn't enough. Take a look around, Trevor." Howard gestured to the cellar full of Reaper clutter. "Is this the life you want? Are you prepared to shun your own happiness, to push Sophie away just to make more room for the monster? I can promise you, it's not worth it."

Trevor listened between the words and found his in. Howard was speaking from personal experience and all Trevor needed to do was crack open his vulnerability. "Who did *you* push away, Howard?"

The old man's face drained of color as he turned away, whispering. "Emma . . ."

"I don't want to make the same mistake." Trevor had struck a nerve and wasn't going to let up now. "Please. Tell me what happened to Emma."

## 48

Howard hadn't consciously thought about that night in so many years.

The night he lost Emma.

It was as though the memory lay entombed here in the cellar with everything else, but now was the time for all that pain to come out of the dark and into the light, flooding back to him and flowing out of his mouth as he told Trevor everything.

"After the first four films, back to back with press in between, I hardly had time to be home with her. But we had made plans, once the franchise ended, to settle down and start a family. With the Reaper burned and buried, I thought we were in the clear, and we'd already started trying for a baby. But then Chuck called. He said that *The Final Reaping* was too big a success to stop now. The fans wanted more. It was time to dig the monster from his grave and make another film. I begged him for a break, just a year off in between, but he assured me that the films would go on, with or without me. So I told Emma, I said I didn't have a choice. She said that I did, that I *always* had a choice. But that I'd already made it. I had chosen the Reaper. We never fought before, not really, but that night was a blur of pacing and screaming."

Howard looked up through the open cellar door now, watching the memory on replay as two shadowy figures moved back and forth across the threshold. Their muffled shouts echoing overhead.

"Until finally, she declared that she needed a break. If I was leaving again for filming, then she would go stay with her mother. I watched help-lessly as she opened the cellar door to get her suitcase, in such a hurry as she started down the stairs. Then I heard the awful sound as she tripped, tumbling down every step, all the way to the floor."

Howard watched now as Emma came falling down the stairs toward him, limbs splayed and cracking until she slammed down on the hard concrete at his feet. She looked up into his eyes, gasping wordlessly.

"I didn't know, she hadn't told me," he uttered, reaching down for her as blood pooled between her legs. "That she was already pregnant."

He squeezed his eyes shut to stop the tears. When he opened them, Emma was gone. It was too late and had been for many years.

"If I had known, if she had told me that I was already becoming a father, then maybe I could have chosen differently." Howard hung his head now, haunted by the life he never lived. "But I didn't. The child was lost in the fall. Emma left me as soon as she was released from the hospital. She sent her mother to collect her things and then the divorce paperwork came in the mail. I never heard another word. She left me here, alone with the legacy I chose."

Howard looked around at the cellar once more. It should have been filled with the memories of a family. Boxes of outgrown children's clothes and stacks of vacation videos. Instead, it was teeming with cheap Halloween costumes and unrated collectors' tapes. The makings of a monster.

His eyes landed back on Trevor, who was frozen in shocked silence. Howard was an open wound in the aftermath of his solemn confession, desperate for some kind of healing recognition. He hoped that if anybody could understand, it was Trevor.

All he could do now was wait for the young man to speak.

## 49

"I get it," Trevor started.

The story was fucked up, but if he had any hope of getting through to Howard, it was going to be through empathy. Sharing your most shameful truths was an important part of recovery and he needed to open up with some honesty himself now, to create the same kind of trust he'd found in his sponsor.

"*Family Genius* robbed me of my childhood. The money tore my parents apart, and my friends resented my fame. Eventually, even my fake family deserted me. I know how you feel, Howard. You really have given up everything for this role, and I can see that it's tearing you apart. But can I suggest something that might help?"

Howard paused before answering, clearly doubtful that Trevor could offer any helpful advice. But Trevor was being honest and maybe that made the difference in Howard finally asking, "What do you suggest?"

"Make amends to Emma. You're carrying around this guilt for a choice you made years ago, for an accident that wasn't your fault. You have to find a way to clear your conscience and let it go if you ever want to be free."

Trevor was speaking from a place of secondhand hope, sharing the experience he heard other fellows share in the rooms. He still hadn't made amends to Sophie and he could only hope that he'd get the chance. If he ever got out of here. That hope was hanging by a thread now on Howard's response.

"I tried the cathartic route at HorrorCon. It didn't go so well," Howard confessed. "Besides, this has nothing to do with her anymore."

"From where I'm sitting, it has everything to do with her. You can't escape the Reaper because of everything you sacrificed for it. But if you come to peace with losing Emma, losing your baby . . . if you finally get some closure, then the monster won't have any power over you." Trevor was speaking Howard's language now, hoping to break through.

Howard looked deep in thought before he finally shook his head. "No, I could never drag her back into this. All I can do now is see it through. And make sure that you don't take my place." Trevor deflated as Howard held up the Moleskin again. "You're right about one thing, though. This *is* preparation. It's the Reaper preparing *you*. In case I fail." Howard smiled sadly. "My understudy. He got to you so quickly, didn't he? Perhaps your addiction primed you. Feeding your id like that only made you an easier target."

Trevor bristled as his patience ran out. "You don't fucking know me."

"Perhaps not. But the Reaper does. He's seen into your soul now, figured out how to pull your strings. How to make you do things you would never do." Howard punctuated that last comment by scooping up the dead cat again. "I'm sorry, Trevor. I'm sorry that it's come so far. But you will never know the full burden. I'm going to see to that. It's my job to feed the beast. My legacy, not yours. I gave it life and I shall see to its death."

Trevor no longer had the will to fight back as he closed his eyes, listening to Howard lumber back up the stairs. A strange sensation washed over him now, something like a calm resignation. Back when he was working Step One with Dr. Liz, he had to admit out loud that he was powerless. But he'd never actually felt it the way he did right now, like every cell in his body was opening wide in surrender.

Trevor had no control over this situation, but something about that was freeing. He was terrified at what might come next, trapped in this madman's delusion, but he knew he had no control over that either. For the first time in his adult life, he did what every sober person said you should do when you feel truly powerless.

Trevor bowed his head and prayed.

## 50

"Funerals are pretty compared to deaths." Howard quoted Blanche DuBois over Stanley's freshly dug grave in the front yard. He kept vigil until sunset before leaving his furry companion in that final resting place.

Curling up in the big empty bed that night, the absence of Stanley's soft purr was pure agony. Still, Howard didn't blame Trevor for the violent act, and it had felt good to share so openly with his unexpected confidant. Even when Trevor made that ludicrous suggestion of making amends to Emma.

All those years ago, when she left without a word, Howard did try to reach out to her. But Emma's mother played gatekeeper and made it clear that she didn't want to see him or hear from him again. It was understandable, wanting to move on from the trauma of the miscarriage. If he did want to reach out to her now, to make amends, he wouldn't know where to begin finding her.

He supposed he could try calling Emma's mother again. He didn't know the number by heart anymore, but it was listed on the divorce papers he still had stashed away in the study. Then he could put his acting skills to use by putting on a false voice and pretending to be an old friend of Emma's, from Springwood High, hoping to reconnect for an alumni fundraiser.

It was a ridiculous plan. But it worked. Howard soon found himself sitting on the edge of the bed with the phone to his ear as he transcribed Emma's phone number onto a Post-it Note.

"Thank you so much, Mrs. Weston," he spoke in his best DuBois drawl. "You have yourself a lovely evening now." Howard hung up and stared at the Post-it.

Emma was just ten numbers away now. Could he really call her to apologize after all these years? Was Trevor right about the freedom that lay on the other side?

He decided that he had nothing to lose as he dialed the number. His heart went quiet as he sat there, listening to the endless silence between every ring until someone finally answered on the other end.

"Hello?"

It was Emma's voice, clear and bright. He hadn't heard it in years, not outside of his dreams, but he was certain it was her.

"Emma. I'm sorry to be calling so late."

". . . who is this?" she asked.

"It's me. Howard."

A long pause on the other end.

"What do you want, Howard?" she finally asked, her tone dripping with dread.

"I know this might seem strange, I just . . . I wanted to apologize. For everything. You were the most important thing in the world to me, and I never should have gone back to the Reaper." Tears were quietly streaming down Howard's cheeks now, but he wouldn't let that sadness creep into his voice as he tried to remain strong. "The night you fell, the night we lost our child . . . I only wish I could go back and—"

"I fell?" Emma repeated on the other end. "Is that how you remember it?"

A weight sunk in Howard's stomach as he breathed an uncertain response. ". . . Yes?"

*Sorry!* The Reaper beamed like a demented quiz show host. *That's the wrong answer.*

"I didn't fall, Howard." Emma said with authority. "You pushed me."

The memory returned like a bolt of lightning, igniting a vision. Emma, turning her back to him, opening the cellar door. Howard's arms shooting out to shove her across the threshold.

He nearly dropped the phone now, remembering with painful clarity. "I pushed you . . ."

"Mom?" The voice of a teenaged boy in the background. "Can I have the car keys?"

"Here you go, buddy," a man's voice responded.

Howard listened to the sounds of a complete family on the other end of the line as he sat alone on the empty bed.

"Howard, listen to me," Emma spoke firmly. "I have a new life now, a good life. If you try to reach out to me again, I will call the police."

"Why didn't you? All those years ago, after what I did?" Howard was desperate to understand now. "Why didn't you tell the police, the divorce lawyer, *any*body?"

He heard Emma take a deep breath, like she was weighing whether or not she wanted to tell him the truth. "Because I heard it in your voice that night. I saw the look in your eyes before you did it. It wasn't really you who pushed me. It was . . ."

*Say my name.*

Howard could hear the phone trembling in Emma's hand. "It was someone else," she finally said.

Howard opened his mouth to speak, wanting to ask her more, to tell her everything that was happening to him now, but she spoke first. "Goodbye, Howard. Don't call again."

A loud click resounded before the dial tone kicked in.

Howard sat with the phone to his ear for a few moments before finally turning it off and lowering it to his side. He had gotten closure, just as Trevor had suggested. Emma was gone for good, and Howard deserved to be alone for what he did to her.

He couldn't believe he'd forgotten what actually happened that night. This meant that the gaps in his memory had started much earlier than he realized, decades before his Alzheimer's diagnosis. He struggled to process the implications of this revelation as two heavy hands crept up from the bed behind him, resting on his shoulders with a harsh whisper in his ear.

*It's just you and me.*

Howard looked at those ragged hands missing fingernails.

*It's always been you and me.*

He understood now. The Reaper's dark influence had been active all along, ever since Howard birthed the monster into this world. A silent puppeteer, no longer quiet.

*It will always be you and me.*

The hands squeezed Howard's shoulders tight as he leaned back into the arms of the beast.

*Forevermore.*

# 51

Trevor sat in the dark, repeating the Serenity Prayer over and over again like a force field to protect against the murky memories that were trying to resurface.

"God, grant me the serenity to accept the things I cannot change . . ."

Something about Howard's story had needled Trevor's unconscious as he started to think about the night he didn't want to think about.

". . . the courage to change the things I can . . ."

The night he hadn't told Dr. Liz the whole truth about.

". . . and the wisdom to know the difference."

The night of the accident.

Sophie's coworker had invited them to a party and Trevor reluctantly agreed. But when they got to the cramped studio apartment, he saw that it wasn't a real party, at least not like the ones he was used to. The group gathered around in a circle to play tedious board games, each nursing a glass of wine while Trevor sipped a seltzer. He promised Sophie he wouldn't drink that night, that he would be on his best behavior, and he was determined to do so. Even though the excruciatingly slow game of Settlers of Catan was driving him fucking crazy.

When his agent Greg called with some news, he managed to sneak away to the bathroom to take the call. Another audition hadn't gone his way. They just couldn't see past that adorable little boy from *Family Genius* to envision Trevor in any other role. He was used to this response by now, but tonight, he found himself at a breaking point. He was done with

Hollywood, done with all the tap dancing and the bullshit. He wanted to burn the whole goddamn town to the ground.

Sophie had pushed her normal one-glass limit by having a second serving of red wine, so she asked Trevor to drive home. He agreed, of course, since he hadn't been drinking. What he didn't tell her was that he'd lit up his pipe in the bathroom.

Trevor tried to focus on the road, to act as normal as possible while Sophie studied him from the passenger seat. But he could never hide from her.

"Trevor. Are you high?" she asked in her motherly tone.

Trevor denied it, which escalated into an argument as Sophie begged him to pull over, to let her drive. But he refused, saying she was overreacting and he was fine. He kept saying that right up until the crash.

It was an accident. That's what the police report said. Trevor had been under the influence and when he finally did try to pull over, to let Sophie drive, he had tugged the wheel just a little too quickly and they veered off the road, right into a palm tree on Ventura Boulevard.

But the police report didn't know everything.

As Trevor sat alone now in the basement, strapped to his chair, he felt as if he were under interrogation. He could vaguely sense another presence in the room, someone standing behind him in the darkness. A devil breathing down his neck, urging him to dig back and face the truth.

To remember that he'd made up his mind that night to end it all.

Yes, Trevor had pulled the wheel just a little too hard. But he'd done it on purpose. He crashed the car because he didn't want to live anymore. He wanted to put himself out of his own misery, and in that split-second decision, he didn't care that he was taking Sophie with him.

When he woke up in the hospital with barely a scrape and learned that Sophie was still in a coma, he didn't understand. How could he have fucked this up, too? He failed to take his own life, and he might have killed the woman he loved in the process.

The only way he could make sense of it was to believe that he'd been granted a new lease on life, a second chance to make things right. If Sophie came out of that coma, he wasn't going to waste the chance to do things differently. He would get clean and stay sober and make it all up to her. He would stop being so wrapped up in his own bullshit and focus on making her happy. He would change.

But he hadn't changed. Not yet.

Trapped in his cellar prison cell, Trevor's mind was finally clear as the last dregs of withdrawal flushed from his system. He felt strong and sure as he pressed his muscles against the bindings. He wanted to break free and run all the way home, wrap his arms around Sophie and tell her how sorry he was. Promise her that he'd never hurt her again and mean it. He wanted to take the second chance that he'd already thrown away, dig it up and give it new life.

And if he had to kill Howard Browning in order to do that, he decided that he would.

## 52

Howard hadn't slept a wink with the Reaper cradling him through the night, whispering in his ear and keeping him awake. But he felt a profound sense of clarity as the morning sun blazed through the windows.

The light of day stung his vision as he got up to close the curtains, but not before he saw a car pulling up to the house below. At this distance, he couldn't quite make out the face of the man who climbed from behind the wheel and surveyed the house before approaching the porch.

Howard had feared some sort of detective would come calling eventually, but he wasn't prepared for it today as he got dressed as quickly as possible. By the time he made it down the stairs, the man still hadn't knocked as Howard watched the shadow through the window roaming about the porch. He opened the door to find the stranger squatting over the floorboards in an unsettlingly investigative fashion.

"Hello," Howard feigned surprise at the sight of him, closing the door behind him. "May I help you?"

The olive-skinned man stood and turned to face him with a sparkling smile, framed by an expertly trimmed goatee. "Howard Browning?"

"Yes?" As Howard shook the man's offered hand, he got a good look at the handsome stranger and realized that he recognized him, though he couldn't quite place where from.

"Danny Alvarez." Of course. Howard had seen that face on comic book movie posters plastered all over town. So he wasn't a detective after all. Just another actor.

"Pleasure to meet you, Mr. Alvarez. But may I ask what you're doing on my porch?" Howard asked. Was that too defensive? No, it would be strange *not* to be suspicious of a man snooping around outside your home.

"I'm sorry. I was gonna knock and then I realized how early it was, so I figured I'd just wait. But since you're up, you mind if I come in for a cup of coffee?"

"I'm afraid I don't have any coffee and I was just on my way out." Howard stood firm as Danny nodded.

"Right. Well, I won't hold you up too long. See, I'm a friend of Trevor Mane." Danny paused after saying the name, as if trying to get a read on Howard's reaction.

Howard remembered the call Trevor had received and fumbled to find the right words. "Yes, I saw that the boy had gone missing. You think I know something about his disappearance?"

"Now why would I think that?" Danny played "taken aback" well. The actor might not be a detective, but Howard felt like he was under interrogation, being baited into saying too much.

"Well, I can't imagine why else you would be here."

"Guess that's true," Danny acknowledged. "I'm here because I just met with Sophie, Trevor's girlfriend. She told me you two had a nice chat."

Howard knew that little tea time would come back to bite him. What was he thinking?

"Yes. I have great sympathy for the girl. We ran into each other by chance on the Pinnacle lot."

"Right. Because you're taking over the Reaper film, now that Trevor's gone."

"'Gone' seems a harsh way to put it, don't you think?"

Danny squinted at Howard. "Sophie mentioned that about you. That you seemed pretty convinced Trevor would come back. It's actually the main reason I'm here, to ask what makes you so sure."

Howard should never have reassured her so cavalierly, but he tried to shrug it off now. "I suppose I'm an optimist, Mr. Alvarez. Aren't you?"

Danny shook his head. "No. No, I'm afraid I'm nothing more than a grim realist. Can I be honest with you, Mr. Browning?"

"Please do."

"Trevor isn't just a friend. He's my sponsee, in Narcotics Anonymous. And I've seen enough kids in program fall off the wagon and go missing, only to get found facedown in a gutter somewhere, too late for saving."

Howard felt sudden relief. Perhaps the cover story he'd fed to the press was working better than he thought. "I'm sorry to hear that, Mr. Alvarez. But I do hope you're wrong about Trevor."

"So do I. That's why it's worth taking every shot in the dark, no matter how unlikely. So Mr. Browning. Have you heard anything from Trevor lately?"

Howard shook his head. "No, I'm afraid I haven't seen him since HorrorCon."

Danny held Howard's gaze for a long beat. "Okay. Well, like I said. Shot in the dark. Guess I'll be on my way. Thanks for your time."

"You're welcome. And good luck." Howard turned back to the front door.

"Thought you said I caught you on your way out," Danny said.

Howard froze with his hand on the doorknob. "It's colder than I expected this morning. I'm going to need a jacket." He opened the door, desperate to escape inside.

"Oh, one last question." This man was relentless.

"Yes?" Howard turned back to face him.

Danny took a step forward across the porch. "Are you in program?"
"Program?"

"AA, NA, GA? Any of the anonymous groups?"

Howard was puzzled by the question. "If I were, telling you wouldn't be very anonymous, now would it?"

"No, I guess it wouldn't," Danny smiled.

"Regardless, the answer is no, Mr. Alvarez," Howard said. "I am not in program. Why do you ask?"

Danny dangled a red plastic coin from a beaded keychain. "Because I found this on your porch. It's a three-month chip. Just like the one I gave Trevor, right before he went missing."

Howard's heart clenched. It must have fallen out of Trevor's pocket when he collapsed on the porch. He'd meant to scrub down the whole area that night, but he was too exhausted by the time he'd gotten back from disposing of Trevor's car.

Howard was caught now, speechless. There was no coming back from this.

"So what say we cut the bullshit, Mr. Browning." Danny took another step forward, uncomfortably close now as his already-large frame seemed to grow. "And you tell me just what the hell is going on?"

Howard weighed his options in a fraction of a second before the words spilled out. "Trevor's inside. He came to me, stressed about the role, very much under the influence." The truth flowed easily, which made the lie that came next sound all the more convincing. "He was looking for a place to get clean, off the grid where no one would find him. Especially not the paparazzi. So I took him in, and I swore I wouldn't tell a soul until he was absolutely ready."

Danny sighed. Had he bought the story or was he about to call Howard out on his lies again?

"You're a good man." Danny put a hand on Howard's shoulder and it eased down with relief. "But Trevor needs real help now. So why don't you take me to him?"

A new tension filled Howard's body as the Reaper commanded.

*Open that door and show the man what he's won.*

Howard opened the door and stepped into the house with Danny following close behind. He didn't know what would happen next, but he knew it wasn't up to him anymore as the door closed behind them, shutting out the light of the day.

## 53

Trevor heard a scream, echoing down from somewhere up above, followed by the thumping sounds of a struggle.

Something was happening up there, someone else was here.

"Help!" Trevor screamed to the ceiling, hoping that someone could hear him, that he would finally be rescued from this pit. But the sounds above soon went silent and he stopped yelling to listen. A single set of slow footsteps descended the stairs overhead, coming down the hall now as the cellar door opened.

"Howard?" Trevor called to the silhouette at the top of the stairs.

"Yes," Howard softly replied, drifting down the cellar steps in darkness and leaving the overhead bulb off as he stood beneath it.

"What was that scream?" Trevor asked, afraid to find out the answer.

"Scream? I didn't hear a scream. It's the Reaper, Trevor, he makes you hear things that aren't there."

Was that true? Had Trevor imagined the sound? No. No, he wasn't fucking crazy. Not like the maniac who was stalking back and forth in front of him now.

"But it's okay," the shadowy Howard spoke. "I understand everything now. He explained it all to me last night, his motivation, like you asked. You see, I thought that I had chosen the Reaper over Emma. But I was wrong. I never had a choice. I was chosen, possessed. He needs the films to survive, to live eternally. Every cinematic massacre is a ritual, a blood sacrifice, immortalized on celluloid. The fans, they play their role, too, in this cycle of worship. He feeds on their souls, these witnesses to his ascension, and he's been waiting, in hibernation, living off the scraps of conventions. News of another film awakened the beast, hungrier and louder than ever. Desperate for the next true offering."

Trevor watched helplessly as the madman forced the fractured puzzle pieces of his psyche into place.

"Emma, she wanted me to stop the films, she threatened to disrupt the ritual. So he pushed her."

"Wait . . ." Trevor responded. "You *pushed* her?"

"*He* pushed her, Trevor, the Reaper did!" Howard bellowed. "He won't let anyone get in his way, not Emma, not you, not Danny . . ."

A wave of horror crashed over Trevor. That scream. He recognized the voice now.

"Howard. Was Danny here?"

"Yes, such a sweet man. He really does care about you. But he's gone now."

Trevor suppressed a painful shudder. "What did you do to him?"

"Nothing. I didn't do a thing," Howard responded with a little too much emphasis on the "I." Trevor couldn't see well in the dark, but it looked like there was something streaked across Howard's hands, glimmering when the dim light from upstairs caught it. Was it blood? Did he even want to know?

"Howard, listen to me." Trevor focused his attention on his crazed captor. "You are not possessed. You're sick. And so am I, I'll be the first to admit that. We're just a couple of weak little men, lashing out because our daddies beat us and our mommies didn't love us. It's a clichéd backstory, man, and it's no fucking excuse." Seeing himself reflected in Howard gave Trevor a newfound clarity. A spiritual awakening, just like they promised in program. He didn't want to end up like the broken man before him. He had to get through to him.

"The Reaper is a role," Trevor continued, "an outlet for our worst fucking selves. But you can't blame anything you've done on some fictional character. It's *you*, Howard, and you have the power to end this. You always have a choice, just like Emma said. And it's not too late to take responsibility for your actions and let me go. Please."

Trevor waited with bated breath for a response to his honest plea.

Howard nodded quietly. Had Trevor actually gotten through to him?

"Don't worry, Trevor," Howard replied. "It's almost over. Production begins tonight. The devil will get his due and soon we'll both be free. One last film, that was the deal. This remake is special, you see. It serves as a sort of bookend for the beast, brings everything full circle to the beginning, to completion. Then he can rest, too."

"Howard." Trevor spoke calmly, playing into the twisted mythology that Howard had cooked up. "If you truly believe that the Reaper is real, then you have to know that he can't be trusted. So what if this last film isn't enough? What if he wants more?"

"Then I'll end it myself," Howard replied with confidence. It was clear he'd already thought that through, already decided. "You have my word."

Trevor saw the resignation in those worn eyes, the suicidal glint he knew all too well in a man with nothing to lose. There was nothing left to say as he watched Howard leave. He might feel sad for the old man, if he wasn't so scared for his own life.

If he wasn't so sure he'd heard that scream.

If he wasn't so sure that Howard Browning had just killed a man.

## 54

Howard emerged from the cellar and walked down the hallway toward the front door. He tried to remember what had happened with Danny once they crossed that threshold, when his memory went blank. He could peek out the window right now to see if Danny's car was still there, but no, he was sure the man had left safe and sound. Howard went straight up the staircase instead, determined to get some rest before filming.

As he walked past the spare bedroom, his makeshift darkroom, the smell behind the door was overwhelming. Chemicals, for sure, but something else as well. The truly foul stench stopped him in his tracks as the memory flooded back into his mind.

"Trevor's just in here," he'd told Danny.

As they entered the darkroom, Howard reached for the bottle of acetic acid from the shelf. He didn't have time to slip on his safety gloves as Danny flipped on the light, the red bulb casting the room in a crimson glow.

"Where is he?" Danny asked, looking around the empty room.

*"Here."* The Reaper growled through Howard.

Danny turned back just as Howard's arm swung down with the glass bottle, smashing it over the unsuspecting man's head. Danny screamed as the acid burned through the flesh of his face, skin dripping as he gurgled blood. His hands shot at Howard's throat, gripping in an angry clutch with those bulging arms as his eyelids melted over, mouth twisting in agony.

Howard gasped, his hand still gripping the broken bottleneck as he jabbed the sharp glass into Danny's throat with one deep puncture.

He pulled it out and blood flowed like a garden hose as Howard shoved Danny back over the table, toppling to the floor in a heap of flailing limbs. Howard left the room and slammed the door behind him.

The door that he was now stopped in front of, smelling the sickening aroma of burnt flesh. But was he really smelling it? He saw the blood on his hands now, but couldn't be sure that was real, either. Was Danny really dead behind that door or was it just another hallucination?

It all seemed so absurd now as Howard convinced himself that the Reaper was playing tricks on him. Still, he decided it was best not to open the door and find out. Better to leave it closed, take a nice long bath and go to bed.

After washing himself clean, Howard crawled beneath the covers with a sense of calm resolve, hoping that the beast would let him sleep through the day now. Tonight would finally mark the end of the Reaper, and he needed to be well rested for his final performance.

*Night of the Reaper Part VII: Seed of the Reaper* (1988)
Script Pages Courtesy of Pinnacle Studios

INT. ASHLAND GENERAL HOSPITAL - NIGHT

Jess SCREAMS on the hospital bed with Andy by her
side and the Doctor between her legs.

> DOCTOR
>
> Push!

> JESS
>
> I'm pushing!

> ANDY
>
> You've got this, sweetie!

Andy squeezes Jess's hand as she looks up into the
sterile fluorescent lights above. She gives another
big push as a nearby monitor frantically BEEPS.

> JESS
>
> What's going on?

> DOCTOR
>
> It looks like the umbilical cord
> is caught around the baby's neck.

> JESS
>
> No! I will not lose my baby!

> ANDY
>
> Hey. That's not gonna happen.
> (turning to Doctor)
> Right?

The doctor wipes the sweat from his brow.

> DOCTOR
>
> Jessica. On the count of three, I
> need you to push as hard as you
> can. Okay?

                              JESS
                    Okay.


                              DOCTOR
                    One . . . two . . . three!

Jess SCREAMS as she pushes with all of her strength,
until her scream is overtaken by the sound of a
BABY'S FIRST CRY.

                              DOCTOR
                    Congratulations!

Andy kisses Jess's head, both gushing with joy.

                              ANDY
                    Is it a boy or a girl?

                              DOCTOR
                    It's . . . it's a . . .

The doctor's eyes go wide in horror as the fluorescent lights FLICKER. The baby's CRY turns into a
wicked little CACKLE.

                              DOCTOR
                    It's a monster!

A slimy umbilical cord chain WHIPS around the doctor's neck. With a sickening CRACK, he collapses
out of sight.

                              JESS
                    Oh my God . . .

Jess grabs Andy's arm, terrified.

                              JESS
                    Andy . . .

But Andy backs away from the bed.

                    ANDY
         What the hell was that thing?
         Jess. Who's the father of that
         baby?

The lights CUT OUT, bathing the delivery room in
PITCH DARKNESS. A strange VOCAL HUMMING resounds
as the lights FLICKER BACK ON to reveal . . .

A TRIO OF BLACK-CLOAKED FIGURES behind Andy.

                    JESS
         Andy!

CLOAKED FIGURE #1 puts a ceremonial dagger to
Andy's throat, SLICING it open as blood splatters
on Jess's face.

                    JESS
         No!

Andy's limp body drops to the linoleum floor. CLOAKED
FIGURE #2 wraps the bloody baby in a white blanket.

                    JESS
         Don't touch my baby! Who are you?!

The third figure steps up to speak, face hooded in
darkness.

                    CLOAKED FIGURE #3
         We are the Sacred Order of the
         Harvest Moon. We have presided
         over Ashland for centuries,
         cutting the wheat from the chaff.
         The Reaper is our eternal servant,
         but he must be reborn. He must be
         nurtured. And he has chosen you,
         Jessica.

Cloaked Figure #2 places the swaddled baby in Jess's arms. She looks into its face, horrified to see the SHREDDED FLESH OF A BABY REAPER.

                    BABY REAPER
          Mama . . .

Tears stream down Jess's traumatized face, unable to deny her motherly instincts.

                      JESS
          Mommy's here.

She snuggles her newborn into the crook of her neck.

                 CLOAKED FIGURE #3
          So it is written that you shall
          give your life unto the Reaper.

The Baby Reaper opens its tiny mouth to reveal rows of FANGED TEETH. It chomps into Jess's neck, feeding on her blood as she CRIES. The cloaked figures CHANT IN UNISON.

                 CLOAKED FIGURES
          For blood holds a sacred power to
          the Reaper of Souls. And it shall
          give him life eternal. Forever.
          And ever . . . And ever . . . And
          ever . . .

# PART VII:
# RESTRICTION

## 55

The costumer really had done an excellent job. Overalls snug around the shoulders, right sleeve perfectly adjusted to Howard's request, and just enough dirt and blood caked into the flannel to tell a story of past mayhem. As Howard admired himself in the dressing room mirror, he could feel the beast within silently settling into its skin.

"You ready, Mr. Browning?" The makeup artist asked from the other side of the curtain.

Putting on the Reaper's face was the next step, an arduous process that he was not looking forward to. But Howard pulled back the curtain with an agreeable nod toward the young purple-haired makeup girl. "I'm ready."

She fitted a bib around his neck as he got settled in the chair, looking in the mirror at the dark circles under his eyes. He hadn't slept through the day as he'd hoped, but it made no difference now as he prepared himself for the tedious five-hour prosthetic application process.

"Would you happen to have a small pillow for my lower back?" he asked. "I can hardly sit for thirty minutes these days without it aching."

"Oh, I'll have you done in twenty," she assured him.

Before Howard could question her, the girl was already dipping her brush in a small canister of bright green paint and lathering it on his face.

"I'm sorry, am I in the right truck? I'm meant to be the Reaper, not the Grinch."

"They're doing your scars in post," she explained.

Howard looked himself in the mirror as his face disappeared under the ridiculous green hue. She couldn't be serious. Cheaply polished computer-generated imagery could never bring the Reaper's iconic visage to life. Where were the visceral practical effects? The hanging flesh and exposed bone, streaked with wet blood?

*This isn't my face.* The Reaper growled his displeasure. *Where's my pretty face?*

Howard's cheek began to twitch.

"Hold still please," the artist requested. "I need to get your lips."

Howard's eyes locked on a large pair of metal scissors resting on the makeup counter, his fingers inching toward them now.

*Let's give her an extreme makeover.*

He gripped the armrests tight to keep his hand from grabbing those sharp blades, stomaching the monster's rage.

"If we don't finish the makeup, there will be no film," Howard responded aloud to the beast in his mind.

"I'm going as fast as I can here, Mr. Browning," the makeup artist replied, turning away to dip her brush again. In the mirror's reflection, he saw her huff at his perceived rudeness. He wanted to apologize, but thought it best keep his mouth shut and focus all his energy on staying in control until the process was finally complete. Then he rushed out of the trailer without so much as a thank-you, for fear that something else might bubble up from his mouth.

"I am doing what you asked of me," he said out loud as he walked from the trailer toward set. "Hurt someone now and you will not get what you want."

*I'll have my harvest. One way or another.*

"What does that—?"

"You need help running lines there, chief?" A familiar voice came from behind Howard's shoulder as he turned to find his old friend approaching.

"Joan? What are you doing here?"

"I wish I was doing my job." She motioned to Howard's green face with her lit cigarette. "Christ, look what they've done to you. But no, I'm just here to watch. You think I'd miss the return of the one true Reaper?"

Howard gave a grateful nod, "That's very kind of you."

"How are the birds?" Joan asked, following Howard toward set.

"The birds?"

"Yeah, did the camera work out all right?"

"Oh yes," Howard replied, remembering his cover story. "It worked like a charm."

"I hope you're being careful in that darkroom."

The melted face of Danny Alvarez flashed behind Howard's eyes, a frighteningly clear memory now.

*Poor Danny boy's gonna need new headshots.*

Howard quickly shook the vision, the voice from his head.

"I should start getting into character," he told Joan, grateful for her support, but eager to get away all the same.

"Of course. Give 'em hell." Joan gave him a pat on the shoulder just as Howard arrived at the edge of the set.

The overhead lights were covered with orange plastic gels, casting a harvest moon glow onto the cornfield below. Beside the field lay the big red barn, that fateful structure from which Lester Jensen was pulled and dragged into his dark destiny. Howard's nerves tingled as the voice buzzed with joy.

*There's no place like home.*

Howard took a deep breath as he crossed the barn threshold, into the realm of the Reaper. The film crew was working feverishly to set the stage for murder, and the sheer energy of being back on set excited him to his core. But tonight wasn't about Howard and his ego. It was about the Reaper, the necessary offering. That was the only reason he was here.

As Howard moved through the barn, he found Andrei beside a haystack, preparing Mandy for the scene to come. "Scotty is your mate. You wish to love him, in the hay, writhing with ecstasy. Your flesh, together, as one. But now, he is lost. You must find your mate. You must—" Andrei stopped short upon seeing Howard. "Mr. Browning!" He turned to the crew. "Everyone! The Reaper lives!"

An encouraging applause broke out among the group as Howard felt himself blushing. "Thank you, thank you all."

It felt good to be appreciated, but the hot lights were already making him sweat and he could feel beads of green paint gliding down his cheeks.

Howard met eyes with Mandy, who quickly looked away as Andrei threw an arm around his shoulder, guiding him toward a darkened corner to review the scripted action.

"You wait for line here. Appear from hay. And kill."

"Simple enough," Howard replied.

"Now. Motivation. She is mouse. And you?"

"I'm going to assume I'm still the cat."

"Yes! See. Professional." Andrei patted Howard's chest, then turned to the crew, throwing up his arms. "Places, everyone! Time to make art!"

The prop master approached Howard in the corner, handing him a large fake scythe made of dull plastic.

"Looks a bit cheap, doesn't it?" Howard asked, feeling the hollow weight of the weapon in both hands like a child trick-or-treating.

"It's safer for wide action shots," the prop master explained. "We only use the real deal in close-ups," he said, pointing to the heavy metal scythe resting against the wall.

*Give me my blade and I'll show you the real deal.*

Howard choked down the voice inside as he thanked the prop master, waiting to be left alone. Then he hunched over and spoke to himself out loud again.

"You listen to me. When they call action, I will be in control. Understand? I will be acting, just like the old days. You do not control me."

Howard watched as his own hands rose in the air, as if pulled on strings.

*Dance, puppet, dance!* The Reaper laughed as Howard's limbs flailed.

Howard forced himself back into control as he reached for the real scythe blade and placed the sharp edge at his own throat.

"Try me again and I'll cut the strings for good."

The beast grumbled within, relenting to the threat as Howard placed the heavy weapon back and picked up his prop weapon.

"Now shut up. And let me do my job." Howard closed his eyes. He could do this. Stick to the script. Don't go too far into character. Just act.

"Action!" Andrei shouted.

Howard opened his eyes, watching as Mandy wandered the darkened barn on the other side of the haystack.

"Scotty!" she called, her voice trembling ever so slightly. "Scotty, where are you?!"

Howard took a step forward from the shadows as he gripped the prop scythe tight, digging out his best Reaper voice.

*"Scotty says you give great head!"*

He swiped the dull blade toward her neck, eliciting a chilling scream.

"Cut!" Andrei shouted. "Beautiful!"

Howard effortlessly slipped out of character, smiling at the director's approval. He was doing it. He was acting, no different than he had in eight previous films, with the Reaper nothing more than a costume, a character. He was even present enough to notice that Mandy's performance was actually quite good, which only added to the thrill.

"Mandy," he felt compelled to tell her between takes. "I wanted to apologize for the way I behaved in my audition."

Mandy shook her head. "No, *I'm* sorry. That was totally embarrassing. I just wasn't prepared to work with such a professional. But I've been studying really hard ever since. I even took a real acting class at the Strasberg Theatre."

"Oh, I can tell!" Howard responded. "What you just did, *that* was professional. Some actors, they dial the fear too high right off the bat, as if the character knows they're about to be killed. But you hit just the right notes, the subtlety of a creeping terror that—"

"Mr. Browning?" she gently cut him off. "I appreciate the feedback, I really do. But I'm trying to stay in character as Riley, and that's kind of hard to do when you're giving Mandy so many compliments."

"Of course, my apologies. *Now* who's being unprofessional?" Howard chuckled. "Let's get to it, shall we?"

They filmed the scene from a few more angles and Howard forgot all about the beast lying quietly within. He was simply doing the work, being a professional actor once again and reveling in the joy of pure performance. This is what he had been missing all these years, the lifeblood of an actor engaged in the collaborative endeavor of true creation. He was finally back, and he hadn't felt this alive in ages. Howard remained in control all the while, until Andrei turned to his cinematographer for a new direction.

"Now, camera." The director made a frame with his fingers. "Point to haystack here. Effects team, splatter blood. With this, Riley is dead. That is wrap for Mandy!"

Andrei led the crew with claps and cheers as his actress blushed and bowed. "Thank you, wow! It's been such an honor, really."

A confused Howard approached his director. "Is this where we bring in the prosthetic head for me to sever?"

"No prosthetic," Andrei replied. "Too fake. We use cinema. Image: Reaper strikes. Image: Blood spray on hay. Montage. Like Eisenstein film."

Joan scoffed from the sidelines, echoing Howard's own dismay.

"I'm sorry," Howard started, "but the script calls for a rather gruesome decapitation."

"Yes, movie magic. Violence happens in the audience *minds*," Andrei explained, tapping his index finger on the side of Howard's skull.

*I will snap off that finger and jam it through his ear.*

"Mr. Dalca," Howard began his appeal as calmly as he could, "I understand you come from a more reserved cinematic background, but that's not how the Reaper films work."

"This is remake. Chuck says PG-13," the director shrugged, "We make PG-13."

*No . . .* The beast rumbled angrily through Howard's bones.

". . . PG-13?" Howard couldn't believe what he was hearing.

"Parental Guidance." Andrei indicated the height of a small child by holding a flat hand at waist level. "Under 13. Make more money from children."

*I will slaughter the children!*

The Reaper fumed as Howard argued. "But the Reaper's rage is brutal, violent . . ."

*A blood-soaked sacrifice . . .*

". . . and it is most certainly Rated R."

*The ritual . . . my rite . . . or else . . . a reckoning . . .*

With the Reaper threatening, Howard leaned closer to Andrei, whispering in his ear, desperate to get through to him. "If we don't feed the monster, I don't know what he'll do."

Howard prayed that his treatise would get through to the director, who rubbed his chin now, squinting in apparent consideration of the actor's suggestion.

"You method," Andrei said with a grin. "I like this." He turned to his camera operator, energized. "Give me camera. I shoot myself."

Howard felt a swell of relief as the inspired auteur took charge of the set.

"We need close-up of monster, thirsty for blood. Handheld camera over Mandy's shoulder, verité effect. Audience won't *see* Riley's death, but *feels* her death. In three dimensions."

*Oh, they'll feel it.* The Reaper prickled in Howard's blood, unappeased but empowered.

"Please . . ." Howard's voice was lost in the bustle as the film crew prepared for the next shot.

*I'm ready for my close-up.*

He had to get out of here, had to leave before something bad happened. He couldn't fight it from taking control now. The current was too strong, already guiding his feet back to the darkened corner when all he wanted to do was run for the door.

"Mr. Browning." The prop master appeared, holding out the heavy scythe. "It's time for the real deal."

Howard's mind went blank as the weapon was placed in his hands and the prop man walked off. The oak handle was heavy in one hand as he ran his other fingers along the blade's sharpened edge, looking into the glistening curve of metal. It wasn't green-faced Howard reflected back in the silver, but the warped reflection of shredded flesh, a cracked grin opening wide to speak with Howard's mouth now.

*"Let's make some magic."*

Howard was helpless as his eyes locked in on Mandy, his mouse, and the summoning word echoed in the hollow barn.

"Action!"

"Oh my God! Cut!"

Howard didn't know whose voice was bringing him back into consciousness, but as his vision returned from the blackout, he saw Mandy trembling before him, blood splattered on her cheek. He searched for the wound, but found nothing. Mandy was safe. The Reaper didn't get her.

The set medic pushed Howard aside, dropping to the haystack at their feet. Andrei was collapsed there, blood gushing from the torn tendons of his neck, gashed open wide. The camera was still running beside him as blood flowed onto the lens.

"Somebody call 911!" The panicked medic pressed her hands to the wound against an endless torrent of red as Andrei's limbs began to twitch.

The set descended into chaos as Howard looked at the scythe in his hands. Fresh blood stained the blade as he searched for the monster in the reflection, but saw only himself.

Andrei's skin went chalk white, the life draining from his body as Howard gasped a question he wasn't sure he wanted answered. "Is he . . ." But the Reaper's voice overtook his own ". . . *happy with his director's cut?*" He cackled as his head swiveled toward Mandy. *"And you, my little seedling. I'm not done with you yet."*

Mandy shrieked in true horror, a bloodcurdling scream that brought Howard back to his senses. He seized the opportunity to throw the scythe to the ground and take off toward the open barn doors, away from this set full of potential victims.

"He can't leave!" the medic called behind him. "Someone stop him!"

Everyone was frozen in shock, or perhaps fear, as he heard Joan's voice call after him. "Browning!" He rushed to his car now, quickly getting behind the wheel just as Joan appeared at the passenger-side window, gravely serious. "Don't run."

The engine turned over and Howard hit the gas, speeding away from his friend, from the barn, from the bloodshed he had created. He glanced in the rearview mirror at himself, searching for the beast.

"This was not the deal!" Howard responded, his voice volleying aloud with the beast.

*"I'm going off script. It's blood for blood."*

Howard's fingers clenched the wheel.

"Fine," he replied, making a sharp turn off the service road, onto a two-lane thoroughfare. "You want a sacrifice? I'll give you one."

A truck was barreling toward him in the oncoming lane as Howard swerved into its path, lining up the . ~adlights for a head-on collision. He could end it now, just like this. No one else had to get hurt.

*"Except for that poor truck driver,"* The Reaper responded to Howard's own thoughts.

The truck honked furiously, mere feet away as Howard realized there was a human being behind that wheel, about to die with him. He quickly swerved back into his own lane, spinning out onto the shoulder.

When the dust settled, his heart still racing, Howard sobbed on the side of the road as the Reaper laughed. Looking in the rearview mirror again, he saw his tears mixing with the green paint.

"What do you *want* from me?" he asked.

His reflection answered. *"I want to see my true face."*

Howard wiped at the tears as his cries became more hysterical. Shifting into laughter now, bubbling up from his belly. The tips of his fingers pressed against the skin beneath his eyelids, knuckles arching as his fingernails dragged down the length of his cheeks, shredding skin. His body convulsed with a manic cackle, feverishly scratching away at his own face as warm blood coursed down his knuckles.

Howard tried to close his eyes to the horror, but he was being forced to stare at his own reflection. Laughing as the flesh shaved away beneath his fingernails and he watched the Reaper's monstrous face become his own.

## 56

Trevor heard footsteps enter the house above, but they were heavier than Howard's familiar light footfall. When the door creaked open, he quickly recognized the figure in the doorway, face dripping over the flannel shirt and shabby overalls.

The Reaper skulked down the steps.

No, it couldn't be. He must be having a nightmare, or else he was hallucinating the monster, just as crazy as Howard.

The Reaper advanced toward him, and even in the dark, Trevor could see a flap of cheek hanging, blood oozing down the shirt. He turned his head away from the gruesome sight.

"This isn't happening," he assured himself. "You're not real."

"But he *is* real, Trevor," the monster spoke in Howard's voice.

Trevor slowly turned back as the figure tugged the light bulb cord, illuminating the familiar features beneath all those crimson scratches.

"Howard? Jesus, what happened to you?"

"He's angry, Trevor. So angry." Howard looked at his own blood-stained hands as Trevor noticed chunks of flesh beneath the fingernails, horrified to realize that Howard had done this to himself. "The ritual has been compromised, it won't feed him anymore. He wants real blood now, 'blood for blood' he said, just like Farmer Joe. I can't hold him back, his vengeance is insatiable."

The sheer mania in Howard's eyes told Trevor that there was no hope in guiding this man out of his delusion anymore. If Trevor wanted to break through the insanity, he had to meet Howard on his level. He needed to join the madman in his delusion, make Howard believe that *he* believed.

"We can fight him together, Howard." Trevor's words stopped Howard in his tracks.

"So you *have* seen him?"

"Yes," Trevor lied. "I just didn't want to admit it. The Reaper told me he wants me, too. But he can't get us both at the same time, right?"

"Right," Howard's eyes lit up. "He may have prepared two vessels, but he can only inhabit one."

"Exactly." Trevor would have agreed with whatever Howard said at this point. His plan was working. "You can't do this alone. So untie me now and we'll end this."

"Yes, of course." Howard nodded as he moved toward Trevor, starting to untie the knots. "I'm so sorry, Trevor, about all of this."

"It's okay, Howard. I know it's not your fault." Trevor still didn't believe the Reaper was anything real, but he knew that Howard was afflicted with a mental illness, a disease, no different from addiction. He could sympathize with the man's plight, just another lost soul who'd become a danger to himself and others. But that wasn't going to stop Trevor from punching him in the face and smashing the chair over his head as soon as those knots were untied.

Before the rope fully loosened, Howard dropped to the ground, covering his ears and moaning as he crawled away across the floor.

"Howard . . . What's wrong?"

"Don't you hear it?!" Howard shouted over a sound that wasn't there.

"Hear what?"

"The chain! The clanking chain! He won't let me!" Howard curled into a ball on the ground like a helpless baby as Trevor looked toward a pile of junk by the stairs, where the rusty chain lay motionless and quiet.

Howard was clearly crippled by his own hallucinations as he spoke softly up at Trevor now. "There's still hope for you, but I can't help. Only the final girl can end this now. Sophie, she's your hero. Don't let him take her from you, like he took Emma. Like he took my baby." Howard ran his hand along the cold cement floor, as if trying to evoke the spirit of his unborn child. "Don't let him make you a monster, too."

The thought chilled Trevor as an older woman's voice boomed from somewhere upstairs.

"Browning?"

Before Trevor could open his mouth to scream, Howard was on his feet, hand over Trevor's mouth as he leaned in with a gravelly *"Shhhhhhh . . ."*

Trevor swallowed hard, looking into Howard's eyes and seeing something else behind them, threatening in the Reaper's tone.

*"Not one peep. Or I'll rip out your tongue and make sweet Sophie choke on it."*

Trevor's breath stopped as a wicked grin stretched across his captor's bloody face. For the first time, he thought that maybe Howard really was possessed by something truly monstrous, some demonic force that wouldn't let him go. As he watched the mangled man slink up the steps, all Trevor knew for certain was that whoever was calling out up there was in trouble.

And he was powerless to stop it.

## 57

Joan spent the whole drive from set to Howard's house scolding herself for ignoring the signs. Her friend had clearly been struggling, and even though she did try to help, she hadn't realized just how bad it was. She'd wrestled with her own demons after what she witnessed in the war, but Howard's trauma looked more like the mental breakdown she'd seen Tony Deptula succumb to in the trenches. The poor bastard swore that bugs were hatching inside his brain, eating him alive as penance for his sins. After two days of beating himself senseless, Tony finally ate a round from his own .45 to end the madness.

Joan feared the same dark fate for Howard now. He'd clearly lost his grip on reality and now that poor director might be dead. Joan felt it was her duty to stop her friend from making the situation any worse.

She called Howard's name through the open front door, but nobody answered. That's when she noticed another door, down the hall, was also open. It had been a while since she'd been inside this house, but she was pretty sure that was the basement. She stepped across the threshold and started down the hall, calling out once more.

"Browning? You here?"

A figure jumped out from behind the basement door, nearly knocking Joan back to the floor.

"Hello, Joan." Howard smiled pleasantly through torn flesh, dripping with blood as he shut the door behind him.

"Jesus. Your face." It looked like he'd caught a face full of shrapnel worse than Sergeant Flesher as ribbons of red skin dangled down to his chin. Was that a piece of fingernail stuck in his cheek?

"Oh, this?" Howard said, raising his hand to casually press a loose flap into place. "Stanley got a little overexcited when I returned home. Separation anxiety, I'm afraid."

Joan didn't feel like she was talking to her friend right now. It was more like a stranger doing a weird performance of Howard Browning, someone trying desperately to pass for sane in the face of utter insanity. She feared he might be more far gone than she thought, the bugs already burrowing deep into his brain, but she tried to get through to him regardless.

"Listen," she started, slow and calm. "I know it was an accident." She really hoped so, but seeing him grinning through torn flesh now, she wasn't so sure. "But you running away from the scene isn't helping your case. If that man doesn't make it to the hospital, and I don't think he will, then the police will be coming here for you."

Howard didn't seem to be processing the gravity of what Joan was trying to tell him as he nodded like a bobblehead doll. "I understand and I'll be happy to comply when they do. What do you say we wait for them outside on the porch? It's such a beautiful night. Harvest moon, you know."

Joan couldn't help noticing that Howard's back was pressing up against that basement door now. She knew a diversion tactic when she saw one, but she just nodded in response.

"Sure, Browning. That sounds like a great idea." She had a few tactics of her own. "But I could really use a drink."

"Lovely idea," Howard smiled, his own blood now staining his teeth. "I'm afraid I don't have your usual bourbon, but I believe there's still a half bottle of chardonnay chilling in the fridge. You go ahead out and I'll bring us two glasses."

"Great." Joan forced a smile as she watched Howard move around the corner to the kitchen. She looked to the basement door as a sinking feeling told her to leave. Get back in the fucking truck, drive away and let the police handle it. But something else was urging her on, tugging her toward that door. She waited for the sound of the fridge opening in the next room and quietly opened the basement door at the same time, descending creaky steps into darkness. God, it stank to high hell down here.

The light cast down behind her as she heard a quiet voice, whispering in the dark below. "Please. Help me."

"Oh my God . . ." Joan didn't trust her cataract eyes these days, but she was sure that she was looking at a young man tied to a chair in Howard's basement right now. Stepping closer, she recognized him as Trevor Mane, the new Reaper who'd been missing for over a week. What had Howard done? "It's okay, it's okay," Joan assured him with a whisper. "I'll get you out of here."

The young man hung his head, looking like he might cry as Joan pulled out her keychain, clicking out her trusty flip knife. She bent down on one knee and started to cut away at the rope wrapped around Trevor's torso, almost getting all the way through the first layer when the kid screamed in her ear.

"Behind you!"

Something flashed over Joan's eyes and then the cold metal links were pressing hard against her throat, pulling her up and off her feet. Gasping for air, she dropped the keychain and clawed at the rusty chain that was now crushing her windpipe. Confusion came next as she caught a glimpse over her shoulder at her attacker, Howard, gritting his teeth in an unfamiliar rage.

"*You trespassed on my land.*"

Howard growled in the Reaper's tone as Joan's glasses slipped from her face and clattered to the ground. She tried to break free, but her strength wasn't what it used to be. Her vision started to blur, the aperture of her eyes slowly closing to shut out the light. The last thing she saw were flashes of the jungle, a slideshow of quick memories. Bullets whizzed past her head while land mines blew fire and dirt into the canopy above. She was certain her life was going to end back there in the war, getting riddled with lead or blown to bits in the mud by a faceless enemy. Not like this, at the cold hands of a dear friend.

## 58

Trevor tried to warn her, but it was too late now as the old woman pawed helplessly at the chain around her neck, spittle flying from her lips. The best thing he could do was focus on getting free, now that the rope was cut nearly all the way through. He struggled to rip through the fraying strands with sheer force and tried not to look at the wheezing woman in front of him, whose face was turning a deep shade of purple. Howard fell backward to the floor now, squeezing tighter on the chain as his victim flailed on top of him.

Trevor worked his fingernails at the rope, tearing away little by little at the final threads. He couldn't help watching as the woman's feet slowly stopped kicking, her bloodshot eyes stuck wide open. Trevor had never witnessed someone die before and the shock of it racked his whole body. But he wasn't about to let himself be next.

He felt the final threads pop loose behind him. The rope was finally broken as he frantically pulled himself out of the bindings and to his feet, standing for the first time in days. His legs were wobbly beneath him as he reached down and grabbed the keychain from the floor, rushing to the steps as Howard rolled the fresh corpse off his chest with a gleeful snarl.

"I told you . . . I love a good chase."

Trevor was halfway up the stairs when he felt the hard *thwack* against the back of his leg and screamed, a firecracker exploding in his calf, dropping him to his knees.

"But you'll have to run faster than that!"

He looked over his shoulder to see Howard cackling as he reeled the chain back in, *clack-clack-clack* across the stairs, readying for another swing. Trevor wasn't going to give the fucker another shot as he scrambled through the open basement door, dragging his limp leg behind him.

When he finally made it out onto the porch, his lungs pulled at the fresh air harder than any hit he'd ever taken. He was free and something in his body knew in that fleeting moment that he'd never touch that golden junk again. Especially when he saw Danny's car outside, confirming his worst fears. But there was no time to mourn his sponsor now.

Stumbling down the porch steps, he went straight for the dead woman's truck, jumping behind the wheel and starting the engine with a rumble. As he threw the car into reverse and pressed his foot to the pedal, his right leg lit up with hot pain and he cried in agony. Something was definitely broken inside, but he had to suck it up. Howard was already bursting out of the front door, swinging the chain overhead like a deranged rodeo clown as he galloped down the porch steps.

Trevor used his left foot to slam the gas just as the chain smashed through the driver's-side window, showering shards of glass into his lap. He swerved hard, nearly backing into the big tree in the yard as he bounced over the curb and onto the street.

Trevor leaned through the hole where the window used to be and looked Howard in the eye one last time. "Chase this, motherfucker!"

He threw the car into drive, savoring a moment's victory before Howard shouted from the lawn. *"You can run, but she can't hide!"*

Trevor looked in the side-view mirror as he sped away and saw Howard getting into his own car.

Shit. He was going after Sophie.

Howard warned him about this, that the Reaper would come for her. But maybe the psycho was just baiting him. Trevor had no phone and no time and he just needed to get to the police. That was the right move to make in every horror movie he'd ever seen, the moment where the audience would shout at the screen and call him a fucking idiot if he didn't do it.

Go to the police.

But what if the Reaper got to her first?

No, not the Reaper, just a man. A crazy old man in his shit-brown Cadillac.

This wasn't a horror movie, it was real life. Either way, Trevor couldn't take the chance. He had to go straight to Sophie, to protect her from the monster.

## 59

Sophie hadn't slept in days, spending every waking moment wrestling with the possibility that Trevor might actually be dead this time. This could be the final bender from which he'd never return and one night soon there'd be a knock on her door and it would be the police. "So sorry to break the bad news."

But tonight, as the exhaustion finally caught up with her, she lay in bed thinking of simpler times, when she and Trevor were just a couple of kids on the playground, falling in love. As she drifted away with visions of honeybees dancing through her head, a banging on the door pulled her out of the reverie and into reality.

This was it. The police were here and tonight was the night. Trevor was dead.

"Sophie!"

Trevor's voice. Was she dreaming?

"Sophie, wake up!"

No. She was wide-awake and Trevor was alive.

Sophie jumped out of bed and rushed down the stairs, where the front door rattled with the banging of his fist. That's when she remembered that she had made up her mind. Even if Trevor was alive, he was still Trevor. He would always be Trevor. Her sister reminded her that Sophie had done this time and time again, taken him back after every mistake, always swearing that this time was the last time. "You almost died, Sophie. How much lower are you going to drop the bar for this guy?" No, she couldn't let him in again. Every time she let him in, she got hurt. It was an endless cycle and she needed to take a stand tonight.

"Go away, Trevor!" she shouted. She hated to shout.

"Sophie. Oh, thank God you're okay." There was a strange relief in his voice. Why wouldn't she be okay? "Listen, you have to let me in."

"No. And if you don't leave, I'm calling the police." She had to be firm, resolved. Like they said in program: when dealing with an addict, don't be a doormat and don't make threats you don't intend to carry out. She was serious, she really would call the police if he didn't leave.

"Good, great. Go call the cops right now," Trevor responded through the door.

What? He wasn't making any sense, but he didn't sound high. He just sounded scared. She needed to see his face. She could always tell what was really going on with him if she was looking him in the eye.

Sophie unlocked the door and peaked through the crack, seeing the utter panic trembling through Trevor's whole body. "Where have you been?" she asked. "What's going on?"

"I'll explain everything if you just let me inside, honeybee, I promise." So many broken promises through the years. Using their pet name now to prod her sympathies. "Please, you're in danger."

Tires screeched somewhere around the corner, people always driving too fast on these winding hill roads. But the sound clearly meant something else to Trevor as he pushed the door open, forcing his way inside.

"He's coming!" Trevor slammed the door behind him and locked it.

"Trevor, you're scaring me. Who's coming?"

"The Re—" Trevor shook his head, turning to her. "Howard. Where's your phone?"

"It's in the bedroom. Howard Browning?" She was still trying to catch up as Trevor pulled her in close and put a hand on her cheek.

"Sophie, I love you. And I'm so sorry for pushing you away, for hurting you so many times. But I'm done with that and I'm not going to let anything bad happen to you ever again, okay? You're the most important thing in the world to me and when we get through this, I'm going to spend the rest of my life proving it to you, every fucking day."

Sophie was speechless. Even in his manic state, she'd never seen Trevor more clearheaded, more sincere about anything than he was in this moment. Something truly had changed in him. The man she was promised, the man she always knew he could be was finally standing right in front of her now. He smelled like he'd been sleeping in a dumpster, and maybe he had, but it was all she could do to pull him closer as the tears filled her eyes.

"Trevor . . ."

"But right now," he continued, his fear more urgent than her joy, "I need you to go upstairs, call the police. And get ready to run."

She pulled back to look him in the eye. "Will you please just tell me what's—"

The lights cut out as darkness fell on the house and a chill rattled down Sophie's spine. Something wasn't right.

"Sophie." Trevor's voice was firm. "Go."

She nodded and started up the stairs, trying to piece together what was happening. Howard Browning? Why would that poor old man be after Trevor? He was so sweet and sad, it just didn't make any sense.

Sophie went into the bedroom and slipped her shoes on, wondering what she should say when she called 911. My boyfriend's back from his drug-fueled disappearance, but he's being chased by a geriatric actor?

She reached for the phone on the nightstand and shivered with a sudden chill, drawing her gaze to the sliding balcony door. It was cracked open, barely an inch, and the wind whistling through the gap was just loud enough to mask the footsteps creeping up behind her, giving Sophie no time to scream.

## 60

Trevor darted into the kitchen and grabbed the biggest fucking knife he could find. It looked a lot sharper knowing what he planned to do with it. But if Howard Browning came through that front door right now, was Trevor really going to stab the old man? Could he really kill someone?

He hoped he wouldn't have to find out.

What was taking Sophie so long? He called her name up the staircase, but got no answer back. Terror gripped his body as he clenched the knife, taking the steps two at a time until he arrived in the shadowy hallway.

Was Howard in the house already? Could he have moved that quickly? The Reaper could.

But crazy thoughts like that weren't helpful right now as Trevor reached the bedroom door. He needed to stay grounded as he took a deep breath, ready to fight with the knife raised high as he leapt across the threshold.

The room was empty, but the sliding glass door was wide open. Sophie lay collapsed on the balcony. Trevor screamed out for her, not knowing if she was dead or alive as he ran across the room and through the open door. As he bent over her body, he sensed another presence on the balcony, lying in wait in the darkened corner behind him.

*"Ready to work the steps?"*

Trevor spun around to see a flash of Howard's twisted grin before two hands shoved against his chest like a wrecking ball. He tumbled, head over feet down the balcony steps, still gripping the knife as the blade caught him across the ribs before his skull slammed against the hard ground, bottoming out into blackness with the bitter taste of blood and failure.

<u>*Night of the Reaper Part VIII: Moon Reaper*</u> (1990)
Script Pages Courtesy of Pinnacle Studios

INT. CARGO BAY - STARSHIP VEGA - NIGHT

Zara's panicked breath fogs her spacesuit helmet as
she types on the ship's interface keyboard. Briggs
paces behind her.

                    BRIGGS
          You really think this will work?

                    ZARA
          All we have to do is travel back
          to Ashland in 1957, kill Farmer
          Joe before he kills Lester Jensen,
          and then the Reaper will be
          history.

She crunches a few more keys.

                    ZARA
          But just to be safe? I say we nuke
          him in the present, too.

Zara slams the final key and the ship's intercom
resounds.

                    SHIP INTERCOM (V.O.)
          Self-destruct sequence will
          initiate in . . . sixty seconds.

                    ZARA
          Okay. We better hustle to the time
          pod.

She turns around, but Briggs is nowhere to be seen.

                    ZARA
          Briggs?

Zara hurries down the hallway toward the time pod door when——A PAIR OF SEVERED LEGS drops from the pipes above, plopping at her feet.

                    ZARA
          Briggs!

                    THE REAPER (O.S.)
          That's one small step for man . . .

The Reaper lowers himself from the pipes, landing in front of Zara.

                    THE REAPER
          And one giant reap for mankind!

He raises his futuristic alloy space-scythe as Zara clocks the airlock button on the wall beside her.

                    ZARA
          Eat stardust, Reaper!

She SLAMS the button with her fist, then wraps her gloved hand around the emergency handle. The air-lock door HISSES OPEN and the Reaper FLIES across the hangar, toward the open door.

But he WHIPS his rusty chain across the cargo bay and it SNAPS around Zara's leg as she clutches the emergency handle tight.

                    THE REAPER
          Do or do not! There is no try . .
          . when it's time to die!

The Reaper dangles in midair, ten feet from the open door.

                    SHIP INTERCOM (V.O.)
          Self-destruct sequence will
          initiate in . . . 30 seconds.

Zara fights the gravitational pull as she reaches her other hand for the star-saber handle on her belt.

> ZARA
> If you love the harvest moon so much, why don't you go there?

Her star-saber ZAPS alive with a pink glow as she slashes the blade through the rusty chain. The Reaper tumbles back, but catches his arms and legs on the doorframe.

> THE REAPER
> Sorry, Zara. But I've got the right stuff!

The Reaper CACKLES, holding on tight as the moon and the stars burn bright behind him.

Zara's grip is weakening as she looks to the time pod door. She reaches out an arm, but can't quite make it. She could make a leap for it, but it's a stretch.

The force of the universe is pulling her in one direction and one direction only as she makes up her mind.

> ZARA
> Okay, Reaper. Let's phone home.

Zara lets go of the handle and flies across the hangar, SLAMMING into the Reaper. They both sail out of the airlock door, into the abyss of space.

> SHIP INTERCOM (V.O.)
> Self-destruct sequence . . .
> complete.

EXT. THE ABYSS OF SPACE - CONTINUOUS

Zara wraps her arms around the monster, clutching
him tight as the ship EXPLODES behind them. The
force catapults them toward the glowing harvest
moon.

                    THE REAPER
          I always knew I'd be a star!

The Reaper CACKLES as the lunar atmosphere ignites
them both, flaming like a two-person meteor. They
SLAM into the moon's surface, leaving a crumbling
crater in their wake.

Gray dust settles over this silent grave as the
rusty chain floats away . . .

Into the depths of space . . .

Toward the earth, rising on the horizon . . .

# PART VIII:
# RECKONING

## 61

Trevor felt the coarse hay against his cheek before he opened his eyes, blinking awake to see the rotting wooden structure around him.

He was in a barn. Why was he in a barn? Holy shit, was he actually trapped inside a Reaper film?

Rolling onto his back, his eyes clocked the big lights hanging from the rafters above, switched off in the dark.

The film set. Of course that maniac would take him here.

He touched the gash in his side where the knife had clipped him during the fall. Not deep and already crusted over, but it stung like hell. Trevor pushed himself up on the pile of hay and his hands came back red and sticky. He couldn't have bled much, but the hay was soaked with it and it smelled metallic, not like the sugary fake blood they used in movies.

This blood was real.

He remembered what Howard had said when he came back from filming, that the Reaper wanted real blood now. Trevor saw the yellow crime scene tape next, torn and fluttering from the open barn door. He shuddered to think of what happened here, what Howard had done on set. But he stayed focused on one thing and one thing alone as he crawled off the hay to his feet, his shattered leg barely keeping him up.

"Sophie!" he called out, limping toward the barn door. He spotted a scythe resting against the wall and reached for it, arming himself. But it was just a cheap fucking Halloween prop. Trevor tossed the fake scythe and reached for a pickaxe, heavy and real.

"Trevor!" He heard her voice, somewhere out there, as he crossed the threshold into the night.

The first thing he saw was the police cruiser parked outside with a shadowy figure sitting behind the wheel. Trevor had seen enough *CSI* to know that they always left a cop behind to guard the crime scene after a cleanup.

"Hey!" he called, rushing toward the driver's side window. "We need help!"

It looked like a cigar was jutting out of the cop's mouth, until Trevor leaned into the open window and realized that it wasn't a cigar at all. It was the handle of Trevor's kitchen knife. The blade was buried deep inside the man's open mouth, piercing out the back of his neck and pinning his corpse to the headrest. Trevor gagged at the gory sight, but quickly steeled himself as he reached over the dead cop's body for his gun holster. Empty.

"Trevor!" Sophie called out once more and he spun around to see the cornfield, lit up with an orange glow from the full harvest moon. No, not the real moon. Just more set lights, blindingly bright as Trevor started into the crops, dragging a limp leg behind him.

"I'm coming, Sophie!" He tried to follow the sound of Sophie's cries. "Keep screaming!"

*"Yes, it's music to my ears!"* came Howard's mocking Reaper voice, somewhere in the distance.

Trevor pushed harder through the dry cornhusks, scraping his skin as he gripped the pickaxe. "Touch her and I'll kill you!"

The monster laughed back and began to sing.

*"When the seeds are sown, but the stalks grow dry!"*

"Trevor!"

"Leave her alone!" He changed direction toward the sound of Sophie's voice.

*"And the harvest moon burns in the sky!"*

The monster's voice came from a totally different direction now.

*"Don't set foot on Lester's land!"*

And now another direction, but closer. How was Howard moving so fast? Sophie's cries were coming from just ahead. He was ready for anything as he sprinted through the stalks, clutching his pickaxe.

*"Lest you're slain by the Reaper's hand!"*

The Reaper's voice was right behind him now as Trevor burst into the narrow aisle between two rows of corn and spun around to face . . . nothing. His head was still throbbing from that fall down the steps and the ringing in his ear may have messed with his hearing. But he swore he'd heard—

"Trevor!" He turned back around to see Sophie, lying on the ground with her arms above her head. The rusty chain was wrapped around her wrists, the length of it going off into the distance, disappearing into the rows of corn. Trevor looked around once more for Howard in the shadows, but saw no one as he rushed to Sophie, dropping beside her.

"It's okay, I'm here." He assured her. "I'm gonna get you out of here."

He started working on the giant tangle of chain around her wrists, but it was a maze of rust, and he couldn't find the end of it.

A mechanical whir resounded from somewhere in the field, like the starting of an engine.

"What is that?" Sophie asked. "Trevor, what—"

Sophie shot across the dirt as the chain extending from her wrists went taut, yanking her into the cornfield on her back.

"Sophie!" Trevor ran after her screaming body, the pain in his leg going numb with adrenaline. He kept pace with her as she crushed through dry stalks, getting dragged toward the sound of mashing gears.

He ran past her now into a clearing where he saw the source of the sound.

A roaring combine tractor with a giant thresher wheel.

The other end of the rusty chain had been fed into the wheel, pulling Sophie toward a certain death in its spinning metal teeth. He had to stop it.

Trevor jumped up into the tractor cab, but the controls were smashed. He couldn't turn it off. He jumped back out and saw Sophie in the clearing now, being dragged closer and closer to the chomping mouth of the machine as she screamed. "Trevor!"

Trevor ran to the moving chain, reared his pickaxe and swung.

*CLANK.*

The chain sparked but didn't break. It just kept moving like a slithering snake.

*CLANK.*

A second swing almost broke through, but the weakened link just got pulled right along, away from Trevor. He repositioned himself with the chain running through his legs now. Sophie was six feet from the spinning blades with Trevor in between as he threw his whole weight into the next swing.

*CLANK.*

The chain finally broke as a spark shot into the cornstalks, igniting a flame. Trevor dropped to the ground to help Sophie untangle the few feet of chain hanging from the ball around her wrists.

"You're safe. You're safe," he told her as the machine clanged to a halt behind them. He put a hand on her cheek and looked into her eyes, which filled with relief. But the relief quickly flashed to terror, her eyes looking over Trevor's shoulder.

She didn't have time to speak, but she didn't need to. Trevor was ready, white-knuckling the short chain as he spun, swinging with all his strength.

He saw the glint of the sickle in the moonlight as Howard sliced down at him, but the hard metal links of Trevor's chain landed first, cracking against Howard's grinning jaw and dropping him to the dirt.

Trevor let the chain clatter to his feet as he reached down to grab the sickle. He gripped the weapon in his hand as he stepped closer to the slumped body on the ground, ready to slay the beast. Howard rolled to face him with cracked teeth falling from a bloody frown. There was no trace of the Reaper left in those empty eyes as the old man begged through the tears.

"Do it, Trevor. End this madness. Please."

The sickle trembled in Trevor's hand. It was the right thing to do, a mercy kill, putting this rabid dog out of its misery before someone else got bit. When he framed it that way, he decided he could live with the blood on his hands as he reared back the blade, aiming to deliver the killing blow. Until he felt another hand wrap around his, holding him back.

"Don't." Sophie's soft but sure voice in his ear. The angel on his shoulder.

Trevor didn't have to turn and look into her eyes to remember the light that dwelled there. If Sophie watched him kill someone, if she saw the true violence in his heart, there would be no turning back. He would never get to make amends for all the harm he'd caused her. He would lose her forever, doomed to eternal darkness like the sad old man in front of him.

Trevor lowered the weapon with a deep exhale. "I'm not the monster."

Howard's face twisted back into the Reaper's grin. *"I will rise again. I always ri—"*

*THUMP.* The thick heel of Sophie's white sneaker crunched against Howard's nose, sending his head flapping back into the dirt and knocking him out cold.

"How's that for a jump-scare, asshole?" Sophie said.

Trevor turned to face her now. Covered in cuts and bruises, but standing tall like a total badass as the crops blazed behind her. It was her, it was always her. The final girl. He grabbed her and kissed her deeply as the warmth from the fire swept over them.

When Sophie finally pulled back to look him in the eyes, she was still trying to make sense of it all. "What the hell happened? Was that really Howard Browning?"

Trevor knew there was hardly anything left of Howard behind that marred face, no humanity left inside the warped shell of a man. "No," he shook his head. "It wasn't."

He turned to look back at the unconscious man, only to find an empty patch of dirt. Howard was gone. No, there was no way. How could he have—

*"Pathetic little boy."*

The Reaper's hoarse voice was right over Trevor's shoulder.

*"You'll never stop—"*

Trevor spun and swung the sickle without hesitation, the blade quickly finding its home with a sickening *thud*. His stomach sank as he looked into the eyes of his victim. Not the Reaper. But Sophie. Her face twisted with pain and confusion as she wavered on her feet.

". . . honeybee?" she sputtered, blood bubbling over her lips.

The blade was planted firmly in the side of her head as Trevor released the wooden handle and all the breath left his body.

No, this wasn't happening. He'd heard the monster's voice, right there.

A gravelly laughter came from the ground behind him now as Trevor turned back to see Howard cackling in the dirt. Still lying there, unmoved with a broken nose. But Trevor was sure that Howard wasn't there a second ago.

*"What's the matter, Trevor?"* Howard spoke through a bloody smile, as if reading Trevor's thoughts. *"Hearing voices? Seeing things?"*

Trevor was racked with horror as he turned back to Sophie and her limp body began to drop. He caught her in his arms, trying to hold her upright. He wanted to believe it was all just a bad dream, but he knew it was real and he was helpless to undo it.

"No, no, no . . ." Trevor's knees gave out and he fell to the ground, clutching Sophie close. How did this happen? He wasn't high, he was through the withdrawal. He wasn't fucking crazy.

*"This is your brain on Reaper!"* Howard answered with a cackle.

Trevor ignored him as he struggled to pull the blade from Sophie's head, finally prying it loose with a bony grind. Blood poured endlessly from the hole in her skull, pooling into his lap as her body tremored.

"I'm sorry, Sophie, I'm so sorry. I didn't . . . That wasn't . . ."

*"You can't blame anything you've done on some fictional character,"* Howard mocked Trevor with his own words.

Trevor shook in agony as Sophie's eyes spun all the way back until only the whites remained. As if her final gesture was to roll her eyes at him for being such a total fuckup.

*"It's time to reap what you've sown,"* Howard sneered.

"Shut up!" Trevor screamed, releasing Sophie's corpse to the ground. His hands were slick with her blood as he reached for the sickle and stood.

*"Yes. Show me your rage,"* the beast in Howard beckoned as Trevor turned toward him. *"Give me your vengeance."*

Trevor felt himself detach, disconnect from his body. Watching through his own eyes as he stepped toward Howard on the ground. He gripped his weapon tight, knowing full well that this time, he was going to use it.

*"Reaper . . ."* Howard splayed his arms wide, closing his eyes, inviting what was to come.

*Rise.*

The voice wasn't coming from Howard anymore. It was echoing inside Trevor's head as he looked into the blade to find the Reaper reflected back. Not Howard or the character from the film, but Trevor's own torn face dripping with blood, face muscles contorting into a venomous grin. Seeing himself as the monster.

Trevor couldn't stop what came next as he finally surrendered to his Higher Power.

## 62

Howard had died as the Reaper eight times before. But looking into his killer's eyes now, he knew that this was the death from which he would never return. Trevor was brimming with rage as the flames rose around them. The first swing of the sickle landed in Howard's shoulder. It was a dull pain, much less than he expected. The second blow landed in his stomach, a sudden heat burning within. With the third strike, square in his chest, Howard heard metal scrape bone as everything went numb. But he could still feel the blood running out of him, pooling in the dirt beneath his body.

Trevor kept hacking away, tears streaming across his face in a madness that Howard recognized all too well. As his vision began to blur, he knew that Trevor wasn't there anymore. The Reaper had won, had found its new vessel. Howard once thought that he'd grown tired of playing the role, but he knew now that he'd had it backward all along. It was the Reaper who'd grown tired of the human role he was cast in. Howard Browning was nothing more than a character, a mask to be shed. He wished there was something more he could have done to save Trevor from this fate, but he couldn't even save himself now as the darkness consumed him.

When his vision returned, he wasn't in the burning cornfield anymore. He had retreated to that inner sanctum, the black box theater of his unconscious. There, he found scared Lester Jensen waiting for him beneath a solitary spotlight, reaching out with open arms. Howard rushed across the dark space and embraced his younger self.

"Is it time to sleep now?" Lester asked, burying his face in Howard's chest.

Howard nodded, holding the young man tight like the son he'd never had.

"Yes, Lester. It's time to sleep."

There was nothing left to fight or mourn as the spotlight dimmed and the stage faded to black.

*Night of the Reaper 3D* (2006)
Script Pages Courtesy of Pinnacle Studios

INT. INTERROGATION ROOM - POLICE STATION - NIGHT

Riley sits shell-shocked at the table with a blanket draped around her shoulders. She stares at her reflection in the two-way mirror, tries to wipe the dried blood streaking across her face. The door creaks open and Sheriff Tillman enters.

> SHERIFF TILLMAN
> Riley. How you holding up?

> RILEY
> Did you go where I told you? Did you find him?

> SHERIFF TILLMAN
> We went out to the old Jensen farmland, yeah. What we found was Paula Carson with an axe in her chest. Scotty Delgado's head on a pitchfork. And what was left of Tori Atchison in a burned-up sleeping bag.

> RILEY
> I told you. It was the Reaper.

> SHERIFF TILLMAN
> Yeah. You mentioned that. Problem is, the Reaper is nothing more than an urban legend. He's not real, Riley. But those dead bodies are. And the state police on the other side of that mirror are gonna need a better explanation of just what the hell happened out there tonight.

Riley's eyes flash on the two-way mirror, then refocus on Tillman.

                    RILEY
          Did you look inside the barn? I
          killed him. Hung him from the loft
          by his own rusty chain.

                    SHERIFF TILLMAN
          The chain was there all right. But
          there was nothing hanging from the
          other end.

                    RILEY
          What? I heard his neck snap, he's
          . . .

Riley jumps to her feet with the sudden realization.

                    RILEY
          He's still alive, Sheriff. Which
          means that no one is safe. He'll
          come for me and he won't stop
          until I'm dead.

                    SHERIFF TILLMAN
          Riley. I'm gonna need you to calm
          down before——

Riley leaps across the table, reaching for the sheriff's firearm. He catches her wrist and handcuffs her to the bar in the middle of the table.

                    SHERIFF TILLMAN
          Riley Harlin, you are under
          arrest. You have the right to
          remain silent. Anything you say
          can and will——

BANG! A gunshot outside the room.

                    SHERIFF TILLMAN
          What the hell?

SCREAMING and more GUNFIRE as Riley sinks into her
seat.

                         RILEY
          He's here.

The sheriff draws his gun and rushes out the room.
The sounds move to the other side of the two-
way mirror now. Flesh TEARING, blood SPLATTERING,
voices YELLING.

The glass TREMBLES as Riley watches. The sheriff's voice BOOMS and the mirror SHAKES again. A
bloodcurdling SCREAM echoes and the mirror finally
EXPLODES toward camera.

Shards of glass fly at the audience in 3D as Sheriff Tillman's body follows, SLAMMING down on the
table in front of Riley. Like a gruesome meal being
served by . . .

The Reaper, climbing through the gaping mouth of
broken glass, sickle in hand. The room behind him
is soaked in blood, a mess of severed limbs and
dead cops.

                    THE REAPER
          It's a pigsty in there.

                         RILEY
          I killed you.

                    THE REAPER
          You can't kill what's already dead.

Tillman moans as the Reaper shoves him off the
table to the floor, focused on Riley as he raises
his sickle high.

                         RILEY
              Get it over with, you son of a
              bitch.

Riley closes her eyes as the Reaper swings and --

CLANK! She opens her eyes to see that the monster
has just cut the chain of her handcuffs.

                      THE REAPER
              I love a good chain, but handcuffs
              are a bit too kinky. Even for me.

The monster grins, casually taking a seat across
the blood-smeared table from Riley.

                         RILEY
              What do you want from me?

                      THE REAPER
              I have a proposition. A proposal,
              really. See, harvesting souls for
              all eternity is honest work. But
              it sure gets lonely. So I'm looking
              for a partner, someone special to
              be my one and only. My final girl.

Riley stares in deadpan disbelief as the Reaper
shrugs.

                      THE REAPER
              What can I say? I'm a romantic.

                         RILEY
              What makes you think I'd ever want
              to join you?

                      THE REAPER
              I saw the look in your eye. That
              cold little twinkle when you
              pushed me from the loft. I saw you
              smile. You're a killer, Riley. And

                    I just hate to see good talent go
                    to waste.

The Reaper places the sickle on the table between
them.

                         THE REAPER
                    So what do you say? Will you be my
                    bloody bride?

Riley stares at the blade on the table as --

                         SHERIFF TILLMAN
                    Help!

Sheriff Tillman pulls himself up by the table's
edge, blood-soaked and fear-frenzied.

                         SHERIFF TILLMAN
                    The Reaper! He's here, he's real--

SHUNK! The sickle blade slams into Tillman's open
mouth.

CAMERA PULLS OUT TO REVEAL -- It's Riley holding
the weapon! She leans toward the sheriff's face as
blood flows from his mouth over her blade.

                         RILEY
                    You have the right to remain
                    silent, Sheriff.

Riley yanks the blade from his mouth, fresh blood
SPLATTERING her face as the sheriff collapses back
to the floor, very much dead now.

                         THE REAPER
                    Bravo! Encore!

The Reaper claps excitedly. Riley's face twists with
rage as she puts the blade to the monster's neck,
leaning across the table toward his shredded face.

The Reaper himself trembles at the sight of that special twinkle in her eye. The cold stare of a killer.

> RILEY
> Okay, baby. Let's reap.

The Reaper grins as they seal their wicked union with a bloody kiss.

# PART IX:
# REQUIEM

# 63

Trevor hardly recognized his own face in the mirror. The dark circles under his eyes with creases at the corners, carved deeply into his skin as if dug by a dull blade. He shouldn't have let Sophie talk him out of that plastic surgery.

Sophie.

Howard Browning killed her. That's what he'd told the police about that night. It was an easy sell after they found the bodies of Danny Alvarez and Joan Poletto in Howard's house of horrors. Not to mention the spectacle of Andrei Dalca's murder in front of an entire crew of witnesses. Trevor was clearly the victim in all this. Howard killed Sophie and then Trevor killed Howard in self-defense. It was cleaner, easier than trying to explain the truth, because Trevor still didn't understand what really happened, how it happened. The more time passed, the more his story started to feel like reality anyway. Memories were funny like that. In the end, all Trevor knew was that he couldn't blame himself for all that bloodshed.

There was only one person, one thing to blame.

"REAP-ER! REAP-ER! REAP-ER!"

The fans were already calling out to him from the conference hall next door. The last time he was in this bathroom was the day he'd thrown it all away with one hit from the pipe. He was approaching one year of sobriety now, and he didn't even crave it anymore. Then again, he didn't crave much at all these days, didn't really *feel* much outside of a numb acceptance. Ever since that night in the flaming cornfield, it was like he was being pulled along in a strong current. A passive participant in his hollow life, day after endless day.

"REAP-ER! REAP-ER! REAP-ER!"

He shouldn't keep them waiting any longer.

Trevor left the bathroom and worked his way backstage to the curtain. He took a deep breath before stepping out onto the stage, where a sea of Reapers erupted in sheer mania before him. The fans at HorrorCon 2006 had outdone themselves with elaborate costumes and makeup, emulating their beloved beast.

*Night of the Reaper 3D* was the highest-grossing horror film of the decade, thanks in no small part to the true horror story behind the scenes. Chuck was right. Everybody loves a good comeback story, and Trevor's had become even bigger than anybody could have expected. He had survived his own slasher film to star in his own slasher film.

After a few softball questions, the interviewer didn't shy away from the ugly details. "I have to ask, after everything he put you through, everything he did . . . Do you have anything to say about Howard Browning now?"

The crowd went silent, thousands of Reaper eyes staring back in the dark as Trevor looked down. "Howard Browning gave his life to this role. He gave it everything and he lost everything. Including his mind."

Trevor knew what that meant now. It was all he could do after losing Sophie to pour himself into the film, to detach and lose himself in the fiction so as not to wallow in the cold reality. He cleared his throat before looking back out at the rapt fans. "I just hope that when people remember Howard, they remember the man. And not the monster."

A solemn silence, then respectful applause. "Beautiful," the interviewer nodded. "Well, with the success of this film, I think the biggest question on everyone's minds is . . . Will there be a sequel?"

The chanting began once more, slow at first but gaining force.

"REAP-ER! REAP-ER! REAP-ER!"

Trevor glanced off-stage, where Chuck Slattery waited in the wings, nodding in encouragement. That was the whole point of this interview, the big official announcement that Chuck had already prepared for him.

After all the mayhem, the producer hadn't taken any chances with the reboot reshoots. He reverted to a hard R-rating and insisted on some last-minute script changes to make sure the franchise could keep going, even if Trevor fell off the wagon and overdosed himself into an early grave. It was Mandy Ray who pitched Chuck the idea for her revised role as Riley Harlin, the final girl turned co-killer. The vision for this inspired character arc had come to her during a brief stint in the psych ward while recovering from her on-set trauma. Chuck couldn't have planned it better himself, but Trevor wondered now whether the producer ever really was the true puppet master behind the immortal franchise. Or if a much stronger force had been pulling the strings all along, just like Howard suggested.

Either way, that climactic story twist made the film less of a remake after all, and while fans celebrated the fresh story, they rejected the lame 3D label, concocting their own subtitle on the message boards. Pinnacle Studios took advantage of the unofficial *Part IX: Bride of the Reaper* moniker, embracing the next film as the tenth entry in a successful franchise that never died. As for Trevor, he wasn't going anywhere. With nothing left to fill his empty existence, he'd already signed his contract to return in the next film.

*Night of the Reaper X: Curse of the Reaper*

"REAP-ER! REAP-ER! REAP-ER!"

"Trevor?" the interviewer asked, still awaiting a response. "Will the Reaper be back?"

Trevor had slipped away from the moment. He'd been doing that more and more lately, having little blips and blank spots in his consciousness. But he was back now, looking out into the crowd as their chant seemed to echo in that gaping hole inside his chest. As he leaned into the microphone, he knew what he was supposed to say. Chuck had teed up the question in advance and scripted Trevor's answer—"Not without my bloody bride!"—to cue Mandy Ray's big entrance. But Trevor couldn't stop the words that bubbled up instead now, the gravelly voice that haunted his waking days and sleepless nights.

*"I always rise again."*

The crowd shrieked with glee at the sound of their murderous idol. Cameras flashed, blinding Trevor as he shielded his weary eyes. He remembered now what Howard said, about the fans playing their role in this cycle of worship. Maybe there was a little piece of the Reaper in each of them, casting a collective spell to summon their own private beasts of burden.

"REAP-ER! REAP-ER! REAP-ER!"

Over their ravenous din, Trevor swore he heard another sound. Faint at first, then growing louder. Piercing its way through the wall of screams in front of him.

The rusty chain began to *clank . . . clank . . .*

*CLANK.*

## Acknowledgments

This story has been haunting me in one form or another for over a decade, which makes it damn difficult to thank the many people who have helped along the way. I'll start with my teachers and classmates at Columbia University's Film MFA program for all the fantastic feedback on the screenplay version, especially Andy Bienen, Frank Pugliese, and Henry Bean. Once I transformed this monster into a novel, Kate Maruyama gave the most excellent revision notes, along with fellow workshop members Lauren Wilson and Jennifer Ritenour.

Thank you to my amazing agent, Dan Milaschewski, for making my dream come true with his steadfast support and infectious enthusiasm. And to Mary Pender and Orly Greenberg at UTA for championing this story beyond the book.

Erin Seaward-Hiatt designed the most killer cover I could hope for, and I'm grateful to everyone behind the scenes at Skyhorse for the tireless efforts that turned my wild words into a tangible tome. Extra gratitude goes to my editor, Lilly Golden, for her insights on the page and guidance through the process.

I'm lucky to swing in the orbit of many creative brains and giant hearts, but I'm especially grateful to friends like Anthony Deptula, Tracy Dawson, Matt Doherty, and Tori Amoscato, who were only a phone call away when I needed them.

Thanks to my parents for never ceasing to support my journey into the precarious world of the arts, and to my brother and sister for being early arbiters of a well-balanced pop culture diet.

Thank you, Morgan, my first reader and favorite person. You inspire me every day to dream bigger, and I'm so happy we get to keep building this life together. But we still have to walk the dog.

I can't sign off without acknowledging all the incredible artists behind the countless horror films that inspired this book. Too many to name them all, so I'll restrict myself to two.

Wes Craven and Robert Englund. . . . Thank you for the nightmares.

Here's hoping, dear reader, that I've given you some fresh ones.